A LAND IN NEED ... MAKE OR BREAK

George Counsel is a Western Australian wheat and sheep farmer who obtained a university degree in history and politics at the age of sixty five, followed by a post-graduate diploma in economics and historical geography.

Make or Break is .... *Need* and
describes events .... lia. The
story continues th .... O'Leary
families and the fe .... ore free-
thinking immigran ....

It is written from the viewpoint of one who has experienced the rigours of a rural pioneering upbringing and the hardships demanded for survival on the land.

Other novels in the trilogy *A Land in Need*:

GEORGE COUNSEL

A Land in Need

Book 2

MAKE OR BREAK

AUSTED PUBLISHING
COMPANY

Acknowledgements

I offer special thanks to:

Mary Hicks for her editing and dramatising; Marie Longworth for her map drawings; Bill Bassett-Scarfe for his outstanding cover art; and my wife Marjorie for her patience, understanding and encouragement.

A special mention for Keith Tyler, who has been such a help and inspiration to me after reading my first book *The Challenge*.

This novel is true to the spirit of early Western Australian colonial life. However with the exception of the assumption of the major historical events, all characters, families and situations are entirely imaginary and bear no relation to any real person or actual happening.

Copyright © 1990 by George Counsel.

First published 1990.

Published by Austed Publishing Company, 12 Keegan Street, O'Connor, Western Australia.

ISBN 1 86307 001 X (set)
      1 86307 009 5

Printed by Singapore National Printers Ltd.

In them at last the ultimate men arrive
Whose boast is not: 'we live' but 'we survive' ...

A.D. Hope

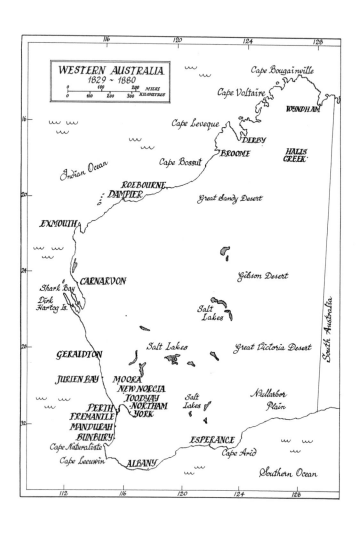

WESTERN AUSTRALIA
1829 ~ 1880

0   100   200   300 MILES
0   100   200   300 KILOMETRES

Cape Bougainville
Cape Voltaire
WYNDHAM
Cape Leveque
DERBY
BROOME
HALLS CREEK
Cape Bossut
Indian Ocean
ROEBOURNE
DAMPIER
Great Sandy Desert
EXMOUTH
Gibson Desert
Shark Bay
CARNARVON
Dirk Hartog Is.
Salt Lakes
South Australia
Salt Lakes
Great Victoria Desert
GERALDTON
JURIEN BAY
MOORA
NEW NORCIA
TOODYAY
NORTHAM
YORK
Salt Lakes
Nullarbor Plain
PERTH
FREMANTLE
MANDURAH
BUNBURY
Cape Naturaliste
ESPERANCE
Cape Arid
Cape Leeuwin
ALBANY
Southern Ocean

CHAPTER 1

"Governor Weld has certainly proved different from Hampton, hasn't he?"

The speaker was David Baker, who on this day in September, 1873, had turned sixty. The occasion was a celebration on the Baker farm near York, close to seventy miles east over the Darling Ranges from Perth. Mary, David's wife, was also due to turn sixty in November, the period when they would be busy with harvest. Prominent guests were Liz and Henry Lovedale, who too had turned sixty during the earlier months of 1873. Also attending the celebration, was the Baker daughter, Judith - and by her side was Michael, the Irish rebel transportee, who after escaping and falling in love with Judith had married her, changing his name from Rooney to O'Leary.

As usual, Henry Lovedale led the conversation.

"Aye Davy, you're right about Governor Weld, but he's got himself in so much trouble lately, they say he's to be replaced. What with him accusin' Darcy McAllum of murder, my goodness, he shoulda learnt in the four years he's been here, you can't accuse one o' the well-to-do of anythin' like that."

David smiled at Henry's cynicism, realising that in the long years since they had first met in CapeTown on the voyage out, his friend had changed little, not only in nature but appearance. The same pleasantly angular features with the penetrating steel-blue eyes, the same thick brown thatch of hair, except now flecked with grey.

"Yes," David elaborated. "I suppose our Governor should have. Weld's position is strikingly similar to that of John Hutt, who was ostracised so much when he was Governor during the early 1840s. But as with Hutt, it seems that trouble always boils over when there is some attempt to protect the

1

Aborigines."

David's son-in-law, Michael eased his lanky frame in the cane-bottomed chair.

"But according to our gentry families, the northern Aborigines have been extremely obstinate." There was cynicism in the handsome auburn-haired Irishman's tone.

"Aye," cut in Henry, his eyes too, showing contempt. That's just what the swells would say. Still, from what you hear, the natives up north have proven far wilder than down south. O' course, there's not many left hereabouts now. What with so many gettin' knocked off in the early days with guns, besides later gettin' cleaned out with diseases an' such."

"Now, now, Henry," scolded Liz. Henry's wife had still retained much of the pleasant dark-haired buxomness which had always attracted Henry, even when they had played together as children on a village green in Lincolnshire. Nevertheless, Liz also had a certain moral discipline about her, which was now revealed as she interrupted her husband.

"As I've said before Henry, what's happened to most of our Swan River natives is a subject well left alone. All I can say is I wish there'd been a better way."

David nodded in agreement, his grey eyes sombre. In his old age, David's formerly average build could now be regarded as squarish. His pleasant ruddy features gave hint of the same design. He had also lost much of his formerly light-brown hair, leaving his pate bald and pinkish. The silver-specked fuzz left around the edges, combined with his stocky build and serious manner made him appear almost monkish. Nonetheless, his grandchildren adored him, as they did their Grandma Mary.

"Yes," lamented David. "We've said it so many times before, and certainly Governor Weld must feel the same. Anyhow, though Darcy McAllum would doubtless have been found guilty if he had shot a white man, it seems public opinion is such that he will soon be released."

Judith now entered the discussion. At forty she still

retained much of her former beauty, luxuriant dark hair framing a perfectly oval face, with intelligent hazel-grey eyes. These appealing attributes combined with a neat figure, had caused her to be admired by many men before she'd met Michael.

"Both the *Perth Gazette* and the *Inquirer* have published the petition, haven't they? Well over two thousand signatures to have McAllum set free. Both papers had also talked about what a fine upstanding citizen Darcy has proven, and if you remember, both papers have pointed out that when he shot the savage on the run, he had only been out to teach him a lesson for stealing."

Henry spat. "Them couple o' rotten rags, those papers. Why, they'd print anythin' as long as it supported the nobs - who own 'em, anyhow. An' as we know, both editors are intrepid Anglicans." Henry's face wore a contemptuous grin.

"But public opinion is well on the side of McAllum," broke in Michael. "One could well admire Governor Weld for the way he has stuck to his guns."

"You are sure it's not because Frederick Weld is a Roman Catholic, Michael?" teased Judith.

Michael's strong blue eyes twinkled. "Well, partly, of course," he laughed. "But apart from his denomination, it must be admitted that Weld has been sympathetic to the downtrodden. Look how he banned extreme punishment in Fremantle gaol as soon as he took over. Look how he forbade hangings in public, besides helping destitute prisoners to find work. In fact, he still employs a host of them in the Residence gardens."

David agreed. "Yes, I believe as with Hutt years ago, sending out a man of liberalist tendencies such as Weld, was an earnest attempt by Britain to make amends for the previous Governor, who in John Hampton's case, was far too ruthless, even as the head of a convict establishment. With Britain having decided to cease transportation in 1868, I suppose a man like Weld was a kind of peace offering."

3

"Aye," growled Henry. "As you said, Davy, the exact opposite to Hampton. I s'pose the only good the rotten blighter did, was to have all those extra guv'ment buildin's put up. But my God, at what cost? I'd say much o' the mortar 'tween the bricks shoulda been pink with the blood o' the poor bastards who'd suffered the lash."

David gave a grim smile. "Well, I understand some of the mortar still shows stains. Of course, there is that huge broad arrow, one of the convict masons built into the clock-tower of the Perth Town Hall."

"It's a wonder Hampton didn't make 'em remove it," scowled Henry. "But he didn't. Let's hope it stays there till Kingdom come."

"An' the way you're holdin' the floor, my Henry," interrupted Liz, "we'll be here till Kingdom come waitin' for this celebration. Can't you see Mary's gettin' anxious."

Mary smiled a little tiredly. Although she had been forbidden by Judith and Liz to help with the repast, she found the flies had become troublesome, and when it grew dark, she knew it would be the moths and even the occasional bush bat diving at the least speck of artificial light.

They had prepared the meal on the open verandah of Judith and Michael's home, a French style bungalow, walled with farm stone, shingle roofed, and only completed the year previously. Judith had designed much of the interior herself, deeply grateful to her parents, who were more than satisfied to spend their declining years in the old wattle and daub homestead.

The Baker workman, Timothy, now over seventy was there also. Though Timothy was now only capable of hobbling around doing odd jobs and shepherding sheep in a light cart, in gratitude for the wiry old ex-convict's long service, David had told him he could stay on the farm as long as he wished, as well as receiving a small wage. Timothy, who for years had been brewing a special ale from barley, had now from the same source, distilled a very potent whisky.

He had brought along a small keg for the celebration.

"Hell's bells Timothy," roared Henry, when he had taken a sip. "It's got a kick like a mule. Where'd ye' get the recipe?"

"From one o' the expiree sheepwashers," grinned Timothy. "Real good colonial spirits, aint it?"

"Aye," grinned Henry, after he had taken another swig. "We've been sellin' a bit o' colonial spirits in the tavern. Under the lap o' course. But this one o' yours, why I'd say it's got more sweet bite than the best Scotch or rye." He turned to Liz. "Righto, barlady, try a taste."

"No Henry," snapped Liz. "With apologies to Timothy, I will not have a taste. For this evening I will stick to beer an' wine. And as for you, my Henry, stop bein' the life o' the party an' let someone else have a say."

After dusk a cold wind had sprung up from the sou-west, and they all moved inside to Judith and Michael's large kitchen-living-room. An open hearth fire blazed at the opposite end from the cooking range.

With the dishes all cleaned away, Judith's next duty was to breast-feed her youngest one, Rory. Retiring into the bedroom, she called to Michael to put the two older boys to bed. But the five year old John and the three and a half year old Patrick, (nicknamed Paddy), were reluctant - being bright-eyed and expectant to hear the elders talk about tales of long ago. Their father not always so indulgent towards his boys, gave in, telling them to sit quietly on a rug by the hearth.

Although David was not usually a hard drinker, he had been well plied with colonial spirits. He put his arms round both Liz and Henry, his voice slurred.

"Well, my old friends, though it's a question Mary and I have asked each other many times, I must now ask it of you. Are you glad you stayed in the colony?"

"Well, I for one certainly am," laughed Liz. "What more

could you want than ownin' the only tavern in York? Yet I will say that I had me grave doubts way back in Clarence in 1830 - when we'd been forsaken by both Thomas Peel an' Guv'nor Stirlin', with people dyin' all over the place, especially wimmen an' kids." Liz arched her attractive eyebrows. "But since that time I've completely changed my mind."

"Aye," agreed Henry, in maudlin mood. "That was really a bad time, especially when Stirlin' an' his cronies took all the good redlands at Guildford an' left Peel's yeoman tenants with all the useless grey sands. But I think the worst I've hated the place, was in the 1850s, just after Jim Dunbar an' I came back from Americcy, when we saw what was bein' done to the poor transportees. With gentry ladies ridin' by in carriages on new limestoned roads, all put down by convicts, the ladies not even turnin' a hair - not even when the warders laid in the lash. Aye, that really disgusted me. Fact is, when I saw it, I wished I'd never come back."

"But how do you feel now, Henry?" asked David.

"Well, right now, as Liz says, with our tavern doin' so well, we're probably better off than ever we coulda been in England. But that's not what I'm really gettin' at. What I'm really on about, is how the place gets to yuh ... sorta grows on yuh, just as Jim Dunbar, my old Yankee friend often says." Henry took a big swig from his mug, to cover his embarrassment.

"I agree Henry," said Michael, who too had had his share of spirits. "Although I've only been here a comparatively short time, the colony's already grown on me. And besides, there's always the challenge."

"Aye, at one time, I'd reckoned this was the last place on God's earth, an' I must say it's still not much better. Yet you keep on feelin' that if you keep on tryin' sensibly, things could improve, even beyond your wildest dreams."

David laughed loudly. It was unusual for him to be so raucous, but it was a special night.

"Well, since you and Jim Dunbar returned from America, you have so often talked about finding gold Henry. Way out there in the never-never, as you call it."

"Aye, not only well east of here, but they've been also pickin' up colour inland from Champion Bay, which they now call Geraldton, and in what they're callin' the Murchison. Yet the gold's still not enough to make it pay." Henry took another swig from his mug. "O' course, there's other things happenin' up there. The Irwin an' Greenough areas where Alistair Strange an' I explored in the 1840s - well, they reckon they're provin' better for growin' grain even than the Avon an' Toodyay Valleys down these parts."

"And further north too," broke in David. "Way up in the subtropical and tropical grasslands where they are successfully running sheep and cattle. That's where I will admit, our sons of the gentry are really proving themselves. Not only Darcy McAllum, but Josiah Trigwell's son Damon, and of course Colin, son of Ian Anderson."

"Aye, they're provin' tough all right," agreed Henry. "Tough with the niggers, as they call 'em, too, as Darcy McAllum has shown. Yet I s'pose they have to be to survive up there. Who'd o' thought the kids from those few posh families which stayed behind in Swan River, could've proved so strong. Still, that's not to say that we've got to like 'em - the bastards!"

David gave a shrug. "Well, at least some of the males should have proven resilient, Henry, since all the originals had held high rank in the Napoleonic Wars. Some should have been shown to have British pluck, surely?"

"Aye," snorted Henry. "An' just seven families out've thirty or more, with the rest all clearin' back to England. Not much odds, is it? But there you are, we've still got the blighters."

"Hasn't one of the seven recently gone broke?" asked Michael, who had been listening intently. He turned to David. "We were only talking about it the other day, Father?"

"Oh, aye, o' course. Dennis Atcheson north o' Toodyay," grinned Henry, answering for David. "Tom Callahan, the conditional pardon convict finally got the family property. I think the Atchesons are now left with practically nothin'. An' there's that wily Callahan, who after his ticket of leave in 1853, only began by peddlin' women's wares on foot from Guildford to Toodyay." Henry gave a chuckle. "O' course, I forgot about him an' his mate grabbin' unbranded poddy calves off the road an' sellin' 'em under the lap. An' to cap it all besides ownin' half o' Toodyay, Tom Callahan's now bought half the buildin' blocks in Perth."

"Callahan's become almost as famous as Jamie Baldeck, said David. "Though he was not a convict, Jamie was still only the son of a teamster. His first big purchase was when he went against his bank manager and wrote out a cheque to buy that big pastoral lease at Dandaragan, nor-west of New-Norcia Mission. Like the Atchesons, that owner had also been foreclosed on. Yes ...," mused David. "I suppose Jamie wouldn't mind us putting him among the ordinary folk."

"Aye," agreed Henry. "From what I've heard o' Jamie, I'd say he would be proud."

Mary too, had consumed more than her share of liquor, which was unusual for her. Having been strictly brought up as the daughter of a well-to-do family, she knew that particularly at parties, she must always keep her dignity. Not always had she behaved herself. She remembered often with shame her flirtation up on Mount Eliza above Perth with Pierre, the French naval lieutenant, to whom she had become pregnant. Mary's parents had made the mistake of allowing their golden-haired blue-eyed teenage daughter - said to be the belle of Swan River at the time to fraternise with the young French officer.

Mary had never forgotten that it was that plunge down the social ladder which had been the means of her marrying David, a commoner, yet a part of it she never regretted.

Though Judith was the child of the illicit union with the Frenchman, David had always treasured her as his own. Mary knew that David's love for Judith, had over the years of marriage grown even stronger with the loss of David's own two children, Charles, drowned in the Avon River in 1839, and Paul, taken by the disastrous measles-diphtheria epidemic in 1864 at the age of twenty nine.

Mary smiled, the fine worry lines etched into her still attractive face.

"Yes Henry, persons such as Tom Callahan and Jamie Baldeck, are bringing out what David and the newspaper editor Robert Black had hoped for so long in our colony. You know, the rise of the bold peasantry?"

"Aye," said Henry. "But I don't know about the rich peasants. I'd say Jamie Baldeck an' Tom Callahan are now so wealthy they'd have joined families like the McAllums an' Andersons, who not only own most o' the big sheep stations, but also most o' the city businesses, includin' the banks."

Henry took a gulp of his colonial spirits. "What I'd call the bold peasants, are the ones still workin' on their own farms, even though they've become so successful they could employ more labour like a landlord. You know, not only the ones who moved out into the Avon Valley in the 1830s after they'd been forsaken by Thomas Peel, but the expiree convicts like Ernie Watkins north o' Northam - you know, the one who married the pensioner guard's daughter. There's so many in the Avon an' Toodyay Valleys like Ernie Watkins, now. A good third o' the smallholders, in fact."

"I do agree," replied Mary. "They are the ones who still do an honest day's toil on their farms, even though they could now afford to only give orders. Such should make them the genuine peasants or yeomen. Of course, even before they were transported, those prisoners with farming backgrounds had applied for agricultural grants to be due after their conditional release in the colony. Certainly many had had hundreds of years of farming tradition behind them, be it in England, Scotland or Ireland."

"Yes," laughed Michael, taking a swig from his tankard. "Similar to what I am, even though I did come from an Irish feudal family. Along with the O'Reillys and the O'Haras, we have always sided with the ordinary folk. That's why our families supported the Fenian Rebellion."

Henry grinned, spilling his spirits. "Pity we couldn't skite you off more in York with your true identity, Mick. In fact, it mightn't be long before we can. If Governor Weld stayed here longer, I reckon we could've marched you through the streets o' York carryin' the Fenian Irish banner, no trouble. I tell, you matey, if they took a vote among the majority, which is most o' the workers an' smallholders, they'd be all for you, an' no mistake."

Michael became serious. "You forget, Henry, that the military Fenians are still locked up in Fremantle gaol, even though transportation has now been abolished for more than five years."

"Aye," said Henry. "I don't know what Britain's on about, still keepin' 'em there, seein' it's quietened down in Ireland. Why, apart from workin' outside under guard, those poor blighters could stay in the gaol forever."

" When Britain declared an amnesty for all Irish political prisoners back in 1869, why didn't she release the military prisoners?" queried Judith. "It would have been so much better for Michael."

"It's revenge," said Michael. "Britain doesn't like her military officers revolting, and I guess it's far more so with those who come from Ireland."

"The stupid part about it, though," said Henry, "is that there are only seven o' the Fenians left in Fremantle Gaol."

Michael smiled. "Anyhow Henry, those seven have not been forgotten by John Boyle O'Reilly, because he has a plan to get them out."

Henry gave a gasp. The mention of O'Reilly's name had

stirred him up. In the six years since escaping on a whaler, the Irish Fenian had been much in the news. Though for obvious reasons, not one iota of O'Reilly's escapades had been printed in either of the Western Australian newspapers, much had been written in American publications which were often dropped in the colony by Yankee whalers. According to the papers, not only had O'Reilly been in the forefront of a premature Irish-Yankee invasion of Canada, but he had also become editor of a prominent American newspaper.

"Hell," said Henry. "O'Reilly's certainly done impossible things since he's left, but stealin' out the prisoners from Fremantle gaol, well now, that's too much. O' course, unless the Yankee navy's goin' to sail in an' bombard the gaol like that rotten Governor Hampton was scared they'd do. You know, when Britain first landed the Fenians here back in '68."

"Well, not quite that," returned Michael. "What O'Reilly's doing, is gathering Irish-American donations to charter a vessel, probably a whaler. I have already corresponded with him over the years in fact, and he recently wrote back to me because he wants to make contact with a Frank Mulcahy, an Irish immigrant, who works as a clerk in the Fremantle gaol. He didn't want to send a letter via the gaol, for obvious reasons. All he wants me to do is give Mulcahy O'Reilly's American address and tell him to write. From a post-box well away from the gaol, of course."

"Aye, I s'pose O'Reilly wants Mulcahy to keep an eye out for the ship an' pass the word on to the Fenian prisoners," returned Henry. "But contactin' this Mulcahy character would still be a bit dangerous for you, Michael. Those gaolers aren't like our brave Cap'n de Burgh, who deliberately failed to recognise you that day and who has now left the colony."

Judith again entered the conversation. "That was why we were wondering about you, Henry. You sometimes travel to Fremantle to buy liquor for your hotel from the port warehouse."

"Aye, I do go to Fremantle occasionally, but what about Father Flaherty, the padre? He goes to Fremantle sometimes too, to talk to the Irish prisoners. In fact, he cadges a ride with me sometimes." Henry hesitated. "I s'pose the padre can still be trusted? A lot o' the warders are Catholic Irish, you know, former ticket o' leavers. You must admit the padre's a bit of a chatterer."

"Of course Father Flaherty can be trusted," Michael almost exploded. "Why, he was the one who gave me my new name Michael O'Leary, when I decided to stay in the colony and marry Judith. I should have thought of it before, Henry - as one to contact this Mulcahy, Father Flaherty is the logical choice. Thanks!"

Henry gulped the last of his spirits. "Anythin' to oblige, Mick."

"Look Henry, " scolded Liz, "when are you ever goin' to act respectable an' stop callin', Michael Mick? God knows, I've warned you enough!"

The Irishman gave a loud laugh. "It's all right Liz, if Henry called me anything else I'd be offended. The same with Timothy. It goes with their natures, and I love it."

"Sorry," laughed Liz. "I guess I should have learnt by this time."

It was now 1876, three years after the anniversary out on the farm, the property now known as the Baker-O'Learys. Although Henry had mentioned to Michael that indeed the padre had made contact with Frank Mulcahy and passed him the message about corresponding with O'Reilly, Michael had heard not a word since. He had come to believe in fact, that as far as O'Reilly was concerned, the whole plan had fallen through.

Again over the years, the concerns of the farm had eclipsed all else. Not only had wheat and wool prices fallen drastically, but those years had proven the driest the York district had ever experienced. Already many of the smaller farmers had resorted to cutting and carting sandalwood, which unlike other exports, had increased in demand.

The Baker-O'Learys were no exception, having had to borrow heavily from the bank to plant their 1877 crop. Michael too, considered using the sandalwood trade as a supplementary means of income. But when he mentioned the subject to Mary and David, they were not in favour. Mary had remembered the ruthless exploitation of the sandalwood stands in the York district in the 1830s. Even the Baker farm had been ravaged. Though David had let the cutters into the property, knowing it was an independent means of income for former shepherds who had come to detest working for the big pastoralists, it had been found later that the sandalwood tree did not re-seed or sucker. The result was that the whole of the Avon Valley, including government reserves, had been stripped of its sandalwood, which could never be replaced.

"Yet what alternative is there, Father, but join in the sandalwood trade?" argued Michael. "It is not so much that grain prices are so low, but the fact that in the last three years we've hardly recovered enough from our crops for seed-wheat. This season looks no better! Here it is almost the end of June, and much of the crop is hardly out of the ground. And I must say we are not the only ones in trouble. Most other small farmers have been out on the sandalwood track for the last two years."

"And not only small farmers," supported Judith. "Last year, the Trigwells and Andersons each had two big wagons on the go."

"That's just what I mean," said Michael. "There is no room for sentiment. We can't stop the wealthier farmers joining in, so we may just as well be in it ourselves. Anyhow, I intended to travel out much further than just the York district. More than one hundred miles in fact. And while I'm out there, I might even look for a grazing lease." His eyes twinkled. "Who knows, I might even strike it rich."

David was now far more amenable. "Sounds like you've been listening to old Henry again." He smiled. "I should have known it was more than just sandalwood - especially so far out. Not that Henry and Jim Dunbar ever found any gold worthwhile. Just a few specks, as Henry would say."

"Yes Father," admitted Michael. "Still, it was Henry who told me about the big stands of sandalwood out there, just in case there is no gold. In fact, when he called in the other day he suggested he go with me as an offsider."

Mary laughed. "Just as well Liz didn't hear him say that. She forbade him going out there nearly ten years ago."

"Yes," said David. "From what I've heard, you could easily leave your bones out there, even in winter."

Michael smiled wryly. "Well, especially this one. With the fresh water claypans still dry from summer, all the graziers have been able to rely on is the deep wells they had the convicts put down. But I understand even those are drying up."

David looked puzzled. "Well, how do you expect to travel out so far then? I understand the last convict well is less than seventy miles out."

"Oh, Henry told me about some good supplies of water near granite outcrops."

"Yes, gnamma holes," replied David. "Most of them are supposed to have been dug or deepened by the Aboriginals. A great credit to their ingenuity." David's brow creased once more. "But in a year like this, all the waterholes could be totally dry. You are still taking too much of a risk, Michael. Apart from your own needs, think of all the water you'll need for the animals. Remember the six horses you'll have for the big wagon."

"I'll be taking a saddle-hack as well," returned Michael, "in order to ride ahead while the wagon and team is left in a convenient position. As a matter of fact, if when I ride ahead and find that the gnamma holes prove to be dry, I'll use the last convict well as a base."

David's long silence showed he was becoming less and less enthusiastic.

"You are talking about going out alone Michael, but you know damned well it's so necessary to take an off-sider. Timothy's far too old, and of course, even if I was sprightly enough to accompany you, there are still those essential jobs on the farm which are now beyond Timothy."

"Well, I just might have someone," Judith suggested brightly.

Michael looked sharply at his wife. "Who, for goodness sake?"

"Daniel Hordacre! He's a journalist working part-time for the *Fremantle Herald*, a free-lance reporter. He first came over here from Victoria to find out what effects convictism has had on our poor downtrodden colony, as he calls it. I met him when he called into the government school the other day where I've been helping out the new teacher. Government schools in the country areas are now mostly staffed by ex-convicts, or expirees. We have an expiree teacher in York, and that is the reason Daniel called in. Part of his commission is to write a paper on the preponderance of transportee teachers in our Western Australian schools. He says it doesn't say much for our educational standards in pre-convict days."

"That's what comes of having had Anglican governors who were dead against educating the rabble," David agreed.

"He suggested the very same thing," replied Judith. "When he found that I'd previously been in charge of the Anglican-sponsored school here, we had quite a discussion. In fact, while working in Sydney, he became a protege of Robert Black, the former editor of our *Perth Gazette*. Of course, under Robert Black, the *Gazette* was far more liberal, more a newspaper for the people."

"Well, the *Gazette* certainly was more democratic in those days," rejoined David. "But Black's editorials were so heavily censored under Governor Charles Fitzgerald, who was sent out from Britain to make sure that this colony was turned into a penal establishment, that he moved over to New South Wales in disgust. The powers that be have owned the *Gazette* ever since."

David hesitated.

"This young journalist having been an understudy of Robert Black is welcome news, Judith. But we were talking about an offsider for Michael. Why, did he mention something about it?"

"Well, he did mention the sandalwood trade, and that he'd like to do a write-up on it."

"That doesn't mean that he'll want to spend a couple of months out in the backblocks Judith," Michael cut in. "He could gain enough information from all the old sandalwooders who hang around Liz and Henry's tavern. And even if I did take him, would he know how to handle a wagon-team? What's his experience with horses?"

Judith smiled. "Well, the way he sat that flighty pony after he rode away from the school yesterday, I could say, need you ask?"

"All right then," replied her husband. "Where is he staying in York?"

"At Liz and Henry's pub, and I believe he'll be there for a week."

Michael now gave David an almost self-satisfied grin.

"Well now," he said. "In that case I'll ride in and talk to him first thing tomorrow."

"There's no need," advised Judith. "I could leave a message with Liz at the tavern in the morning. With all the extra pupils, it looks as if I could be helping out at the government school for some time." She became serious. "Also Michael, although it's been years since you elected to stay incognito in the colony, we must still agree that until Britain grants a pardon to the rest of the Fenian prisoners in Fremantle gaol, you must continue to keep out of York as much as possible."

At Michael's hesitation, David spoke. "I agree Judith, but Michael's become so popular among the small farmers, especially the ones with Irish wives, I think it might be dangerous for the troopers to pick him up, even if he was recognised."

Judith smiled. "Yes, those Irish wives alone could be a formidable force. In fact they are already trying to run the government school in there, even though they were mostly illiterate when they were brought out."

"Up the Irish," laughed Michael, raising his fist. "We'll make a stand yet, even if we can't in dear old Erin. Anyhow Judith, seeing that you have to travel in to teach school, I'll leave this Duncan to you."

"No," corrected Judith. "Daniel, Daniel Hordacre."

CHAPTER 2

On the next Tuesday morning, after Judith had sounded out Daniel Hordacre about accompanying Michael on the sandalwood track, the young man rode out to the homestead. As he dismounted from his high-spirited pony, Mary was particularly impressed by his looks; his slim figure and his delicate tapered face under the fashionable wide-brimmed hat. He was dressed neatly in well-cut trousers, and sported a fine checkered waistcoat. He obviously cared about his appearance, his light blue shirt looked freshly laundered, his boots carefully polished. As Mary greeted him, his companionable easy-going manner reminded her much of the younger Henry Lovedale. Yet his eyes were far more serious and searching - so much like David's. Yes, if Robert Black needed someone to study the progress of Swan River Colony at first-hand, it seems he couldn't have chosen better.

David and Michael had been busy behind the shed checking the big wagon, but after a call from Mary, they appeared, Michael wiping wagon-grease off his hands with a piece of old sacking.

"Well Daniel," said David after greetings were exchanged. "So you are a protege of Robert Black. It is now just twenty five years since he left here. How has he been keeping? We received letters for a few years, but it has been so long now, we've almost forgotten his handwriting."

Daniel tipped back his hat, casually. "You know of course, he is now married with a family."

"Yes," replied David, impatiently. "But what I really would like to know, is he still fighting the good fight - if you know what I mean?"

"Of course," laughed Daniel. "He told me all about Swan River Colony when I first started working for him at sixteen, over three years ago. What an excellent experience it had been and although he had left because the freedom of the press had been stopped as a requisite to Swan River becoming a penal colony, it had made him even more determined to carry on the good fight over there."

David felt he was liking the young man more and more. "Once a liberal, always a liberal," he laughed. "Even though I realise Robert also had his disappointments in New South Wales."

"Oh, you mean republicanism and Eureka in Victoria and all that. He still talks longingly about it, even though he admits that he and others like him underestimated the power of the squatters, who even with their convict backgrounds, still stayed loyal to Britain."

"It was all to do with the wool trade and the contracts the squatters had with the big British merchants," said David. "Did you ever meet Charles Harpur, the political activist and writer?"

"I did. He and Robert Black share the same ideals."

"How about you?" asked David, looking the young man straight in the eye.

Daniel smiled. "Well, unlike the sons of the ex-convict squatters, I've stayed true to my rebel heritage. Both my grandparents were transported out in the first fleet. My father did well for himself as a government printer, and is certainly less political than his youngest son. No, Mr Baker, I feel I have an axe to grind. That's why I became a journalist."

"I fully understand," was the reply. "And call me David."

"As far as I'm concerned, you can dispense with my surname also," contributed Michael. He gave a wry grin. "And speaking about axes to grind, you'll be needing more than just metaphors if you want to come out sandalwooding, my young friend."

"Well, I will admit I've had little to do with axes, apart from chopping up firewood. But I'm certainly willing to learn."

Murmering her apologies, Mary moved indoors. It was

almost nine-thirty, and with Judith away helping to teach school, it was Mary's duty to prepare morning tea.

At her call, they all went into the old house, David yelling for Timothy, who had just arrived back in the old spring cart, after having driven round the sheep. Daniel liked the atmosphere, the sweet motherliness of Mary, the stoicism of David, the strength and capability of Michael and the warmth and wittiness of Timothy. He had already met Judith and her three children, and he felt that if there was ever a family he could take to, it was the Baker-O'Learys.

"Well, it looks like you're hired, Daniel," said Michael, as they left the house after the cup of tea with scones. "What about your belongings?"

"Oh, I'm travelling light," returned Daniel, airily. "I've everything in my saddle-bag."

"Well, I hope you've a change of clothes," suggested Michael, not unkindly. "After you've put away your horse, I want you to help us remove the wagon wheels. You'll be battling to stay clean."

Daniel laughed, realising that Michael was testing him out, wondering whether a journalist could prove a good practical assistant out in the bush.

"I've brought out a change," he replied casually. "As a matter of fact, I came out in my best just to create a good impression."

"You did then." Michael liked the young man's straight-forwardness. "So now get in your work togs and give us a hand. I want to get moving as soon as possible, otherwise we could be out there half the summer. Now, hop to it!"

"Right!" Daniel realised that though Michael was friendly enough, he was not a man to be trifled with.

Late in the afternoon, Judith returned home from school with her three boys, Rory, the youngest, though only five, having been taken along by his mother to learn the ropes.

Having met Daniel earlier in the more disciplinary confines of the school, the boys were now able to entertain him in their own free environment. But while John, assisted by little Rory, proudly showed off the farm's machinery, including a Ridley stripper and a McCormack mechanical mower, Paddy was more inclined to reveal to the visitor a couple of magpies, sitting high in a nest on an old white-gum, explaining how every year in the spring when the birds were nesting, the adult magpies would attack the boys, especially singling out Paddy, who had been deliberately throwing stones at the nest. Paddy was the one who also showed Michael what was left of the Avon River, now only a string of stagnant pools, after such a run of dry seasons. Though obviously the daredevil type, Paddy was also the one who showed the visitor his school books, proudly giving a demonstration of his reading ability. Nonetheless, Daniel took to all the boys, joining in a game of marbles - or aggies as the lads called them - while they waited for the tea-bell.

Within three days, Michael and Daniel were ready for the track. Daniel's pony was tied alongside Michael's behind the wagon. Though it was just after daybreak, the family were all there to see them off, the two older boys climbing all over the wagon in a last desperate attempt to travel out with their father. Like any a brave member of Robin Hood's band, about which he had been encouraged to read by his parents, Paddy's bold inquisitive grey eyes were alight with adventure.

Just as they were about to leave, Judith climbed quickly and agilely up to the driver's seat, giving Michael one last kiss. Michael gaily responded like a young lover. Judith's looks had already impressed Daniel, as had Michael's strong masculine stature. The young journalist's mind now conjured up thoughts of romance and an enduring love between the pair.

After Michael and Daniel had left the precincts of the farm, the first part of the road or track wound east-north-east through terrain which to anyone familiar with the district was commonplace. First York-gum and white-gum woodlands, underlaid with jam-bush and black wattle acacia, soon to change dramatically into great stretches of sandplain, covered in tamar, tussock and the occasional clump of mallees.

In the first three days they covered around sixty miles, and found themselves skirting north around a large area of sandplain which had been obviously dodged by earlier travellers with wheeled vehicles owing to the treacherous soft surface.

By midday next day they were in higher much firmer terrain, so hard in fact that every so often the wagon wheels clattered over patches of solid sheet ironstone. Late in the afternoon the track dipped down into a pleasant glade, on the edge of which was a white-dumped convict well with windlass and bucket. Turning a windlass handle each, the pair drew brackish water from the well, pouring it down a chute into a trough for the animals. After watering and feeding the horses, they had just sat down to a rough meal, when a little procession pulled in. Accompanying the drays, was a huge wagon, its flared sides torn and splintered from years of use.

"They are sandalwooders permanently engaged in the trade," remarked Michael. "They spend a lot of their spare time in York."

"In the tavern, too, by the looks," said Daniel, with good humour. "Look at 'em passing the bottle round. Anyhow, I suppose we would not be very popular. Too many wagons like this one could put them out of business."

Michael smiled to himself, realising that Daniel's journalistic appraisal of the sandalwood trade was already beginning. "Of course," quipped Michael, "but we are going well beyond their normal territory."

"There's gold out there also, isn't there?" added Daniel, with a half-smile.

Michael jerked up his head. "So Henry told you about that

also. I guess that is the real reason you wanted to come out with me?"

"Well partly," admitted Daniel, feeling better because Michael seemed to be taking it in good heart. "Though Henry had already told me, back there I didn't want to let on, because you may have thought me insincere. Anyhow, there's been so much talk about gold since I arrived here, what with them finding good signs well inland from Geraldton, I suppose it's only a matter of time before you find it in payable quantities, as they did in Victoria in the 1850s, and later in Queensland."

Michael shrugged. "The trouble in Westralia is that the likely spots are only to be found in the most inhospitable country. As Henry and his American mate, Jim Dunbar have so often pointed out, the men who find it will need to be made of the right stuff."

"Yet this colony needs capital so much, I can't understand why the authorities won't encourage more prospecting parties, as they did in Queensland with such great success? Certainly you haven't lacked exploration in the last few years, but as with your far north, it seems only for the purpose of running more sheep and cattle. Chasing grass so to speak."

"I agree," said Michael. "I think it is all to do with the types of people who still run the colony, or I should say dominate the Governor's Council. They're the same people who own or lease the bulk of the colony's arable lands. To them exploration is largely about looking for new pastures for their livestock, as you inferred. Also, as these men are all powerful, and as they themselves or their sons usually accompany the exploration teams, the top families always get first pick of the new pastures, as has happened up north in the last ten years."

"I know Michael. It hasn't really changed, has it? As I mentioned to David, just after we first met, Robert Black has instructed me well. Since Black left of course, the colony had its detestable convict era, initiated by the same families, the McAllums, Trigwells and Andersons and the like who by then after eating out the Avon and Toodyay Valleys, had grabbed most of the rich redlands around Geraldton or Champion Bay. But now they say all the natural grasses and edible shrubs in the Geraldton region have begun to disappear, so the same families have had to take their flocks and herds even further afield, conquering the northern blacks, there to establish domains around the Gascoyne, the Fortescue, the Pilbara, and finally right up north in the tropical Kimberleys."

"As David, er Father says," replied Michael, "with them it's all about land, as it always has been. Though they also still dominate most of the businesses in the colony, they can't feel secure unless they also hold dominion over the soil. And that does not mean they look after the soil, because as agriculturists, they've proven pretty damn poor." Michael laughed. "According to Henry, rather than try and grow feed for their animals, they'd prefer to eat the country out and move on."

Daniel nodded his head slowly. "The way they've spread their flocks and herds around up north, certainly proves they're efficient nomads, at least." He gave a grim smile. "Maybe it's still left for these few astute families - as we cannot deny they are - to find payable gold. Or I should say, put some of their wealth into better prospecting methods so that gold may pull this backward colony out of the mire."

Michael's lips firmed. "Not if I can prevent it. I'd like to make sure it's just the ordinary folk."

The former Fenian was suddenly quiet, realising that he was just spouting empty words. Here he was still living a bogus existence. A man who should still be serving time in Fremantle Gaol with his other rebel compatriots. What chance had he against men who not only held dominion over most of the colony's arable lands and its commerce, as well as its Parliament - but also over its judiciary. In fact, besides

24

Perth and Fremantle, every Government Resident or District Magistrate, be it in York, Northam, Toodyay, Bunbury, Albany or Geraldton, had some sort of blood connection with the Landed Six - the McAllums, the Trigwells, the Andersons, the Mainwarings, the Bartletts and the Clayton-Brownes.

The ex-Fenian got to his feet. "Look, I think I'll turn in," he grunted but suddenly smiled apologetically. "Yet not before a whisky. Or should I say, Timothy's colonial spirits." He retrieved a bottle from a pack in the wagon. "Here Daniel, take a swig."

"Yes, thank you," replied Daniel politely, having been puzzled at Michael's sudden silence, yet realising he could do little about it. He would be living with the man for six weeks or more, so he'd better get used to it.

The next ten days saw them travelling due east through miles of flat country, growing thick stands of black wattle and jam under salmon gum and gimlet. So far all the area had appeared to be under lease, as indicated by painted pegs or brand signs gouged into trees. In cynical fashion Michael remarked that the brands were those of the Landed Six. Next day it seemed that they were in unoccupied territory. Michael realised that they would now have to look for water, because the end of the leases meant the end of the convict wells. But because the weather was cold and the mornings dewy, they decided to journey on for at least a half day. They travelled along a winding track for about ten miles through a red ti-tree flat, overlaid with gimlet, salmon and a species of York gum.

With the sun at its meridian, they hobbled the wagon horses, and after a quick lunch saddled the ponies, not only to search for sandalwood, but as it was virgin country, to search out prospects for grazing. By nightfall they had circumnavigated a large area, finding not only a dearth of sandalwoods, but an over-abundance of ti-tree, so much in fact, that the shrubs as they really were, choked everything else out bar the big trees.

Michael realised that the thick ti-tree scrub also made it extremely difficult for shepherding sheep, without large amounts of it being cleared, which on a pastoral lease was forbidden by the authorities. In addition, the almost impenetrable ti-tree, not only prevented the growth of the jam acacia, but also the growth of the winter native grass, both of which were essential to flockowners.

Nonetheless, the Irishman decided to mark out a location, gouging the Baker brand into a series of trees along the track bounding what he calculated was around ten thousand acres of possible grazing lease.

"If it was much closer to York, I'd say it would be a better agricultural prospect than one for running sheep," remarked Michael. "But this far out, I'm afraid it could be very short of rain."

"Yes," returned Daniel. "By the look of the dust on our wagon, I'd say you could be not far wrong, and here it is the middle of winter."

"Well, it's been an exceptionally dry one, similar to the last three years. That's why you haven't seen any sheep on the big leases back there. The nob families, as Henry calls them, have had to keep all their sheep back in the valley. As a matter of fact, they have been importing chaff and oats by ship from South Australia. It makes woolgrowing damned expensive."

"Well, I suppose it's good for South Australia Michael. Unlike you, they've had a run of good seasons."

"And they've even been exporting wheat here," replied Michael unhappily. "Of course, the sad fact is, they can ship wheat from South Australia to Fremantle, cheaper than we can cart it by wagon to our capital from York. Even if we had the wheat to sell."

"I can't understand why a struggling colony like Western Australia stands by Britain's free trade principles," replied

Daniel. "This situation with South Australia proves it."

"Yes. With the Home Office advocating free trade, how can a backward colony like this one survive? I realise South Australia was settled years after Western Australia, but there you have it, a large wheat producer dumping its surplus on its neighbour. Free trade, pah! It's all right when everyone is equal."

Daniel smiled cynically. "As regards free trade, there's the old story about alligators in a pool. The big ones usually survive by gobbling up the little ones. In a frontier situation, the new agriculturists just have to be protected. Still, it makes me wonder whether the Home Office really cares about grain production here? Looking at Australia as a whole, Britain probably sees Western Australia largely as a wool-producer, with the t'othersiders like South Australia quite fit to look after the weaker colony's table needs."

"I agree," said Michael. "Certainly a colony needs more than just wool to make it a success. What I mean is that as well as pastoralists, we need our smallholders or yeomen, as we have in the Avon Valley, and not without proven production, I might add. If only Mother nature would give us a decent winter!"

"Anyhow, enough said!" Michael took a mouthful of home-grown whisky, and handed the bottle to Daniel. "Here, have a nightcap - seeing that all the claypans are dry, tomorrow we'd better make tracks back to the last convict well."

After he had taken a swig, Daniel gave a grin. "Well, believe it or not, it looks like rain coming up in the west. Who knows, we could be lucky."

And lucky they were, for that night a good half inch of rain fell, filling a small claypan close to where they were camped. Now, rather than returning to the convict well, they hobbled the wagon horses by the claypan, and struck out west on their ponies to find out the extent of the rain.

Moving at a jog-trot, by midday they found themselves

in vastly different terrain, showing the occasional gravel ridge, the soil on the slopes a deep metallic red. There was also the semblance of a low range to the east. Michael recognised it as the area described by Henry, where he and Jim Dunbar had found traces of gold.

They decided to press on and soon came across a good untouched stand of sandalwood, which Henry had also talked about. They were also pleased to discover that the rain had indeed penetrated this far, replenishing a gnamma hole down from a big granite outcrop.

They made camp for the night, and next day they returned to the claypan to find they had company. Encouraged by the rain, and curious to find out what Michael and Daniel were up to, the sandalwooders had also pressed on.

With only a nod for a greeting, Michael and Daniel hitched up their wagon horses, realising that the wily sandalwooders would be soon following them. Yet both realised that there was little they could do about it.

With the slow wagon it took them a good day and a half to reach Henry's sandalwood site, and after they had selected a good place for a permanent camp, they were not at all surprised when the sandalwooders pulled in behind them, finally halting their wagon and drays, only a stone's throw away.

Towards evening, playing the diplomat, Daniel walked over to speak to the opposition. The leader, Sam Wescott, was a hard-bitten type, who was not frightened of hard work. Although he drank heavily, he had saved up enough to buy his own wagon and team and had joined up with the others who owned the two drays, which though convenient in the bush, were not practicable for long hauling.

After the exchange of small talk, Daniel suggested that they might be trespassing.

"Like hell we are," swore Sam, scratching his unshaven jaw. "All the sandalwood in this country belongs to us cutters. It's our means of subsistence."

He gave Daniel a glare. "I don't know about you, but that Mick O'Leary's married to the Baker daughter. They're farmers, an' they shouldn't be out here!"

"But they are not big farmers like the McAllums and Andersons who also have their hands in city business," pointed out Daniel. "I understand they have far bigger wagons than even yours on the go."

"I know that," said Sam. "But there's big pirates as well as little pirates. They say even back in the days of Guv'nor Stirlin', the sandalwooders were allowed a free rein, so you'd better move on."

Daniel could not argue, for the sandalwooder had a strong point. But when told, Michael was obstinate.

"But this far out, surely the first finder has the choice. We are staying here, and that's that."

Taken aback, Daniel said no more, realising in all truth, he was only Michael's workman.

Michael put his hand on the young man's shoulder. "Sorry, Daniel, I suppose I'm a bit hard, but I guess this far out in the wilderness, ideals get swept aside. Sort of dog eat dog."

"Yes, rule of the frontier," smiled Daniel. "Of course, the editor of the *Fremantle Herald* where I work part-time, could think differently. Seeing that he is an ex-convict, he is very much for the little man."

Realising he was a transportee himself, made Michael think twice, but his stubbornness remained. "Well, I'm usually for the little man, too. But it looks the best patch of sandalwood around, and we've come a long way." He grunted, as if still not sure of himself. "Anyhow, let's forget it, I've got a damper in the camp oven. Tonight we'll have supper in style."

Next morning the pair prepared for work as if the sandalwooders were nowhere in sight. But the opposition was not to be beaten that easily. Sam and his mates hurled taunts every time they came near, even to the extent of firing shots,

29

after they'd been primed by a few rot-gut whiskies. But these proved nothing more than scare tactics, and Michael and Daniel just kept their heads down, apparently engrossed in their labour.

The usual practice after a good rain, was to pull the sandalwoods out by the roots with a couple of horses, the whole tree being of value. Then the branches had to be lopped off and the wood stripped of its bark. The pair also profited by watching the veteran sandalwooders, noting how they let the precious timber lie and dry as long as possible, to make it lighter for the wagon. They also copied the sandalwooders method of cutting wagon-hurdles from the straight-growing gimlet trees.

Here Daniel showed that he was better with the axe than he had made out, increasing Michael's respect for him. Daniel also showed he was no novice with a rifle. It was necessary for them, as for the sandalwooders, to supplement their rations by shooting the occasional kangaroo, which with the long-legged emu-bird were there in plenty. Also white cockatoos and smaller green parrots kept up a chatter as if protesting at the human intrusion of the wilds. The birds and native animals also frequented the replenished water-holes and claypans, prompting a comment from Daniel that it was a mystery how they survived in the drier periods, especially in summer.

"Yes, it is a mystery," Michael had replied. "But they do survive, and apparently when water does become available they make a welter of it."

The work went on for more than a month, the drying sandalwood timber whitening in the sun as it lay lined up in small stacks ready for the wagon. But though the pair worked diligently, their more experienced neighbours worked better. The huge old wagon was loaded before Michael and Daniel's was three-quarters filled. A further advantage with the contractors were the drays, which they used to ferry the sandalwood to the wagon from the more inaccessible spots. All the sandalwooders had to do now was to stack their drays high, ready for the road similar to their wagon. The problem now for Michael and Daniel, was that the grove was cut out.

The disgruntled pair were now obliged to saddle their horses and ride ahead looking for another patch, which they found ten miles ahead. They had almost reached the new location with the wagon, when a heavy shower of rain fell, and the wagon became stuck in the sticky clay soil. It rained all that night and next day; three inches were measured in a tea billy. There was little they could do now but wait for the soil to dry out.

It was now a chance for the pair to ride ahead and search for gold, about which they had talked so much while cutting and loading the sandalwood.

Following a narrowing trail for around two hours they came across the reef previously described by Henry. The rain-washed quartz showed obvious traces of the precious metal. Grabbing each a pick and spade, which they had strapped to their horses, they set to work shovelling out more quartz from the dark-red alluvium. But though they dug out to a good three feet, smashing up piles of quartz rock in the process, the yield was no better than on the surface - only the occasional glimmer.

Not beaten, they rode onto a second reef, also described by Henry, but they ended up with the same result.

Disgusted, Michael threw down his pick.

"At this rate, we'd need to take back a whole wagonload of rock to make any profit!" he swore.

"We are far better off with the sandalwood," replied Daniel. He looked longingly east towards the distant range. "You know, I'll bet there's payable gold out there just the same. The geology is too much like the goldfields in Victoria, even though it's a far drier climate."

"Exactly what Henry says. Similar terrain to around Ballarat and Bendigo, also the goldfields of California."

Michael stroked his chin. "You know, I'd say to have had so much rain out here is unusual. If ever there was a time to strike out further it's now." The Irishman looked mournful. "The trouble is we've been away nearly seven weeks already. At home they'd be sure to be worried."

Daniel was eager. "Well, they wouldn't be worrying much about me, surely. After we've loaded the wagon, what about leaving me here with my horse and a few stores? I'm beholden to no one. Why, if I did find payable gold, I could really write a story, couldn't I?" The young man's eyes were shining.

"No," replied Michael, emphatically. "I feel kind of responsible for you. If you failed to return, I'd never forgive myself. Now, cut out the pipe dreams and let's get back to the wagon. It should be dry enough to shift it out."

"Well, you're the boss," replied Daniel unhappily.

They returned to the wagon, and within three days had it topped up with green sandalwood, ready to move out. Passing the old campsite next morning, they noticed that the sandalwooders like themselves, had been held up with the heavy rain. In fact, going by the fresh mud tracks, it seemed they had left only recently.

As they drove down from the higher slopes to the red ti-tree flat, Michael and Daniel found it slower and slower going, the horses down to their knees, as they strained through the wetter patches. They found it even worse where the sandalwooders had damaged the track, and felt almost triumphant when next day after rounding a bend, they came across the sandalwooders' wagon bogged to the axles, the ground around already beginning to set. Sam and his two offsiders were cursing freely, as they contemplated unloading the wagon to make it lighter.

Although Michael was still annoyed over the sandalwooders' belligerent attitude, he knew he could never leave them in such a predicament.

"Do you want to borrow our team for an extra haul?" he called from the wagon seat.

Sam, formerly hostile, was now ready to take any help that was offering. They had already tried the dray horses in front of the wagon team, but still with no result.

"Aye, we could at that," replied Sam, grudgingly, realising he had little choice.

"Right, we can't see them stuck," grunted Michael to Daniel. Let's unhitch!" But Sam's offsiders had already beaten them to it, in case the pair changed their minds. They then quickly cut wooden swingle-trees to spread the chains between the horse-teams.

There were now eighteen Clydesdales lined up in rows of three, ready for the pull. As Sam gave a bellow, each man laid hold of the wagon, heaving to his utmost. After much creaking and twisting, the large wagon began to emerge out of the bog like some prehistoric monster, its mud-caked wheels gripping on the ti-tree brush which had been laid out in front like a mattress. Soon the lead horses began to bolt forward, chains clanking, the men yelling happily, as the wagon rolled easily over the dried out surface.

Sam was now all smiles. "Well, now," he said, "you may as well stay an' partake in a whisky."

"Sure an' begorrah, lud," laughed Michael, putting on an act. "We might at that, because we've run out of the good life-blood ourselves."

That night they shared the hospitality of the bushmen, as the permanent sandalwooders were so often called. Daniel as a reporter, found out much about the men's colourful pasts, something he had been unable to do back in the sandalwood patch - even though they had been camped so close together. As always, he knew it had taken just a simple act of kindness, to create good fellowship.

Next morning they even aided the sandalwooders to reload their wagon, the plan now being to travel together just in case one of the wagons became bogged again. It proved a good

33

tactic, because even after they had safely negotiated the treacherous ti-tree flat they found formerly dry creek-beds awash with mud-stained water.

As they drew closer to York, the evidence of a good rain was even more pronounced. Although it had meant a much slower journey returning home with the sandalwood, Michael felt joyous, knowing that it had been the best winter rain the district had experienced for years. As they entered the precincts of the Baker-O'Leary farm, Michael pointed out to Daniel the lush green wheat-crop.

"What a difference," rejoined Daniel. "When we left more than two months back, much of it was like a red fallow paddock."

"Yes," said Michael. "They must have received that earlier rain besides. Also, because the winter rains blow in from the coast, they probably got much more than we've seen." He laughed. "Well, seeing that most bad seasons here come in cycles, the recent good rains could mean another run of plenty. If we are to be free of droughts for say another three years, it could be that long before I'm out on the sandalwood track again."

"But what about the gold?" queried Daniel, somewhat sadly. "You know, over the last few days, I've been thinking that instead of returning back east, I feel I'd like to stay here. As a matter of fact, I was hoping I could go out with you again next year. That range in from where we were camped, I can't get it out of my mind."

"Neither can Henry," smiled Michael. "But as he estimated, the range could be another good fifty miles beyond that spot. Anyhow, Henry's far too old, and if predictions are correct, next year I'll be far too busy on the farm."

"Pity," replied Daniel, wistfully. "If we found payable gold I could write that good story. And think what it could do for this broken down colony."

As they sat together up the front of the wagon, Michael

gripped the young man's shoulder affectionately. "Looks like you've become one of us, then, Daniel. One of the newer Westralians, looking for the end of the rainbow."

But on arriving home all such sentiments were temporarily cast aside. The family was tearful and overjoyed to see them after so long without news. The boys were highly excited also, not unexpectedly climbing to the top of the lofty load of sandalwood. Paddy brought screams from his grandma as he hung perilously over the edge.

Yet the family looked so serene, Michael was certain that there was something else besides just his and Daniel's welcome return and the fact that the farm looked to have a bumper crop. It was so well expressed in Judith's eyes.

"Michael, the Americans have rescued the Fenians from Fremantle Gaol," she said simply. "The family insisted that when you arrived, it was me who should give you the glad tidings."

Michael's reaction was to grab Judith and waltz her around the floor. The news of the daring rescue of the Fenians by their American Irish comrades had left him ecstatic. Judith was as one with him, having already thanked God for the courageous men who had put their lives at risk to perform the hazardous deed.

CHAPTER 3

Though as a journalist he was not unaccustomed to startling news, Michael's performance had left Daniel open-mouthed. The way the Irishman grabbed the latest copy of the *Fremantle Herald*, made him even more mystified. Certainly the headlines were sensational ...

FENIANS MAKE DARING ESCAPE BY YANKEE WHALER. AUTHORITIES DEEPLY EMBARRASSED.

The last few days in Fremantle have contained all the trappings of a comic opera. On the afternoon of August the 15th, a man came galloping madly into Fremantle from Rockingham, with word that an American whaleboat had been seen in the vicinity of Warnbro Bay, manned and armed with rifles. He went on to report that the boat had taken on nine men from the beach, some dressed in prison clothes.

With the report, the Fremantle police immediately attempted to telegraph Rockingham, only to find that the line had been cut. Finally, reports from a fisherman revealed that the Yankee whaleboat was still battling heavy seas on its way out to a vessel anchored well west of Garden Island. In great haste the military commandeered the coastal steamer *Georgette*, arming it with a six-pounder.

The *Georgette* eventually steamed through

the South Passage, between Garden and Carnac Islands, to find the whaleboat still struggling towards what has since been confirmed to be the American barque, *Catalpa*. But before the *Georgette* could reach the whaleboat, the run-aways had climbed aboard the Yankee vessel.

According to an eyewitness, the *Georgette* immediately hailed the *Catalpa* calling on it to give up the prisoners, or be bombarded with shell. The Yankees retaliated by running up the Stars and Stripes and threatened to rake the *Georgette* with rifle shot.

Reluctant to create an international incident, the Commander ordered the Georgette to steam back to Fremantle, letting the *Catalpa* sail away with the Fenians ...

Our report ends with the news that the escape of the prisoners has thrown Fremantle into a gala mood - the population obviously well on the side of the underdogs.

Michael brandished the newspaper, finding it hard to control his elation.

"Look, with such sympathy in the colony, why should we still keep my secret from Daniel here?"

"Why should we indeed?" sang Judith, her eyes alight. "The way I feel, I'd like to shout it to the world." She turned. "Yes Daniel, as you must have guessed by now, Michael is one of the brave Fenians."

Daniel's eyes showed a little hurt, as though annoyed that Michael had not taken him more into his confidence. Still, journalists had a reputation of being obligated to pass on information to the public. In fact, his reporter's intuition had already told him that the Irishman was someone out of the ordinary. But this news was beyond all bounds of the imagination.

Judith told Daniel how she had first met Michael during a winter storm while driving to teach school. How they were attracted to each other, and how later, Liz Lovedale had suggested that Michael disguise himself and stay in the colony, at the same time deluding the authorities that he had fled the country on a whaler with his compatriots, John Boyle O'Reilly and Timothy Regan.

Daniel's eyes were still wide open with wonder. At the same time his mind again conjured up romantic thoughts, as it had that day when the pair had kissed goodbye on the wagon seat.

"Well now, what a story! But of course it is still not safe to print it. Not that it won't be. You may be sure that when the news gets out about the Fenians being taken off by the Americans, both the authorities here and in Britain will have to eat humble pie. I only wish the overland telegraph was completed from here to t'otherside, so I could contact Robert Black. Once he hears the news, I tell you, he'll have it all over the globe in no time. Robert has already written some pretty potent stuff about the Irish prisoners being locked in Fremantle Gaol unnecessarily, far away at the ends of the earth. Now he can really do justice to it." He turned. "Yes, Michael, it will be so good for you. After this, Britain will feel so humiliated she is sure to hand out pardons to the military Fenians, even though they have all absconded, including you, my friend." After taking a good measure of colonial spirits from Timothy, who had opened a bottle to celebrate, he went on. "What did the other papers say? They weren't on the side of the Fenians, like the *Herald*, I'll bet?"

"No, not by a long chalk," agreed David, who along with Mary had been happily surveying the scene. He handed Daniel a copy of the *Inquirer*.

"The very fact that both conservative papers talk about Yankee impudence," David went on. "... Well, I guess that's all you need to know."

"But you must remember, Father," corrected Judith. "The other papers have had their front pages filled with the trial of Roger Bartlett, who shot his wife."

"Goodness," said Daniel. "He's the son of one of the top families, isn't he? Here I am a reporter, and look at all I've been missing. So what happened?"

"It was more than a month ago," explained Judith. "But you can read all about it in one of the earlier issues of the *Gazette* - or in a copy of the *Fremantle Herald*. Naturally, they both give different versions. While the *Herald* says he should face the music similar to a member of a lower class family, both the *Gazette* and the *Inquirer* are calling for a plea of unsound mind, in the hope of his only receiving a light sentence."

"They are trying to get him off similar to Darcy McAllum who shot the savage," broke in David. "Which I guess you already know about, Daniel."

"Yes, I do. The Bartletts like the McAllums and Clayton-Brownes were among the first settlers around Champion Bay, weren't they? But why did Roger Bartlett shoot his wife? I don't go such people, but I will say it's a bit unusual. In domestic strife such families generally uphold their dignity, or strength of character, or whatever they call it." Daniel pursed his lips in distaste.

"Well, Roger Bartlett did have his problems," David said. "Back in 1864 he lost his first wife during the terrible measles epidemic. That was just after he first moved to Champion Bay. Since that time he became obsessed with breeding blood-stock, especially race-horses. Also in recent years, he began to gamble heavily. In fact, he met his second wife in Victoria, where he had been living it up, so to speak. Drink of course, went with it. The second wife became an even worse alcoholic than her husband. I understand they both used to get badly inebriated together, and according to the papers in one dreadful argument he pulled out a pistol and shot her." David gave a sigh. "But

I must say Roger Bartlett was one, different to the rest of the upper crust. In fact, he has admitted his guilt and says that he's ready to take the consequences, even though the conservative papers are trying hard to protect his character. Roger Bartlett has also favoured responsible government here, unlike his peers. This would mean lifting us from our degrading status of just a Crown Colony under a Governor, and if such did eventuate it could also mean full voting rights for all adult males."

"The top families wouldn't like that, would they?" Daniel laughed cynically. "Especially as they say there are still over six thousand conditional pardon convicts in the colony. They would never vote for the gentry in a thousand years, even though their children might. Yes, being from the chosen few, who traditionally believed they were born to rule, Roger Bartlett sounds very liberal. It is certainly a pity. Still, justice must be done. Even if he does come from a privileged family, he should not be protected."

"That's what the *Herald* points out," continued David. "If he had been from a worker or a smallholder family he wouldn't have stood a chance. It would have been the gallows and no mistake."

Daniel's brain was active. "When I return to Fremantle, I might ask the editor of the *Herald* if I can take up the case. In New South Wales it was my forte, writing all about one of society's worst imperfections. Different rules for the rich and poor." "Spoken like a true journalist Daniel," said Michael. "While wealth or position is placed in front of principle or morality, your kind will always be needed."

As he took another draught of colonial spirits, the Irishman laughed heartily. "Anyhow, let's think of nicer things. Seeing that we have both returned safely and with my future almost assured with the Fenians' escape, I feel in a jolly mood. Who'll volunteer to ride into York and invite Liz and Henry to a thanksgiving?"

"Goodness," exclaimed Mary, looking at the clock. "It's

almost three o'clock. "I must bake some cakes."

"No need," laughed Michael. "Jerked mutton and damper will do, Daniel and I have become quite accustomed to it."

"No," insisted Judith, kissing him. "You'd be surprised what Mother and I can rustle up. Now Michael, seeing that you suggested it, you can be the one who rides into town for Liz and Henry."

"No I'll go," volunteered Daniel with good humour. "After all that walking behind the wagon, my pony could do with a gallop. See you all later."

So the Baker-O'Learys had another celebration, this time with Daniel included. When the young man told David that he had made a decision to stay in the colony, David was pleased. The colony badly needed such men, even though Daniel as yet may not have shown his true colours. While there were those who spouted the time-worn philosophies of the high-bred Anglicans, and who also ran both conservative newspapers, there were those like the editor of the *Herald*, the ex-convict, whom David believed could be just as vitriolic. Though Robert Black had often been anti-government, he had only been in opposition when he believed a government's policies were immoral, or against the teachings of Christ. But it seemed the expiree intellectuals, as the proprietors of the "Herald" were called, often preached downright atheism, which David with his upbringing could not accept. He only hoped that Daniel would remain true to Black in that respect. But there was so much being thrown up to learned young people like Daniel these days. Not only the evolutionary dogma of Charles Darwin and Herbert Spencer, which only strengthened the old adage that might was right, but also the socialism of Karl Marx, which in many ways was similar to the teachings of Christ, except that the Almighty was replaced by an ideal and man was left with no Spiritual Light for guidance. Having been so much influenced by his Quaker mother as

41

a child, David felt that without a belief in the Inner Light, which also meant belief in oneself, humankind might again revert to a Dark Age, this time under the sway of rationalists and bureaucrats rather than Popes and Bishops.

Less than a year later, Britain as expected, granted pardons to all former Irish rebels, including the Fenians. It was the cue for yet another celebration, but this time it was held in Liz and Henry's pub in York. Though the Anglicans generally voiced their disgust that Britain had weakened so - as had the British Governor regarding Michael - the other denominations welcomed the news, particularly the Catholics, who were mostly Irish anyhow. Also, many an English convict had been converted to Catholicism after taking an Irish bride. By this year of 1878, the children from these unions had themselves become adult - and had themselves taken wives, their children attending the various schools along the Avon and Toodyay valleys. Even so, to Liz and Henry's dismay, society in towns such as York, Northam and Toodyay, now showed a definite split between what was still called the bond and the free.

While the families such as the McAllums and Andersons still held themselves aloof, the more middle-class Anglicans had also formed their own institutions. One such in both Northam and York was the Mechanic's Institute, more the domain of bank managers, lawyers, and men who liked to profess themselves untainted by a convict past.

In opposition, the men with bond backgrounds had formed Workingmen's Associations, even though some of these men were more literate than many of those who patronised the Mechanics's Institute. This was especially so of expiree schoolteachers, similar to Ray Phelan, who had been originally transported for larceny. As Daniel Hordacre had found out since the end of the convict era in 1868, every schoolteacher assigned to the country areas had been an ex-convict. Just lately Daniel had compiled a story on Robert

Mewburn, also transported for larceny, who only a year previously had opened a school in Mandurah, forty miles south of Fremantle. According to Daniel, Mewburn had already become extremely popular, even to the extent that he was courting the daughter of a prominent local identity. In fact, in order to gain the education that had been previously lacking in isolated towns such as Mandurah, the young woman had elected to become one of Mewburn's pupils.

The same stories could be told in the smaller towns throughout the Avon and Toodyay valleys, where besides scores of conditional pardon teachers, there were also many expiree clerks. Two of these had become secretary-engineers of both the Northam and Toodyay Road's Boards. Also there were proven men of business and commerce, such as Tom Callahan, who though one of the wealthiest men in the colony, still lived in Toodyay, and being a loyal Irishman, had naturally attended the get-together in Liz and Henry's York pub. Also celebrating the pardoning of the Fenians, was Father Flaherty, who before the *Catalpa* episode, had shifted temporarily to Fremantle. With Frank Mulcahy, he had passed secret messages to the Fenians in the Fremantle Gaol. Unlike the Irish padre, who had a certain protection as a priest, Mulcahy had believed it safer to flee to America with the others.

To make room for the swelling crowd, Liz had opened the wide doors into the hotel lounge, giving access to all except the children. She had also employed extras behind the bar so that she and Henry could join their old friends. Yet sadly, some were missing.

Teamster Joe, of wagon-track and sandalwood fame had passed away. So too had Angus Macregor, the wily Scot from the North Toodyay district, who with Jock Douglas had come out from Scotland in the late 1830s as professional shepherds, or flockmasters. Both had become large graziers in their own right. Angus was represented by his daughter Jeannie, who had married Henry's American mate, Jim

Dunbar. The ex-whaler and adventurer had taken up the now well-known property of Mt Rupert, north of Northam. On the way, Jim and Jeannie had met up with the Watkins family. Ernie was the resourceful convict who had successfully sought the hand of Mary-Jane, the pensioner guard's daughter. Since their marriage and settlement near Jennapullin north of Northam in 1853, Ernie had really made a name for himself. Previously he had grown wheat on a small patch on Crown land not yet released for agriculture. But Ernie now held sway over six thousand acres. His four grown sons and three daughters had all settled down on the same property. Just recently, despite violent protests from a number of the district's early families, Ernie had been elected president of the Jennapullin Agricultural Society as well as having been surprisingly voted in as vice president of the Northam Workingmen's Association.

Daniel and the editor of the *Fremantle Herald*, Len Chandler, had also arrived at Liz and Henry's pub. The editor soon sought the company of Tom Callahan, who also had a financial interest in the *Herald*.

After Henry had started the proceedings from the top of the bar and offered a round of drinks for all, the crowd merged into groups. Liz and Henry were soon in the company of their old friends, including Jim Dunbar and Jeannie. Judith and Michael's boys had been told to behave themselves in a back room with other children - not without protests from the active young Paddy.

Daniel had been filling his time circulating through the crowd, making mental notes. Yet he had much on his mind. A rumour had spread that Roger Bartlett had fled the country. In fact, despite the efforts of the *Perth Gazette* and the *Enquirer* for leniency, a people's jury had sentenced him to death. Daniel, backed by the expiree editor of the *Fremantle Herald* had campaigned heavily to have this jury selected not from the top echelon, but "from the streets", as the *Herald* expressed.

"But how did the blighter manage to get away?" asked Henry incredulously. "He was supposed to have been locked up in a special section for the swells in Fremantle Gaol, with all the privileges. Christ Almighty, they musta left the cell door open for him!"

"Yeah," spoke the white-haired Jim Dunbar. "Fremantle Gaol's gettin' a bad name. What with the Fenians less than a year ago, an' now Bartlett. But they don't know whether he got on a ship or what, do they?"

"Well, it couldn't a been a whaler," smirked Henry. "Bartlett talks too much with a plum in his mouth. Those rough Yankee sailors would never have let him aboard. No, it couldn't a been a whaler."

"Yet he was secreted out somehow," said Daniel. "And I tell you, I haven't got to the bottom of it. I suspect a couple of Magistrates who were desperately trying to get him off."

"Yes," said David. "Not only friends of the family, but relatives, not that you could blame them I suppose. You only have to put yourself in the same position. It must be terribly distressing for them."

"But what would've happened if it had of been you or I, David?" argued Jim. "The bloody rope within a month, I'll bet, especially for an ex-whaler like me - even if the excuse was that I was drunk out of my mind." The American changed his expression and put his arm round the still attractive Jeannie.

"But I could never harm me darlin' wife, could I sweetheart? Even if I was boozed to the eyeballs?"

"Well, we've certainly had our arguments Jim, me darr'lin'," rejoined Jeannie with her delightful Scottish burr. "Especially when you were determined to go out gold huntin', leavin' me to run the properr'ty."

"But that was years and years ago," replied Henry. "As a matter of fact, now you mention it Jeannie, I had been about to ask Jim to hit the gold trail agen'."

"Now, now, my Henry," interrupted Liz. "Sounds like the rot-gut talkin'. Don't ye' realise your nigh on seventy."

"No, sixty eight," retorted Henry. "An' fit as I ever was. What say you, Jim?" He turned to the ex-whaler.

"Yeah, if it wasn't for our wives, we'd have struck it rich out there years ago."

Though the talk about gold was casual and carefree, Daniel's eyes had lit up.

"Those reefs of yours out there? As you know, Michael and I dug well into them, but found near enough next to nothing."

"So did we," said Henry. "You probably dug through the same material, because after ten years it would've all weathered down. Aye, I told you that there was nothin' there much but the signs. But this means that it's bound to be better out further."

"Yeah," said Jim. "Those reefs are near the start o' the greenstone country - probably the edge o' the Eldorado."

"Why didn't you pair find it?" asked Liz, scornfully. "You went out there every winter for a good six years. Call yourselves prospectors."

"Well my girl, if we'd struck a decent rain out there durin' those years, like Michael an' Daniel were lucky to get, we might have been able to go out further," expostulated Henry. "An' remember there were no convict wells along the track in them days, you had to carry your own good water just about all the way from York."

"Yes, it is much easier now," said Michael. "And after the good rain out there, we were certainly tempted. But we'd run out of time. We were out there to get sandalwood, not gold."

"I would have stayed," cut in Daniel, his eyes shining again. "As a matter of fact, if I had the money I'd be out there now. Of course, what it needs is a well-equipped expedition, even to take out drays converted to water carriers."

Jim laughed grimly. "The trouble is that you need horses to haul the water-carts, an' in a dry winter, the nags'd soon drink all the water in the carts. So you'd be no better off. No, probably what it needs is a few more convict wells."

"Who'd put 'em down?" laughed Henry. "Seein' the good water's down so deep, they're too hard a work for the average labourer, even a contractor. I s'pose that's somethin' the rotten convict era did do for us, have things done like puttin' down deep wells in hard country, which only poor bloody convicts under guard would do."

"The gentry are talking about bringing in the Chinese," suggested David.

"Aye, they would," said Henry. "Anythin' for cheap labour."

"It could be one way of finding the gold," said Daniel. "The Chinese have done very well in Queensland. They don't mind digging deep holes either, as they've proven. Maybe they could put down our deep wells out there, and even dig for gold?" The journalist changed his tune, smiling mischievously. "No, better to find the gold ourselves - eh?"

"But you are only a newcomer, Daniel," teased Jim. "Though a Yank, I've lived here permanently since 1853, an' the older ones here, they've been around since the first landin' in 1829."

"Aye," laughed Henry. "It's not up to you t'othersiders to find the gold, Daniel, it's us."

"Well, you'd better hurry up then," taunted Daniel. "I know some very tough diggers over in Victoria and Queensland who are just waiting their chance to check out the potential of the far-off west as they call it - especially for gold." He grinned sarcastically.

"So if you Western Australians want to find your own gold, you'd better be quick about it."

"Yeah," returned Jim. "We might even have some Yanks over here from Californy if we don't watch out. An' if the foreigners do beat us to it, I guess it's our own fault.

Take my kids now, my boys up at Mt Rupert. As far as gold is concerned, they couldn't care less, even though we're still findin' specks round the Wongan Hills."

"Well you keep 'em too busy on the properr'ty. O' course, now that they have proven the lands can grow good crops, even the lightlands, I suppose there's the added interest." Jeannie smiled at her husband. "Not like their scallywag father, always chasin' the rr-rainboow."

"That goes for you, too, my Henry," chimed Liz.

"Talking about rainbows," smiled Daniel. "I guess it's the scallywags chasing rainbows, who usually break first ground. That's what I meant about the t'otherside diggers, if ever you'd find adventurers and ne-er do wells, it's among them - the Victorian diggers especially."

"Yeah," agreed Jim, a faraway romantic look in his eyes. "Many have fathers who fought in the Eureka Stockade. Them were the days, weren't they, Henry, when on our way back from Americcy we stopped off at Ballarat lookin' for gold an' met Peter Lalor."

"They were good days an' all," grinned Henry. "Pity we couldn't've stayed over for the Eureka Rebellion. With that rotten Governor La Trobe makin' the diggers pay license fees whether they struck gold or not. Anyone could see the revolt was sure to happen."

"Look here," declared Liz, "we all know you both regretted missin' Eureka, but it's not about that it's about what's goin' to happen right here."

She waved her arms indicating the proceedings. "For Godsake take a back seat for once, Henry."

Jim Dunbar answered for Henry, putting his hand to his silvery forelock.

"Ye-e-s-s, Ma-a-aam," he grinned.

Two men had joined them. Tom Callahan, a man of around fifty, strongly built and red-faced, and Len Chandler, the editor of the *Fremantle Herald*, himself leaner than Callahan, with dark swarthy complexion and handle-bar moustaches.

Unlike Callahan, who had been originally transported from Ireland for cattle-stealing, Chandler had been accused of fiddling the books of his employer in East London. By his accent he was obviously a cockney, but an educated one at that. Like Callahan, since gaining his conditional pardon, Chandler had made his name in the colony, not so much for gaining quick wealth, but as a quick-witted newspaperman, often accused by the landed gentry of muck-raking and trying to up-end society.

Callahan placed his hand on Michael's shoulder.

"Well Michael," he suggested. "Seeing it's your evening, it's only appropriate that you say a few words."

"Aye," grinned Henry. "Up on the bar with ye', Michael."

"But the British pardon was not only for me," protested Michael. "But for all the Fenians."

"Yes, but you represent all your comrades here," persisted Callahan.

"Yeah," said Jim. "Up on the bar with you matey."

Although Michael had addressed a crowd before, not only as a military officer but as a rebel leader, it had been a long time.

"Go on, Michael," urged a proud Judith. "They want you. They need you."

The cheers and clapping that came as Michael vaulted onto the bar proved Judith right.

Stumbling with emotion at first, Michael quickly found his bearings.

"Friends and relatives," he began. "As this speech has been sprung upon me, I hope you'll excuse me for my wanderings. First, I would like you all to charge your glasses for the Irish, not only the Fenians, like myself, whom Britain has at last condescended to pardon, but for every Irish man and woman who has emigrated to this colony, some by force and some of their own choice. The British gentry who unfortunately still hold so much sway here try to tell us that unlike t'otherside, where a good half of the colonials are of Irish stock, here they say the percentage is insignificant. Certainly records show that before the arrival of the Fenians in '68, only two shiploads of Irish convicts had been sent to Westralia. The *Phoebe Dunbar* and the *Robert Small* arrived in Fremantle in '53, each carrying around two hundred prisoners. So not counting the Fenians that is only four hundred out of a total transportation list of close on ten thousand."

Michael laughed loudly.

"But I tell you my dear friends, the Irish have certainly made their mark. According to records, not only have far more of their proportion been hanged, others have also made their mark in commerce." He swung his arm. "Here we have Tom Callahan, a reluctant passenger on the *Robert Small* in '53, and now I'm proud to say, one of the richest men in the colony. Even that apart from very generous donations to Catholic welfare, as the Father here will tell you." Michael indicated the padre, who nodded his head to the crowd.

"That's true, but charity should be done in secret," reminded the Priest with a smile.

Callahan laughed. "Well, the fact does slip out at times." He focussed his eyes toward the top of the bar. "You're up there to pay praise to Tom Callahan, Michael, get on with your speech."

"Thank you, but still on the Irish we must not forget the two thousand Irish sewing girls, who though not transported, were indeed encouraged out here by the British with hardly a penny to their names. A great many of those women are with us this evening as wives of expiree settlers, including of course, the wife of Tom Callahan. If you don't mind, ladies, will you all please put up your hands?"

A host of hands went up, including that of the wife of Len Chandler. Nearly every transportee of worth had married an Irish bride.

"Anyhow, enough about the Irish, Michael," called Ernie

Watkins, who had also taken an Irish girl, except that she had been the daughter of an Irish pensioner guard, sent out in 1851 to manage the transportees.

"Aye Michael," spoke up another Britisher, who too had taken an Irish bride, but before being transported had been the son of a tenant farmer. "Talk about our future here. You're well eddicated, so, aye, talk about our future."

"Well, I guess seeing we are now all free men," Michael went on, "we can all face the future together. And I for one have faith in it, even though after ten years here I realise that this place is no picnic. No South Sea island where you can loaf around and pluck your necessities off trees. No my friends, no American prairie, where the land is all cleared for you and you just have to put in the plough. Nor is it a land of regular rains like dear old Ireland or Britain. Here we've just had three droughts running, which must surely come again. Yes, my people, this is a harsh unpredictable land, of which only a tiny part can be utilised for agriculture." Michael hesitated.

"I guess by now it's become a cliche, yet there's something about this land isn't there? Maybe it's the way a good rain can magnificently transform the countryside after years and years of dry. As my good wife Judith often tells me, it's worth the waiting for."

Michael was becoming emotional but the crowd was far from finished with him, and after a sustained clapping, a man yelled:

"Yet a land's no good without good leaders, Michael. When are we goin' to be rid o' the rotten nobs, who've got their noses in everythin', the sheep an' cattle stations, the banks, the shops, the pubs, an' o' course, flamin' politics?"

Michael took a deep draught from a full glass of Scotch, handed to him by Henry. "I suppose what you mean, Sir," he called, "is that when are we going to have some equality, some democracy? I must say, that while other Australian

51

colonies have had full male voting rights since 1850, we in 1878, are still fully under the jackboot of a British governor. Over t'otherside, the governors are mostly just for ceremony now, yet our few well-to-do families here tell us that we were granted an elected government in 1870. But I ask you, who are the electors? Those with wealth and those who must own more than a specified area of land. In fact, none but the same families who have dominated this colony from the outset - the McAllums, the Andersons, the Trigwells, Mainwarings and Clayton-Brownes and so on."

Michael smiled sarcastically. "Indeed, the grandsons of the old ones have lately been talking about liberalism, in the hope I believe that if Britain does grant us full male voting rights and a People's House of Assembly, these so-called liberals will still gain the vote. One candidate being groomed, I believe, is William Groves of Bunbury. But as my wife Judith and I have discussed, Groves is married into the Landed Six, and spends all his time with the genteel society."

"Aye," yelled a man. "Groves call himself a liberal. Why, he won't even let you call 'im Will."

"That's what I mean!" bellowed Michael from the top of the bar. Also I understand the *Perth Gazette* is to change its name to the *West Australian*, to give it a more liberal flavour. The *Gazette* no doubt brings too many reminders about convictism, which the proprietors instigated." Michael threw up his arms.

"But we haven't forgotten, have we? I also remind you that the editors of both the *Gazette* and the *Inquirer* have recently gained knighthoods, as had James McAllum, Brian Trigwell, Eli Anderson, indeed and others, all implicated in converting this colony into a convict establishment." He hesitated. "I suppose you could say, that if they had not got their way, we ex-cons would not be happy here in this colony today. But that is not the point, my friends, it is the principle. So with the coming people's vote, be watchful of wolves in sheep's clothing."

"Well, certainly the ones with knighthoods," growled Callahan. Although the ex-convict was far wealthier than anyone in the colony, and indeed had given far more to charity, Callahan knew that because he was a former transportee, any creditable awards from British Royalty in the future were out of the question.

Michael was becoming bored. "I've said enough," he called. "I'm just an Irish rebel, though I must say I'm still proud of it." "And we are proud of you, too, Michael," roared Callahan. "In fact, you've enlightened us so well on the colony's political problems, I think when Britain does condescend to grant us responsible government we might make you our candidate."

A loud cheer came from the crowd.

"HOORAY, Michael for our representative."

"And the way he presented himself, probably our first Premier," remarked Daniel to Judith.

"Not very likely," growled Len Chandler. "You wait and see, they'll find some way of preventing the ex-convict vote, mark my words. And as for one running as a candidate, well, now!"

"Yet it is not so much that the establishment allows the ex-convict vote, Mr Chandler," contributed a serious-eyed David. "Of which I doubt will ever happen. The problem will be our ex-convict's offspring. To forget the sins of their fathers they will naturally try to lift themselves by voting conservative. The philosophy which the *West Australian* is attempting to bring out, could trap them. What I mean is that we must be ever watchful, as Michael just implied."

"My very sentiments too, Mr Baker," replied the editor.

CHAPTER 4

For one who believed in the advantages of learning, Judith was disappointed in her two older boys. She had thought that with her encouragement, at least one might have proven studious. Yet the eldest one John, was far too practical, always anxious to be at his father's side preparing machinery, or making repairs in the blacksmith's shop. But Paddy was the one Judith was more concerned about. Though his reading ability was well above average he would not be pushed, and she felt he spent too much time following normal boyhood pursuits, such as clearing off into York three miles away and mixing with larrikin farm lads of the same nature. Though nearing fifty, Judith was determined to keep up with her part-time teaching. She felt that the family needed the money. The farm had been going through another series of dry years, making her wonder if the Baker-O'Learys were ever going to escape from a state of respectable poverty.

Judith had never regretted giving up her job teaching at the York Anglican school, where she had begun at sixteen, until leaving in 1868 to Marry Michael, a Roman Catholic. From her position in the community school assisting the ex-convict Ray Phelan, she realised how selfish the colony had been in the old days, with the children of workers and smallholders growing up with hardly a jot of schooling.

Already in York she could see society levelling out - helped also by those conditional pardon convicts who had been well educated before committing the crimes which had caused them to be transported from Britain. Judith was also inspired by the mothers, especially the Irish women who had married convicts and who now seemed determined that their children should gain a name in West Australian society. Certainly the wives themselves had never had the chance in Ireland, or in

England, to where many had been forcibly transferred to work in clothing factories.

Yet compared to Judith's experience of Anglican children, who had usually been trained in the airs and graces even before they began school, the community school children had a certain roughness about them, often coming out with unrepeatable swear words, which they had doubtless learnt from their parents. However she was pleased to find that despite the uncouthness, the children appeared endowed with a primitive code of honour. There was far less sneakiness among them than had gone on in the church school. Whatever these children did, it was usually done openly.

Even so, in such an environment she was worried about her boys, especially Paddy. Almost from the time that they spoke their first words, she had insisted that her children sound their words correctly, urging them to listen to Grandma Mary, and Grandpa David, who had never been heard to drop a "g" or misplace an "l". To make her boys more respectable, Judith had also been tempted to take them to church. But there was an agreement she and Michael had made before their marriage - though she had renounced her Anglican faith to wed in a Catholic church, any children born of the marriage were free after a certain age to stay away from religion if they so desired.

Judith had thus followed the example of her father, David, who though trained for the church in his early youth in England, had come to believe more and more in the teachings of his Quaker mother. Bring a child up to the age of seven to believe in Christ's teachings - particularly the Sermon on the Mount - and as far as religion was concerned, the child should be able to find his own way. But Judith was becoming less and less certain about her Paddy.

Even the local Padre had noticed. By now Father Flaherty had been transferred, and the new Father, true to his tradition had begun to pay visits to those whom he believed should be practising Catholics. In this decision he was spurred on by the reputation young Paddy was gaining around town. However Michael, true to his promise to Judith, would not compromise with the Priest, saying that he would prefer to regard himself simply as a non-practising Catholic, similar to his wife. But the Priest was not to be beaten so easily.

One day in York he cornered Paddy and warned him in his strong Irish brogue, that if Paddy and his family failed to attend Mass on Sunday mornings... "Paddy's whole family might go to the Divil ...!"

Despite threats and expressed doubts about the O'Learys being allowed through the Pearly Gates, Paddy's mother was already convinced that the only way to heaven, if there was one, was through good works and setting a good example, and not from weekly visits to church and torturous bouts of confession.

If there was anything Judith encouraged her boys to pray for, it was not so much for oneself, but for a better world where there was far less inequality. Michael, her rebel Irish husband, was usually in full agreement - and even if he wasn't, the deep love and respect they held for each other always won over.

Michael retained his fame as the escaped Fenian who had married the Baker daughter. Though he would sometimes stride arrogantly through the town like a military man - which in the Irish Army he had been - the more high-bred Anglicans still had a certain respect for him. Part of it undoubtedly was the correct speech, which with that blarney flavour, was even enough to charm the most respectable Anglican wife.

Having proven he was good at rhetoric, Michael had been urged to join the Reform League, which had been raised in the colony to prepare for Western Australia's long-awaited independence. But though Tom Callahan the ex-convict and successful property owner was involved, both Judith and Michael suspected the League's motives. Many of its members had connections with well-known families, including its present chairman, William Groves of Bunbury. David was exceedingly suspicious about the Reform League also, pointing out that he believed that Michael was not really wanted as a future people's candidate, as had been offered. Instead it was more likely he was required as a local organiser - one who with his popularity could gain many a smallholder or worker to a cause which was only to enable the landed gentry to retain control in the guise of moderates.

David was still an avid reader, not only of the colony's newspapers when available, but also of books and novels. While much of the reading material was now purchased from an ex-convict bookseller in York, a portion was still brought home from school by Judith, who had long come to understand her father's tastes both for the philosophical and the political.

The combination of the Baker-O'Learys in progressive ideas and intellect was said by some to be unsurpassed in the colony. Nonetheless Mary could still not be classed as a free-thinker. Despite all, she had remained loyal to her church. Though frail in her older years, she regularly attended the weekly Anglican service in York. Through a concerted effort David now accompanied her in the sulky and while his wife attended church would spend his time under a tree in the town park, enjoying his favourite relaxation, reading a book.

Still angry with the Anglicans for spurning him as an Evangelical, David had never forgiven Britain's church in Swan River for putting aside Christian compassion in favour of the demands of the prominent settlers. He still resented the fact that the Anglicans had spurned him for his ardent support of William Wilberforce, who in his old age had formed the Aboriginal Protection Society. Wilberforce had hoped that in Swan River, Britain's newest colony, the natives may have been treated more humanely than in Tasmania. There, as David knew, the Aborigines had been systematically exterminated by the white settlers, under the jurisdiction of a series of Anglican Governors.

Then came Western Australia's detestable convict era, beginning in 1850. David's hostility had increased in 1853, when Judith at the age of twenty was molested by an escaped felon, who had been transported for rape. It was only the timely intervention of her brother Paul which had prevented Judith from losing her virginity in the most vile way. David had felt that it was bad enough the prominent Anglicans having demanded that the colony be turned into a penal establishment, without Britain sending out her most violent criminals along with more minor offenders.

His attitude often brought scathing comments from the church ladies in Mary's presence.

"With a father like David, small wonder Judith is the way she is - and as far as her marrying a Roman Catholic - well!"

"And remember he's also a Fenian," said another. "Heaven help us!"

But as always Mary turned a deaf ear, keeping steadily to her faith as a true Christian, which she believed was above such spiteful small talk.

Not that the gossip had quietened down about Mary's grandson, Paddy. They even called the lad an unfortunate product of a mixed marriage between Anglican and Roman Catholic. "Far worse even than the proverbial black sheep!" as one devout Anglican lady put it.

Certainly Paddy was maintaining his reputation. Judith was forced to admit that her second son may have inherited much of her independent thought. Though she knew that the bulk of this nonconformism had been influenced by her stepfather David, there was also her bitterness against the Anglican-dominated establishment after she had been molested by the convict. The trauma had almost immediately caused her to break off an engagement with Duncan Macregor, son of Angus, and left her for years with an abject fear of men. It was only the chance meeting with Michael which had re-awakened her womanhood.

The fact that she had been made an outcast after marrying

Michael, made her detest her former Anglican mentors even more. Indeed, she wondered if all this venom hadn't been passed down to Paddy along with the independence. There were also those rebellious ideas of Michael, the father, to contend with.

Just lately Paddy had been bragging to other children that his father had started the Irish Fenian Revolt - according to Paddy, almost alone. Not that these tales weren't well received in the community school, because most of the parents sympathised with Michael.

But it was a great disappointment to Judith to hear Paddy deliberately not sounding those "g"'s in particular, besides saying "yeh", "yeah" or "yep" for yes - or even "aye" like Uncle Henry, an expression many of Paddy's fellow students still used, obviously an inheritance from fathers who had hailed from the English back-country.

Paddy at times also took on the lilting brogue of his Irish father, making him popular with girls at school. Yet if he did feel physically attracted to a girl at any time, he would usually show it by tying her pigtails together as he had done to a winsome girl called Trish Forward while he sat behind her in class.

Most girls liked Paddy's looks, especially the snubbish nose, laughing grey eyes and determined jaw. His clear pinkish skin also fortunately tanned easily to a reddish bronze. And though it seemed by his build he would probably grow up a couple of inches shorter than his six-foot father, Paddy already had a body like an athlete. He therefore excelled in school games, making him even more popular with the girls.

Yet because Paddy also had a certain softness about him, his father was even more determined to make him tough. But from outward appearances, Paddy revelled in it, especially when expected to sit a horse as good as his brother John. The father also taught his boys at an early age to handle a gun. Paddy could be seen when only six, the butt of the small bore rifle under his shoulder, gripping the barrel like grim death, sturdy little legs well splayed and with head comically twisted sideways, determined to do a better shot than his elder brother. As yet the littler one Rory, was only allowed to be a spectator, which he firmly though rigorously resented. It was then that the father taught his children the rudiments of safety, warning them never to walk in front beyond the shoulder of a shooter, never to point a gun at another person even in fun, and always to make sure a firearm was unloaded before putting it away.

To Judith's horror, Michael also taught his boys the art of boxing, in which he had excelled as a young man in the military in Ireland. She was sure this was a mistake, especially for Paddy, giving him more brash confidence than he already had. Indeed, it was not long before he got himself into a fight at school on behalf of a girl. In this case the object of his chivalry was Bessie Sissons, whom everyone knew was about as ugly a lass as one would find. A pale pimply complexion, violent red hair, and always untidy in her dress. Even worse, Bessie was pigeon-toed, and during school recess she was teased unmercifully.

"Always ready to trip over herself, the silly bitch," was so often said of Bessie.

Paddy was sick of it. In fact, the latest disgusting insult from the children was that Bessie had a face like a pig's posterior.

"Oh, why don't you give the poor girl a go?" Paddy yelled angrily to a group of boys.

The response was immediate and hostile.

"What's it to yuh, O'Leary?" a lad yelled, himself two years older than Paddy and much bigger built. "There you go again, yuh bloody sissy." The reminder to Paddy about his weakness concerned a live frog of which the big lad had torn off a leg, just to bring on the expected reaction. "Call yerself tough," the big lad went on. "Why, the next thing we know, yer old lady'll be puttin' those prissy locks o' yours in pins."

That was enough for Paddy. He put up his fists - one against his chest, and one out, as his father had taught him.

"Come on McGraw," he yelled. "I'll show who's a sissie."

Without a word, the bigger boy rushed in with fists flying. Paddy warded him off with his left, in imitation of his father's action. Then as the lad came rightabout to have another go, Paddy gave him an uppercut right under the chin. The larger lad was obviously surprised as well as dazed, and the other boys cheered wildly.

"Finish the rotten mongrel off Paddy," one lad yelled. "He deserves it." Even the girls joined in from the outskirts of the crowd.

But Paddy foolishly waited for the big lad to recover. In came the adversary again, but this time in a flying tackle, his sheer weight pushing Paddy to the ground. Now his hands were around Paddy's throat, fingers pressing in, making Paddy's eyes bulge. But Michael had also taught his boys wrestling, and Paddy using all his strength spun the lad over, then quickly applying a half nelson, pushed up an arm behind the back, causing the lad to scream out in agony.

"It's all right O'Leary, you win, I give in! I give in!"

But once again Paddy was too kind-hearted, and as he released his opponent and turned to face the cheering crowd of youngsters, McGraw "whopped" him one with the edge of his fist right on the back of the neck. The former hero dropped to the ground almost senseless. It was then that the more quiet elder brother John too put up his fists in anger. But by this time the school bell had rung calling the children to classes.

John told his parents about it later, as did little Rory, who though only seven had been an excited witness. Judith had been away from her teaching that day. The school had obtained another literate ex-convict and she was now only needed occasionally for guidance.

Both parents praised Paddy for his action in defending Bessie. But when John told his father about the bigger boy suddenly striking Paddy down with a king-hit, Michael jumped to his feet and banged his fist on the table.

"You damned idiot Patrick! How many times have I warned

you never to turn your back on an adversary? Sounds like I've been wasting my time. Fighting fair does not mean fighting foolish, my lad. From now on never give an opponent an advantage, that's all I have to say." It was just one of the things Paddy was to remember in later life.

As the two older boys had already become expert horsemen and rifle shots, they would in the rare quiet times, urge their father to go out riding. Michael had already ridden with them out to the Merredin lease, which besides being unsuitable even for winter grazing, had still not been released for the growing of crops. Michael had even gone further east with the boys, pointing out the range in the far distance. The range where old-timers such as Henry and Jim had said there was gold in plenty. These expeditions had excited the boys no end, especially Paddy, who on the last trip had urged his father to ride out even further. But that winter like others, had been terribly dry, with empty gnamma holes and claypans. Much to Paddy's distress, his father elected to turn back.

The following year, 1882, the boys urged their father to go out riding and camping again. With seeding and mid-winter jobs such as fallowing and scrub-cutting behind him, Michael at last relented, leaving Grandpa David to look after the farm. Old Timothy had since passed away.

As usual, when his older brothers were off on a long ride with the father, there were violent protests from young Rory, who though an accomplished rider at the age of ten, was regarded by his mother, as still too young to go out adventuring in the backblocks.

This time rather than reconnoitring east, Michael and the older lads had planned to ride due north as far as the Dunbar property at Mt Rupert in the Wongan Hills. They hoped to spend the night there. The aim then, was to return by a roundabout way through the Darling Ranges to Toodyay on the Avon - then upstream east to Northam and then back due south to York.

The object of the boys' insistence that they ride through

the ranges however, was to do a gallop with the wild brumbies. The brumbies were the result of Arab-Timor cross ponies which had gone wild after breaking out from poorly fenced properties, many years earlier.

The lads revelled in the thought of it, making their mounts dance as they made off, tantalising young Rory even more. It had turned out a better season than usual, the crops and livestock on this sunny balmy August day looking their best, and everyone along the track in a jolly good mood.

It was a Saturday and the taverns which were situated every ten miles, around a half day's run for a wagon, were crowded. Between the taverns, at intervals along the roadsides could be found the more industrious Irish wives, peddling their bottles of home-grown whisky or colonial spirits. Even though Michael knew this was breaking the law, the atmosphere caused him to encourage his boys to take in the colour of it all. He even laughed loudly as he pointed to a quick-thinking ma-am, who on sighting a squad of troopers approaching had swiftly placed her baby and cradle - the cradle itself only a deal box - on top of a crate of the bottled home-brew. Instead she now held out a small hessian bag of oranges, enticing the smiling policemen to buy.

But the boys were still more interested in the brumbies. They talked excitedly about playfully chasing them through the rough high-range country as they approached Mt Rupert station. But they were to be disappointed. Though the white-haired Jim Dunbar welcomed them warmly, he told them how the brumbies had been declared vermin by the authorities and an order was already out for them to be eradicated.

"But I thought up in the hill-country the brumbies weren't much trouble," replied a disappointed Michael, while his lads just stood there with doleful expressions.

"Wa-aal, the point is," Jim drawled on, "one o' the nob families, the Trigwells, have recently purchased a huge parcel o' high hills country to join onto their property sou-west o' Bolgart Springs. The Trigwells want to get rid o' the brumbies because they eat up so much pasture. Mind you, we have a few o' the wild ponies round here, an' though we put up with 'em, I tell ye' they're a goddamned nuisance. One o' their worst habits is smashin' down fences. Anyhow, they've been declared vermin, and fact is, the shooters could be already out. That's why it mightn't be safe to ride through them there hills."

The boy's faces fell even more, as their father answered. "Yes, but there's been talk about getting rid of the brumbies for years, hasn't there? Are you sure it's official, Jim?"

"Yeah," replied Dunbar. "This time it's dinkum. As you know, Harold Trigwell is on the Legislative Council, and as the big families still run the show, includin' the Governor, I guess you'd find it's already been made law. I already know that certain kangaroo-hunters, because the price of skins has dropped to hell, have already been askin' to take the job on."

"Yes, ruffian-types, too," replied Michael. "Mostly the worst of the ex-cons, and the sort who'd make a rough sandalwooder look like he should wear a skirt. Henry and Liz have a lot of trouble with them in their pub at York."

"Yeah, that's them all right," said Jim. "So if you take the boys ridin' in them there hills, you might strike trouble. With that crowd there's no beg pardons."

"But Dad, surely we could ride into the hills careful-like an' just take a look?" queried a very disappointed Paddy. "At the brumbies I mean."

John agreed. "Yes Dad, we've ridden this far, surely we are allowed to just ride back the roundabout way through the hills as we planned?"

"All right then," said Michael, himself also wanting to see the brumbies. "We will go. But I must say that if we do strike trouble with the shooters, as Uncle Jim here implies, it's straight back home to York."

Michael was to wish he had used his better judgment.

On first negotiating the lower slopes of the range country, they did come across around fifty brumbies with a fancy stallion in front, all galloping along playfully, manes and tails flying. "Let's follow 'em Dad," yelled Paddy, his eyes alight. "Just for the fun it."

Putting caution to the wind, an exhilarated Michael rode with his boys up into the high country.

It was while riding due south after losing the herd that they came across the first dead brumby. The thrash marks in the soil showed that the horse could have kicked in agony for some time after being shot. Fifty yards further on was another pony which also had been shot, then another until they had counted more than twenty.

"God in Heaven," swore Michael. "If they have to shoot them, at least they could make a proper job of it."

They rode on further. A sign already indicated they were on the Trigwell property. From the position where they rested their mounts in a patch of tall white-gums, they could see east down into the Toodyay Valley. The cleared paddocks of pasture and crop appeared peaceful and picturesque.

"OH, LOOK, DAD....!" suddenly screamed John.

There in front stood two ponies, legs apart, eyes transfixed, blood pouring from slits in their throats.

Without a word, Michael tore his Winchester from its sheath, and working the lever-action like lightning, swiftly and mercifully despatched the animals.

"Well boys," he said to his white-faced sons. "I guess I will have to tell you - yet it makes me wish so much that we had taken more notice of Jim Dunbar and kept away from the blasted place. You see what these cursed hunters do to save time and money is to first round up the ponies and drive them into a corral, and this one certainly must be located on the Trigwell property. Though mind you, we must always be careful before we accuse."

"But what happens then Dad, for gosh sakes?" asked Paddy, yet in his mind knowing what his father was going to say.

"Well Son, what happens is that not satisfied with shooting the ponies on the run, as they did further up in the hills, they drive them into a yard and there cut their throats one by one. Yet not too much, leaving the poor beggars just enough energy to stagger up here to die and rot away out of sight. If the ponies were shot dead around the yards, either the hunters or property-owners like the Trigwells would have the trouble and expense of dragging them away."

Paddy was distraught. "But can't we do somethin' about it? Can't we go down an' stop 'em?"

"No, I'm afraid not Son. You see it is the law which allows them to be disposed of in any way fit, as long as they are no more trouble to the property-owners. In fact, my sons, it is the same law which allowed the property-owners to have the power of life or death over convict workers, as well as over the Aborigines up north who happened to have existed on a station-run before it was taken over. What angers me though, is that these same influential families, so often talk about a love for horses, similar to us Irish. Yet here they are disposing of these ponies in such a horrendous way. These horses I might add, have the same feelings as any of their own blood-stock."

Paddy replied. "As Grandpa David says, animals have feelings just the same as humans, and if we do have to get rid of 'em for some reason, we must not do it because we enjoy it, but because it is something that has to be done."

"Yes," said Michael, "what we as humans must learn to acquire is a reverence for all life, even when swatting a fly. That's not to say that we must never kill or eradicate for our own survival, but we must do it mercifully, which means that if we have to do it, we must do it as quickly and efficiently as possible."

Though satisfied with the explanation, Paddy was still curious, and he suggested to his father that they try to find the corral where the hunters were doing their dirty work. With some misgivings Michael agreed, and following the blood-trail they emerged out into the open to sight a big stock-yard not far from the imposing two-storied Trigwell homestead.

More than a dozen hunters were busy pushing yet another herd of ponies into the corral.

Michael had taken out a small telescope which he always carried in his satchel.

"Well, would you look at that?" he cursed. "What damned hypocrisy!"

"What Dad?" expostulated an excited Paddy. "Give me a look!"

"Mind your manners Paddy! But take a look. You might learn something about how the other half lives. Train the glass on the homestead."

"Goodness," said Paddy. Pulled up by the homestead was a carriage, from which a group of young ladies had just alighted, no doubt paying a visit from the city. Close by were two young women on horseback, possibly the Trigwell daughters, who were well known in the colony's social set.

"But the corral's not far away," said a distressed Paddy, handing the glass to John. "Surely they must know what's goin' on."

"Yes they must," answered Michael. "And I've a mind to ride down and have something to say, especially to those damned hunters."

"Well why not!" replied Paddy, speaking for his elder brother. "We have rifles, we can help."

"No Son, it's too risky. Here, take a good look at those men, and you'll know what I mean." Michael took the glass from John, handing it back to Paddy.

"Streuth," this time Paddy almost swore. The hunters had knocked off for afternoon tea after locking the gate on the ponies. But afternoon beverage for most of them obviously consisted of colonial spirits, which they were socking down out of huge flagons. Also the men looked more villainous than any Paddy had ever seen, even in his scallywag sojourns around York. Most had long unkempt beards and were in motley dress, some wearing big bush hats and some wearing worn-out bowlers. All wore a cartridge belt and pistol and carried knives, obviously well-used to despatch the ponies.

"Yes Dad," said Paddy, as he handed the glass to John. "They'd be certainly hard ones to tackle."

"That's right, my lad. They also have the law on their side. Which means if we were to challenge those men at their grisly task, they could legally shoot us down for interfering - and the Trigwells probably wouldn't even turn a hair. Those ruffians have been authorised to do a job by the government and in that regard would have as much authority as policemen - and that means something." He turned his horse. "So let's get going. We've a long ride for home - we'll probably spend the night beyond Toodyay by the banks of the Avon."

It was a sombre ride. Both Michael and the boys found it hard to get the sight of the tortured ponies out of their minds.

In his school years, Paddy had other adventures, but not quite as gruesome as the experience with the brumbies. In fact, though he was reluctant to be a criminal, what he had seen gave him a certain disrespect for the law, preferring to adopt the philosophies of his Grandpa David, which were indeed those of the whole family. Don't do to others what you wouldn't wish done to yourself. Or when unsure, just do as Jesus would do. But such direction for Paddy, as his mother well understood, might often be a pretty tough proposition.

Paddy had long pestered his mother to be allowed to leave school at twelve, which was the usual age for children to cease their studies in the colony. But despite the fact that the farm needed them, Judith insisted that all her boys must attend school an extra two years, even though this often meant that she had to help out in the fields in the busy times. Grandpa David was not getting any younger.

Judith's experience of teaching all types of children over the years, had convinced her how necessary it was to have an education to get on in the world, even as a farmer.

It was now 1886. John, the eldest of the O'Leary sons had turned eighteen and had become a steady hand on the farm. Also, Rory, the youngest, had left school that year at the age of fourteen, and though short in stature similar to his grandfather David, was extremely muscular for his age. Also, Rory, like John, saw the farm as his only future. But Paddy at sixteen was still unhappy. With his natural yen for adventure, farm life to Paddy was terribly boring. So one day he packed his belongings, saddled his own pony and rode into York, where he took a job with Cobb and Co, which for long had held the monopoly over passenger traffic. With his natural way with both people and horses, he was soon allowed to drive a coach from York all the way to Mahogany Creek, close to where the new railway was now snaking its way through the ranges from Guildford.

Yet Paddy was bright enough to know that with the advent of the railway in the colony, his future with Cobb and Co could be limited. Not only was the railtrack due to proceed onto York for the next stage, but there was also talk when the government could afford it, of the line proceeding on further south from York to Albany, taking in agricultural settlements such as Beverley, Narrogin, Wagin, Katanning and Mt Barker. There was also talk of connecting York to Northam to the north, and also rumours of the government even laying a track the whole two hundred and fifty miles north from Perth to Geraldton, to service the growing agricultural and pastoral districts there.

Much to his mother's disgust, Paddy decided to take work with the construction teams, pushing ahead with the rail to York. But after six months, as the track neared its destination, Paddy again became restless, frequently talking to another youngster about searching for gold beyond the old sandalwood tracks. Besides intrigued by old Henry Lovedale's tales and his own glimpse of that faraway range while visiting the Merredin lease, Paddy was also inspired by Daniel Hordacre, the roving journalist who still visited the farm periodically, and often discussed his favourite subject -

GOLD.

During his last visit, Daniel had been far more enthusiastic, telling how payable gold had recently been discovered near Hall's Creek, accessible only from the far northern port of Wyndham in the Kimberleys. Daniel, with his usual disdain for the slowness and backwardness of Western Australia and Western Australians in general, talked proudly about a group of Victorian and Queensland prospectors who were attempting to charter vessels to take them around the north of Australia to Wyndham.

To the adventuresome young Paddy, such news was like a tonic. There were also more rumours about the gold prospects well to the east of Northam and York. One afternoon, while talking to a young workmate on the rail-gang Paddy made up his mind. After work that evening he rode home to tell his parents that he and his friend Tommy Tetlaw had decided to ride out beyond the sandalwood tracks looking for gold.

With the colony already infected with gold-fever, Michael was not surprised by his son's request - more an ultimatum. But his answer was short and to the point.

"You're a damned fool Patrick. Why, only last weekend you were telling me how the foreman said you were such a good worker, that after the track was finished to York he could find you a permanent job with the maintenance gangs."

"That foreman's left," said Paddy, simply. "Anyhow, everyone's talkin' about gold."

"There's also a good future for you now on the farm Son," argued Michael. "With the rail through, not only will our freight costs come down enormously, but the government has at last had the sense to tax imported grains and livestock. And there is also a whisper that they are going to open up land well east of Northam. I mean for agriculture, which could also mean our lease out at Merredin. With all the new wheats they are developing over in South Australia, they say you can now grow grain in almost desert country."

But Paddy was hardly listening. "No, Tommy and I will do all right, I tell you. His dad says that there is more gold out there than anyone imagines. In fact, he was telling us a tale about two convicts who were diggin' deep wells out there for the gentry pastoralists years ago. The pair cleared off thinkin' they could cut across country to South Australia. Anyway, the troopers eventually found 'em dyin' of thirst on their way back. But they'd already picked up some small lumps of pure gold, which they'd hid an' did not tell the troopers. Tommy's father, in fact, met one o' the convicts."

His father gave a snort. "Where, in gaol I suppose?"

Well, yes," nodded Paddy. "But that was a long time ago. Anyway, Tommy's father's got a rough map showin' where the gold is."

"What's the matter with him, then?"

Paddy looked downcast. "Oh, Tommy's father you mean? Well, as a matter o' fact, he's doin' another spell in gaol; wasn't much though, only a few railway sleepers to build a pig-yard."

Judith so far had kept out of the argument, torn between whom she should support, the son or the father. But she could contain herself no longer.

"Goodness me, the company you keep Patrick. Why can't you remember what I've taught you, especially the difference between right and wrong?"

"Well, I didn't steal those sleepers Mother. And neither did Tommy. Anyhow, you forget I'm nearly seventeen, an' I'm goin' out, an' that's that!"

Judith could see that her son had acquired a certain early wisdom, but she so much wanted to guide him, knowing that unlike his elder brother, he was so headstrong.

"If you don't want to come back to the farm, what about that job as a junior reporter on the *Fremantle Herald* that Daniel offered you? You know you are capable Patrick. Even though you won't speak correctly, writing for you was never any trouble."

"Yes, I had thought about it Mother, especially as Daniel says he might go right up north in time to catch all those t'otherside diggers landing up at Wyndham. They might let me go with him." Paddy's eyes lit up once more.

"Yes," agreed his father. "Though I doubt if they'd let you go with Daniel, as a learner you'd probably be stuck for a couple of years around the office. Even so, at your age, it's certainly better than dying of thirst out in the backblocks. You don't know what it's like."

"Yes I do," returned Paddy. "That range you can see beyond our Merredin leasehold where Uncle Henry reckons the gold must be. I can't get it outa my mind. That's why I want to go out."

"NO...!" roared his father. "You are not going out. It's been a hell of a dry winter, and you could both leave your bones out there."

"All right then," rejoined Paddy, with fire in his eyes. "I'll go an' talk to Uncle Henry."

"My God," said Michael. "Of all the people to ask for advice about prospecting?"

"Maybe Liz will talk some sense into Paddy," remarked Judith hopefully later, as they watched their son ride off towards York.

CHAPTER 5

Liz and Henry in their declining years had leased their pub out, but were still living only a few doors away in an imposing rock-walled, shingle-roofed home. Determined to keep in touch with a lifestyle they both enjoyed, they still visited the old pub almost every night, spending a half hour in the bar.

Disgusted with the way railway workers were performing in the streets of York during their time off, Liz was not disappointed about Paddy giving up his work with the gangs. But when the youth began to talk about going out prospecting with another sixteen year old, she wasn't so sure.

"By Hades, Paddy," Henry mused, his gnarled hand stroking his jaw. "It all sounds so damned excitin'. As a fact, I reckon I coulda heard that story about the convicts before."

Liz gave a snort. "Don't tell lies, Henry, for God'sake. If you'd heard that story, you could have never shutup about it. Now for heavens sake stop stringin' the kid along. You know damned well he's too young to rough it out there."

She turned to Paddy, looking him straight in the eye.

"Now you go an' tell that no-good Tommy you can't go, an' we want you to take a job closer to the coast, where we can all keep an eye on ye' till yer old enough."

Paddy took notice, because he had always admired his Aunty Liz, even though she was of no real kin. But when he returned to Tommy with the verdict next day, the youngster was full of abuse.

"The old people always say that," he stormed. "Look, why don't we clear off just the same? We've both got our ponies and our wages. Tommy's lips curled. "Yeh, to hell with 'em. Just imagine if we really found gold. Why Paddy, we'd be heroes. Not only because we'd be rich, but because our colony needs gold so much to get it outa the mess it's in. Hell's bells, Paddy, they might even make us Lords or sump'n."

But all Paddy could say was. "Look, I'll think about it. I'm still worried about my parents."

Tommy's eyes blazed with contempt. "Yeah-hh! I knew you didn't have what it takes. All bloody talk, that's what you are. That's what comes o' havin' a mother who's a schoolteacher. Books, pshaw, what's the use of 'em if they don't teach you the necessary. Guts!"

Paddy felt miserable. "All right, Tommy, I guess you're right. Parents an' teachers do hold you back a bit, don't they? I wonder why?"

"Oh, they call it learnin' to do the right thing, or suchlike," replied Tommy in a far happier tone. "But while you're worryin' about that, someone's slipped in in front o' yuh. Like what could happen with the gold. You've just got to be smart. Anyway, we'd better talk to the foreman an' tell 'im we want our pay."

But getting paid off was not so easy. "You know you're s'posed to give notice," shot back the tough-looking boss-ganger. "Looks like I'll be takin' out a fortnight's wages."

That worried the lads, because they knew their funds were limited.

"Anyway, why are you young coves clearin' orf?" asked the foreman irritably.

"Gold!" said Tommy. The magic word had slipped out. "We're off out east."

The foreman laughed scornfully, looking them up and down. "What, you pair go out there alone? Have you asked your dear muvvers' permission?" At the lad's stony silence, he went on.

"Anyway, there's too many o' my workers talkin' about gold. Why the hell can't we get this railway finished, even just to York?"

"Well, we're the only ones leavin' so far," argued Tommy. "It's just that we wanted to be first. To find the gold, I mean."

"Gold, gold ...! That's all I've been hearin' of late. Still,

I'd reckon my workers like the pubs too much to go chasin' out there in the never never. Let's hope it's all just flamin' talk."

Muttering to himself the foreman turned on his heel towards a corrugated tin shed set up as a temporary office.

"Right, foller me an' get what's due."

What was due was still minus the fortnight's wages, so for good measure, Tommy, as he walked out, slammed the tin door and told the foreman to stick the rest of the wages up his backside!

Tommy's words were mild compared to what the foreman thundered in return. The obscene epithets still rang in their ears as they mounted their ponies.

The first part of their plan was to ride to Fremantle and talk to Tommy's father Bill Tetlaw about the gold map. Bill was still a guest of the government in Fremantle Gaol.

After riding down through the ranges, the boys stayed the night in a ramshackle residence with Tommy's mother in Guildford. To keep the family during her husband's frequent spells behind bars, she did part-time cleaning work in the Stirling Arms hotel. Becky Tetlaw was another of the imported Irish stitch girls. She had married Tommy's cockney father, a typical "lag", who apparently believed that to be periodically in or out of goal was living a normal life. But it was obvious she was proud of Tommy, her son, who, she believed, unlike her husband had the ability to make a name for himself, albeit, honestly.

It was a fine clear day in late September, with the verge-side grasses drying off, a sign that spring was on the wane. After negotiating the well-used Guildford Road to Perth, the boys detoured into Riverside Drive, slowing their horses as they passed below the foot of Mt Eliza, enjoying the sight of the paddle-steamers plying their way across the river to South Perth, or on their way downstream to the port of Fremantle. After the Drive came the busy Stirling Track, which took them all the way to North Fremantle where a strong timbered bridge spanned the Swan around a half mile from the reef-filled entrance. The wooden bridge had replaced the horse-ferry which had been located further upstream near a place called Rocky Bay. Here though the river was conveniently narrow, the high limestone cliffs made it too expensive for bridging.

On the hill over the bridge reared the massive Fremantle Gaol. This bleak greying limestone edifice had been first built in 1853 to house the more obstinate of the imported felons or transportees. As the boys drew closer, the great grey wall, with its spiked top, and rows and rows of tiny cell windows strung up the main structure, gave them grim reminder how fortunate they were to be free on this sunny pleasant day.

Nonetheless, Tommy's father, possibly because he was not a dangerous criminal, had been enjoying life outside the gaol also. When the boys found him after they had enquired at the huge steel-studded gate, Bill was busy with broom and shovel picking up horse-dung along the fronts of a row of warden's cottages backed against the wall of the gaol.

Tommy's father was reluctant to give up the map. For him it was a good conversation piece, and with the newspapers all talking so much lately about gold, it was especially handy with the warders.

"But we could find all the gold Pa," argued Tommy. "Just think what it could do. You could buy your way out, just like the sons of those rich families do when they shoot a black or sump'n. You can do anythin' with money."

Bill quite believed it, having had experience of paying off the warders even with a few pence.

"Yus, all right Tommy," he said, his dark little round eyes shining in his hawkish, cockney features. "But cripes, you young uns 'ad better watch yersel' from what I've 'eard. They say it's real dry out there. An' it's gettin' close to summer."

Paddy realised it was just what his own father had said, but as he went to give an answer, Tommy got in first. "That's why we can't waste much time Pa. We've got to get out there an' back. Remember what I said about the gold buyin' you outa gaol. Now where's the map?"

Bill reluctantly pulled the map from his pocket, more a tattered yellowish crumpled piece of paper.

"'Ard to make 'ead nor tail o' this."

But Paddy thought differently. As Bill spread out the rough chart, it seemed the design though now faded, had been drawn surprisingly well in pencil. There was also an arrow aligning the map to grid north.

"Yes, look, there's the range of hills to the east," said Paddy excitedly.

"An' look, there's the gold," cut in Tommy, pointing to the pencilled cross next to what looked like a patch of trees. The convict artist, as he certainly had been, had also drawn a typical reef or outcrop, even to calling the broken quartz by name.

At once Paddy became despondent. He was experienced enough to know that there were probably thousands of reefs like that out there, even within sight of the range. And it was also so close to summer, as both his own father and Tommy's father had reminded them. He realised much later that he should have been much firmer with Tommy, especially as Paddy was more experienced. But at that late stage he didn't have the heart. The truth was that at the time he'd been so full of adventure himself.

Worried about his parents finding out, Paddy suggested to Tommy that rather than travelling east by way of York, it might be safer to ride by way of Northam. This was more in line with their destination, anyhow. It was in Northam where they purchased the old decrepit packhorse, because after buying picks and spades, leather satchels for victuals and canteens to hold water, they were running desperately short of cash.

With high hopes they left Northam at daybreak, riding through twenty miles of the old agricultural lands, chequered with ripening crops and red patches of fallow, ploughed ready for the following year. Around forty miles out they came across the old sandalwood track from York. Paddy pointed this out to Tommy, telling him it was the road they took from the Baker-O'Leary farm to the Merredin lease.

They were now in the winter grazing country - grazing of course only applicable in a wet winter, owing to the lack of rivers and permanent good water. Much of this land was still held under a peppercorn rent by the wealthy genteel families, the same families still despised by the ordinary folk, as Paddy expressed colourfully to Tommy.

Two day's ride and they had reached the O'Leary lease at Merredin. The blazing midday sun made the boys realise that winter was now well behind. Also they had now passed the last of the convict wells, the run of dry years having not only lowered the water-table, but reduced the quality. This was expressed strongly by Tommy as he spat out a mouthful.

"Hell, it tastes like dunny water!"

Paddy was unhappy also. "Well, the water was never much good for people, only animals. So do you reckon we'd better turn back, Tommy?"

"No! We can get used to the water, tastes a bit crook, I know. But seein' we've come this far out, we must go on - an' remember we've got the map."

"But remember there's no more convict wells," said Paddy. "We could both die out there."

"We-e-ll, yeah-hh, I s'pose we could kick the bucket out there," replied Tommy thoughtfully. "But I'm still willin' to take a chance for the gold. Aren't you matey?"

Paddy felt humbled at his friend's show of courage, and it was so important to find the gold - even for the good of the colony. "All right, we'll be off like a shot as soon as we've watered our ponies an' filled our canteens," he grinned.

"That's better," said Tommy. "Talkin' like a man."

The boys rode for two more days, finally reaching the location where Michael and Daniel had spent weeks cutting and loading sandalwood, and where they'd had for neigbours the regular, and at first volatile sandalwood cutters.

The lads were surprised to find the nearby gnamma-hole half-filled with water.

"Thought it was dry out here," remarked Tommy happily. "It's like a picnic place."

Paddy realised Tommy was right. Good rains had apparently fallen in the last month, not only replenishing the gnamma-hole but miraculously bringing to maturity donkey orchids, spider orchids and delicate rainbow creepers.

Next morning fresh of heart and with their waterbags filled, the boys struck out for that distant range - since called the Yilgarn Hills. But after riding for another two days, they were disgusted to find that the rainstorm which had replenished and transformed the area back there, had only been localised. With their horses thirsty and their canteens near empty, Paddy suggested they turn back. "An' remember we just about emptied that gnamma-hole," added Paddy.

"But look at all this quartz an' stuff," protested Tommy, looking around. "It's just like it says on the map, an' look, there's the trees."

"Look matey," Paddy said persuasively. "There's so many reefs out here like that one on the map, this could be one of a hundred - yet still in sight o' that blasted range. Trouble is we could perish of thirst lookin' for the right one. An' look at the old packhorse, he's so tuckered out I doubt if he'd last the distance."

Tommy looked towards the range, which in the clear desert air looked so comfortably close, but which to the more experienced Paddy, could still be a good two days ride away.

"But we know it's out there, don't we?"

"I know, Tommy, I know. But we need to be better equipped. An' even if you've got more horses carryin' more water, the extra nags need water also, so you're not much better off."

"Yep, that's one o' the reasons we only brought one

packhorse, apart from not havin' the money." Tommy firmed his jaw. "Look Paddy, what about riskin' it for another few miles?"

And risk it they did, with the old packhorse dragging its feet in obvious distress. But they did find a two-ounce nugget of gold within only a day's ride of the Yilgarn Hills. Tommy picked it up where it lay embedded in dark red alluvium down from a typical quartz reef, so much like the one described on the convict map.

But the lads were now completely out of water, with the old packhorse just standing there with legs apart, reminding Paddy of the dying brumbies that terrible day in the hills.

They tried to lead the old horse along, but in answer he just collapsed on his belly, his eyes in torment.

"Looks like we'll have to shoot the poor old bastard," said Tommy.

"Yep," replied Paddy, trying to act casual. But one thing he hated doing was shooting a horse, or even a cow or sheep. But as his father had told him, it was a task at times that had to be done.

Tommy appeared to be made of sterner stuff so Paddy let him have the job.

"CRA-A-AACK!" The echoes of Tommy's rifle split the air.

The old horse slumped over, blood pouring from its nostrils.

They had already unloaded the gear, and now had the problem of sorting out which they could conveniently carry. However, their mounts were also exhausted, and reluctantly all they took from the dead packhorse were two extra water-containers, even though they were dry. They were forced to leave all their spare clothes, their hard-tack tucker and their picks and shovels.

It was now late afternoon. But with the sun still as hot as ever, the lads decided to wait and travel at night under cooler conditions. Fortunately the moon was out, and they let their weary ponies gradually pick their way back west towards the gnamma hole. Two more nights of travel and they had still not reached their destination.

"We're here. We're here!" suddenly yelled Tommy, kicking his heels into his famished horse.

"Ugh! Jesus! Look!" said Tommy as he poked his head down the gnamma-hole.

Paddy focussed his eyes down to see a dead goanna floating on top of the water. Steeling himself, he bent down and grabbed it by the tail.

"Ugh!" gasped Tommy again, as it came out oozing black blood and slime.

"Yep," replied Paddy, almost bravely. "It hasn't been in there that long, but it's all gashed. Probably bitten by an eagle or somethin'."

Tommy screwed up his face. "Gawd, it pongs worse'n a dead cat. What about the water? How the hell can we drink it?"

"Well, if it was my dad, he'd make us boil it before we drank it," said Paddy, miserably. "But you know what we've gone an' done, left our tea-billy with the old packhorse. All we've got are our canvas waterbags."

Tommy tipped back his floppy hat and scratched his head. "Well what the blazes do we do now?"

"Looks like the horses may as well have the lot," suggested Paddy practically. "There's not much left down there, anyhow. At least the horses should then have enough spurt to get us to the convict well."

They let the horses each drink in turn, knowing that the polluted water would have little effect on the animals. As it was, the small amount left in the gnamma hole went far from satisfying the horses either, and the boys mounted up, worried about the increasing heat, so hot that the metal clips on the saddles and reins burnt the skin when touched.

The distance back to the last convict well was still almost a day's ride, and long before sundown the lad's were gasping, their lips parched, their tongues swollen.

"Hell," croaked Tommy. "You were right Paddy, we could

really kick the bucket out here."

"Yes," replied Paddy very soberly. His mind was now so much on his mother. Indeed, he had been thinking about home and his whole family.

Now the horses had again begun to stagger, as they had before they'd drunk at the gnamma hole.

Even the brave puckish features of Tommy had become frightened.

"Now we're really in the soup," he moaned. "Better rest these poor bloody nags."

"Yes," gasped Paddy. "Trouble is, we could still be a good ten miles from the convict well."

The boys sat down in the shade of a tree, the horses just standing there dejected, their bridle reins trailing.

This was how Michael found the little expedition as he rode around a corner leading a packhorse. He had anticipated the worst after receiving word a fortnight after the boys had passed through Northam.

With hardly a word, Michael now jumped from his horse, holding a waterbag to each of the boy's lips in turn, making sure they swallowed slowly.

"Jesus, that's good!" cried Tommy.

"Well, let this be a lesson to you both," exclaimed Michael, as the boys began to recover. He turned to his son.

"It was lucky that your brother John is friendly with one of the lads who works for that Northam horse-dealer. He told John about you pair purchasing an old packhorse."

"Yes Dad, and it died," replied Paddy, gravely.

Paddy felt like clasping his arms round his father and bursting into tears. But he could never do such a thing in front of Tommy. He admitted how foolish they both had been; how lucky they'd been even to get back to the gnamma hole; lucky also that the moon was out and they'd been able to travel in the coolness of night.

"Yes," replied Michael soberly. "You'd both better give

thanks and say your prayers."

But Tommy was fast recovering, and he handed Michael the tattered old map, as well as the shining slug of gold.

"Well, you did find something then," smiled Michael, grimly. "But by not seeking professional advice before charging out into the backblocks in summer like you did, you may have broken the law. I believe there has been a similar rule in the colony since the first landing. It could have been worse, you know, costing the government hundreds of pounds to send out a search party. And then worse still, you could have both perished." Michael's face was serious, reflecting the emotional strain he had been through.

"But someone's got to find the gold, don't they Dad?" a recovering Paddy now demanded. "You know it's out there, don't you? An' what with us findin' that nugget."

"I agree, I agree," returned Michael. "But it's going to take much more planning and care to find it in such harsh waterless country. Anyhow, the newspapers are talking about three experienced t'otherside prospectors, who have been contracted by a Fremantle businessman, himself a former Victorian. They are apparently going out there next winter."

While Tommy was excited, saying that he was going to apply for a job with the prospectors, as long as he could get back out there, Paddy was downcast.

"There you are, I knew it would happen," he said with a long face. "Just like Daniel has said so many times. It's goin' to take the t'othersiders to show us the way."

"Perhaps you're right," replied Michael, giving credit to his son's astuteness. "But as our colony needs the gold so much, it doesn't really matter who finds it, does it, my lad?"

"But you really don't mean that Dad, do you? About them bein' the first to find the gold I mean."

"No I don't, but what can we do? You must remember these men are professional prospectors. It's their job. And over in the Eastern Colonies they've had so much more experience in finding gold. The newspapers also tell more about that small army of diggers who have already charted ships in Brisbane to sail around the north of Australia to Wyndham, so that they can trek inland to Hall's Creek and the gold." Michael hesitated. "As a matter of fact Paddy, if you are still set on not coming back to the farm, that newspaper job's still open for you. Daniel was only talking about it when he called into the homestead the other day."

"Yeh," replied Paddy, casually. "An' maybe I can still talk Daniel into takin' me with him when he goes up north on that assignment."

His father shook his head. "Well, as I told you before, I doubt that very much. Anyhow lad, you apparently don't want to be a farmer, so as far as taking that newspaper job's concerned you have my blessing, and of course, more so your mother's. As she told you before, with your ability with the written word, it should be well within your capabilities."

"Yes Dad, I have decided to do what Mother wishes," replied Paddy formally, and with finality.

"Right then, let's get back to the last convict well. I'm afraid despite their condition, from then on you boys will have to push those ponies. I want to get back and prepare for harvest.

Though Michael's hunch was right about his son being refused permission to travel up north with Daniel, Paddy at least made a last-ditch effort.

"But the paper doesn't even need to pay me Daniel," he insisted. "I've still got a bit of money left. My friend Tommy I was tellin' you about gave me two pounds ten, as my half o' the gold we found."

Paddy had such a soulful look in his eyes, that Daniel was almost tempted. But having heard that the two hundred miles from Wyndham inland to Hall's Creek was even more waterless than east of Merredin, he felt he should not risk someone else's life, especially Paddy's.

"No matey," he said to Paddy. "I'll take you into Len

Chandler. It's already arranged anyhow. As another reporter will be taking my place, there will be that spot at the bottom for you."

So Paddy became a junior reporter, taking to the work so easily that it was not long before he was on personal assignments. After six months away, Daniel returned, thin and gaunt, his experience on the gold trail nothing short of agonising. Much of what had come to pass had already been transmitted to Perth by overland telegraph, but the real story was far more graphic.

Daniel told how hundreds of hopeful diggers were dumped off the ships in Wyndham, and had then walked and pushed barrows the whole two hundred and sixty miles in the middle of summer, the so-called wet season, around one hundred and twenty degrees in the shade. He told of how they were forced to drink polluted water, scores dying of dysentery even before they reached their destination.

"But what about the gold?" demanded an anxious Paddy.

"For the average prospector, damned disappointing," said Daniel. "Certainly there's gold there all right, but it's going to take expensive machinery to recover it, similar to Victoria and Queensland after the diggers had covered the surface. The trouble is, up there, and probably in any gold-bearing country in the west I'd say, you're not likely to get rich on top. Unfortunately it's a job for the big companies."

"Certainly must have been heartbreakin' for the diggers," said Paddy. "Anyway, I don't know whether you know or not, but those t'otherside prospectors have already gone out to the Yilgarn. Matter o' fact, my friend Tommy has got a job with 'em as billy boy. It's a start out there though, isn't it?"

"Good-oh for Tommy," teased Daniel. "Looks like one Westralian's out there at least. Those prospectors are Victorians aren't they, similar to most of the diggers up north."

"Well, aren't all the Victorians goin' broke or somethin'?" retaliated Paddy, who since becoming a reporter was more in touch with the wider realm of events. They say that what money's left, they'd rather put into gold prospectin'. Just the same, Daniel, I guess you're right about Westralians. Look how they won't bother to go out searching for gold, even though they all talk about it." He screwed up his face in mock fashion. "Not that I blame 'em after the experience Tommy an' I had."

Daniel put his arm round Paddy's shoulder. "Who knows Paddy? One day we might go out there together. Even if that exploration party gets in first, there should be plenty more gold for others. Westralia's a vast country. Just the same, apart from yours and Tommy's trials, my own experience tells me to take it damned cautious too. To see hundreds die of sickness along the track, is not very nice. I tell you. In fact, as far as the north's concerned I don't want to be sent up there again for a long time."

Daniel was wrong. Just over a year later he was assigned north once again, but this time to Carnarvon, in distance only around six hundred miles from Fremantle, about one third as far as Wyndham. This time it didn't concern gold, but native problems. Paddy had again begged to go along, compassionate about the problems of Aborigines through the Quaker philosophies of Grandpa David, and Paddy's mother, Judith. She had also taught her boys about William Wilberforce, Grandpa David's greatest hero. Judith had impressed on her sons how Wilberforce despite his great humanitarian endeavours including the British Anti-Slavery Bill and the Aboriginal Protection Society, had never received a knighthood from his own country. Britain preferred to give her awards to her swashbuckling military leaders and her piratical entrepreneurs, as long as they advantaged her commercially.

Daniel had also made mention of such hypocrisy by a so-

called Christian nation - and this was one reason he had taken
so much to the free-thinking Baker-O'Learys, and to Paddy
in particular.

But though this time, Paddy was certain that he would
be allowed to accompany Daniel up north, the request was
again refused by the editor, Len Chandler. With Daniel again
away, Paddy was too useful at home as a news-gatherer.

Daniel returned after two months, his sufferings this time
more mental than physical. The purpose of his trip had been
to investigate complaints sent to the H*erald* from the
Reverend John Gribble, an Anglican curate, who was
attempting to found a native mission in Carnarvon. Although
reports had been telegraphed down, and much had been
published in the conservative *West Australian* condemning
the foolishness of the young rector, it took Daniel to tell
the full story. Yet when he first landed in Carnarvon from
the coastal steamer, the mood was such in the little settlement
that he believed surely the young rector was wrong. As
Daniel explained to Paddy and Len Chandler.

"... but it did not take me long to find out, I tell you. The
settling of the north has only been a repeat of what happened
down here, the grab for land by a few families. Yet you
wouldn't believe how the grandsons of the same families
are carrying on up there. Not only roughing it under the
most primitive conditions, because these sons are mostly not
yet married, but taking in native lubras as concubines - and
I might add, usually against their wishes."

"Yes I know, Daniel," said his editor almost irritably.
"But unlike down here in the early stages they've been able
to make great use of native labour. But get on with Gribble!
You say that they literally ran him out of the place?"

"Well, it did amount to that, because while there he
certainly offended them, including Colin Anderson, the local
Magistrate, who incidentally is also the largest station-
owner."

"Yes," interrupted Paddy. "Gribble sent word about the local Magistrate acting like a tyrant. He also said how Anderson was allowing the grazier families to put the fear of death into the natives with guns - herding them onto the stations for use as slave-labour."

Daniel laughed cynically. "Well, didn't I say that the Resident was also one of the station-owners. It's so easy when you can make your own law. Legally each native is supposed to be signed on like any ordinary worker. But naturally if the natives refuse, the threat of a whipping soon brings them to their senses - which means ensuring the old English Master and Servant Act, by means of a tarred thumbmark on a piece of paper. Some of the pastoralists have even branded their station boys, as they call both males and females. Like cattle!" Daniel again twisted his lips. "And you may be sure also in this regard, that the gift of a little flour or baccy works wonders."

"Yes," returned Chandler. "And of course, if Gribble was to start up a mission like Salvado did down here at New Norcia, the natives could become too well-educated, even to possibly running their own flocks."

"You are so right," replied Daniel. "But what made Gribble even more unpopular was when he demanded that certain station owners be arrested not only for scourgings and beatings, but also for murder. Also scores of natives have simply been shot for trying to run away from their white masters. But for Gribble to try and protest officially up there with Anderson simply a law unto himself, is all just a joke. He gives orders to the local constabulary when need be, or shuts his eyes when it suits him. Similar to down here, it is the general practice to fit the disobedient natives with neck collars, chaining them together."

"So I've been told," said Chandler. "Gribble sent word about a group of natives who were chained together in a corrugated iron hut for three weeks awaiting trial, with only just enough food and water to keep them alive."

"That is so," confirmed Daniel. "I had the occasion to visit that same prison hut myself in one hundred and ten degrees in the shade. The stench! My God! My experience as far as natives are concerned is that free in the bush they have their own strict code of hygiene. But to lock them up fast like that for three weeks without vital personal liberties, besides just throwing them a few meat scraps occasionally like dogs. By heavens, one wonders who's really civilized, us or the Aborigines."

"If I know anything about our top families," growled Chandler, "they'd treat their dogs far better. I believe many natives have died while in the chains or while locked up also. Is this true?"

"True all right, and many hundreds more with the gun, as I've already explained, life up north is damned cheap, I tell you. Or should I say the life of a native."

"All the same it looks like the unfortunate Gribble has lost out," said Chandler. "I've tried to do my best for him, and I must say the majority of the people sympathise with him. But when you've got the ruling Anglican hierarchy as well as its mouth-piece the *West Australian* against you, it makes it a hopeless task. An article in the *West* points out how Gribble has been a total embarrassment to the Anglican church. According to the paper, he was sent north not so much as a missionary, but to look after the spiritual needs of the white settlers. Of course he made the mistake of interfering in legal procedure. The law says that disobedient natives can be beaten, as the law also says that offending Aboriginals can be chained up, especially while awaiting transport down south to Rottnest Island."

"And you may be sure those places where they are chained up awaiting shipment are no better than stockyards," replied Daniel. "Or I should say pigsties, the smell even worse than that tin hut I was telling you about." Daniel gave a sigh. "The trouble is John Gribble has upset the comfortable status-quo, which has gone on pretty well with the Anglicans since the first landing."

"You're so right," scowled Chandler. "But I guess the worst hypocrisy is where the *West Australian*, though not denying that these atrocities have been carried out against the Carnarvon natives, including further north in Broome where white pearlers slaughtered those sixty five Aborigines for refusing to work as divers - all these are admitted, yet the paper's attitude seems to be that because Magistrates such as Colin Anderson have decided in favour of the whites, the cases are closed. Finished."

"And even if they did condescend to allow the poor natives a jury," said Daniel bitterly. "Which I must say under British Law they should - you can be sure the jurists would be white."

"Too true," replied Chandler. "Too true. It makes the whole aspect of our judicial system a farce, doesn't it?"

"It reminds me of my grandfather David talking about the Reverend Agostini," ventured Paddy. "He was another Anglican Priest who stood up against his church calling for a better deal for the natives. Tried to support two of them in a trial in York, but was slandered so much by his fellow Anglicans that he decided to get out of the colony."

"Robert Black, the editor of the *Sydney Herald*, when he was over here was Agostini's greatest admirer," rejoined Daniel. The cases are so similar, and so embarrassing to our government and the Anglican Church, one wonders if they'll tear up the records."

Chandler with his ink-stained fingers had been busy taking a cheroot out of a flat wooden box.

"If I know anything about dear old England's church," he growled, "they'll certainly keep those records away from official historians." He struck a wax match on a striker, lighting his cheroot. "Anyhow, with the *West Australian* having become a power unto its own, and with it about to produce a daily into the bargain, I'm afraid our *Herald* could be in real trouble."

"I must say the *West* was pushing us out before I left,"

Daniel replied. "With its so-called middle of the road view it's been stealing the show. Certainly different to its forerunner, the *Perth Gazette* which was boycotted by the workers and smallholders."

"In some ways the *West* is making space for more concerted opinion," said Chandler blowing smoke. "At first glance you could say the letter columns have been totally democratic, allowing scathing opinions from both sides."

"But that's only a ruse," Daniel almost spat, wondering if his editor was losing his drive. "The *West Australian* is still under the same ownership, including its patronage from the Anglican Church."

"And that same ownership means capital," replied Chandler, stubbing his cigar in distaste. "With our drop in sales, it is something we are finding hard to come by."

"What about Tom Callahan?" asked Daniel. "He's become even richer hasn't he?"

"And more respectable too," gritted Chandler, his face long. "I suppose you know that another one of his sons has come back from Ireland after gaining his medical degree in Dublin College. That's the second one, and unfortunately they have both returned with well-bred wives who prefer to mix with gentility. Of course, Callahan's been hobnobbing with the high echelon himself lately, similar to Jamie Baldeck - himself only a teamster's son. His own son, incidentally, has also become one of the infamous northern frontiersmen. No Daniel, my old friends are deserting me wholesale to become respectable." The editor finished with a grimace.

"Well, it's 1888 isn't it Len?" Daniel had suddenly become more familiar with his employer. "Most of the transportees who settled down married here in the fifties, didn't they? Their grandkids, now, especially the wives, could be trying to ward off the old convict stigma, and if they've done well financially, could have become middle-class. Now you see why the *West* is selling so well."

"Grandpa David and Mother and Father often spoke about this," said Paddy, rejoining the conversation. "Even before I left the farm. That was why Father refused to join the Reform League."

"Yes I knew about that," returned Daniel quickly. "And full marks to your father for refusing to join. The League's financed by the very people it's purported to be against. Yes!" Daniel snorted. "They are getting ready for democratic government, and my God, with the riff-raff possibly having the vote, the Old Guard, as our Six Ancient Families have begun to be called by their adherents, is going to make sure its candidates can reach the people - even if a mite insincerely."

"We need a few more of your tough t'othersiders over here Daniel," grinned Paddy. "If they stayed here, they'd certainly not be backin' the Old Guard, would they?"

"Well, if it's the diggers up at Hall's Creek you mean, certainly not! Most still look up to the rebel Eureka flag. I tell you, there'd be no worries about them seeing through this political sham down here." Daniel smiled cynically. "Still, even if all the Eureka men did decide to stop here, the local powers that be would find a way of preventing the digger's vote, there's nothing surer."

"My sentiments too," agreed Chandler. "Anyhow, our paper is not beaten yet, we'll go down fighting." He turned to Paddy, apparently having put himself in a better humour. "Now, young fellow. Talking about our paper, you've been doing the rounds like a good reporter I hope. What's the latest on Perth and Fremantle's society life? What's going on in the bars and clubs?"

"Which reminds me," said Daniel with a grin, also turning his gaze on Paddy. "They tell me you've become friendly with a certain chorus girl. You certainly have been doing the rounds like a good reporter, haven't you? But my goodness, what would your mother say?"

Paddy found that one hard to answer.

CHAPTER 6

Paddy first caught Ann Fogarty's eye while she was high-stepping with a troupe of young ladies in the Colonial Club in Perth. More an amusement hall, the club was called by some a "knees-up", where the ordinary citizens were both entertained and could entertain themselves. The Colonial Club also had its bar, where young Paddy not only liked to indulge - he had been taught to drink on the sly on the farm by old Timothy - but also where he could gain social information for his newspaper.

Paddy could not deny that he enjoyed the atmosphere, people there either celebrating or trying to forget their troubles.

Although the well-to-do families were more likely to frequent the better-class entertainment houses, such as the Queen's Theatre, some of the gentry still attended the Colonial Club.

One was Ashley, son of Darcy McAllum, the businessman pastoralist who in his younger days had got himself into trouble shooting a black on the run. Ashley was expected to ultimately take over the managership of one of the many big McAllum properties, including the enormous leasehold inland from Carnarvon. It was here the gentry families had had problems in the Kennedy Ranges with the belligerent native bucks known as Myalls. The Aborigines had rebelled because too many of their lubras had been abducted to serve as helpmates for the graziers.

After spending five years in Britain attending a finishing college, Ashley on his return had decided that he preferred the society of the city to roughing it out in the backblocks, even though much of the station land would eventually be his.

Like Paddy, young Ashley took a job with a newspaper

as a junior reporter. But certainly not the *Fremantle Herald* which was promoted by ex-convicts, and long the bugbear of the Old Guard or Landed Six, or what was left of the original genteel families.

It was befitting he work for the *West Australian*, since the majority of shares were owned by his father, now Sir Darcy McAllum. The *West* was also still trying to prove it was a newspaper for all classes, of solid intellectual worth, and not a dangerously rabble-rousing rag like the *Herald*.

As they were both now in the same vocation, Paddy soon came in contact with Ashley - and knowing the gentry lad's background, Paddy with his natural wit, was soon having a go at Ashley. But Ashley was also of tough fibre, and what made them more alike in nature, was that they both became rivals for the favours of Miss Fogarty who with her natural good looks had claimed the attention of other young men besides Paddy and Ashley.

But while Paddy himself had fond thoughts towards Miss Fogarty, he was sure that Ashley's motives in chasing a dance-hall girl were not so sincere. It was well-known that the colony's well-to-do males besides wooing their prospective brides or wives, often sought women of easy virtue.

Daniel had explained that he believed the landed families as such, appeared to produce males of strong libido. This meant that they not only had an inborn drive for taking over most of the colony's arable lands, businesses, banks and so forth, but also had an overwhelming urge to procreate, which did not always mean with their own kind. As Daniel had concluded. "... it is being proven more and more out in the backblocks, where half-caste children are being fathered galore!" Paddy had this in mind, when he first confronted Ashley, not really despising the youth, but almost with a feeling of elation, like a warrior going into battle.

When Paddy had glanced at Ann that evening for the first time, she too had responded, liking him at once. The young ladies were dancing in a troupe, arms linked and kicking their legs. After the act was over and the girls walked out to mix with the crowd, Paddy daringly sought her out, talking naturally and carelessly, as he had spoken to girls while at school in York.

"You perform well, don't you, sweetheart?" he said, putting on his best smile. His eyes searched hers, which were an attractive grey-green complimenting her honey-blonde hair.

"Well they tell me so," she answered, lowering her lashes. "But they probably don't mean it."

"Of course they do," returned Paddy quickly. "You are a good dancer an' a darn good singer besides."

Her eyes met his, a tantalising look which seemed to be reserved for him alone. But apparently he had embarrassed her a little.

"Thank you. But I think I know you. You work for the *Herald*, don't you? Father never misses a publication." She became more serious. "Still, he's only a railway porter."

"An' a good one, I'll bet," smiled Paddy, reassuring her. "Feel like a drink? I'd like to talk for awhile." Paddy indicated an empty table.

For a moment she hesitated, wondering whether Paddy for all his youth and charm, was just another gigolo-type after a pick-up.

She suddenly smiled "Yes, all right. But only for a few minutes. I have to go on again."

Paddy escorted her to an empty table. "About that drink?" he enquired. "What'll it be?"

"Oh, just lemonade please," she replied, her face colouring a little, as if ashamed that in a beer-hall she should not be asking for something more potent.

But Paddy respected her all the more for it, already having decided that this particular dance-hall girl was different.

"Yep," he said. "Then you won't mind if I have a beer?" Her eyes met his again with that half-shy intimate look.

"No, not at all, in a place like this, you shouldn't need to ask. Let me get the drinks, it's my job as a part-time waitress, anyhow."

"No," offered Paddy, motioning her to sit down in her chair. "You're my guest, an' a real sweet pretty one at that."

It was all half play-acting, an attribute Paddy had learned from his Irish father. But the look in his eyes hinted at something more serious, and it moved the girl even more deeply.

They talked animatedly, Paddy fully conscious of her femininity sometimes clouded with an air of uncertainty. It was then she mentioned Ashley McAllum, saying how he'd been trying to pay attention to her, but that she did not like him. Paddy had given a quick answer, at the same time nodding his head discreetly towards the handsome dark-haired though foppish-looking Ashley, who only a few tables was sitting there glowering, even though he was with another young woman.

"Oh Ashley," laughed Paddy. "He's a bit of a joke, really. Making out as if he's an apprentice reporter, when we all know his father has the controlling interest in the *West Australian*.

"We girls treat him as a joke that way also," she replied. "Still, I doubt he'd be a joke if he had one of us alone."

Paddy laughed loudly. "Yes, you've certainly got his measure." He became more serious. "I don't know your name, do I?"

"And after all this time we've been together," she bantered. "It's Ann Fogarty. Born of a conditional pardon convict and an emigrant Irish bride."

"And you should be proud of it," he replied. "But I've got a feelin' you know my name?"

"Yes I do. Patrick, son of Michael O'Leary, the well-known and respected Fenian.

"I don't know about respected," grinned Paddy. "But certainly well-known."

"My parents think the world of your Pa," replied Ann, "and so do I."

She laughed teasingly. Whether she intended it or not, Paddy could see she was a natural attraction to men. No wonder Ashley was sulking.

Suddenly she became more serious. "Look Patrick, sorry, but I'll have to go."

Paddy took her arm gently. "Call me Paddy," he said softly. "Now, where can I meet you again?"

"Here of course, I work four nights a week. And when I'm not performing, I'm waiting on tables."

Paddy left later, believing he had made more than a conquest. As with all young men, it was always a thrill and an achievement to catch a pretty girl's eye and to be able to make her acquaintance. He realised Ann had attracted him far more than any other lass he had met, including Trish Forward, for whom he had developed a crush during his school days.

In the two years before 1891, Paddy saw much more of Ann, even visiting her home, but never trying to take advantage of her. He respected her too much.

Ann dared to believe that Paddy genuinely liked her and dreamed that one day he might ask for her hand.

In those two years Paddy was to lose much of his youthful boyishness and brashness. The role of a reporter, mixing with all classes, helped him to mature, never losing that attitude for fair play, as had been taught him by his parents and grandparents. Though Paddy had come to realise that there had to be rulers, he believed that these rulers in Western Australia, at least, were getting too big a slice of the cake.

In December 1890 after more than sixty years of mostly despotic rule by a series of British Governors, the colony was at last granted responsible government, the right of the people to elect their own House of Assembly.

Although the *Herald* was becoming more and more overshadowed by the *West Australian*, this was an energetic time both for Paddy and Daniel. Paddy had more and more confrontations with Ashley, who had become increasingly arrogant. Political men related to the families of the Old Guard began to gain more adherence from the lower ranks, largely through the efforts of the *West*, the colony's only daily.

The non-partisan nature of the coming election meant that all candidates were independent of each other. Yet it was no secret that most of the competitors were connected by birth or marriage to either the McAllums, the Trigwells, the Mainwarings, the Bartletts, the Andersons, or the Clayton-Brownes.

Just recently in a fit of frustration, Len Chandler had dubbed these prominent families the "Hungry Six", even printing it in his newspaper.

"Though it's close to libel, full marks to our editor for his Hungry Six title," Daniel remarked to Paddy. "Here they are not just satisfied with owning most of the colony as well as controlling its politics, but in the *West Australian*, they're calling themselves moderates."

"Yep," replied Paddy casually. "Just a ploy to catch the vote from the lower ranks when it comes. They are so damned sure of themselves they're even talkin' about William Groves as future Premier. An' here he is married to a Mainwaring."

"Well, all the candidates are from the same old brood, come to that," gritted Daniel. "So how can they lose? What has happened to all the democracy we spoke about? Where are all those bold peasants who were going to take over the colony in the name of the yeomanry?"

"A lot o' the bold peasants are ex-convicts, aren't they? Now there's the big rush by their sons an' daughters to aspire to the middle-class, just as my Pa an' Grandpa David were afraid of."

Daniel's reply was curt. "Yes, they obviously want to cast

off their roots, which leaves them completely at the mercy of that infernal *West Australian*. God Almighty, speaking as a Victorian, what's the matter with you lot over here?"

Paddy laughed cynically. "My God, you should talk. I've learnt enough of history to know you had your chance after Eureka, Peter Lalor an' his digger's parliament an' all. And you muffed it, letting the landed gentry and their erstwhile friends the ex-convict squatters once more rule the roost. I guess in some ways it's the same over here with our expiree families trying to lift themselves in society. It's what's helpin' to give our fake liberals so much confidence, William Groves being typical of the new, er, expedient breed."

Spoken like a true journalist," replied Daniel, raising his eyebrows. He continued soberly. "Of course, the whole strength of it, is capital. To me a People's House will never be truly democratic until the government pays a Member's salary. That is why the businessmen pastoralists will still dominate Parliament, even though the old Governor's Council will soon only be a house of review."

Paddy nodded his head. "You're so right. Grandpa David used to talk about it years ago. Until land, wealth and social position are taken out of government, the ordinary folk will never get their say."

"Of course, the underdogs too need an organisation," grunted Daniel. "Like this Political Labor group the workers are trying to form."

"And I'd say you've been urgin' 'em on, haven't you chum?" grinned Paddy.

"Yes I have, but unless we can get backing from wealthy people like Tom Callahan and Jamie Baldeck, men who've been through the mill themselves, a union will never raise the cash to fund its candidates."

"I do agree, I do agree. Of course, rather than help their own kind once they make money, they'd prefer to elevate up with the nobs. Talk about loyalty to their own kind."

"Again spoken like a good newspaperman Paddy," said

Daniel.

Aside from her political and social problems, Western Australia still had her economic woes. Compared to t'otherside, she had consistently lagged behind. While the South Australian press had coined the phrase a bunch of sandgropers looking for the light, another t'otherside paper had gone as far as to say that the backward colony was like a Cinderella waiting forlornly for her handsome Prince.

Proclamation Day 1890, nonetheless, proved one of fervent celebration. Perth was crowded with cheering citizens, the streets at dusk lit up with Chinese lanterns, dangling from the balconies of dwellings and business-houses. The city's spanking new fire-brigade sported itself out at the head of a torch-lit procession, with Perth's military band once again that day striking up tunes dear to the heart of England, not so much Western Australia. "Rule Britannia", "Men of Harlech", "Land of Hope and Glory", and so on.

Public and private parties were held throughout the capital, and while a people's ball was held in the Colonial Club, the people who really mattered joined with the Governor in a more formal arrangement in the Town Hall. The day proved a bonanza for the publicans, irrespective of their political leanings.

As Paddy and Daniel expected, the outcome of the election saw the new House of the People under the sway of the same few families who had controlled the Governor's Council - the Hungry Six. The only difference was that while the new Upper House, really only a remnant of the old Governor's Council - still contained the older originals, the lower house held either the blood relations or those who had become connected by marriage, similar to William Groves, now the Premier. As Paddy and Daniel felt to their sorrow, the *West Australian* with its ability to reach the people with its daily message of bogus liberalism, had won hands down.

Len Chandler was in a black mood.

"Well my friends, it looks as if we're finished. It was

bad enough a weekly trying to compete against a daily, but now with the *West* getting ninety five percent of its sponsored candidates in, I guess it has shown the mood of the populace."

"But you know that's not true Len," protested Daniel. "You only have to talk to the people in the streets - or in the pubs."

"Well what's the matter with them then?" cursed Len. "I think I should have seen the writing on the wall when that two-timing Tom Callahan took his backing from my paper."

"Yes," returned Daniel, gloomily. "Everyone's trying to be so damned respectable, trying to shut out their convict pasts. Of course, I suppose seeing the "*Herald*" was begun and is still promoted by expirees, it's too much of a reminder. Anyhow Len, I believe Robert Black would say that the *Fremantle Herald* deserves to be held in memory by every lover of liberty and freedom. You started it up even before transportation was ended back in the sixties, and the way its staff courageously portrayed the monstrous abuses of those times under Governor Hampton, I too believe that it should be recorded on the Tablets of Truth." Daniel finished with a theatrical gesture. "Far more indeed than these damnable knighthoods which in the last few years have been handed out so liberally to our well-to-do."

Chandler close to tears, shook Daniel's hand. "Thanks Daniel for the bouquets, but it does not alter the fact that we must close down."

"Jesus!" said Paddy.

"No, not even He can help," replied Chandler, grimly. And with that the ex-convict left, his shoulders bowed.

"Well," grimaced Paddy to Daniel. "What the hell do we do now?"

"I tell you I'm not finished," declared Daniel firmly. "Even if the *Herald* is. You wait, some day I'll own my own newspaper, you see."

"But how are you going to do that Daniel? You were only

saying the other day how you didn't know where your wages went, even though you don't drink heavily."

"Oh, I've still got a bit. I was going to suggest we pool our resources and take off to the Yilgarn. They're finding more and more gold out there. Who knows, within months we could make our fortunes."

Paddy's eyes lit up.

"Now you're talkin' Daniel. My God, that is a good idea. As a matter-o'-fact, I had visions of goin' back to the farm."

Paddy's eyes grew even wider.

"But what are we thinkin' about? What are we waitin' for? In fact, there's a train up to York tomorrow night. It's on the way."

"My God, yes," laughed Daniel, in as carefree a mood as Paddy had ever seen him. "We'll purchase horses and equipment in York or Northam - and then strike out east."

Paddy's face turned serious. Dammit all, he'd forgotten all about Ann. It certainly proved he did not love her. Different from what he'd whispered to her on more than one occasion.

Daniel gave a half-smile, catching Paddy's mood.

"Forgot about young Annie, didn't you?" Daniel had almost come out with "that little trollop!", but he thought better of it, he valued Paddy's friendship. Yet as far as Daniel was concerned, if Paddy was becoming too serious, the less he saw of Ann the better, even if she was very pleasing to look at. But a dance-hall girl - all right to relax and have fun with, but to become over-attached - never. Probably it was all for the better that Paddy was going away.

"Well you'd better make up your mind then hadn't you, my friend?"

"Yep, I had forgotten all about her," Paddy said slowly. "I feel a bit rotten about it too."

Daniel again gave that twisted smile. "Oh, she'll soon find someone else," he said. "Of course, there's always Ashley."

"No Daniel!" Paddy shot out, far from amused. "I'm going to make it my business to see her tonight in the club. As

I said, I feel rotten about it."

"All right, have it your own way. But remember you were the one who was so anxious to hit the track in search of gold."

In the Colonial Club that night when she was given the news, Ann tried to hide her distress.

"But it's only for the winter sweetheart," soothed Paddy, holding her hand over the table. "It's too damned hot to prospect in summer out there, so we'll be back to the big city."

"All right Paddy," she replied, trying to avoid tears.

Paddy now wondered why he would ever want to leave her. Misinterpreting his silence, she suddenly got to her feet, almost angrily.

"Look, I have to go! They want me on again."

All Paddy could do was give her a quick kiss goodbye.

"Bear up darling, I'll be back."

But as Ann resumed with her troupe, she wondered. Though Paddy had always protested that he was not above her, Ann felt that if he ever asked for her hand - which she sincerely hoped he would - there would be problems and disappointments. Though Paddy had often talked about his mother in admiring and affectionate terms, he had never suggested that Ann travel to York to meet her. In fact, she suspected he was afraid to even mention an entertainment girl in his own home.

Paddy decided that while in York, he would visit his folks with Daniel. On arrival in the town and not yet having purchased their horses, the pair decided to travel out to the old farm on foot, leaving their belongings with the York publican. In an adventurous mood they strode out towards the farm, making comments about the glorious country air, even though the weather had turned wet and blustery.

Certainly Paddy's father proved to be in a happy mood also, because good rains in early May usually heralded an excellent season. By the end of the day the weather had become bitterly cold, and after an enjoyable meal in the O'Leary living room they drew up chairs around a big log fire.

Mary and David also came over from the old cottage. Paddy noticed how frail they had become. They were both now nearing eighty, and Paddy felt himself wishing that when they did pass the divide, they would pass it close together.

He also noticed how young Rory had become even stockier, with muscles like a blacksmith. The darker-headed John looked muscular, too, but leaner, his brown eyes intelligent and determined. Looking at his two brothers together with their eyes full of confidence, Paddy felt a certain envy. The whole atmosphere as his father gave the celebratory toast in colonial spirits, made Paddy almost wish he'd stayed on the farm.

What a good future they now had. In the three years since Paddy had left, the railway had proven a boon. There was also a rumour that the O'Leary leasehold at Merredin might soon be opened for agriculture - a further rumour that the railway might be extended all the way from Northam to Southern Cross, the route passing through the O'Leary lease.

Paddy was now even more determined to prove himself out in the goldfields.

Two days later Paddy and Daniel headed for the Yilgarn. In York they had purchased two reliable saddle-horses and two sturdy pack-animals. Rather than take the old sandalwood track which was a short cut to the main route to Southern Cross, they decided to ride by way of Northam. Although far younger than York, the Avon Valley centre was now at least a dozen times its size. That evening, Paddy and Daniel enjoyed the company of prospectors, like themselves on the way to the goldields for winter.

Leaving Northam just after daybreak, by midday the pair

had reached Meckering, a new town, which with the extension of agriculture had become a typical frontier settlement, dominated by the general store and tavern. An addition to the tavern of course, was the Cobb and Co coach stop. Even with the advent of the railway, the long famous "people mover" had found a new lease of life with the establishment of the colony's first genuine gold-town, Southern Cross.

As the pair rode beyond Meckering, they passed a new bungalow homestead, built right close to the track. The farmer's young wife waved cheerily to them, three children by her side. Behind the homestead was a large recently cleared area, two horse teams working, the newly ploughed strip strikingly red against the black of the recent burn.

By sundown they had reached Tammin, another coach stop, built where the old sandalwood track from York struck the now well-used public road. The night was clear, so again to save money they tethered their horses on a grass-patch and slept under the stars close to a big granite outcrop, by which there was a good government well of excellent water which had been recently put down. It was one of the few wells along the route to Southern Cross fit for human consumption. Water had to be carted from the Tammin well to replenish the travel stop at the Doodlakine Inne, twenty eight miles further east, and already famous as the halfway house between Northam and Southern Cross.

Paddy and Daniel reached the Doodlakine Inne the following night, and after riding through the O'Leary lease at Merredin next day, the Yilgarn Hills began to rear up to the east - still elusive and mysterious, despite the fact that they were now inhabited by goldseekers.

Two days later they were in The Cross, an untidy straggling place, with its horseyards, blacksmiths' shops and rows of hessian-walled corrugated-iron huts, watched over by the occasional tall salmon-gum or gimlet. Yet a large hotel had already been built, and by the din erupting from within it was obviously well-patronised by the miners and prospectors. The observant Daniel soon picked out the odd character who was out in the "never-never" not for the love of gold alone. As he had discovered up at Hall's Creek, some were simply there to escape from nagging wives or bad debts. Some too were on the run for robbery even murder.

Next day they visited the one and only company mine, situated high up in a section of the Yilgarn Hills behind the town. There they interviewed the mine-manager who informed them that he was heartily sick of new-chum prospectors asking where was the best place to search for gold. As far as he was concerned, the Yilgarn could go to hell. It was too bloody hot in summer!

Yet the manager had no complaints about the mine. Though not a bonanza, it was doing well, employing nearly fifty men.

"Taciturn cove though, isn't he?" remarked Paddy to Michael.

"Yes, a typical Victorian digger of the old school," laughed Daniel. "Apart from the usual one or two remittance men and what-have-you, from what I've seen of the regular diggers, if they're not Victorians, they're Queenslanders, and there's even some New Zealanders." He became mildly apologetic, but still with a trace of cynicism.

"There I go again matey, knocking the stuffing out of you Westralians. Not that you don't deserve it."

Paddy nodded his head. "You've already reminded me so many times Daniel. Still, we both know that the powers that be in this colony have never worried much about minerals, except for a bit of lead north of Geraldton. With them, it's still all about land, just like Grandpa David says. Like the mad scramble still going on up north, for the families of the Hungry Six to grab the lot, even though most of it would take at least twenty five acres to support one sheep, let alone a cow."

"It's in their blood," returned Daniel. "They have to set

up their sons as overlords like the old feudal system. I saw enough up north when I was reporting on that poor devil Gribble. Talk about the feudal system! One of the Anderson sons even had a set of stocks in which he placed runaway natives, whom he believed belonged to him, even if he only paid them the little token wage for Aborigines allowed by the British Government."

"Yeh," scowled Paddy. "As Grandpa David said also, these are the same sorts of people who settled the American south, and who had to be conquered to stop slavery. Former British gentry, who as he said, believed serfdom or slavery was Holy Writ."

"And it's not to deny that the adventurous colonial types are a tough breed," rejoined Daniel. "But because they are so set on land or property, their minds are limited, so I guess as far as the gold is concerned, it's going to take the little person to open the way, and trying not to be nasty again, I might mention the Victorian digger."

"But surely the Hungry Six cohorts are aware," replied Paddy shrewdly. "Maybe they are just biding their time. The little bloke doesn't usually get much out of gold-prospecting in Australia, does he? It's the big British companies, which I recall Grandpa David mentioning, are largely owned by the British gentry anyhow."

"Along with the London Jews," grimaced Daniel. "Our newer British capitalists. Share capital which is sharing with the gentry in running the tea plantations in Ceylon and India, banana and pineapple plantations in the Pacific Islands, coffee and sugar plantations in South America. My God, there is no end to it is there? If the gold here is good enough for the British companies to invest - and I mean including the Jews - the McAllums and Andersons and the like will buy shares later, there's nothing surer."

The "New Chums", as Paddy and Daniel had quickly been dubbed by the mine-workers, were quickly warned about carrying plenty of water while out prospecting. After purchasing two extra water-containers at an exorbitant price, they were directed to call on the man who ran the big and so necessary condenser plant. It was fired by local timber and converted the salt water, of which there was plenty in the company mine in the hills, to fresh.

"That'll be a shillin' a gallon," said the man on the condenser. "An' if you want any extra for a bath, you'll 'ave to pay double."

"Christ," said Paddy. "It's damn near as costly as their grog."

A couple of old hands had warned them about venturing too far out, particularly as their horses also needed to drink. The standard procedure appeared to be to spend three or four days in the bush, then head back to The Cross.

"Unless you're lucky enough to find a native gnamma hole," explained a grizzled t'otherside prospector. "But I tell ye', they're as scarce as emu's teeth." "Yeah, they're as plentiful as the kangaroos," grinned Paddy. "Where they all get their water, God only knows?"

"I doubt if He does either," wisecracked the prospector. "Haven't you heard o' the place God forgot?"

Daniel and Paddy spent the next two months doing exactly what the other prospectors were doing - carefully searching the quartz and greenstone areas, which ran in a strip around thirty miles wide and about fifty miles north and south of The Cross. A likely little field to the nor-west had been Golden Valley, named not so much for the gold, but for the resplendent wattle acacia blossoms in spring. It had also been the first area where payable gold had been struck in the Yilgarn by Dick Greaves, Ed Payne and Harry Anstey, the three professional prospectors engaged by the Fremantle merchant. But now in digger's terms Golden Valley had petered out, and Daniel later lamented, that as far as surface gold was concerned it seemed the whole of the Southern Cross region could be given the same old tag - "Petered Out".

All winter they had been hearing tales in the bar about an energetic young Victorian Arthur Bayley, who with his Queensland mate William Ford, had come down to The Cross from the Pilbara just south of the Kimberleys in the far north. Skilled and toughened prospectors, Bayley and Ford, according to rumour, had already come across some likely spots well to the east of The Cross. The only problem was that to get there, it was necessary to travel through well over a hundred miles of mostly hungry waterless sandplain. A local character who appeared to know all about it was Wally Truslove, prospector turned mine-worker, who had taken the job because it paid well and gave Wally plenty of time to indulge in his favourite pastime, boozing.

It was getting near the end of winter, so almost in desperation one evening Paddy decided to pump Wally, shouting him a drink for good measure. With a free beer under his belt Wally soon let forth, relating how Bayley and Ford had cobbered up with a Gil McPherson, who had come in nearly dead with thirst, and how the pair had looked after McPherson till he was better.

"So what happened then Wally?" asked Paddy, all ears.

"Well," went on Wally, after Paddy had re-filled his glass. "Apparently what made Bayley an' Ford so friendly with McPherson was that he had shown them some big lumps o' solid gold which McPherson had picked up more'n a hundred miles east." Wally drained his glass, pushing it over to Paddy again. "The trouble o' course, is gettin' there through all that damned waterless scrub country. Otherwise I'da gone out meself."

"So that's where the pair went," said Paddy, excitedly.

"Yeah, they did cobber; followin' what's called Hunt's Track, which is not much wider'n a kangaroo pad."

"But they couldn't have found much, could they?" reasoned Paddy. "Bayley and his mate have cleared off back to Perth again. Some say they are goin' up north for the summer wet."

"Yeah," said Wally. "Back up the Pilbara. That bloody Marble Bar, hotter'n a furnace, better down here."

Next day Paddy and Daniel discussed the possibilities. Paddy suggested it might be an idea to visit the District Warden.

"It's certainly part of his job to know," agreed Daniel.

The Warden, who had been in The Cross almost from the outset, was cooperative only to a point.

"Yes, Bayley an' Ford did come in with some samples," he admitted in an Irish brogue. "But as far as lettin' you spalpeens know how much the samples were worth. Well now, it's just not my place to tell, as you both should know. Looks like you're still only new chums."

Though obviously stung by the unpopular title, "New Chum", Daniel was still persistent.

"If I may ask, Mr Finnerty, have you any idea what the country's like out there? I've heard it's pretty tough going."

The bluff red-faced man now seemed ready for conversation.

"Well as Warden I've had to visit the place, an' I don't dislike it, certainly a change after all that hungry sandplain. The land is red and rich and well-timbered, similar to the country more to the west of here. The difference is, that like round here there's big outcrops of ironstone and quartz. Likely gold country, I can tell ye'. It's good pasture land too," he went on. "As a matter o' fact, one o' the Clayton-Brownes has a station a long way nor-nor-east o' here. Runs his flocks over there where we're talkin' about some winters. But this season's been so dry he's kept 'em up in the mulga where there's permanent good water."

"One o' the nob families again," swore Paddy, as they left. "There he made mention of the Clayton-Brownes. Can't get away from the bastards."

"Yes," laughed Daniel. "Even dear old Ashley might turn

up. Anyhow, back to things more pleasant. Gold. Although we could be crow-bait out there, seeing there's no permanent water, what about giving it a go?"

"Why ask?" returned an excited Paddy. "An' we'd better make it quick smart, it's now the middle of September an' approachin' summer."

After purchasing and filling up extra water-bags next day, Paddy and Daniel left early the following morning, picking up Hunt's Track about twenty miles out. They were soon into the plain country, which apart from the isolated few acres of timbered redlands, was covered mostly in low heath, with the periodical stands of wodgil and broombush ti-tree. The weather for the time of the year had turned exceptionally hot, and by nightfall they realised that they had consumed far too much water. Next day the trek seemed even more slow and torturous. The broombush was alive with sandflies, annoying the horses as much as the humans. The monotonous scrubplain seemed never-ending, bringing to the pair feelings of gloom and inadequacy, only allayed by the possibility of gold.

Near sunset on the fifth day, the weary travellers at last entered a huge stretch of open forested redlands. With their water almost gone, the parched exhausted pair sat down in the welcome shade of a large salmon-gum and contemplated their future.

They used the last of their water, giving some to their horses from a large flat pannikin. Recklessly, they pressed on and by sundown had come across a likely reef where they picked up some quartz specimens specked with the precious metal.

But with all the rockholes and claypans dry, there came reality. Paddy was reminded of his earlier experience with young Tommy Tetlaw, within sight of the Yilgarn Hills.

"Christ Almighty, if we're goin' to die out here through lack o' water, the gold's not likely to be much use, is it?"

"Well, not to us anyway," replied Daniel grimly.

It was early next morning when they met Wilga, an Aboriginal. He was one of a family clan claimed by the Clayton-Brownes on their station. Wilga had decided to wander, as was the wont of many of the native bucks, much to the wrath of their white masters. In fact, the attractive redlands area with its magnificent forest glades and tall outcrops of green granite, ironstone and quartz, was to Wilga's clan like some gigantic faraway sacred retreat, yet only to be enjoyed by the bulk of the tribe in a wet winter. It was for the same reason that white families like the Clayton-Brownes used the area for shepherding sheep in a good season.

Though Wilga was a runaway from a station he had got to know prospectors fossicking well north of Southern Cross, and in fact had more than once led them to water. Dressed in tattered blue dungarees, Wilga introduced himself by name, and then at a half-run led them a mile further east, showing them a deep gnamma hole near the edge of a granite sheet, down from a steep rocky outcrop.

Wilga only used what was necessary for communication. Typical was his vocabulary concerning the gnamma-hole. "Fella water - not much," he grinned. "Men along you. Drink!" He waved his arm as if pushing aside the obviously thirsty horses.

"No," said Paddy, putting his hand on Wilga's shoulder in friendly fashion. "Horses - first."

That was when Wilga really took to Paddy, realising he had something which many white men lacked, compassion.

"Anymore water?" asked Daniel of the still smiling Wilga. After they had satisfied theirs and their horses' thirsts there was none left for the canteens.

Wilga showed his even white teeth, waving his arms eastwards.

"Long way in, 'bout day's walk. Only little bit, though.

But more longa here," he grinned, indicating the hole. "...though take long time."

"Oh, it's got a spring feed," said Daniel, looking into the recess. "But by the looks, a damn poor supply. Still, it's better than nothing. I guess all we can do is wait around for a day or so till we've enough to fill our canteens and return to The Cross."

Paddy was unhappy. "Looks like we came all the way out here for nothin'." He turned to Wilga. "Gold, Wilga, you know what it is. We've found some, anymore out there?"

The native gave a hearty laugh and pointed his finger to the north-west.

"Out there, plenty!"

"Well I hope he's right," said Paddy, after the young native had slipped away. "Anyway, what about it, we could risk going in a few miles while this spring's makin' up?"

"Why not?" was the reply.

After around five miles they found themselves riding up a rocky slope, scattered with white quartz. They dismounted, and almost immediately Paddy gave a yell.

"Christ, look at this!" In his hand was a nugget weighing at least three ounces. But a frantic search in the heat, netted them nothing more and they returned to the gnamma hole, as jaded as ever. Fortunately the hole had made up enough to quench their own and their horses' thirsts again. But then there would be that many hours wait for enough to fill their canteens for the trip back to The Cross.

Finally after an anxious twenty-four hour vigil, they were able to make their way, only to find that after three days travel in the intense heat, they were almost out of water again. Nothing now but to keep going. The next two days were torture. Each twenty miles distance from clear hillbrow to hillbrow across the low scrub, seemed like an infinity, the next long expanse the same. And so it went on, the heat ever-increasing, the flies in the occasional shade-patch ever more plentiful. Emus and kangaroos were also in quantity.

Paddy made comment, as he had with the rugged prospector when they had first arrived at Southern Cross.

"Christ knows where they get their water?"

Daniel replied soberly through parched and blistered lips. "Your father and I discussed that years ago when we went out on that sandalwood trip. The wild animals either get enough moisture out of the natural herbage they eat, or they must have the capacity to travel a hell of a long way for a drink."

"Yeah," agreed Paddy, desperately. "Wish I knew how far. We could follow 'em."

"Oh I guess it's been tried before," mused Daniel. "And I'd say Wilga back there would know all about it, but I think right now it might pay to rely on our waterbags."

"Or what's left in 'em," was the gloomy reply.

Considering the trials they were going through, it was just normal conversation - and it was fortunate that two days out from The Cross, they met a party of prospectors doing an end of winter search along the edge of the greenstone belt, well to the east of the mining town.

Rather than sympathy back in The Cross they met derision. They were called all kinds of fools, including the dreaded New Chum. It was obvious they hadn't prepared themselves enough. But still not deterred, they were soon making plans to return to that distant locality. With its prospects for gold, its graphic colours and its shady attractive woodlands it was like some far-off Shangri-La. The only drawback was water - or the lack of it.

However, such plans were for next winter. With summer fast approaching, the best bet now was to make for the cooler climes of the coast.

Another drawback was that they were desperately short of cash, so each took advantage of taking a job in Northam, Paddy with the local flour-miller, and Daniel as a temporary clerk in the District Roads Board Office. Paddy was also surprised to discover Ann Fogarty working in one of the

Northam pubs. While Paddy was pleased to see her, Daniel took the news with tongue-in-cheek.

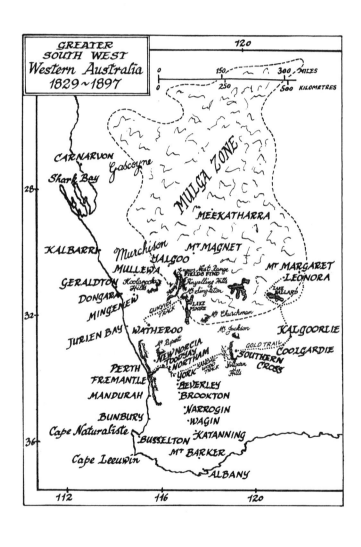

GREATER
SOUTH WEST
Western Australia
1829~1897

120

0   150   300 MILES
0   250   500 KILOMETRES

MULGA ZONE

CARNARVON
Shark Bay
Gascoyne

28

MEEKATHARRA

KALBARRI
Murchison
YALGOO
MULLEWA
GERALDTON
DONGARA
MINGENEW

Mt MAGNET

Mt MARGARET
LEONORA

Emus Nest Range
FIELDS FIND
Payalling Hills
Mt Clingleton
Koolanooka
Hills
GUNYIDI
TRACK
LAKE
MOORE

LAKE
BALLARD

32

Mt Churchman

JURIEN BAY
WATHEROO

Mt Jackson

KALGOORLIE

Mt Pupunti
NEW NORCIA
TOODYAY
NORTHAM
YORK
SWAN
WOOL
TRACK

GOLD TRAIL
SOUTHERN
CROSS

COOLGARDIE

PERTH
FREMANTLE
MANDURAH

BEVERLEY
BROOKTON

Yilgan
Hills

BUNBURY
Cape Naturaliste

NARROGIN
WAGIN

KATANNING

36

BUSSELTON
Mt BARKER

Cape Leeuwin

ALBANY

112   116   120

CHAPTER 7

As was their plan, Paddy and Daniel again spent the winter prospecting. Arthur Bayley and John Ford had also returned from the Pilbara. In that year of 1892, heavy rains had fallen in late March, giving hopes of a good season around York and Northam. Well east of Southern Cross, the rains also fell, washing down the alluvial gullies and exposing the glint of gold. It was the time to make the most of it, as any experienced prospector knew.

Signing off from their temporary jobs in Northam, Paddy and Daniel made preparations to ride for The Cross. But before leaving, Paddy once again had to say goodbye to Ann Fogarty.

In those summer months in Northam, Paddy and Ann had become more emotionally attached. Paddy had even suggested to Daniel that they take lodgings in the same hotel where Ann worked as a part-time bar-girl and entertainer. But Daniel disagreed, mainly as he said hotel board was too expensive. Yet also in Daniel's mind was the feeling that the attachment between Ann and Paddy should not be encouraged.

So the pair stayed on in a second-rate hostel on the edge of town. Even so, for the two young men, apart from drink, there was the temptation to spend part of their off-duty hours in the bar. Many a prospector had taken temporary work in the agricultural centre like themselves - and so much of the talk was about gold and how the end of summer couldn't come soon enough for them to be back out fossicking.

In the late evening after the bar closed, a disgruntled Daniel was often forced to return to their quarters alone, while Paddy walked off with Ann, usually to the town park. The young pair would perform the same ritual on Sunday afternoons.

As in Perth, Paddy and Ann enjoyed each other's company.

Ann felt they were meant for each other, and more and more wished he would ask for her hand. Of late she had begun to talk about her love for children, and how if she had not been a pub-girl, she might have wished to have been a children's nurse, or even a governess. But her poor education was against her.

To capture Paddy, Ann often thought about giving herself to him completely. But she had already had enough experience to know that to give in easily like a tart to a man she loved and admired enough to marry, might also be the means of losing his respect.

Paddy too, respected Ann, and it was the reason he had not attempted to use her, as he would have to any other attractive girl who was willing. In fact, on that last evening when they were saying goodbye, he felt that he and Ann had been acting privately more like some sort of moral-minded Puritan courting couple. It was certainly different to what some of the hard-bitten drinkers at the Northam hotel believed - especially with Paddy taking Ann to the Northam park most evenings after she knocked off.

"Gettin' yer bit matey, I'll bet!" was a typical comment, the character in question making sure Ann was at the other end of the bar. "Lucky you, with a good-lookin' piece like that."

Paddy found it unnecessary to explain that their dallies in the park were only confined to sweet talk and the occasional kiss and embrace.

It was all so ridiculous. Paddy had to admit to himself that though he enjoyed Ann's company, he still preferred the life on the gold-trail. The very fact that he was so excited about leaving for The Cross tomorrow only went to show. Ann felt it too, and it was the reason that last evening she burst into tears. "Paddy, do you still love me?"

"I'm buggered if I know sweetheart, I'm not quite sure?" might have been his answer. But he simply held her tighter in his arms, telling the usual white lie.

118

"Of course I do, my precious."

"Will you be returning to Northam then after winter?"

"Of course Ann, of course. It's too damned hot out there in summer, even chasin' gold."

Ann knew that he had given himself away. If the winter was to last all year, he'd stay out there forever. But she left it at that, still loving him and wondering why?

Arriving back at The Cross and knowing all the claypans and gnamma-holes would be filled, Paddy and Daniel were soon on their way to what they now called Wilga's Find. With extra pack-horses, they also carried enough gear to put down a shaft. But though they worked hard at it digging sifting and cracking up quartz for more than four months, they realised they were not getting enough gold out to make it pay.

What had made Paddy and Daniel even more frustrated was the resourcefulness of the pair, Bayley and Ford, who had called in from time to time. The seasoned prospectors were now using camels both for riding and transport. They had brought them down from the far north, where camels had been introduced first to make easier the tough waterless trek between Wyndham and Hall's Creek. With their ability to carry heavy loads and survive for days without water, camels were the answer to a prospector's prayer. Such was proven when Bayley and Ford, while doing extensive fossicking in the area where Paddy and Daniel had their mine, were able to make many trips back to The Cross with apparent ease. To Paddy and Daniel, the more than one hundred mile journey was a nightmare - to be avoided as much as possible. But forced by a shortage of stores and yearning for a welcome break - even if only in a frontier town - the pair made their way back to The Cross.

As it was now near the end of August, Paddy and Daniel had even contemplated returning to Northam. But though Paddy had revived some endearing thoughts about Ann waiting there in the agricultural centre, he finally agreed with

Daniel that they spend a few days "hanging around" the mining town before they made up their minds.

Also some interesting rumours had begun to spread around The Cross. Paddy still had his penchant for pub-life, even if it was only yarning at the bar. Not that he always drank heavily, but just enjoyed the company. It was also here where one could pick up the latest information, often highly coloured as was usually the case with Wally Truslove, who still spent most of his time with his hand around a glass of ale.

The previous winter Wally had come to appreciate Paddy's natural wit, possibly because unlike most of the other miners and prospectors, Paddy was more resilient to Wally's "ear-bashing", as the diggers made it known.

"Look cobber," slurred Wally the night before Paddy and Daniel had finally decided to return to what Daniel called, civilisation. "Seein' yer such a good mate, I c'n let you into a secret. You were sayin' you're pullin' up stakes. Maybe I could make you change yer mind. But if it turns up trumps, I also want a cut?"

"What the hell are you gettin' at Wally?" demanded Paddy.

Wally's voice fell almost to a whisper. "Bayley an' Ford've struck it rich, an' I mean, RICH."

Knowing Wally's reputation, Paddy still wasn't impressed. "You're sure it's not just another tall story Wally, there's been such a hell of a lot round the place lately."

Wally seemed hurt, but his tone was still low and urgent which made Paddy believe he might be genuine.

"No, o' course not!" went on Wally. "Fact is, accordin' to a mate, Arthur Bayley came in yestiddy with over six hundred ounces."

"God Almighty!" Paddy whispered fiercely. "How did your mate find out?"

Wally looked around suspiciously. "From another mate!"

"Knowin' your mates Wally," returned Paddy. "Can you depend on 'em?"

"O' course I can," said Wally. "As it happens the Warden's away in Perth, an' Bayley had to leave the gold with a clerk, who put it in the care o' Mike Fitzpatrick, the local policeman."

Paddy had become excited. "Well, with a big find like that, the Warden's supposed to go out and inspect it. Where's Bayley now?"

"He's gone back. Who wouldn't?"

"Look Wally," shot back Paddy. "Have you told anyone else?"

Wally looked sheepish. "Well, that other mate, he does talk a bit."

Paddy ran his eyes around the bar-room. "Yeh, an' that's why there's a few faces missing. From now on for Chris'sake shutup about it. An' if it turns up trumps, as you say, you'll certainly be rewarded."

With that Paddy moved swiftly out of the hotel, motioning Daniel who had been talking further along the bar, to follow him.

"Wally reckons Bayley and Ford have struck it rich," said Paddy, quietly, outside the door of the pub.

"Jesus," exclaimed Daniel, trying to keep his voice down, despite the noise from the bar. "With their expertise, it certainly could be on the cards. It might pay to change our plans."

In the darkness, Paddy gave a grin. "Looks like we'll be ridin' east again instead o' west. Certainly suits me. When do we start?"

"The sooner the better," declared Daniel excitedly. "Our horses are handy and our canteens are full, so let's make it first light."

But next day in their eagerness, they pushed their mounts and pack-animals too hard. The weather had turned exceptionally hot for the time of the year, causing the horses still with their winter coats to pour with sweat. By three-o'clock in the afternoon they were forced to rest, losing valuable time.

"Christ, I thought we'd learnt a bit by now," cursed Paddy.

"But we haven't, have we?" grumbled Daniel, wearily sliding down from his mount. "Still just plurry new chums, as they'd say back there in the bar. Anyhow, let's make the best of it and rest the horses till morning."

They were away again by dawn, the sun rising yellow and molten in a clear desert sky. From then on for the next five days it was unendingly the same, the now familiar scenery boringly changeless - the only spur for the anxious pair - Gold. On the third day on the top of a hill, Paddy climbed a pile of granite and looked back towards The Cross through a pair of field-glasses. Across the wide expanse of scrubland, he detected a small dust-cloud.

"God Almighty," swore Paddy. "Looks like Wally's blabbed a bit more."

"Knowing him, it's not surprising," called Daniel. "Anyway, if the strike is true, it makes one realise the urgency."

"Yeah, first in first served," grinned Paddy, jumping onto his horse.

Two days later they reached the forestlands, watering their horses and filling their canteens at Wilga's Soak. With still a few hours of daylight left they rode east-nor-east, taking a line on a high feature about fifty miles distant, already known as Mt Youle.

"I was wonderin' about that mob behind us," said Paddy, as they rode along. "Maybe it might be an idea to press on through the night."

"Tough on the horses," but yes, could be an idea."

But with hardly a track to follow, and with the moon in the wrong quarter, the pair were forced to abandon their plans till first light. That night they had very little sleep, talking for hours about the possibilities both for themselves and the colony, if Bayley and Ford had really struck it rich.

But around nine-o'clock on their way they were suddenly confronted by five men on horseback trailing three laden packhorses. Paddy recognised them as the group of Wally's mates who had been missing earlier from the bar when Wally had told Paddy the good news about the gold. The men were apparently on their way back to The Cross.

"Out of your territory a bit, you fellers, aren't you?" suggested Paddy half in jest. "You wouldn't have taken a visit to Bayley and Ford's claim by any chance, would you? We've heard a bit of a rumour."

An unshaven Victorian, stuck out his jaw.

"An' what's it to yuh, O'Leary? If you want to see what's goin' on, ride on an' take a look yerself." He gave a wider smirk, exposing nicotine-blackened teeth. "In fact, it's like a bloody jeweller's shop. We snuck in an' took a look early this mornin' before Bayley an' Ford were outa bed."

"What's that you've got in your saddle-bags?" asked Daniel suspiciously. "It looks a mite heavier than just tinned tucker."

"Bloody what's it to yuh?" gritted the grizzled character again. "If you want to know, go an' take a look yerself." And with that the men pushed their horses past on the narrow track, and rode on.

"Jesus," said Paddy to Daniel, after the men had left. "What do we do now? Go back an' tell the police or what?"

"There's only one policeman in The Cross to tell," Daniel replied, half amused. "Those same coves have probably done similar over t'otherside. They'll cash the gold in small lots, making out they got it around The Cross. Anyway, let's ride on and just pay Bayley and Ford a casual visit."

"Yeah," agreed Paddy. "At least we're honest."

It was only about a half mile further on that they met Wilga, who had visited their main claim more than once that season. He was with a companion, who unlike Wilga with his cast-off station clothes, was clad only in an apron-like breech-clout.

It seemed the natives knew exactly what was going on.

"Plenty bloody gold," smiled Wilga. "We show you."

"Too bloody right Wilga," said Paddy happily. "Lead on."

They cantered their horses along the narrow track, the two natives sprinting easily in front. Five miles further on they rode into a large semi-open patch of salmon-gums and gimlets, which lay below a jasper ridge to the north. All at once they came upon Bayley and Ford digging away on their claim.

The lean, bronzed Bayley, gave greeting. "Well now, you pair," he smiled. "Bit out of your territory, aren't you?"

"We said the same thing to a bunch of coves a few miles back," grinned Paddy. "In fact, we suspect you could have misplaced a bit of ore."

"The bastards, that we have," swore Bayley. "So it was them. We're missin' a good two hundred ounces, pretty well pure gold."

"Good heavens," broke in Daniel, "they did take a heap, but I'd say by the looks you'd hardly miss it would you?" Daniel indicated the lumps of quartz the men had picked out loaded with gold. "Do you mind if we take a look?"

"No go ahead," said Bayley generously. "In fact, we were just about to put on the billy for lunch. You may as well join in."

The reef was around four foot wide and two hundred foot long, and wherever the pair had dug lay exposed huge chunks of practically pure gold.

"Mother McCree," breathed Paddy. "As that cove back there said. Like a bloody jeweller's shop."

"Whew," gasped Daniel, as they walked over and sat with the prospectors. "Any more reefs like this one?"

Bayley handed each one a tin pannikin of tea. "No, nothing like this one. Not close, anyhow." The prospector smoothed his beard. "But there's another likely reef about a half-mile east." He had a broad grin on his face. "And I'd reckon you'd better peg it while your luck's in."

"Thanks mate," said Paddy. "Much obliged. Anyway, if you don't mind me askin', did you just stumble onto this patch, or what?"

Bayley again broke into a laugh. "Well, in a way, yes. But as often happens, we were looking for water and we met Wilga here." He indicated the smiling natives, who had just replenished their thirsts from the nearby gnamma-hole.

"Well I'll be damned," swore Paddy. "I thought we were the only ones he associates with. He found us a handy supply last year."

"Of course, Wilga doesn't really discover the gnamma holes," replied Bayley, as he took another sip of tea. "You see, his clan has known about the gnamma holes since God know's when. And in the first place the holes were doubtless dug out using the Aboriginal's incredible rock-cracking ability with fire." Bayley pointed down the slope. "Like the one Wilga showed us down there. In fact, his people call it the Colgardy, almost like some sacred place."

"My God, a sacred place, it's that and all," declared Daniel in admiration, his eyes on the gold reef.

"Yes," smiled Bayley, getting to his feet. "And we've called it Coolgardie, it comes better off the tongue."

"Good on you matey," said Paddy to Wilga later, as they were mounting their horses. "You should get a medal."

"Not very likely," cut in Daniel, cynically. "Bayley and Ford might, but not Wilga, he's only a native."

But Wilga just grinned happily, glad to be free of the Clayton-Brownes, whom he knew were still out to punish him for absconding from their station.

"We go," said the other native, running on the spot and highly pleased with his new vocabulary.

"We'll have to teach that one the proper King's English," said Paddy, as they rode along.

"No don't," replied Daniel. "Any more could lower his dignity."

It was not long before they came across the reef Bayley had told them about, but apart from a few specks embedded in the quartz, there appeared to be nothing of real value on the surface. Paddy drew a chipper from his belt and began to pick into the red soil.

"Christ Almighty," he yelled. "A real beauty." He held up a nugget of almost solid gold.

"I'll bet it goes ten ounces or nothing!"

Daniel had also picked out another rich piece, and the natives had joined in the enthusiasm, digging amongst the quartz with calloused fingers.

Paddy and Daniel quickly stepped out the bounds of the reef, including the mass of dark red colluvium radiating down from it, in all around ten acres. They then marked the corners of the lease with cairns built of loose stones, placing in each a steel peg on which had already been engraved their prospector's rights numbers.

They were none too soon. All at once more than a dozen excited men broke through the scrub, the ones who had been on their tail after they left The Cross.

"You pair of bastards," yelled one. "Anyway, any more good reefs around?"

"Go an' look for your bloody self, Flanagan," yelled back Paddy. "It's a big country."

By nightfall there were at least one hundred more men in the vicinity, many of them mine-workers from the hills up from The Cross. They had stolen a few picks and shovels from the company for good measure. When they reached Coolgardie, one look at Bayley's Reward, as it had already become known, was enough. In the language of the digger, it was the richest strike in the colony by a mile.

Southern Cross was now connected by overland telegraph and word of the find rapidly reached the centres of population. As with other towns, all work in Northam and York came to a standstill. Everyone's thoughts were on gold. And while some conjured up hopes about personal gain, the odd one had thoughts more aspiring - about what it might do for the Cinderella colony.

Within a month, Coolgardie had a population of more than a thousand, all living in tents or hessian huts. It was now almost December, the height of summer, when normally most white men made their way to the coast, to be revived by the refreshing south-west breezes from the Indian Ocean. The problem in Coolgardie of course, was water, the ancient Colgardy gnamma hole having hardly the capacity to sustain more than a couple of prospectors and their beasts of burden. Bores had been hastily put down, but what water there was underground so far had proven too salty not only for humans but also for livestock. Once again there was the rush to cart and assemble the huge and necessary de-salinator.

But such would take precious time, and it was then the local carriers in faraway York and Northam began to put their wagons to good use, converting them to water-carriers and filling them from good potable water supplies, such as from the well near the granite rock at Tammin. In addition, the York carrier had all the cobwebs cleaned from his idle Cobb and Co coaches - to cope with the ever-increasing passenger traffic. There was even talk of more unused Cobb and Co coaches being brought over from South Australia by an enterprising young man called Sid Kidman, who starting penniless as a lad had made a fortune in dealing in livestock, his aim to acquire a vast chain of sheep and cattle stations stretching from just north of Adelaide in the south to Darwin in the north.

Out on the Baker-O'Leary farm, they spoke with relish of what had already been described by the *West Australian* newspaper, as the Coolgardie bonanza. In fact, though the farm was doing handsomely - that season had turned out a bumper for grain - it was decided to put the big old farm wagon to water-carting to Coolgardie similar to the York carrier.

The energetic Rory believed that with the diggers paying one hundred pounds per fifty gallon barrel for good water, he could certainly put up with the heat and flies on the long trek. Owing to the long sandy stretches between Southern Cross and Coolgardie wagons had to be hauled by bullocks instead of horses, making the journey more tiresome. Oxen, the same stolid breed of beast which had been used in earlier times to haul wagons through the deep banksia sands between the Darling Ranges and the coast.

On the Baker-O'Leary farm, aside from the excitement heralding a rich new phase in the colony's history, there was also sadness. In the last fortnight Grandma Mary had passed away. Although a wire had been despatched to Southern Cross, the news was too late getting to Coolgardie for Paddy to attend the funeral. Mary was buried on high ground not far up from the old homestead, David only looking forward to the time when he could lie there with her. In his old age, David had developed even more guilt feelings about the harsh treatment of natives, often quoting passages from the journals of his beloved William Wilberforce. Yet for some families in the York district, especially the remnants of the old Anglican gentry, there was the feeling that David in his last years had become senile. According to the new Anglican Vicar, he harped too much on the same old worn-out theme. The evils of slavery, convictism, native exploitation and so on, when in all truth without the indentured labour that these unfortunates supplied, the majority of Britain's colonial ventures might have turned out failures, Western Australia included.

The next two months saw the colony's population increase to the extent that Perth found it difficult to accommodate the shiploads anchored out from Fremantle. What made it even more frustrating for the new arrivals, was that after more than sixty years of settlement, passengers still had to be ferried into the Fremantle jetty by small boat through notoriously rough seas and over dangerous reefs. Many more of the gold-hungry t'othersiders left ship at Esperance on the southern coast, trudging the whole three hundred miles north to Coolgardie, many pushing barrows loaded with stores and mining gear. Some of these hopefuls had been previously rich, but lost their fortunes with the crash of the Melbourne land boom in the late 1880s

All this time Paddy and Daniel had been busy on their Coolgardie claim, having by now accumulated an imposing stockpile of nuggets. Wilga also worked with them, and though he had lost his coloured companion to the wilds, he had elected to stay with Paddy, for whom he had developed a deep attachment. Many more male Aborigines had begun camping on the outskirts of the boom settlement, some having brought along their lubras, who were regarded only as personal chattels by the Clayton-Brownes.

Clayton Downs station, run by Julien Clayton-Browne, lay around ninety miles north-west of Coolgardie on the edge of the mulga, the acacia aneura, so highly palatable to sheep as summer-feed. An advantage was that in the dry-looking mulga zone, underground water suitable for sheep was reasonably easy to find at depth. Hence the movement of the Clayton-Brownes back in the seventies to acquire yet another valuable lease.

Since the 1892 season had been better than usual owing to the March rains, the Clayton-Brownes had again used the Coolgardie area as a winter sheep-run. Later during that exciting summer of 1892-93, Julien Clayton-Browne himself had been seen riding arrogantly through the mining town.

Paddy and Daniel with their experience as observant newspaper men in the older more established areas of the colony had never lost their distaste for the traditional families. As well as the fear from Paddy and Daniel that Wilga could be seized and taken back to the station, the presence of Julien Clayton-Browne brought some caustic comments.

"Just like I said, we can't get away from the jumped-up bastards?" remarked Paddy caustically. "Even out here, Clayton-Browne has to ride through our minin' town, lookin' like he owns it."

Daniel gave one of his rare laughs.

"Well, I guess he does own it in a way, seeing he has the unofficial grazing lease of the whole area. Still, I suppose he's only doing what he's been brought up to believe. And in regard to them being the first to push their flocks out here for the benefit of winter feed, though admittedly astute and courageous, it could also mean in the language of the nomad to eat the place out while you've got the chance."

"Just keepin' up the tradition," replied Paddy with a scowl. "Grabbin' all the best while you've got a free rein."

"Well, certainly the early British governors had given them that and all," said Daniel.

On one day alone Paddy and Daniel dug out at least fifty ounces of high-grade gold from their claim. Paddy was gleeful.

"Well cobber, I'd say by now we could call ourselves rich."

"No, not quite," smiled Daniel. "But I tell you, it might not be far off. In fact, I've already thought about starting up my paper. I've got a name for it too, the *Coolgardie Miner*. How's that?"

"Sounds good," said Paddy cautiously. "But it could be back to the flamin' grind again, couldn't it? Why don't we just keep on with what we're about? It's payin' so well."

Daniel was solemn, realising Paddy was becoming so much like the other prospectors, even taking on their careless ways and manner of speech.

"You talked about coming out here to make your fortune," exclaimed Daniel. "Yet you should know from your mother's teachings Paddy, that gold is only the means to an end. She must have read to you out of the Bible how the Good Lord sayeth, that here are riches, now spend them wisely. Gold is only a stepping-stone to self-improvement."

"Well, there's another nugget," wisecracked Paddy. "Look, I'm improved already."

Daniel dropped his shovel with a clatter, setting off a fit of laughter from Wilga.

"Look Paddy, why can't you get serious for a change? Back in Fremantle, you proved yourself a good newspaper-man. You're not without brains, and you've got the personality to mix with all and sundry. But by the way you're behaving it could all be wasted."

Paddy just gave a grin. "Why worry, when we've got plenty o' the necessary." He pointed to the gold.

But Daniel saw little humour. "Look, I meant what I said about the newspaper. I was hoping we might pool our resources. We could still work the mine in our spare time."

Wilga showed his teeth, pointing to himself. "Me work mine no worry."

"Yes," added Daniel. "Wilga can work it as he is helping now, and also getting his share."

"No!" rejoined Paddy. "Running a newspaper's too bloody boring."

"My God!" swore Daniel. "No wonder you had trouble at home Paddy, you've got no patience." Daniel went silent. "Look, I might have to find someone else. You must know by now I'm dinkum."

Paddy looked shame-faced, realising he might have gone too far with someone he had called a friend - even though Paddy himself was still far more interested in digging for gold than working on a newspaper.

"Surely you can take a joke, matey?"

"Well now, that's better."

Far more than Paddy, Daniel felt the mood of the people, as a good newspaper editor should. The fathers of most of

131

these Coolgardie diggers had been diggers themselves in the 1850s around Bendigo and Ballarat. And now the sons of Eureka were over here, hoping to strike it rich.

But as Daniel knew, these gold-seekers lacked the essentials of an entrepreneur. In most ways they were just simple men, as naive almost as little children. Daniel felt that with his education and his liberal-democratic philosophies, it was up to him to look after the average digger to protect him from the ravages of the company men, many of whom were already in Coolgardie.

Christmas in Coolgardie, apart from the grog, was a dry and dusty one. Making it even more dusty were the dryblowers, an innovation born of necessity through lack of water. The dry-blower was simply a small blacksmith's bellows set under a mobile hand-operated shaker and sieves. Air was used to move the powdered ore instead of water. Made on the job, mostly out of local timber, except for the sieves and bellows. By New Year there were literally hundreds of them - spread over what had become called Fly-Flat, sifting out the rich red loam, much of it yielding more than five ounces to the ton. The whole of the area was soon covered in refuse from the dryblowers. Such scenes made Daniel all the more eager to start his newspaper in which he could portray eager-eyed diggers shuffling up to their ankles in fine red dust from dawn to dusk.

The miners did not have to wait long to find somewhere to spend their gains. First a couple of rough hessian-walled grogshops appeared. As well as drink they also offered gambling as a pastime and as a way of relieving the diggers of their gold. Yet the more independent diggers often played their favourite game of two-up, tossing the pennies under the shade of a salmon-gum. This was especially so on Sunday mornings, which in the diggers' religious code, meant time-off, especially for two-up.

By April 1893 the main drinking-house, already dubbed

the Coolgardie Pub, had become far more sophisticated, besides liquor and gambling also offering board and entertainment. One late afternoon Paddy and Daniel walked into the Coolgardie to find Ann Fogarty putting on a dancing act with a group of scantily-clad girls, the diggers cheering them on for all they were worth.

As had happened before, Ann's eyes were at once all for Paddy, even while in her stilted heels, she swung her legs high with her nubile companions, in perfect time to the piano. Though all under twenty, the rest of the girls, like Ann, were all seasoned troupers, and not averse to entertaining a male customer behind the scenes as long as he paid well.

Daniel wasn't happy, still believing that although Ann was a generous sweet-looking girl, she was not good for Paddy. Paddy's trouble with Ann, was that he held her in too much respect. On the other hand other men only liked her for her attractive features and her enticing figure.

Besides a board floor for the girls to perform on, the Coolgardie Pub also supplied tables and chairs for the patrons. Paddy and Daniel sat down to their whiskies, while most of the rest of the diggers lined the bar a good three deep. At the completion of the chorus-act, the girls naturally mixed with the crowd. Ann however, walked straight over to Paddy.

"Well we got here," she said. At the same time Ann thought of Paddy's promise to return to Northam for the summer. With the mania following the Coolgardie bonanza he had apparently forgotten all about it.

Paddy failed to meet her eyes, her delightful feminine nearness at the same time making him wonder why the hell he had forgotten to write, just as he had forgotten to write to his parents.

"Yes Ann," returned Paddy, quietly. "We knew a few dancing girls were on the agenda and with no white womenfolk yet on the fields, I must say we were lookin' forward to it. But it's certainly a surprise to see you."

Ann looked hurt. "Didn't you want me to come?" She now held Paddy's gaze, her eyes though sad, lustrous and appealing.

If they had been alone, he would have taken her straight into his arms consoling her, but with so many of his digger friends watching, he could not bring himself to it.

"Of course Ann," he went on, as if for something to say. "But it's a pretty rough joint."

Daniel realised he was out of the conversation, so he moved over to talk to a mining engineer who he knew could supply the latest information about the expected arrival of Britain's largest mining magnate from South Africa. Britain had been regretting having allowed the Boers in the Transvaal part independence, the formerly struggling province having since proven itself a gold bonanza. There was now a danger of the Boers booting out the British completely, Cecil Rhodes included. With the news of Coolgardie, the mining companies were now looking east across the Indian Ocean to Western Australia.

Ann looked again at Paddy. "It's only the conditions, Paddy. The men here are no less respectable than at Northam, or even in the Colonial Club in Perth."

Paddy looked worried. "I don't quite agree with you Ann. These men are far wilder, as well as having far more to chuck around. I mean gold."

"Oh, you mean us girls could be kept busy Paddy." She looked hurt. "I didn't come up here just for that, I came up to be near you, I don't mind admitting it."

Almost involuntarily, he placed his hand on her's across the table, bringing sniggers from the nearby diggers. "I don't deny I like your presence Ann, but remember this is a boom mining town, with mostly t'othersiders, who are out to paint the place red, far more than they'd be game over home."

"As if I didn't know," she almost tittered. "Why, you are treating me like a sister."

He was still serious. "I guess I am. But I worry about you.

Could we talk alone?" He gave a grin. "But I'm afraid there's not much to offer in accommodation."

"Oh, there's the bush and the stars," she smiled. "That's what I like about this place. Even better than Northam. In summer, you are nearly always sure of a fine evening."

Paddy knew that Ann had described it well. He led her upwards away from the gold rich flat, up behind the jasper outcrop. Away from the din, the lamplight and the tobacco smoke to appreciate the delicious coolness of the desert air, now laden with the tang of eucalypts, acacia and smoke-bush, which grew so prolifically near the ridge. They sat down on a piece of greenstone, nature-carved into a lover's-seat. As he had done before during those evenings in Northam, Paddy put his arms about her, thrilling to the touch of her, and the honey-milk smell of her. Even the cheap perfume she wore could not spoil the effect of her presence.

For a while Ann just nestled close to Paddy, ecstatic in his strength. Yes, she loved him, not so much to lie with, but to be with. She compared this, with being up here alone with another prospector, starved of a woman's company. In that case, if she hadn't come across by this time, she could forget about being paid. As an entertainment girl arriving in a womanless mining town, she knew it was something she was expected to do. As she cuddled there, apparently contented, the old doubts in her mind began to build up once more. After all, though pretty she was still only a glorified prostitute. What chance had she really with someone like Paddy? One who could walk into a bar, and if need be, charm the whole assembly with his infectious grin. Although he was still hitting his straps, as a digger would say, Paddy had a future. She was sure of it. But what about her?

She began to cry, causing Paddy to turn and put his other arm about her.

"What's the matter Ann?"

"Do you love me Paddy?"

135

"I've told you that plenty of times in Northam, as well as Perth."

"But you love your parents too don't you Paddy, surely our love must be different?"

Paddy found that one hard to answer, especially as Ann was now touching his ear with her tongue.

"Yes and I love dry Coolgardie here, apart from the heat an' flies," he muttered, a delightful spasm running through his loins. He held her tighter in his arms, kissing her well-exposed breasts, the soft brush of his beard increasing her raptures. "But you know you're different, little Annie."

The smell of his strong unwashed masculine presence only increased her desire. She was beyond caring, and she ran her hands deep inside his shirt aching to further explore.

"Prove it. Prove that you love me," she breathed.

Paddy paused and at once she began to sob. "Why have you put me on a pedestal Paddy, when you know what I am? If it was one of the other girls, you'd have her on her back by now, wouldn't you?"

He laughed, a bit embarrassed by her directness. "Well, I guess I would. Still, there's an old sayin' about bein' only good for the moment. With you Ann, it's the opposite. Apart from the physical thing, any man would wish to stay with you always."

He crushed her in his arms, kissing her passionately, Ann worried now that if she revealed her true feelings, she could be reduced in Paddy's eyes to just another freely available bar-girl.

She again began to sob, knowing this was only just a further episode of what had gone on between them in Northam. What made her heart ache even more was that as man and wife she was sure she and Paddy would be a worthwhile match. But she knew that with the reputation any girl must develop in the occupation she was leading, he surely must never ask for her hand. As she got older, it could only get worse.

She was trembling.

"Though you like my company Paddy, you are still ashamed of me, aren't you?"

Paddy wondered about that himself. Was he being too high and mighty? Was it something to do with his mother? Yet with her understanding, she would surely accept Ann as she was. But why the hell should he worry about his mother at his age? He felt like letting out a curse, and saying "To hell with it, sweetheart! Let's live dangerously like all the rest in Coolgardie! Let's live for the moment!"

But with Ann he could not. Yes, indeed, he had put her on a pedestal. And of course, if such thoughts did conjure up ideas about what a splendid wife she would make, right at the moment he just didn't want to get tied up - to anybody.

He gave her a swift kiss.

"Look, darling," he said. "I'd better be gettin' you back."

Though Ann wanted to stay with Paddy forever, even without total physical abandonment - which in her heart she knew would be the total culmination of their love - she also realised it was the time to come back to earth.

"Yes, Paddy," she said almost gaily. "They've probably put on the second act by now. I'll be getting the sack."

He kissed her again.

"Not with your looks and style, my precious Ann. No, never! You're already the belle of Coolgardie."

CHAPTER 8

After working on his and Daniel's claim, Paddy was enjoying himself at the bar, even cracking ribald jokes with Nell, the barmaid. Nell had arrived only a week before from Southern Cross. No novice concerning the ways of miners and prospectors, Nell was always ready to retaliate or even promote conversation.

"Why the shine in your eyes tonight?" she asked good-naturedly of one digger who had just arrived back, after weeks out prospecting. "Struck it rich or somethin'?"

"Yeah," replied the digger, with a dry grin. "Drinks on the flamin' 'ouse." With that he pulled out a kangaroo-skin pouch and poured out a glitter of small gold nuggets on the bar.

To Paddy such events in Coolgardie were nothing out of the ordinary, it was just that the feminine touch behind the counter, as added by Nell the barmaid, spiced things up a bit.

"Yeah," yelled the digger with the gold-pouch. "What about a bitta fun. Bring on the dancin' girls."

"Yeah, where the hell are they?" shouted another digger. He was around Paddy's age, yet his good looks were marred by a facial scar that ran down his cheek, and a cast in one eye. But for all that he was physically handsome, and since the pub-girls had arrived had already gained a reputation as a wencher.

What had held the girls up, was that they were preparing to perform the popular can-can, new to the Fields. And soon the diggers muttered in mock disappointment as the girls began to glide over the prepared wooden floor dressed from neck to toe in plain full gowns. The piano player was vamping out a hymn as good as any organist. The girls looked pure, Puritan and maidenly, especially Ann Fogarty.

But suddenly the piano-player increased his tempo. The girls lifted their skirts high. Their stockinged and gartered legs, and their short frilly knickers brought yells of applause from the audience. The wall-eyed young digger happened to be close to Paddy.

"Well now, look at that little Ann Fogarty, would ye," he said to a mate, as Ann swung by. "Good lookin' face an' nice legs. Likes showin' her crotch too, by the looks - but from what I've heard, hasn't she got a price on it."

"Hey," hissed his mate, nodding his head back to Paddy, whom he knew.

But Paddy had heard and now being well primed up, he walked over and stuck out his jaw to Wall-Eye.

"That's no way to speak about a lady."

Wall-Eye let out a guffaw.

"Lady, what in Coolgardie? You must be jokin' digger."

Paddy stood his ground.

"No way to speak about a woman, anyhow. Any woman. Haven't you a mother or a sister?"

"What the hell's that got to do with it?" shot back Wall-Eye. "Anyhow, I don't recall havin' anythin' to do with a mother. Come to that, nor a sister. Matter-o-fact, I was brought up in a boy's home in Fitzroy, Melbourne. Did a spell in jail too, for stealin' a nag." Wall-eye flexed his muscle, the brown sinewy arm like whipcord. "That's where you learn to be tough, in clink. Had a stoush there just about every day." He again popped his biceps. "So digger, next time you make accusations, remember who you're talkin' to." He gave a glare with his wall-eye. "As a matter-o-fact, just to make it sink in, I've a notion to ask that little Ann Fogarty to take a stroll out in the scrub just like I've done with a coupla the others. Don't mind whether she charges a bit more neither, 'cause I reckon she's special. Still, they've all got a price, otherwise why the hell did they come to Coolgardie?" The tough-minded young prospector

139

emphasised his last few words by roughly pushing past Paddy to the bar.

It was too much for Paddy. He grabbed the young man by the shoulder, giving him a shake.

"Righto matey, you've said quite enough. I'll see you outside."

"Why not in here?" hissed Wall-Eye, and with that he dropped his glass and punched Paddy square on the nose, the blood spurting.

No slouch with the knuckles either, Paddy was quick to respond. He drove his fist like a ramrod into the young digger's heart. His opponent's breath whistled as he doubled up in pain.

The diggers roared approval.

"Give 'im a flamin' uppercut Paddy," yelled the grizzled prospector from the bar.

Paddy complied and drove his fist skywards, almost lifting his adversary from the floor.

The diggers were now all around - also the dance-girls, Ann not yet knowing what the fight was about.

"Kill the Irish bastard!" yelled another digger, urging on Wall-Eye, even though the digger was half-Irish himself.

"Not a chance McGinty," roared one of the opposition. "Two to one on O'Leary."

But by now Paddy was coming off second best. The tough young prospector had forced him into a headlock, pounding his temple with the hard edge of his fist. Paddy felt himself slipping into unconsciousness.

"Knee him in the knackers Paddy," yelled a digger, forgetting about the womenfolk.

"I'll knee you if you don't cut down the language, O'Rourke," yelled Nell the barmaid. "Now for heaven's sake pull them apart, they're wreckin' my bar."

But by this time Paddy had taken the advice of the digger, kneed Wall-Eye in the groin, and as he jack-knifed down, obliged with another upper-cut.

Amidst cheers from his few followers, Wall-Eye came back like a steel spring. But Paddy was every bit as quick and deciding to end it all, bent his opponent over his shoulder, hurling him over the bar crashing among the bottles. But Wall-Eye still came back - even though soaked in rot-gut added with a mixture of his own red blood from the broken glass.

Certainly the fight might have lasted all night, except that a digger came rushing into the bar accompanied by Daniel.

"TYPHOID! T-Y-P-H-O-I-D...!" yelled the digger. "We've got the flamin' TYPHOID! For Chris' sake break it up."

Suddenly the barracking died. The contestants froze in their tracks. Their arms dropped limply by their sides.

TYPHOID! The terror of pioneer settlements and mining camps. For some of the older hands who had experienced the scourge, notably in Queensland, it was no surprise. So though the news might have turned the grog into vinegar in their bowels, the reaction for most after the first shock, was to "crack hardy".

"Yeah," spoke the grizzled one who had tossed the nuggets on the bar. "Pity we 'ad to break up the stoush 'cause I 'ad me money on Paddy."

He suddenly stopped, looking more closely at Daniel.

"Any'ow, 'ow de ye know it's typhoid? Want me to take a look? Seen it more'n once before. Fact is, I lost one o' me best cobbers with it near Townsville. Wus kicked off by those slant-eyed Chinks, the dirty bastards."

"Yes, it sounds like you've been through the mill," agreed Daniel. "But I've had experience too, there was a bad outbreak around Ballarat when I was a lad in Victoria. Yes, it's typhoid all right, I know the symptoms."

"Who'n hell's got it then?" enquired the grizzled one. "I've been out in the sticks for weeks."

"Johnnie O'Halloran. First he had the fever, and now he's been vomiting badly and can't keep anything down. He's just come out in those red-brown weals, that's how I knew."

141

"Just about cashed his chips by the sounds?" enquired the grizzled one, without even a blink.

"I'm afraid so," returned Daniel. "And for the time being we must keep him in isolation."

"Well just standing there's not going to help!" cut in the more practical barmaid. "In fact, while you're about it, some of you bastards can help clean up this bar. I'll give you urge that pair on!"

As he walked out with Daniel, Paddy spoke through bruised and bloody lips. "Do you reckon it'll spread? The typhoid, I mean."

"It'll spread all right. Lucky the telegraph line's been put through. I'll get a message to Perth first thing in the morning."

"Yeah, I guess they'll send a doctor quick an' lively."

"Yes, and a temporary hospital and staff as well," added Daniel.

But it was not to be.

The reaction in Perth to the typhoid outbreak in Coolgardie was almost the opposite to what the boom town expected.

"HELP! We'll get no help from that lot!" gritted Daniel to Paddy after a week with twenty diggers already dead. "All they can supply is an old military marquee for a temporary hospital. But the main suggestion - more a command is for us not to leave Coolgardie, in case we spread the plague to the rest of the colony. For a plague they've called it, my God."

"But surely they'll send a doctor?"

"Oh, the excuse is a doctor can't do much. What the patients need is good hospital attention. But where can you get that around here?"

"Well, before the marquee arrives, there's those four tents the Gallatlee brothers set up," suggested Paddy. "You know, that pair that came here to start a hardware business in opposition to Charlie Cousins when he started the general store. Why, you can see Charlie's sign from here across the track."

COUSIN'S GENERAL STORE
OPEN ALL HOURS
ALWAYS READY TO HELP A DIGGER

"Trouble with Charlie," went on Paddy. "He's too easy-goin', too much grubstakin' down an' out prospectors an' losin' money. Different to them Gallatlee pair o' bastards. You know, they've already started to build coffins out of old packin' cases as a quick means o' makin' money. Also those four tents they've put up are supposed to be supplyin' hospital an' medical attention."

Daniel gave a grimace. "Well, not that I blame the Gallatlees seizing on a chance to make some cash, seeing that Charlie Cousins has all the victual trade and most of the hardware. Furthermore, I don't disagree with them putting up those four little tents as a kind of temporary hospital. But it's all that money they're charging for admittance, besides feeding the poor patients on hard-tack. If they can eat it, that is. Talk about kindness to their fellow-men. Why, the sick diggers may as well stay in their own tents."

Paddy shrugged his shoulders. "That won't work either. The diggers nearly all camp in pairs, or threes or fours, an' their mates won't even let 'em back in their own lodgings. They're too scared o' the plague."

"Oh, what difference does it make," queried a distressed Daniel. "The government tells us with our close proximity to each other added to our primitive ablutions, we've all become carriers. So why worry about things like that?" Daniel firmed his jaw. "Anyhow, I've got plenty to say to the community. In fact, the whole colony. So I've decided to set up that printing press."

"But you haven't got one," reminded Paddy.

"Yes I have. I sent a telegraph to Len Chandler about that old Eagle press we used to use with the *Fremantle Herald*.

Seeing that most of the teamsters have refused to cart merchandise to Coolgardie, I'm going to journey to the coast and pick up the press myself."

"But even though you mightn't have the typhoid, you're not supposed to travel west past Southern Cross."

"That won't worry me," said Daniel. "I'll make the coast, never fear."

"But what about a wagon? Or a cart would easily carry the press, wouldn't it?" Paddy's eyes were alight.

"Yes," went on Daniel eagerly. "I already know where I can get a prospector's cart. As a matter of fact, he has died of the typhoid, poor blighter. Anyhow, I only have to take the cart as far as Burracoppin. The railway line's now reached there on its way to the goldfields."

"Yep, an' my saddle-hack will go in a cart," grinned Paddy. "Matter-o-fact, I think I might tag along."

"All right, but what about the mine?"

"Oh, Wilga and his Aboriginal friends will keep an eye on it. There's quite a lot of 'em in Coolgardie now, includin' women. Wilga reckons most of 'em have cleared off from the stations like he did from the Clayton-Brownes. Queer, none of 'em have caught the typhoid, isn't it?"

"Yes, could be immune," replied Daniel. "All right then matey, Wilga and his friends can watch the mine. We'll make our way to Burracoppin together. "Better take a spare horse and trace chains to get us through those sandy patches."

"Good idea," grinned Paddy.

Paddy and Daniel's journey to Burracopin was not as simple as it sounded. First there was the problem of the cart, which with its narrow wheels, even though only lightly loaded, often became half-bogged to the axles in the long stretches of deep sand - softened even more by the hundreds of heavily-laden bullock wagons which had negotiated the track before the typhoid.

Even with the spare horse in front Paddy and Daniel still

had problems. Often they were forced to jump out and push on the wheels. Then as if that wasn't enough after the more than one hundred mile journey, they were halted a few miles east of The Cross by a couple of troopers.

"Where you bastards from?" asked one of the policemen. "We've orders to turn back anyone travellin' from Coolgardie."

Paddy felt like telling him to mind his own business, but realised he had to be cautious. The police certainly had the power to send them back, or even take them back forcibly, as they were already doing to others. "Oh, Yellowdine," replied Paddy. "You know that new little gold show round thirty five miles east."

"Sure you're not from Coolgardie, we've got orders to turn you back?"

"No, we're from Yellowdine," contributed Daniel. "Starting to strike it rich, too." Daniel took out a three-ounce nugget from his pocket.

"Yeah, looks like you have been," agreed the trooper. "Couldn't spare a bit, could you? Pretty poorly paid, us troopers." The trooper squinted his eyes.

"Well it's not a bribe," replied Daniel with tongue-in-cheek. "But yes, we can spare a bit." With that Daniel returned the three-ounce bit to his pocket, pulled out two smaller pieces each about an ounce, and handed them to the troopers.

"Christ," grinned Paddy later, "if that wasn't a bribe, what was it? O' course those bastards knew we'd come from Coolgardie. Talk about a quarantine. Jesus, it's a bloody farce, isn't it?"

"Yes, especially when they've got lowly paid policemen to contend with. Anyhow, it looks like we'll be able to stay the night at The Cross pub, and as far as worrying about handing on the typhoid, I don't feel guilty one bit."

"Nor me," agreed Paddy. "In fact, seein' you can pass on the typhoid even though you're not down with it, I've a good mind to visit Parliament House an' give it to Premier Groves an' his mob. That'd teach 'em to treat us like shit. An' talkin' about The Cross pub, stayin' there will be just like old times."

From then on for Daniel and Paddy, it was reasonably plain sailing. Next day they made for Burracoppin around forty miles west of The Cross - there to leave their horses and cart with a livery-man, and take the train to Northam, Perth and finally Fremantle.

Len Chandler, former owner of the ratbag *Fremantle Herald* as the establishment had called it, was fully in agreement with Daniel's starting up the goldfield's first newspaper.

"Couldn't have picked a better time," advised the ageing ex-convict and former editor. "If I was younger I'd be travelling back with you - even just to get a last crack at that damned Hungry Six mob. As representatives of the Government, the Groves Gang is treating you all like lepers. The trouble is with Coolgardie being new territory there is no one in Parliament to represent your interests, only the big pastoralists. That's where a good editor like you comes in Daniel, in this case almost a holy duty. You are the diggers' only wherewithal, their spokesman, their champion. Otherwise, who else have they got?"

"Thanks for the bouquets Len," smiled Daniel, wryly. "Certainly the old Eagle press is going to help. Just the same, I do wish we could get some medical assistance out there, if no doctors, even to a trained nurse or two."

"No!" returned Chandler abruptly. "This colony's still that backward it can't even staff the few hospitals it has. The trouble is the Government has never looked ahead, never allowed for a rapid increase in population, as they should have five years ago when gold was first struck in the Yilgarn. And as for anticipating an outbreak of the dreaded typhoid - well now - better to keep their heads in the sand."

"Being just businessmen graziers, they still have their eyes on their pastoral leases," growled Daniel. "Their minds are limited."

"Oh not quite," corrected Chandler. "I'd say they have been a bit more astute than that. With benefit to the Hungry Six families, of course. You see it was them who first made the suggestion that a British company purchase Bayley's Reward. In fact, engineers from the African Transvaal are already here to begin deep mining. Furthermore, they've brought a whole shipload of mining construction gear with them from the Cape."

Paddy cut in sarcastically. "An' though we can't get nurses or medical supplies for the diggers, I'll bet that equipment goes through to Coolgardie post-haste."

"Knowing the British company men, no doubt it will," said Daniel. He turned to Chandler. "Anyhow Len, where's the old printing press?"

"In a back shed," smiled Len. "And am I glad for its resurrection."

"And you couldn't get a better Messiah," grinned Paddy indicating Daniel.

"I've already expressed my sentiments about that, laddie," returned Len. "The only thing I'm sorry about, as I said, is that I can't be on the job with you. Anyhow, I've already made arrangements for a local carrier to cart the press to Fremantle to be freighted when necessary. So it's all yours."

"Much obliged Len," grinned Paddy, getting in ahead of Daniel once more.

It took Daniel and Paddy more than three weeks to return. Much of the time wasted was spent on the agonising stretch between The Cross and Coolgardie. The printing press proved a heavier load than expected even though they had acquired a third horse to hook up in front of the other pair. One sandy stretch of more than thirty miles in fact, took them five days to get through. When the pair did eventually arrive back in Coolgardie, it was to find that the typhoid was worse than ever.

Most of the diggers were blaming the lack of rain, even though a quick thunderstorm in March had filled a small dam at the bottom of Fly Flat. But it had soon gone dry.

On the second day of May another thunderhead reared up to the north, its white cone against the black sky to the Victorian diggers, mysterious and romantic, like winter snow on a faraway peak on The Great Dividing Range.

Then came the wind, blotting out Fly Flat in a pall of dust - followed by a torrent.

Many of the diggers had knocked off early to drown their sorrows in the Coolgardie Pub. The sound of rain on the battered tin roof caused a minor pandemonium. Most of the prospectors ripped off their sweaty dust-stained shirts, and ran cheering out in the rain. The girls too, rushed out in their brief costumes, longing to shed all, relishing the touch of the cool-cold rain on their hot steamy skins.

"Send 'er down, Hughie," yelled a digger, throwing his arms to the sky. "Wash away the friggin' typhoid."

But though the lightning flashed and the thunder rolled, the rain began to ease. So after just enough to wet the top of the ground the rain then brought curses from the digger as the half-sticky alluvial stuck to his boots, making it difficult to walk.

Another digger saw the humour. "Serve you right McGinty. Send it down Hughie fer Chris-sake. Why, it's a bloody Scotsman up there you'd be talkin' to. Next time, matey, as an Irish-Victorian, it might pay you to hold your tongue."

But within a week came another violent thunderstorm, which not only filled the little dam, but brought a crispness to the air, washing the dryblower dust from the salmons and gimlets and twinkling their leaves in the sun.

But as far as easing the dreaded typhoid; if anything the rain only made it worse.

Though Daniel had warned the diggers that they could

not run away from the typhoid, hundreds took to the bush on the pretext that they were off to discover some new bonanza. And find more gold they did, even up to ninety miles north and east of Coolgardie. With the plague now spreading around to the outlying camps, the bodies of diggers, often in pairs - typical of bush mateship - were to be found in their hundreds. Some ailing prospectors realising their mistake had tried desperately to return to Coolgardie, some dying on the track. Some indeed did reach the stricken mining town, only to find the place still quarantined by government decree, but still without proper medical attention the sick and the dead everywhere.

Yet despite the tragic circumstances, many of the younger more reckless diggers had stayed in Coolgardie, still operating their dryblowers and working their claims. Some no doubt felt that if they could survive the plague, they could become rich at the expense of their more unfortunate comrades. Survival of the fittest became the law of the camps. Daniel, though sympathetic was also inclined to take this realistic view, as was Paddy, who went on operating their "rich little show" as he called it, with the help of Wilga.

Nonetheless, grim reminders of the dreaded typhoid were hard to escape. The Gallatlees were now performing a half dozen burials a day, the rough coffins dropped into shallow graves where a patch of gimlets had been cleared out just east of Fly Flat - up on top of a slope - appropriately called by an American Irish-Victorian - Boot Hill. In the absence yet of a cleric, the ceremony was usually read by the Warden. When he himself caught the typhoid, this duty was taken over by Daniel. Though now even more a dedicated atheist, owing to his disgust over the way the Anglican-dominated government had neglected Coolgardie during the plague, he agreed to perform the ceremony. With his gift for rhetoric he was not often lost for words. But he found it difficult to express religious sentiment. So standing there over each grave in front of the rough-clothed head-bowed diggers, typical was his prayer.

"I hereby dedicate the remains of this digger to whom or whatsoever he believed in. Whether it be in the spirit and the everlasting life, or simply to become part of the Coolgardie dust - for all eternity."

The way he felt, Daniel could have concluded with "what the hell difference does it make once you're dead?" But most times he was helped by a grieving digger who had lost a favourite cobber. While the odd one would come out with "... goodbye chum, see you in hell ...", there were others who would simply make a gesture into the grave, as if shaking a hand. "Cheerio matey, cheerio. Nice to have known yuh."

This often brought tears from the pub-girls, who dressed more formally - though not in grey or black - when they attended the burials. Along with Nell, the barmaid, the girls helped where they could, but because all were inexperienced with hospitalization, all they could offer was sympathy, and certainly a little amorousness to go with it.

To pass the time, Ann and another adept member of her troupe had taken to hairdressing, charging willing diggers for a shave and a hair-cut outside Charlie Cousin's store. Daniel depicted the scene in his newspaper, telling how despite the typhoid and the general squalor a man could be spruced up by a young woman, alluring enough to grace a Renoir canvas.

This described Ann Fogarty well, even though Paddy was becoming desperately worried about her. He wished she could return to civilisation and safety. But the official ban was there. Female entertainers had to stay where they were and make the best of it.

Late one afternoon, while Paddy was working on the claim after having returned from his usual daily attendance at the growing graveyard, Wilga called out, pointing.

"Look, man longa barra-aa. Look, sick!"

"JESUS CHRIST!" yelled Paddy, as he ran. "You poor bastard!"

The digger moved like a rag-doll, legs flopping, feet dragging. The handles of the miner's barrow virtually held him up. The amazing thing as Paddy told Daniel later, was that he was actually making ground.

But what opened Paddy's eyes further, was the digger's mate - as he truly was - curled in the barrow part-covered by a tattered blanket. The skin of his half-bald head was covered in the tell-tale red-brown weals.

"JESUS," breathed Paddy. "Bloody typhoid agen'!"

"Aye," the man croaked in a Cornish accent.

"JESUS," said Paddy in repetition. "How far've you come?"

"Bout seventy miles," gasped the prospector. "But me cobber, please get 'im to a doctor."

"Some hopes," murmured Paddy to himself, thinking about the attitude of the government. Then he bent down and examined the sick man more closely.

"Oh, my God," he whispered. "The poor bastards gone."

The tears streamed down Paddy's cheeks as he put his arm gently round the digger.

"Look matey, let me take the barrow."

For a few moments Paddy just stood there, a barrow shaft in one hand, his other hand supporting the worn-out digger's mate.

"Hey Wilga," he suddenly called out. "Run an' get someone to look after this bloke here, while I see to the other poor cove. Christ, what a story for Daniel's paper."

And stories Daniel told, not only about the courageous digger, who was to live on as one of Coolgardie's many heroes, but also about the neglect by the authorities, who were still determined to keep the plague from the rest of the colony, even though by now it had spread back to Southern Cross. The whole grim picture however, had not changed very much from Daniel's first editorial:

Dear Residents of Coolgardie, while it is with pride that I print this first issue of the Coolgardie Miner, it is with regret that in this newspaper I must publish a list of those who have fallen to the dreaded scourge.

Dreaded indeed, Readers, especially as our government has so forsaken us. I could well ask our Premier what would have happened if the plague had descended on Perth our capital, especially among the well-to-do which includes many of our Premier's relatives? Would they have supplied only a big tent and told the populace to look after itself?

No, my Readers, the three big public hospitals in Perth and its suburbs would have been reorganised like lightning to take the suddenly ill as they should in any emergency like this one in Coolgardie. But instead here we are being treated like pariahs. In fact, my Readers, I could well ask almost the same question of the Premier. Would he be treating us so if we were mostly Westralian born, and not just a ramshackle mob from t'otherside as they're prone to call us?

Before ending my epistle, I must also thank those diggers who have contributed such witty and appropriate ditties for our location and times on the third page of this newspaper. Please keep them rolling in.

Your Editor.

In later editions, Daniel was to write about how despite the quarantine, well-escorted government gold-coaches were still leaving Coolgardie for the Burracoppin rail-head more than twice a week. He also wrote bitterly of how the British South-African mining company had been allowed to quickly develop Bayley's Reward, with well-paid teamsters bringing in wagon-load after wagon-load of heavy equipment.

"There's no doubt about it," swore Paddy to Daniel. "Once the big companies start, there's no stoppin' 'em is there?"

"The spirit of capitalism," replied Daniel cynically. "Keep the wheels turning, as they do with their factories in Britain. God Almighty, a bit of sickness like this is only a drop in the ocean. Think about the British factory system and the workhouses? What about the sick and dying there? Though reformers like Dickens tried to shame the industrialists, the philosophy of the workhouse is still here among us. No, while there's a profit to be made the wheels will keep turning, just like the wheel on the great poppet-head they've already erected here."

"Well, you could say their wagons are bringing in a bit o' tucker amongst the machinery," defended Paddy.

"And charging through the nose for it, by Gad," cursed Daniel. "I guess there's our capitalist spirit once again. As with our pair of ghouls making the coffins, charging to carry the dead on their wagon, charging to dig the graves, and before the generous donation of the government marquee, charging to set up those miserable four tents as a hospital."

"Well, the pubs are still doin' all right too," grinned Paddy, with black humour. "They've been caterin' for so many wakes after the funerals."

"Of course," grimaced Daniel. "Especially with all these Irish-Victorian diggers, it's a tradition."

Though there was still a fervent hope among the authorities in Perth that the Coolgardie typhoid might burn itself out, it finally took a lone courageous woman to start the settlement on the long road to recovery. Bridget Shane, though of Irish descent was Victorian born like her two brothers, who tragically both succumbed to the dreaded Coolgardie plague in the first month. While practising as a bush nurse in the Victorian mallee, Bridget received word about her brother's deaths and as was her nature, after getting over her tragic loss, and learning that the Westralian authorities appeared to be deliberately neglecting the Coolgardie digger as if he was some sort of sub-human species, Bridget packed her bags and took ship to Fremantle. Even before she left Melbourne the determined sister was warned about the typhoid and what she was letting herself in for. But Bridget had had experience of typhoid before and though she knew there was no cure, she knew at least she could calm it down.

Perth and Fremantle by now had had the odd case of the plague, the residents in abject fear of what might eventuate. As Bridget could see, they were far more concerned about their own welfare than that of the citizens of faraway Coolgardie. What made her even more furious was when the blame was laid on the diggers, whom she knew were mostly Victorians similar to herself.

So after only two days in Perth she caught the train to Moorine Rock, where the rail now reached twenty miles short of The Cross. She rode the rest of the way in a bullock-wagon, apart from the dust heat and flies enjoying the trip, because the tough-talking teamster was part-Irish, similar to herself.

As Paddy admitted to Daniel, after Bridget had been in Coolgardie only a fortnight.

"Certainly she's stirred the place up."

"Yes," replied Daniel. "She's made me ashamed, because with my education I should have suggested all those things she has religiously enforced. The problem has been of course, bad sanitation. Here we have thousands of people just walking behind the nearest bush to respond to the call of nature."

"Most diggers take a shovel, I do anyhow."

"Yes, and bury it about three inches deep," scolded Daniel. "What about that rain we had in March which filled our little dam? And the rain which filled it again in May? As the Sister says, all that filthy spoil just washed into the dam, polluting the water. I should have known."

"Well, so should I," said Paddy. "I was taught all this sort of stuff as a kid from my parents."

"And so should most of the other diggers here," replied Daniel. "Certainly we're all to blame. We should have dug deep ablution and sanitation trenches as the sister has already made us do."

"But what about those bastards in Perth, who are supposed to be runnin' the country, they're always talkin' about bein' well brought up."

"Yes, as I've mentioned in our paper, they still must bear judgment, because it is to them we look for guidance. But they preferred to shut their eyes to it. Out of sight, out of mind."

"Yeah, three cheers for Sister Bridget. Though one thing that's got a bit tough, she's commandeered all Ann's troupe to work in her new hospital."

"No, it's not too tough," replied Daniel soberly. "It's something we should have insisted on earlier, but as usual, in grim things like sickness and death, it takes a woman to organise womenfolk."

Sister Bridget in her determination, had also induced the Gallatlee brothers to exhume most of the coffins and bury them three feet deeper. The burial ground though high, was still located on part of the catchment to the town water supply. She also suggested to the brothers that from their stocks of hardware, they set up community showers to draw water from the one de-salinator which fortunately had been made a going concern before the typhoid outbreak. Though still far from enough for the settlement's needs for fresh-water, its boilers had already used up all the local dry wood, dead logs and branches having to be carted for miles.

The sister saw more immediate use for the boilers than just steaming off the salt-water. She pointed out that to help with her hygiene, hot water could also be drawn from the condenser's boilers before the liquid turned into steam - when unfortunately though freshened most of the original water was lost.

Though difficult to lather, the heated salt-water could be as cleansing and invigorating as a dip in the ocean. It was up to the Gallatlees now to complete the job.

The Gallatlees, dark-visaged hatchet-faced men, argued. The elder one was the spokesman, throwing his arms about like an Arab peddling wares in a bazaar.

"Even using the de-salinator's boiler and pumps," he wheedled. "We still need pipes and shower-heads, besides yards of hessian for privacy. We have you women here, you know."

"Well, you can use ti-tree thatch on end similar to what I had them put around the ablutions," shot back the sister, also with a half a mind to castigate him for his veiled sarcasm about women. "I do agree, anything to save money, because I want these showers to be free."

The brothers could have argued, but realised there were more coffins to make and more graves to dig, and if the sister put her foot down about making a profit on those then they could be really in trouble.

"All right Sister," agreed the elder brother. "I suppose it's for a good cause."

"It's for a good cause all right," snapped the triumphant nurse. "And just think how popular it will make you."

Formerly the brothers had only been concerned with popularity if it meant making a profit. But for their benefit, Daniel took up the brothers' gesture in his paper. Again he paid tribute to Sister Bridget, even telling how since the advent of the community showers, the diggers had begun to look clean and tidy, even shaving twice a week and washing their clothes.

To be sure Bridget had had her problems in instructing the diggers in washing. Previously, owing to the lack of water, it was not unusual for a digger to wear his clothes till they well-nigh rotted off. It was something the girls had helped remedy after they arrived, at least inducing the prospectors to wash themselves and their clothes more. Even Nell, the barmaid told how with only a half-gallon of water, a man could cleanse himself from head to foot standing in a tailings dish, and then with what was left wash out his duds.

But these were only suggestions, and it was the sister who really changed the diggers' personal habits, the men calling it just another of Bridget's miracles.

Though the community showers and Bridget's general hygiene instructions were preventatives, they did not hold a cure, and could do little about those people who appeared well but who still carried the germ. By now the typhoid had spread throughout the colony. The death-rate had reached unmanageable proportions in the shanty-town sections of Perth and Fremantle, which had been swollen in population through the mining boom. In the more well-to-do city neighbourhoods however, the blame was still laid on those disgusting uncouth t'otherside prospectors in Coolgardie, and their filthy habits.

Churches had now taken up the banner. There was even a rumour that religious groups were about to help in Coolgardie. The Salvation Army was in the forefront. All this was good news for Sister Bridget, who still needed any help that was offered. One morning Daniel was again setting out the week's grim death list after having already given more praise to Sister Bridget, besides making further gibes at the Perth authorities. All at once Paddy rushed in with the news that Ann Fogarty was down with the typhoid.

Daniel comforted his friend.

"Well matey, it's not as bad as two months ago with one

half of Coolgardie busy burying the other, but diggers are still dying. God knows what would have happened without Sister Bridget. The plague would have probably wiped out the whole town."

Paddy had tears in his eyes.

"I know that, but Ann's been virtually working night an' day, much more than the other girls who still can't keep outa the grogshop lookin' for customers. It's not just because Bridget's a Catholic Daniel, similar to Ann, but it's Ann's nature to be kind." Paddy nervously wiped his hand down his breeches. "Look Daniel, I know the damned typhoid's catching from others besides through rotten water, but I must try an' visit her. The sister has put her in a little private tent away from the ward, which is full of men."

"I didn't say no, did I?" returned Daniel with some sympathy. "Yes, go and visit her. With the sister having straightened us all up in our personal habits, surely there's less chance of catching it. Now go and visit her Paddy, for Godsake."

Daniel half-wished just the same that Ann had never come to Coolgardie, as he had often wished that Ann had never come into Paddy's life.

CHAPTER 9

Sister Bridget pointed out to Paddy the little tent in which Ann lay. The sister apologised that she had too much on her hands looking after the two hundred or so diggers still gravely ill in the big military marquee. Even as she spoke, the Gallatlee's death-cart pulled in, piled high with coffins. One casket showed plainly a disused label. KEEP AWAY FROM BOILERS. Yet the sister gave Paddy some re-assurance about Ann.

"She's over the worst. The worry is she's been left with a lung infection." The chubby little sister held Paddy with her strong though kindly blue eyes. "Apparently her family has a history of chest problems, so when she's strong enough, I'd like to get her to a decent hospital. The way she is, she needs something comfortable to travel in. A Cobb and Co coach, for example. The trouble is the few coaches that come and go now, seem mostly reserved for company men."

"Oh, don't worry Sister," Paddy reassured her. "I'll even buy a Cobb an' Co coach if I have to. I want to get her better whatever the cost."

The sister looked at him even more appraisingly.

"You do think a lot of her, don't you? Anyhow, she's a good girl. Before she took ill, she worked like a trojan. Not like those other trollops."

She patted Paddy's arm.

"Now go and talk to her. But don't expect too much, she's still very sick."

Paddy was shocked to see how much Ann had changed. Her usually attractive features were disfigured with the red-brown blotches, her usually appealing eyes, hollow and stricken. At the sight of Paddy, she screamed out.

"Don't touch me Paddy! I'm contagious."

But Paddy came on, taking her hand.

"It's all right Ann, the sister says you could be over it," he said gently.

"But I could carry the germ for months," she wailed, though still clinging to his hand.

"I know Ann. I know. Anyhow, the sister wants you in a decent hospital. I'll be arranging for a coach as soon as you can travel."

"But no one would ride with me, even the driver."

"I'll be taking you myself," insisted Paddy. He smiled. "Why, I was drivin' a Cobb an' Co coach at sixteen, my first job away from the farm."

He squeezed her hand. "Now sweetheart, don't you worry."

But acquiring the coach was not as easy as Paddy had made out. Since the typhoid outbreak, the passenger service had been depleted alarmingly. As Sister Bridget had said most of the coaches had been reserved for engineers and mining magnates, who with more and more gold strikes despite the typhoid, were still arriving. Finally, after Paddy had offered the agent three times the worth of a coach and team in cash, he acquired what he sought. He also made sure the coach was one equipped with special wide wheels to manage the deep sand along the track.

Then it was a case of waiting another fortnight after Ann had a serious relapse, and even then the Sister suggested that one of Ann's troupe, who conveniently wanted to return to the city, should travel with Ann and tend to her while Paddy drove the coach. But the other woman still expected to be paid. It was all extra cost, and it was one of the few times Paddy gave thanks to God that the claim was still producing its share of gold.

Finally, all was arranged. Paddy had not only stored enough boiled water and wholesome food for the road, but on the rear and sides of the vehicle, as instructed by the local sergeant of police he had painted, DANGER, TYPHOID, in large white letters.

As Paddy remarked to Daniel, after his handiwork. "Now if I step off the coach into a store or tavern, I could just as easily get a bullet."

He also realised that, with such a sign aboard, he would be refused a change of horse teams at the regular coach-stops, like Yellowdine, which meant that the nights would have to be spent on the track, close to known water-points while the horses were hobbled out. Also though the rail was now getting close to The Cross, there was no chance of Paddy being allowed to take a typhoid patient aboard a train.

It took them a good fortnight to reach Northam, with the other young woman having to look after Ann almost like a baby. Yet it was Paddy who always lifted Ann from the coach. Ann, though fearful of contagion for Paddy, found it more and more impossible to hide her love. She often had severe bouts of coughing. Paddy at times had to stop the team and light a fire, so that the other woman could prepare a steam bowl of tar and eucalypt to ease her patient's congestion.

Finally they reached Fremantle.

Ann's parents were loathe to take her in. The love and affection was evident, certainly, but the family was already aware about keeping a distance from carriers like Ann. Also with Perth and Fremantle in a panic, and the *West Australian* warning about keeping away from affected areas, besides avoiding typhoid patients as a duty to the community, the family believed they were breaking the law even to have her in the house. Though not in so many words, it seemed to Paddy that they would have preferred their daughter to have stayed in Coolgardie.

For the time being Ann was left in the coach, which was comfortable enough even though the young woman in attendance had left for her own home. It was embarrassing to Paddy, who had to stay and look after Ann, the mother at least cooking her meals, though Paddy had to take them to her. There was also the problem of Ann's ablutions, Paddy having to take water to the patient in a large china jug, besides emptying and washing the chamber-pot.

It was even more distressing for Ann. She who had been so vibrant and active before her sickness, was now so wasted and frail. The love in her eyes was mixed with a look of melancholy desperation.

"I'm sorry Paddy," she'd often murmur, lapsing into a flood of tears.

"It's not your fault Ann," Paddy would usually reply, while at the same time tempted to tell her parents what he thought of them.

One morning after she'd had a particularly bad night, he simply just took her in his arms telling her he loved her and trying to reassure her.

"I love you too Paddy," she sobbed in return. "But it's not right that you should have to tend to my every need like this. Not only is it not a man's job, but I know you have to get back."

"Sh'sh, that can wait my love," he'd say.

In those hours when Ann in her illness was not tortured with those hideous spectres in the nether world between awake and asleep, she often thought about men, especially Paddy. Though she knew how much he preferred an adventurous life in the backblocks to a woman's company, she felt sure she wanted him no other way. To compare Paddy with a man who would always wish to be by her side like a faithful dog - No! Even though in need while prostrated by her sickness, she still wanted him the way he was.

"Look here Ann, I don't have to get back," Paddy would repeat. "Wilga an' his friends can work the mine."

"But you really want to get back for your own self, don't you darling?" she whispered. "And I don't blame you. If I was a man, I'd be the same."

Paddy was too slow with his answer, proving Ann's

predictions.

In the next few days Ann's cough grew even worse. It could be heard not only outside the coach, but all through her parents' house. It was the reason the parents were finally forced to find a solution. Ann's father was still friendly with Tom Callahan, the expiree convict who had become one of the wealthiest men in the colony and whose sons had both gained medical degrees in Dublin College. One was the resident doctor in the Victoria Hospital in Subiaco, and was able to arrange for Ann to be admitted into a special isolated annexe.

With Ann in safe hands, Paddy's next thought was to return with the coach and team by way of York, where he felt it was a chance to call in on his parents at the old farm. He arrived to find that Grandpa David had passed away only two days before, and was due to be buried next morning close by Grandma Mary. It seemed, rather than sadness, there was a kind of benign gladness in the air. Everyone was smiling, even old Henry and Liz who were also at the funeral. They had all been around Grandpa David's deathbed, where he had told them not to mourn, but to be glad for one who had finally decided that death was just another adventure, another flight into the unknown, new discoveries, new mysteries, new problems to solve, like reading a well-written journal or novel.

"Yes, that's Grandpa David all over," said Paddy. "I only hope that wherever he goes, Grandma Mary shares it with him."

In York, Paddy got a little of his money back by selling the coach and team to the local agent. He even offered to drive the coach back to Coolgardie loaded with passengers, those for whom the lure of gold was still far stronger than the deadly threat of typhoid. But when Paddy arrived back in Coolgardie he received the welcome news that the plague was easing. Only one burial had needed to be carried out that day. Sister Bridget had performed her task well. As Daniel had stated in his latest editorial:

"If anyone ever deserved a decoration, it surely must be Sister Bridget."

It was also true that despite the typhoid, there had been those rich gold discoveries - Kanowna, Guangarra, Siberia, besides another rumoured strike near Mt Youle, well to the north-east. Paddy had only been back a week when he rushed into Daniel's office - still only a hessian shanty where he was setting up his press for the next issue of the *Coolgardie Miner*.

"Talk about Bayley's Reward," yelled Paddy. "Wait till you hear about this one."

"What are you getting at matey? I hope it's not another tall story, there's been such a lot around, lately."

"No, this one's dinkum. But you should hear the way it was discovered. You know those three boozers, Paddy Hannan, Mick O'Shea an' Dinny Flanagan?"

"Who doesn't? Go on!"

"Well, they've hit it at last."

"What do you mean, at last? They spend most of their time at the bar."

"You wouldn't believe it. There was about a dozen of 'em camped around three miles this side o' that place called the Four Hills, about twenty five miles east of here. You know how those rough Irish-Victorians usually hang out together. Anyway, it was not surprising that two of their horses became lame - you know how they ride 'em without being shod - so they got left behind from the mob and had to spend the night there. Then you wouldn't believe it - Paddy Hannan apparently took a walk in the scrub for a you-know-what."

"What happened then, for Godsake?"

"The story goes that he picked up a coupla big nuggets. But he only let on to his closest mates, Mick an' Dinny."

"Yes, that's possible with them," agreed Daniel. "Well,

get on with it, what happened then?" Daniel felt he was repeating himself.

"What do you think? After searching around further after their other mates had left, they uncovered a reef they reckon would put Bayley's Reward in the shade, an' then it was hell-for-leather into the Coolgardie Warden here. In fact, he's out there inspectin' the site right now."

Daniel threw a dusty tarpaulin over his printing press. "Well, what are we waiting for? Just when our claim here was starting to peter out. Go and grab Wilga and saddle up the horses."

"But what about the paper?" asked a surprised Paddy, knowing how attached Daniel had become to the *Coolgardie Miner*.

"To hell with the paper!" replied Daniel recklessly. "As I said our claim's beginning to peter out. So for the time being the less we tell in our paper the better. Come on, let's get going."

Already the track between Coolgardie and the new strike was clogged with traffic, men walking pushing barrows filled with only the necessary mining tools, men with only a bulky sugar bag over a shoulder, beside men with just the vital necessities held in hand, a small miner's pick and a short-handled shovel. While the more fortunate rode in laden prospector's carts often pulled by donkeys because they drank less water, pushing their way through were those on horseback, similar to Paddy and Daniel. Also the company men, with their measures and tapes in fast coaches, bouncing over the jasper and greenstone rocks, the horses snorting and with ears pricked, as if they too sensed what lay ahead.

But despite the competition, Paddy and Daniel were successful again, and it was not long before Hannan's, or Kalgoorlie, as it became known, was proving far richer than Coolgardie. It was not only the rich alluvials where the gold was first discovered, but in the Four Hills away to the east, which though seemingly capped with ironstone, revealed golden domes beneath. Although prospectors with a knowledge of the district talked later of how they had suspected the richness of the Four Hills, it took two South Australians, William Brookman and Sam Pearce, to prove the Four Hills worth.

The news of Hannan's Find pulled people from far and wide reports of the Coolgardie typhoid had been little deterrent. Not only did the gold-hungry come from t'otherside, but telegraph messages about the richest find of the century brought adventurers from Europe, America, and even from the already rich fields of the Klondike and the Nevada. Following the British South African mining men who had first arrived in Coolgardie, came men holding knighthoods. Men who were active on the boards of at least a dozen British companies - men not renowned for their generosity but for their entrepreneurial skills. It was not surprising that the dominant interests of these men was where gold had already been found in other British colonies in quantity. The South African Transvaal, Canada, New Zealand, as well as the Eastern Colonies of Australia. And now the former Cinderella province, Western Australia, the jewel surpassing them all.

Daniel's *Coolgardie Miner* was now in such demand he could not produce enough copies. In fact he had contemplated moving to the new Kalgoorlie, which by the middle of 1894, was showing amazing growth, even to well-built stone buildings, including a stock exchange and a half-dozen banks. Predominant were the pubs, of which there was already more than twenty. In the Eastern Goldfields as it was now known, the market for shares had become insatiable. The wide streets of Kalgoorlie were alive with carts and carriages, bullock-wagons and camel teams. A new bonanza had been discovered a few miles south of Paddy Hannan's

Find, quickly called the Great Boulder, owing to an obvious natural feature there. Within weeks the mine was in production, complete with shaft, poppet-head and stamp-mill. And not far behind rose a smart new hotel, replacing the usual gum-boughed and ti-tree thatched drinking-joint, but so necessary for the thirsty, weary miners after working below on shift.

Most of these underground workers were former prospectors who had failed to make a fortune by individual effort. Also the diggers had never forgotten that as far as looking after the independent prospector and underground mineworker was concerned, none could surpass the *Coolgardie Miner*.

But as far as setting up his main press was concerned, Daniel had left his move into Kalgoorlie too late. By September, 1894, a syndicate linked to the proprietors of the *West Australian* had started a newspaper in the thriving boom town, calling it *The Kalgoorlie Advocate*, a newspaper as such, which as graphically stated - would look after the interests of all. Not only the diggers who were down and out, and those who were successful, but also the interests of the big mining companies, as well as the sharebrokers.

Daniel was understandingly cynical. "Although they reckon they're not connected to the *West*, they preach the same old philosophy. Catering for a classless society. To me the distrust lies with the ownership, which now includes some of the mining entrepreneurs who have bought shares in the paper."

Paddy nodded his head. "Well they certainly must be connected to the Hungry Six crowd anyway, because we've got dear ole Ashley here as assistant editor."

"Yes, and Ashley's arrival might bring you back in the newspaper game," replied Daniel with tongue-in-cheek. "The personal competition I mean?"

"Could at that," replied Paddy guardedly. "But I'll let you know."

"Yet radical reporters like you are now needed Paddy,"

persisted Daniel, still careful not to get angry. "What with the companies almost demanding that the diggers work down their mines. Next thing you know, the authorities will be rounding them up into a convenient labour force."

Paddy was showing interest. "Well, I suppose there is a lot of digger prospectors in trouble. And you could say most have failed to discover the end o' the rainbow. Admittedly they're still gettin' a crust sortin' out gold from the loose alluvials, but they're spendin' too much time in the dozens o' pubs round the place."

Paddy set his jaw. "An' o' course, talkin' about the alluvials, if the companies win this fight to claim all gold that lies beneath the surface over all the thousands of acres they've now pegged, it'll knock the independent prospector to billy-oh."

"Yes Paddy, it will certainly anger the Victorians whose fathers won their rights back in Ballarat and Bendigo after Eureka. One of the major concessions was for the diggers to be allowed to trace the alluvial or free-flowing gold down as deep as they wished - so long as they didn't interfere with the major ore-bodies. But here these companies from the South African Transvaal will hardly let them scratch the surface."

"Yeah, the buggers want the flamin' lot," gritted Paddy.

"It's not that these big companies can't afford it," went on Daniel, his mind obviously troubled. "Damn it all, they've already proven that most of the wealth here is tied up in the hard quartz veins. But the main tactic of course, is to turn the prospector-digger into a mine-worker by breaking down his independence. Over in Africa they have the niggers, as they call them, but here you'd never get an Aboriginal down a deep mine in a thousand years. Apart from that, there's not enough of them."

"You're so right Daniel," replied Paddy, Daniel looking pleased because Paddy was taking so much interest. "I guess the *West Australian* bosses startin' up their own paper here is all part o' the plot. We already know that the McAllums, Andersons, Clayton-Brownes an' so forth are buyin' shares in the big British companies, just like we said."

"And the Anglican Church is again in on it too. All part of the great plan, just as we predicted - colonial exploitation. As it was with the East India Company and now with the mining cartels, but still all the same people." Daniel drew a breath. "So against such odds it's going to be a pretty tough fight matey. But we must do our best, not so much for the ordinary worker, whom I want to protect too, but for the little self-employed digger, the battler who wants to get out his own bit of gold and still stay his own boss."

"My sentiments too chum," said Paddy. "But with these companies with their engineers peggin' damn near every flamin' acre they come across, it's goin' to be tough for the little bloke. There's hundreds o' prospectors on the bones o' their arses already."

"Yes, and you must remember they're the real genuine diggers Paddy, which they won't be if they become ordinary workers. I guess I'm repeating myself, but we want these fellows to stay true men of Eureka, men who still believe in their own stake in life. This row over the alluvials is truly symbolic."

"Looks like we'd better run up the Eureka flag then," grinned Paddy.

"I've already had our Coolgardie seamstress manufacture one," smiled Daniel. "And now with the *Kalgoorlie Advocate* here in opposition, I could be running it up tomorrow."

"An' I could be pullin' on the lanyard too," grinned Paddy once again. "Especially now that bloody Ashley's in the district."

Daniel was now in a happy mood. It had taken the alluvial crisis to bring Paddy to his senses.

But within the next month Paddy was to again lose interest. He had been receiving letters periodically from Ann, and from her writing he believed she was getting better. He was therefore deeply shocked to receive a short note from Ann's mother, stating that her daughter had contracted consumption and was not expected to live.

Paddy was shattered. He didn't have to be told about the dreaded consumption. Since the first landing in 1829, whole families had died of it. In fact, many families as well as individuals had migrated especially to Westralia hoping that the drier climate would cure the frightening complaint. In most cases it had proven a hopeless task. Henry Lovedale had told the story of the wife of Thomas Peel, the much talked about and somewhat infamous Mandurah Squire, whose wife and daughters had migrated to the colony much later than himself and against his wishes. The wife and the elder daughter Jane had been afflicted with the dreaded lung disease even before they left England. Jane wasted away for years before she died tragically in Mandurah, the mother later returning to England where she had succumbed to the disease herself.

Paddy clenched his fists in despair. And now Ann had it. Though it was not surprising seeing that the typhoid had left her with such a cough.

By now the railway, spurred on by gold was beyond Southern Cross and almost to Yellowdine. Paddy caught the train at The Cross, and after travelling through Northam to Perth, disembarked to take a suburban train to Subiaco. To help prepare himself, rather than taking a horse cab the two miles to the hospital, he decided to walk. It was a perfect spring day, with the wildflowers after a good season west of the ranges, revealing their best. Red and gold banksias, pink Swan River myrtle, bright yellow hibertia and golden coastal wattles. The blossoms of the often-scorned prickly Moses only added to the miracle that could arise in each September from the horrible coastal sands.

For Paddy, the loveliness of the day and the beauty of the

countryside only made the sanatorium more depressing. Rows and rows of white-quilted beds, with occupants no more aware of the beauty of the day outside than if they had already passed the divide. Ann was in a tiny ward with four other patients, all near death's door. Yet despite the whiteness and thinness of her cheeks, her eyes immediately recognised Paddy. As a tear rolled down her cheek, Paddy took her in his arms. She felt as light as a wafer, her bones sticking through her flesh.

Paddy trembled remembering a passenger telling him in the train how the dead bodies in a consumptive ward often had to be wrapped in swaddling cloth to make them fit to grace a casket. He determined to put it out of his mind, trying to remember the delightful curvaceous Ann as she was.

"Ann, Ann," he said brokenly. "If I had known, I would have come weeks ago."

Her voice was barely audible.

"No Paddy. You'd already done enough."

After a silence, she tried to speak again. Paddy placed his ear close to her lips. "Paddy darling, do you still love me?" she whispered, her voice rasping in her throat.

"Of course I do sweetheart, now sh-shhh, you're using up your strength."

"No, Paddy, I'm gone... finished ... Oh Paddy..." Once again the voice trailed off, her eyes desperately trying to focus.

And he held her, staying with her all night and half the next day. For a while there he had thought she had made a miraculous recovery, asking questions about Coolgardie and Sister Bridget? How the pub-girls were? Then the lustrous appealing light in her eyes switched off as if pulling down a blind, causing Paddy to suppress an anguished cry, fearful he should disturb the other patients.

Finally the part of Ann which had been so desperately trying to stay with her loved one, flew - yet leaving the young woman with a look of pure peace.

"She waited for you," said a sympathetic sister to Paddy. "We read her your telegram, otherwise I think she would have gone well before."

Paddy couldn't answer, he was too close to breaking down. As he walked back to the station his mind was not only filled with sadness but with guilt. When Ann had stopped writing, why had he not enquired? As usual, when away from Ann, he had been too enraptured in the goldfields. Sitting on a railway seat waiting for the train, he put his face in his hands and sobbed, regardless of those around him.

It was months before Paddy was back to anything like his old self. Even then Daniel wondered if he would ever be the same. He realised that Paddy had been showing weakness, even before the trouble with Ann. Drinking far too much at night as well as gambling, and surrendering to the temptations of a rip-roaring boom town - more now a glitzy city.

To be sure the attractions were there, especially in the Hannans, by far Kalgoorlie's largest and most popular pub. Already equipped with a chain-long front bar, the longest in Australia, the precincts were always crowded. The Hannans not only supplied refreshments but the usual gambling. Cards - Crown and Anchor - Dice. Two-up was a problem because the coins needed plenty of air. There were also the inevitable pub-girls, serving behind the long bar besides exhibiting themselves in the dancing acts. Yet as far as privately entertaining customers was concerned, they were now under competition. A whole Kalgoorlie street, Hay Street, had been reserved for houses of ill-repute. Many of the hostesses were of Japanese origin. The girls had migrated down from Broome where they had originally come to Western Australia to supply feminine company for Nipponese pearl-divers.

Though most of the Hannans' customers were still the t'otherside diggers, there were also the adventurer types, some high-class English remittance men, but mostly a mixture of Germans, Italians, Swedes, Norwegians, and not less than a few Americans. But they all held allegiance to Eureka and the fight for the right to mine the alluvials.

Paddy had become very friendly with a character called Tim McBride, a stocky, dark, solid-jawed steely-eyed Victorian around thirty, four or five years older than Paddy. Tim, a self-taught though proven geologist, had been bitten with the gold-bug early, and had first worked for mining companies in Queensland. Then wanting to be more independent, he had joined the large group of digger adventurers, sailing round the north of Australia to join the tragic rush to Hall's Creek in the Kimberleys. Later with his mates, Tim had returned to Wyndham on the coast to sail a little south to the tiny port of Cossack, striking out in the Pilbara to Marble Bar, reputed to be the hottest place on God's earth. Still more fascinated with the searching than the finding, Tim and company came even further south to the wool port of Geraldton, to again strike inland, where reasonably payable gold was found around two hundred miles into the Murchison sheep-country.

After getting rid of most of their gold profits on a wild spending spree in Perth, Tim and his mates decided to try their luck in the already booming Eastern Goldfields. Although he would have preferred to stay prospecting with his digger compatriots, Tim knew that an easier way to make quick money was to take work temporarily with the British companies which were now pegging out those vast areas of potential gold plots.

Nonetheless, to have to rely on wages, even the high pay of a geologist, made Tim feel that he was breaking some sort of sacred trust, known to the Victorian prospector as the Eureka Tradition. Tim's father had been one of the original diggers who had mined around Bendigo and Ballarat and had stood by the side of Peter Lalor in the defence of the Stockade.

Tim, also an avowed republican explained it all to Paddy and Daniel in the Hannan's one day.

Daniel, as a journalist and especially as a Victorian like Tim, could well appreciate Tim's allegiance to Eureka, which in simple terms, only eulogised the average Australian's yearning to be free and his own boss. Daniel could also appreciate Tim's argument that the revival of the Eureka Principle was so important in the present confrontation between the diggers and the British mining companies.

Yet it was well-known that when Tim wasn't working he could usually be found in one of the hotels either drinking or gambling. And although Tim did keep himself sober it was said by balancing his bar drinking with playing poker or pontoon, Daniel still felt that Tim might only be helping Paddy to slip further down the ladder.

Not that Tim McBride wasn't interested in politics, as Daniel soon found out. In fact, the rugged digger-geologist had a strong reputation as a miner's agitator. But the problem with Tim was that most of his agitating in the booming Kalgoorlie was at present being done in the pubs. What made matters worse was that Paddy now made the excuse that he was busy discussing the problems of the diggers, including the alluvials, with his new-found friend, Tim McBride - naturally in the pubs.

Certainly Tim was no ordinary digger, in fact unlike the average fossicker, he always dressed well. Not that he was religous about his laundry, but he wore his clothes as though they fitted him, red Kalgoorlie dust and all. Rather than the often shapeless headgear of the diggers, Tim preferred a hat with a narrower brim, with the edges curled and the peak carefully dented. He also smoked a short straight-stemmed pipe and was even known to indulge in the occasional Hàvana cigar, particularly while gambling.

Though he might have played the part, Tim was far from a gentleman. His language at times could make even the roughest of diggers cringe. Also Tim usually wore his hat under a roof, especially in the bar or while playing cards at a side-table.

Yet he was no compulsive gambler, and could give it away if he wished. Indeed, even while winning at cards - which he often was - he would talk about his yen to be back out in the never never with only a couple of mates.

Daniel was sure that it was this romantic image of Tim, that so attracted Paddy to him. In fact, Daniel had threatened to replace Paddy with another reporter, a Canadian, Max Heinrikson. Not only had Max an experience of boom-towns, but he also had liberal democratic leanings similar to Daniel.

Yet the alluvial issue, at least, did revive Paddy's journalistic instincts temporarily. Well attended miners' meetings were now held every Sunday morning before the start of two-up. A new two-up ring had been built well out of town, because the police had banned the favourite digger's game in the streets. With the red dusty ring in the centre unprotected, shade for the spectators and participants was supplied by the popular thatched ti-tree brush propped up by the usual gimlet poles. The shape of the bush shed followed the pattern of the ring in the centre, the whole like an old-time Spanish dollar.

They always held the meetings before the start of two-up. While Daniel roused the diggers with his rhetoric, Paddy usually walked around urging them on. Tim McBride filled this role adequately also, the diggers almost venerating him as a man who called a spade a spade.

This day Tim waved the latest copy of the conservative-minded *Kalgoorlie Advocate*, taking Daniel's place on top of a mine machinery case. He took off the pompous style of the colony's well-to-do as he read out the headlines:

DIGGERS STILL AGITATING OVER
THE ALLUVIALS

According to the Minister for Mines, Edwin Mainwaring, the demand by private prospectors for access to the deep alluvials on company pegged leases is a fruitless attempt to stave off the inevitable.

The future of the Goldfields digger does not lie in running his own show, but in working for the big companies.

The fact that many of these prospectors have wives and families to keep in the Eastern Colonies makes this even more imperative.

After he had finished, Tim slapped the back of his hand across the face of the newspaper.

"THE BASTARDS!" he yelled. "Should you all stand for it? The swines just want you all to go cap in hand to the mine managers for a job. Are you going to be sucked in?"

"No, tell the mongrels to go to blazes," shouted a digger, who indeed did have a wife and kids over t'otherside, and who as an individual prospector was finding it hard to find enough gold to sustain them. It was the same with hundreds of others who made up the thousands who now attended the meetings.

Tim was bitter as he sat with Paddy and Daniel later in the Hannans. The Goldfield's pubs were always open on Sundays.

"Without access to the deep alluvials the poor bastards are finished," he growled into his whisky. "Most of 'em would prefer to stay close to Kalgoorlie in any case for obvious reasons. All the surface gold is gone. The companies have got 'em over a barrel."

"And with access to the deep alluvials denied, they won't even have to pay them decent wages," complained Daniel.

"Well, I will say they've offered 'em better wages than they do to the African nigs," shot back Tim. "But it's the principle. Most of the diggers came over here in the hope to get enough gold to start a farm or a little business of some sort."

"Hardly a one has struck it rich like Arthur Bayley or Paddy Hannan, have they?" agreed Daniel. "And even if they had, they'd probably have been paid a mere pittance by the mining companies. Arthur Bayley made no fortune, and there's Paddy Hannan gone out prospecting again." He went on hopefully. "A cooperative could be the answer. If the more independent diggers are agreeable, I'd be willing to help finance it."

Tim again growled into his whisky. "You could be wastin' your money Daniel. That's just the trouble, these diggers all want so much to be their own bosses, that they are suspicious even of their best mates. Yeah," went on Tim, cynically. "The flamin' companies know this! Talk about divide an' rule. The bastards don't need to! All they have to do is wait! Of course, even though they'd been allowed to mine the deep alluvials, the same eventually happened with the diggers over in Bendigo an' Ballarat back in the '50s an' '60s. What I mean is that despite Eureka an' all the glory talk, most of 'em finished up workin' for a boss down the deep shafts anyhow. You wait! If they don't pull their fingers out an' fight for their rights against the companies together, these diggers could be the same. Most of 'em have wives an' kids over in Victoria - just like that rotten *Kalgoorlie Advocate* said. So with families to keep, whether they like it or not, it's just underground they'll have to go."

At the end of his tirade, Tim gulped down his whisky, telling the bartender for Chris' sake fill up the water-jug, he was bloody thirsty!

"No wonder with all that fire-water cobber," teased Paddy. "Anyway, you're beholden to the companies yourself Tim. You've been down mine-shafts right here in Kalgoorlie."

"Christ Paddy," retorted the digger-geologist. "How many times do I have to tell yuh? My job's just to trace a gold lead, or to check on the safety of a tunnel. To tell you the truth, though they want me because I've got a nose for gold, I'd rather give it all up just for some little show of my own out in the sticks somewhere. Just take out the gold when I need it."

"Hell, I thought you enjoyed doin' the rounds of the Kalgoorlie pubs too much to retire out in the never-never Tim," laughed Paddy "Anyhow, maybe the government could help the diggers who still have little shows of their own, like you were talkin' about. You know, the ones who've sunk shafts down an' the claim's payin' a bit. O' course, they'd need access to the alluvials. The Premier's been a bit sympathetic about the alluvials, hasn't he? Even despite what that rotten Mines Minister said in the *Kalgoorlie Advocate*."

Daniel's eyes flew sparks. "What, you mean when Groves offered the diggers three feet underground? Would you call that generous, Paddy? What's the use of sinking a shaft on that? Why, in places the alluvials go down a good three hundred feet - or more, as with the Ivanhoe mine out past Boulder!" The journalist kicked the boarded face of the bar structure with his boot toe, obviously showing his frustration.

"Why Paddy, you must be joking. That's not what I'd call helping the diggers. By even offering them a mere three feet, I'd say the Bastards of the Coastal Strip, as our diggers call the Groves Gang, are probably only after the digger's vote in the next election anyhow."

"Yeah," grinned Tim, pushing back his hat, still at a rakish angle, revealing dark raven locks. The digger geologist was obviously amused by Daniel's show of temper, especially as from what he'd seen of the editor, he was one who usually remained calm, even when orating to a crowd.

"They could be offering us cursed t'othersiders, male suffrage at last, couldn't they?" said Tim. "Mind you, there's enough of us. They say our population here in the Eastern Goldfields alone already surpasses Perth an' Fremantle."

"Yes," added Daniel, now again reduced to a little

calmness. "You must include me amongst the t'othersiders too Tim. I've been here since '76, and I haven't even had a vote - yet! I tried hard enough in 1890, when the colony first gained responsible government."

Tim laughed cynically. "Responsible government, ugh! After what I'd experienced in Victoria, responsible government here is a bloody farce. The Parliament, if that's what you call it, is still choc-a bloc with the old colonial gentry. It's about time the joint had a change. Certainly all these tens of thousands of diggers could do it." Tim clenched his teeth on his pipe. "Responsible government, my arse! All the Groves Gang has done since I've been here apart from their latest suckin' up to the minin' companies, is to look after the interests of the big pastoralists."

"Well, that's the Groves Gang incorporated," returned Daniel with sarcasm. "As I've said to Paddy here, if the original family names are not on the Ministerial listings, you may be sure their blood relations are."

"You'd better add prick relations too, Daniel," snickered Tim. "William Groves, the Premier's married into one o' the daughters o' the Hungry Six isn't he? Anyway, who says for a few hands o' poker? Looks like there's an empty table."

But Daniel gave his excuse and left. Not that he was so annoyed with Tim for his deliberate use of one of the coarser epithets. But it was because Paddy seemed to prefer Tim's friendship to his own. That was the problem. As a newspaper editor, he knew, everyone, even the diggers expected you to speak just a bit above the ordinary, and also to act that way in public. Not high-faluting, but just educated. Paddy apparently preferred the rougher environment.

CHAPTER 10

A week later Paddy was drinking with Tim in the Hannans pub, when in rushed an excited digger.

"CAVE I-N-NN...! There's been a cave-in!" he yelled.

"Where, for Chris' sake?" cried Tim, dumping his whisky on the bar.

"The Lady Venus!"

"Hell!" gasped Paddy. "Anyone trapped?"

"Yeah," panted the digger. "Geordie Davis, Jimmy Lachlan an' Jack Farrelly."

Paddy leapt from the bar-stool. "God all bloody Mighty! Davis, Lachlan an' Farrelly! Those three were fossickin' in the early days round Southern Cross."

"Yeah," growled Tim. "Just like I said, if they've wives an' kids over t'otherside an' they never strike it rich, it's down the company mines they've gotta go. Anyway, let's get over there!"

As they hurried east along Hannan Street, so wide you needed to carry a waterbag to get across, as one digger put it, Paddy surveyed the mixture of roughly erected shanty stores, pubs and boarding-houses against those far more permanent of beautifully tuck-pointed local stone and precise cement work and plaster. There on the left of the street stood the huge new Town-Hall with its great spire and its round-faced clock displaying the hour. Beyond the end of the roadway, reared the tall poppet-heads, with the dumps of treated ore already up to a height of fifty feet. To Paddy it all graphically contrasted with the original countryside, and the change brought on by the rush for minerals, especially gold.

But as they drew close to the mine-site with its great steel winch-tower hovering one hundred foot above, Paddy had his reservations. Though aware of the challenge and excitement of this enormous enterprise, on Paddy's mind now was a gloomy picture of British industrialism, of which he'd read as a youngster, and which Daniel had often spoken about.

Here down this great hole in Kalgoorlie were men who had suddenly succumbed to the same dangers which had befallen others in the British coal-mines - in Britain not only men, but women and children, since their only alternative was starvation. Certainly the alternative in Kalgoorlie might not have been as bad. The more fortunate diggers often felt obligated to look after their mates. But underground with companies not so worried about safety precautions owing to the cost, the danger was still the same - life held cheap with death just round the corner while proprietors lived it up on the profits.

They reached the mine-site to find around two-hundred diggers loudly cursing an engineer, who had arrived from South Africa two months previously. To be sure he'd had plenty of experience with cave-ins in the Transvaal, but usually when there was a protest over inadequate safety precautions, there a white man's word was backed by the military with guns. In Kalgoorlie, the company manager expecting trouble had already notified the local sergeant of police, but as yet not one trooper had arrived, making the engineer realise all too well that this was not South Africa.

"You rotten bastard," roared one of the diggers, who like the rest, was still working a small alluvial show or a small-scale mine independently. "Our three mates only took work with you to make a little extra money to send back to their wives an' kids back home in Melbourne. They were tellin' us last night in the pub, how loose rocks were all peltin' down from the drive' ceilin' every time they fired a charge."

"Yeah," supported Tim. "I agree with these men about inadequate safety measures. In fact, I warned the manager more'n a month ago when I was doin' some work for the company when one o' the other geologists took sick." Tim gave the man a glare. "You do remember me, don't you?"

"Yes I do Mr McBride," replied the engineer haughtily.

"But the fact is ..."

Before the man could utter another word, Tim erupted. "It's the same ole story, isn't it, my friend? Time is the essence, different if the workers were gettin' a fair cut o' the gold."

"They get it all right," snapped back the engineer. "By theft! In my years as a mining man, I've never seen anything like it is here in Kalgoorlie."

"You'd better pay better wages then, hadn't you chum?" yelled one of the diggers from the crowd. "You're not over in Africa now you know, havin' the nigs work down the mines for next to nothin'. You'd better wake up to yourself matey. But what about gettin' those poor bastards out? They could still be alive."

"We have two men down there clearing away the rubble," defended the engineer. "The trouble is it will take a long time. The mine-face is a good two hundred feet in ... and we are so short of men." The engineer looked over the diggers contemptuously, no doubt thinking "... here we are short of workers with you crowd spending most of your time in the hotels."

"Well what about closin' the rest o' the mine down then?" Tim yelled in reply.

"We have telegraphed the managers in Perth," answered the engineer. "And though they have told us to clear the fallen tunnel, they have also ordered us to keep up production, especially with crushing and the treatment of ore on the surface."

"But this is a flamin' emergency," swore Tim, "Those men in the tunnel could still be alive."

"I told you we have men clearing the debris," replied the man heatedly.

"Well, I want to go down an' check," cracked Tim.

"What! Are you calling me a liar?"

It seemed for the moment that he was going to refuse Tim permission. But as a crowd of diggers surged behind the tough-talking geologist, Paddy among them, the engineer changed his mind. He began to walk over to the winch-house to tell the operator to start working the lift-cage.

"Righto you bastards," yelled Tim to the diggers. "There's only room for half a dozen in the cage, an' that includes me, Paddy here an' the engineer. Also the ones that come make sure you're sober. We want those men out, come hell or high-water."

The diggers were still not satisfied. "Can't you send the cage back up for a few more?"

"You silly bastard," roared Tim. "Call yourself a miner. You know there's only room for a half dozen at a time to work in those goddamned tunnels. But you'll all get your turn, never fear, because we'll have you workin' in two-hour relays. An' while you no-hopers are standin' by, for Chris-sake stay away from the pubs. We don't want a mob a drunks down there."

The cage descended, and apart from the odd wisecrack the men were quiet, revealing the gravity of the situation. It stopped with a jerk at the allotted level and the men piled out one after the other into the narrow tunnel. While Tim and the engineer carried carbide lamps in front, the rest walked along the narrow ore-truck tracks, two abreast, with heads down.

Tim tapped the roof above with a miner's hand-pick. "Look at that," he cursed. "How the blazes does that stand up to gelignite? I warned 'em to shore this up before I left. There's a big seam o' rotten quartz through here."

"We know that, and bracing the roof has been put on our schedule," replied the engineer.

"Yeah, on the schedule," shot back Tim in the gloom. "I've heard that too many times. Like all bloody companies, you're too interested in gettin' out the gold than worryin' about men's lives." Tim shone his lamp forward. "Anyway, here we are. Hey, what's this takin' time off you bastards."

"Lay off McBride," said one of the miners, his face sweat-streaked in the lamplight. We've been at it for hours, we've just taken a breather."

"Sorry McCann," apologised Tim. "Anyway, the relief's here. Righto you lot!" he boomed at the diggers through the gloom. "Don't just stand there, get stuck into it. Think o' your mates!"

"What de ye' reckon on their chances?" Tim asked McCann. "Heard anythin'? You must be only about fifteen feet off."

"Not a thing," replied McCann. "The trouble is she's jammed chocablock."

"So I can see. Anyway cobber, you an' your mates get back up top an' get some rest. We may need you later."

"Geordie Davis is a mate o' mine, I'd like to stay," protested McCann.

"No, get back up top McCann!" replied Tim, sharply. "I know how you feel, but there's no room to rest up down here." Tim's voice softened, as he gripped the other digger's shoulder. "Yeah matey, get your men out of it. They're tired."

Not accustomed to deep-mining, Paddy had been feeling like a passenger, but very soon he was put to work shovelling fallen rubble into an ore-truck with one of the diggers and running it to the cage where it could be lifted to the surface. The engineer rode back up with the first load.

"While you're about it, send down timbers in the empty cage," yelled Tim to the engineer as he stepped into the lift. "We need to shore up the roof as we go along. Otherwise, you might have to dig out the whole flamin' lot of us."

The engineer left without a word, knowing that Tim was different to the run-of-the-mill digger. He was one Australian he could grudgingly admire. Certainly rough and tough in nature like the rest, but he also possessed brains and the power of organisation.

As the timbers arrived, Tim expertly erected them, standing them against the walls, pushing them up to the top and keying the pre-cut sections together to form a strong wooden U upside down. The work went on, the men cursing, but desperately worried about the fate of their comrades.

All at once an agonised yell came from one of the men clearing the tunnel. "OH, CHRIST ...! NO...!"

"OH, JESUS ...!" cursed Tim, as he rushed forward head down shining his torch. Paddy was just behind. He too shone his torch as one of the diggers turned the broken body over.

"Oh hell, it's Geordie Davis!"

"Keep workin' you bastards!" roared Tim at the diggers. "We'll look after Geordie. Here Paddy, don't just stand there, help me carry him."

The men worked on, now resigned to the fact that it would only be a matter of time before they found the other two bodies. But as they cleared desperately with Tim shining his torch forward and upward, they realised the roof was more stable, the debris less high, a space between the debris and the roof. Then they could hear muffled shouts.

"THANK GOD!" yelled Tim. "THEY'RE ALIVE! THEY'RE ALIVE!"

Feverishly they dug at the rubble, throwing down their shovels and pulling out fallen rocks with bare hands hurling them back to Paddy and the other digger, filling the ore-truck to clear the way. The trapped miners were now talking over the rubble. Though weak they had begun clearing fallen rock back towards the mine-face, which being of tougher ore had stayed complete. In the torchlight, it now had the appearance of a small amphitheatre.

"WE'VE MADE IT! WE'VE MADE IT!" roared a miner.

"Thought you'd got rid of me, didn't you O'Malley?" gasped one of the rescued men as he was tearfully embraced by his mate.

"Yeah Farrelly, you no-good bastard," replied the rescuer. "Here, steady now cobber." But Farrelly had collapsed in his mate's arms.

"Don't stand there, get 'em to the surface!" roared Tim. "They need clean air."

Next morning they buried Geordie Davis.

Though a wire had been sent via the overland telegraph to the dead digger's family in Victoria, no answer as yet had been received. Bodies could not be kept too long in the Eastern Goldfields climate as had been proven with the typhoid. There was also talk among Geordie's other mates about how, with no money having been sent over for more than a year, the wife had begun to carry on with another bloke. This was a common problem with itinerate husbands, particularly prospectors and shearers.

Although the cemetery was crowded with diggers, mine-managers and company engineers were noticeably absent. Daniel Hordacre wrote all about it in the next weekly issue of his *Coolgardie Miner*, as usual taking the digger's side. Certainly the conservative *Kalgoorlie Advocate* did offer thanks that the death toll had been confined to only one and that the other two miners had been found alive. But the paper gave no condemnation of the mining company for not timbering up the tunnel. It had already been proven that the rock strata was weak. The paper even gave praise to the company for putting men immediately to work clearing the mine-shaft.

The Coolgardie paper instead gave the diggers' version, castigating the British South African company for its poor regard for a miner's safety, besides extolling the role played by Tim McBride. Much of this side of the story was reported by Paddy.

"What a lyin' bastard you are O'Leary," grinned Tim, as he punched Paddy on the shoulder in the Hannans. "What's this flamin' hero business? I was only doin' my duty as a digger geologist."

"Well Daniel says that even that South African engineer finally admitted you deserved it," laughed Paddy, playfully punching Tim back. "You've just got to take it matey."

"Oh for Chris'sake shutup an' drink your beer," was the embarrassed reply from Tim.

The cave-in, coupled with Daniel's interpretations in his newspaper about men risking their lives down the mines for the industrialists, made the diggers even more vocal about their right to mine the deep alluvials. The increasing yields from the rich sediments down hundreds of feet in the Ivanhoe mine only spurred them on further.

As the diggers lamented ... "In the old days in Victoria after the Eureka Rebellion all that loose gold in the Ivanhoe would have officially been the property of the self-employed prospector."

The next few months saw the diggers engaged in small protest meetings in Hannan St mostly outside the dozen or so pubs. Finally, on orders telegraphed from Perth by Edwin Mainwaring, Minister for Mines, the Kalgoorlie police began to intervene. As a result, on the next Sunday morning out at the two-up ring, the talk was about much more than two-up.

There in the crowded ring-centre, Daniel stood on the packing case and waved his latest copy of the *Coolgardie Miner*. He had the men's attention since, in their eyes he had the guts to stand up for the ordinary man. Right now he was their hero, even though in appearance, he looked far from a regular digger.

Paddy and Tim stood each side of the packing-case like a couple of lieutenants, both admired in their own right. Paddy was popular for his easy-going nature, mixed with his readiness to stick up for a mate, and Tim for his proven ability as the one geologist who had thoughts about people besides rocks. To them Tim was the modern tough rough-hewn epitome of Peter Lalor, an educated man who could have made his fortune just working for the mining companies. But Lalor had risked all at Eureka to lead the diggers' rebellion.

"IT'S THE TIME FOR ACTION!" yelled Daniel.

"YEAH!" roared Tim. "Time to get organised. Time to

round up your mates."

"A lot of our mates are out in the scrub prospectin'," a digger shouted back.

"Those mates are the ones we want," yelled back Tim. "The ones who really want independence an' the right to mine the alluvials." Tim could have gone on with ".....not like mosta you bastards hangin' round Kalgoorlie, who've pretty well agreed to work down below for the friggin' companies."

But Tim didn't really want to offend. All the diggers were needed in the march.

"Anyhow, when's the day?" queried another digger.

"Well, as Mr McBride implied. It's up to you," answered Daniel. "But how does a month's time sound?"

"Suits me," called back the man. "Yeah, a month's time."

There was mumbled support from the crowd, but the meeting was over and two-up was more on their minds. "RIGHT!" shouted Daniel, as the ringmaster began to set the centre. "A month's time! I'll put it in my paper."

Already rumblings about the alluvial problems in Kalgoorlie had reached t'otherside. Eamon Davitt became interested. He was a former Fenian and an old compatriot of Paddy's father, Michael. He was also one of the seven left to rot in Fremantle gaol, who had been taken out by the Americans in 1876. Davitt had since returned from the United States and had been busy organising shearers' strikes in Queensland. Julian Stuart, a Queensland smallholder's son of Scottish descent and a journalist agitator similar to Daniel, was also interested. Both Davitt and Stuart had already gained a reputation throughout Australia as tough union activists. Within the month, they arrived in Kalgoorlie where they got together with Daniel. Paddy and Tim joined in and it was decided to hand over the organising of the protest march to the two very capable visitors, Davitt and Stuart.

On a sweltering day in March 1895, more than five thousand diggers turned up, defying the six troopers who up till this time had kept the miners at bay. But with the diggers now openly brandishing knives and pistols, the policemen could well have believed in the old cliche: discretion was the better part of valour.

Davitt and Stuart had formed the diggers into ranks military style, and despite the century heat, the roughly dressed men marched down Hannan Street shouting slogans against the mining companies, most of them obscene. In front strode a barrel-chested prospector with Eureka flag held high, its white cross and stars on blue already soiled with blood-red dust.

The target was the Mines Office, where the diggers demanded an audience with the Mines Minister, he who had been so vocal in the *Kalgoorlie Advocate* about how the only future for the digger was working underground for the companies. It was he who had ordered the police to use force to prevent the diggers congregating together in a public thoroughfare.

The diggers also resented the fact that Edwin Mainwaring as a businessman pastoralist knew absolutely nothing about mines. Most of the diggers as republicans resented it even more because Edwin was the son of Sir Albert Mainwaring, who along with Oliver McAllum and others of the original retinue of Western Australia's founder, Captain Stirling, had been knighted for their achievements.

It was not surprising that Mainwaring and the rest of his Hungry Six accomplices, proved to be the main topic of conversation between Paddy, Daniel and Tim, as they marched along with the diggers.

"... it's the same old story isn't it?" complained Daniel. "Here we have our Minister for Mines, emulating the exploits of his father, who along with the rest of the gentry brought in the convicts to save the Westralian wool industry. Again there is the need for a ready workforce - this time for the mines."

"Yeah," said Tim. "An' o' course if they let the diggers

have access to all the alluvial gold, too many of the diggers could remain independent. The mining companies then might have to bring in outside labour. Who knows, even those nigs from Africa."

"Well they still might have to," said Paddy, pointing. "Looks like this mob could smash down the Mines Office if their requests aren't granted."

"Yeah, the Warden's telegraphing Perth right now," spoke Tim. "The demands are that the Minister for Mines leaves for Kalgoorlie on the next train."

"Hey look," yelled Paddy. "The Warden's wavin' a piece o' paper."

Warden Finnerty, the same tough old character who had been in Southern Cross and then in Coolgardie, spoke gruffly. "Roight, you mob o' heathens, the Minister's agreed to come. He'll arrive on Friday mor-rrnin'. Now, off with ye', there's enough dust in Kalgoorlie without ye's trampin' the streets. Now, for the love o' Pete, be off."

Paddy gave a grin. "Ye' know, I reckon old Jack's a bit sympathetic."

"Sure he is," laughed Tim. "I tell you, if it was up to Warden Finnerty, he'd be givin' the diggers the full rights to the alluvial - all the way down. The trouble is bein' a government man, he's got to do as he's told."

"Well, let's hope something good comes out of Friday," sighed Daniel.

"I hope," agreed Tim. "But with the government an' the companies in cahoots together, I've got me doubts mate. I've got me doubts."

On the Friday morning standing on a temporary dais in a dusty cleared paddock bordering Hannan Street, Edwin Mainwaring faced the crowd. In fact, even with his large police escort brought with him from Perth, it could be said he faced them bravely - and even a little honestly.

"... you men must understand that these British mining

companies, whom you detest, are vitally needed....," he went on. "You Victorians should know all about it. You remember the disastrous crash, which five years ago not only ruined the economy of Melbourne, but near pauperised the whole of Australia. I tell you, my friends, the crisis is still far from over. The capital which is now being injected by the British mining companies, is badly needed for Australia as a whole to get back on its feet."

"But Westralia was never on its blinkin' feet, was it?" yelled a digger. "In fact it took us Victorian prospectors to find the gold and at last get you out of the manure. Now look how you bloody treat us, lettin' all these flamin' companies in, stealin' all our alluvials an' takin' away our livelihood."

"They are not stealing all your alluvials," replied the Minister levelly. "You have my permission to dig down three feet. It has already been publicised."

"Three feet be buggered!" yelled the burly man, who still held the Eureka flag. "As you've already been told, we want one hundred foot or nothin', an' even then yer gettin' orf bloody lightly. Look how deep the alluvials run down in the Ivanhoe."

The Minister stood his ground.

"I told you that without access to the alluvium some of the big companies would pull out," argued the Minister.

"Well, let the bastards pull out," yelled the Eureka flagman, who was one of the few who was still doing well out of his own little claim. "Let the rotten company men go back to Africa, where they stand over the poor bloody niggers with guns, forcin' 'em down the mines. No, no alluvial gold for the poor bloody niggers." He gave a roar, turning to his comrades. "But we're not bloody niggers, are we mates? So we want our rights."

"Too flamin' right we do!" roared the flagman.

"Look's like the ayes have it," grinned Paddy amidst the general roar of approval. "That flagman's doin' well, isn't he?"

The editor had gained a vantage position along with Paddy and Tim. "Yes, Eamon Davitt's been training him."

"Eamon's had experience as a rebel, I tell you," returned Paddy. "Fact is he was tellin' me he called into York to visit my folks an' talk about ole times when he fought beside my Pa in the Fenian Rebellion in Ireland. O' course they were prisoners together in Fremantle Gaol."

"Paddy," reminded Daniel, almost irritably, "you must remember I had all that story told me back in '76, just after the American barque *Catalpa* daringly took out Davitt and the rest." He turned to Tim. "His father was the bravest of them all though. Stayed behind in the earlier episode in 1869 when John Boyle O'Reilly got away on a Yankee whaler. Changed his name from Rooney to O'Leary and disguised himself and married Judith, who became Paddy's mother."

"Yeah, quite a story," grinned Tim. "Paddy's already told me. Still, I'd reckon Julian Stuart up there could have a bit to tell also. A Stuart, eh. Why, he could be related to Royalty. Unionism in Australia breeds strange bedfellows doesn't it? That pair up there now, one Irish and the other a Scot. Never such a pair would get together in dear old Britain. Yet I guess out here it's all just a part of fighting the good fight. Kind of glory fight."

"Yes," replied Daniel soberly. "The chance in a new country for more equality and decency than in the old. And talking about enmity between the Irish and the Scots," Daniel went on. "With the British as usual, it's been mostly just a ploy to stir up discontent - as happened when she deliberately sent in kilted Scots to quell the Fenian Revolt."

"Spoken like a true republican, Daniel," grinned Tim, handing out more genuine praise than he was accustomed to giving. "Anyhow let's get closer, it seems Edwin is holding his own, worse luck."

"He certainly bloody is," gritted Paddy. "And would you look at that Ashley McAllum, standing there just behind him with his note-book an' pencil an' a smug grin on his face."

"Yeah, talk about a people's journalist," swore Tim. "You'd think the bastard was one o' the Groves Gang."

"Well, he near enough is," said Paddy.

"Will you two keep quiet and listen to what's going on," commanded Daniel.

The Minister, standing there in the blistering heat in well-cut suit with waistcoat and gold watch-chain, pushed back his bowler hat and mopped his brow. Yet the smile on his face was now almost benign.

"It looks like I'll have to make a compromise," he called. "How does six-foot sound?"

Go to blazes," yelled a digger. "What do you take us for, fifty foot or nothin'."

"Oh the bloody idiot," said Paddy. "He's gone and ruined it. He should have stuck fast on a hundred."

"Seven," yelled the Minister, realising he was winning the day.

"Thirty foot," yelled back the foolish digger, the other diggers now strangely silent.

"No, eight foot," roared the Minister, now at his full height, his stance upholding the ancient Mainwaring family pride.

"Twenty," was the cry from the digger.

"Nine," came the confident reply from the Minister. "Look, let's settle on ten," he went on, revealing his ability to turn the heraldic cheek and hobnob with the rabble. "You know Diggers, from what I've heard there have been many fortunes made in the goldfields at less than ten foot down. Take Bayley's Reward, why the first ten foot was a treasure house, as was Hannan's Find right here. And take the Four Hills, a wealth of gold 'neath less than six inches of ironstone, but still classed as alluvial gold. All less than ten foot down. Yes my brave diggers, all you have to do is go out and find it. As you know, there are new discoveries every day.

I can name a list as long as my arm." He smiled broadly. "So we'll settle on ten foot, eh?"

"Like bloody 'ell," yelled another digger. But it was too half-hearted. Now Daniel, Tim and Paddy had joined Eamon Davitt and Julian Stuart, and they all stood together trying to rally the crowd. But they were too late - most of the diggers had already dispersed to talk about it all in the pubs.

"Well I guess they had an excuse," said Tim to Daniel and Paddy later on in the Hannans. "It must be a good one hundred and twenty in the shade."

"Yes," returned Daniel, gloomily. "But it's the same old thing isn't it? Servility to our betters. Just because they might speak a bit more correctly and sound their h's. It's still inbred in us from the convict days. Though we aspire to be rebels, we fear to face the future without the patronage of our traditional masters, the British upper class."

"Count me out," answered Tim, gruffly, putting down his glass. "As I told you before, I'm a Eureka man from way back."

"Well why didn't you do something about it?" Daniel said angrily. He turned. "You too Paddy, you are always talking about your father being a rebel. But you all just stood there."

"Well, so did you, Daniel, so did those union organisers, Davitt and Stuart," reminded Tim. He gave a half-grin. "Well, I guess those two dozen troopers our dear Edwin brought with him made a difference. Our precious Minister wasn't takin' any chances." Tim drained his glass. "Yeah, I guess one or two of us might have taken a bullet, especially as they were gettin' round with cocked revolvers. Anyhow, as far as our illustrious Minister tellin' the diggers there's plenty more gold to be found in the backblocks, I'd reckon he knew full well that most o' the silly bastards have got so accustomed to the sweet life in Kalgoorlie, you'd be lucky to get 'em a half-hour's march from a pub." Tim's lips curled in disdain. "In fact I'd say it's the urge to stay close to the bright lights, that made the diggers give up so easily today."

"That's a tactic with the hierarchy Tim," returned Daniel grimly. "Give the rabble plenty of playthings. Not only pubs and gambling and sleazy entertainment, but football, cricket, and of course, horse-racing, the rich man's sport where the little bloke is more often than not the loser. That's why the big British companies are encouraging all these recreations, even investing in them because it keeps the workers happy. Yes, they'll be workers all right. Especially if they hang around Kalgoorlie, they'll be workers and nothing surer."

"Well I'm glad you've admitted it Daniel," replied Tim, with some humour. "Anyhow it's your shout, our glasses are empty."

"All right Tim. But just one more for the track. I've never been one to drown my sorrows anyhow. And I've got an editorial to prepare."

"Yeah," said Tim to Paddy, after Daniel had left. "I might have a crack at the poor bugger occasionally, but it's a pity there weren't a few more round like Daniel. If ever I've seen a true Australian intellectual, as the nobs would say, Daniel is one."

"Yeah Tim, my family in York said the same thing. Daniel is one of the very few Australians with courage enough to not only say what he thinks, but to try an' do somethin' about it."

Tim laughed cynically. "I wouldn't say that most Australians don't want to Paddy. Trouble is that most Australians can't seem to. We won't try an' finish what we started. Whether it's the penchant to want to drown our problems in booze, I don't know? But we do seem to need someone like Daniel to lead us. Yet I guess in some ways Daniel lacks the lustre - the image. You know, like the ones who started the American War of Independence."

Tim again slid his glass across to the bartender, picking up Paddy's on the way.

"Yeah," went on Tim. "They tower up in history. We've

never had such men. It's probably the reason we've never had a real revolution in Australia, with all due respects to Eureka. Whether we like it or not, we're still forced to look up to dear ole England, more'n twelve thousand miles away. I guess that's why we always finish up givin' in to bastards like that Mines Minister today."

"I guess it takes money," grinned Paddy, sipping his beer thirstily. "What I mean is to break off the ties with the Old Dart, we need to be more wealthy. More rich true Australians."

Tim gave a scowl. "But then can you trust 'em still? "Look at the rich squatters' sons in New South Wales an' Victoria. Currency Lads, they called 'em, like William Wentworth, who pretty well dubbed himself the first true Australian. But did he support the diggers in the Eureka Rebellion? No! Rather he desired to form a New Australia on the pattern of dear old England. Of course the whole thing with the ex-convict Bunyip Aristocracy whom Wentworth represented was that they had to stay sympathetic to the good ole Mother Country because she controlled the market for their wool. No, I'm afraid it will be a long time before us Australians grow up, matey."

Tim handed Paddy a full glass of beer. "Anyhow, we could go on and on about it, but I guess Daniel will need a hand with that special edition won't he?"

"Oh he's put on that Canadian, Max Heinrikson. As a journalist he could leave me for dead."

Tim looked at his friend closely. "With the end of the fight for the alluvials you've lost all interest again, haven't you cobber? But someone like you needs a continuous challenge. As don't we all. Otherwise we try to drown our miseries in grog."

"Yeh, I guess so Tim. The fight over the alluvials did stir me up a bit, an' now it's over as far as the paper's concerned, I couldn't care less."

"But what about your dear friend Ashley? Think about

his column in the *Kalgoorlie Advocate* with all the I-told-you-so's about the fight for the alluvials. Your leaders know best, sort o' thing. Won't that stick in your craw?"

"Yes it will Tim," replied Paddy shortly. "But I'll leave the fight to Daniel and his new reporter."

"Yeah, I s'pose for you it's best matey. What's left is only a sort of protective fight, lookin' after the interests of former diggers now turned to mineworkers. Yeah, though tough, it could be far from excitin'."

Tim grabbed Paddy by the arm, almost spilling his beer.

"Look matey, you mightn't believe it, but it was true what I said the other night about bein' fed up with Kalgoorlie. In fact, like you I've had a gutsful. Kalgoorlie from now on will just be a place where workers can spend all their pay in the pubs after slavin' down the mines. Give me the old days when it looked like just about every man could recover enough gold to be his own boss." Tim sipped his beer. "I guess you've read Henry Lawson in the *Bulletin*?"

"I certainly have," said Paddy. "Even though his father was a Norwegian, an' his mother a Yank, he brings out Eureka so much it's uncanny. With never a one bossin' the other, but all gettin' along just fine, like we did in good old Coolgardie, an' I guess you did with your mates up north. You're right, Tim, with companies an' governments callin' the tune, it's all gone, hasn't it?"

"Let's both make the break an' get out while the goin's good," said Tim.

Paddy looked mystified. "What do you mean matey? I know you just ran down Kalgoorlie, but I thought it was mostly kidstakes."

Tim looked around through the tobacco-smoke, at the lightly-gowned lasses who served behind the long bar, at the occasional entertainer who now sat close beside a digger at one of the less occupied tables. He glanced again at the busier tables where diggers were engrossed in poker or pontoon.

"No, I meant it," grinned Tim. "Kalgoorlie to me's become like one o' these good-lookin' trollops right here. Here to enjoy when you want her, but my God, what an expensive bitch to live with?"

Tim's grip tightened on Paddy's arm.

"Look Paddy, you've still got money and so have I. What about us gettin' an expedition together an' prospectin' up Mt Margaret way, a coupla hundred miles north? I've talked to some prospectors about the place an' though they still call it just the Mt Margaret area, it's really a greenstone range, most of it runnin' around fifty miles from nor-west to south-east with Mt Margaret to the right o' the top end. But from what they were tellin' me, the best show up there so far seems to be Mt Leonora, more to the west."

Though attracted by Tim's plan, Paddy still had a few reservations. "What about that crowd that ran outa water on the way back from Mt Margaret last year? They had to shoot most o' their packhorses to survive."

"Oh they went too far east," advised Tim. "Anyway, if we go we'll be takin' camels. Also rather than followin' the waterless gold trail due north, I'd prefer to detour west round Lake Ballard. More in the settled station country, where there's one or two stock wells. Could be chances of findin' gold there too. Seein' we'll be makin' for Leonora, divertin' round the lake mightn't be that far out of our road, anyhow."

"Yep, I guess that's a good idea but if Wilga comes with us, which I know he will, it'll be goin' close to Clayton Downs station on the western edge o' the lake. I don't know whether I mentioned it or not, but the Clayton-Brownes regard Wilga's little family clan as their own. Under law they could still grab Wilga."

Tim laughed loudly. "Yeah, like the rotten bastards do up north." He put his hand on a revolver he always carried at his side. "But seein' Wilga's a friend of ours, it could be a fine time to break the tradition, couldn't it chum?"

"It sure could," grinned Paddy. "And if you're askin' me now if I wished to go. Well cobber, just lead on, I can't get outa this rotten place quick enough."

CHAPTER 11

"Hooshta...! Hooshta-aa...!

"Bloody hell!" swore Tim. "You awkward long-legged bastards. Give me a nag anytime."

Paddy and Tim were having problems with camels. They had planned a roundabout route to Mt Leonora and were taking no chances with running out of water.

Also Tim McBride had in mind that he and Paddy might later journey north-westward from Mt Leonora into the Murchison, were he and his Victorian adventurer mates had followed on the heels of another t'othersider, J.F Connelly, who in 1890 had found reasonably payable gold on a sheep-run, around two hundred and fifty miles east-nor-east of Geraldton.

The contrary camels Paddy and Tim were attempting to handle were new to the country, being part of a consignment which had arrived from India three months earlier. Accompanying those sent to Kalgoorlie was Ahmud, an Afghan driver.

Besides Ahmud and the faithful Wilga, Paddy and Tim had employed a young half-caste, Lennie Alberts, who had been with the ill-fated party which had travelled to the Mt Margaret area the season before. Yet they were all grateful for Wilga, who knew the country to the north-west where they would be making their detour, better than any other. It was the territory where in the old days his tribespeople had spent their summers, owing to the availability of good permanent water. Yet the danger for Wilga was that in this area lay the three million acre Clayton Downs station. It was now June 1895, the little expedition having hoped by this time for a winter shower, even just enough to fill the odd gnamma hole, which lay along the first leg of their journey. They had felt optimistic when over the weekend, heavy black clouds blew in from the west. But as so often happened, Kalgoorlie hardly received enough rain to lay the dust. Not prepared to wait any longer, after saying goodbye to Daniel, they started out on the Monday, thankful for the camels, even though it took some time to get used to the rolling rollicking gait.

After four days, they had travelled nearly eighty miles, traversing an area already well-known to prospectors, as evidenced by the occasional white quartz kaolin dump next to a small mining shaft. As usual, the digger-prospectors worked in pairs, the general comment being that because most of the gold was locked into the hard quartz seams its extraction necessitated the liberal use of explosives. In the words of one dusty tired digger, who looked as if he hadn't had a bath or shave for six months. "... the flamin' gold's that hard to get out, it looks like a job for the friggin' companies, after all."

"Yeah," agreed Tim, after looking around. "What can a coupla men do without money or good equipment?"

"Yeah cobber, you hit the nail right on the head," replied the prospector.

"I'd say back there's another coupla mates who'll most likely have to sell out for a song, then go back to the deep mines in Kal' just to make a crust," commented Tim later as they rode along. "Flamin' companies! Necessary evil, that's what I call 'em."

So far they had ridden through typical Kalgoorlie territory, gently undulating redlands, wooded on the slopes with salmon and gimlet, the running gullies growing raspberry jam bush and black wattle, descending slowly into ti-tree flats interspersed with dry white lakes, bounded by salt bush, blue bush and samphire. On the way Wilga led them off the track to the occasional rock-hole, which as expected after the previous dry winter, were all empty and littered around with dead kangaroos. By one gnamma hole, Lennie Brown showed them the carcases of the four packhorses, shot the year previously to conserve water for the humans.

By the sixth day they had reached Lake Ballard, leased as part of the huge Clayton Downs station, the lake not so much a dry white expanse, but containing the odd high rocky feature, with great stretches of salt-bush and samphire, so precious as summer supplement for sheep. It was here the party rather than taking a well-defined exploration path to the right took the other to the left, Wilga growing nervous, because the route after rounding the west side of the lake would take them right into the heart of Clayton Downs station.

A day's ride and they were beyond the lake, the endless expanse of mulga - so different after the Kalgoorlie woodlands - like a dull green ocean. Wilga now rode in front and led them to what he knew had been a permanent native well, surprised to find it much deepened, walled neatly with rocks, mission-style, and equipped with a big windmill and huge squatter's tank. A flock of sheep were drinking at a trough.

Wilga had become even more edgy, and Paddy was not sure whether they should water the camels and top up the canteens. But Tim threw caution aside.

"Well, it wouldn't be the first time I've taken water from a station well without permission," he growled. "Most of our prospectin's been along the sheep and cattle runs. Right from up in the Kimberleys to way down here." He looked around. "A good thing about it was that there'd nearly always been a good mob of us diggers together. At one time up in the Pilbara, we were as many as five hundred." He smiled grimly. "O' course then, with so many behind ye' usually carryin' guns or knives, a contrary station-owner had to watch his step."

With that Tim urged his camel close to the trough. The others followed, scattering the sheep. The camels sucked up the water from the trough like so many steam-pumps, the water spurting in through the ball-valve from the big tank.

A shot rang out.

"CRACK!" And then another.

"CRACK! - ZING-G-GG!" The bullets clipped the ironstone rock and kaolin, which composed most of the well dump.

Tim's hand flew to his revolver, and Paddy touched the butt of a rifle which projected from a sheath strapped to his camel-saddle.

"I suppose you realise you are trespassing," came the voice, cultured and clear. "All right, my man," the voice said to Tim. "You won't need that pistol, I've got a Winchester repeater trained right on you."

The man on horseback now came into full view. His creamy white moleskins might have come straight from a Chinese laundry. His light blue shirt looked fresh and spotless and the black waistcoat matched his highly polished riding boots. On his head he wore a rakish wide-brimmed hat with curled edges and plaited leather band. He also wore a revolver and cartridge belt, similar to Tim's.

But although he was dandily-dressed and his speech gave hint of an educated background, his eyes were dark and steely, the jaw out-thrust, the nose beakish over the handsome moustache. He looked one not to be taken lightly.

"Jesus," said Paddy to Tim, almost in a whisper. "Julien Clayton-Browne. It can't be our day."

But Tim was already speaking to the station-owner.

"We've run shorta water."

"Yes, I can see that," answered the man, still cradling the rifle expertly. "But usually travellers ask permission. The station-house is only five miles away."

"Sorry," returned Tim, reluctantly. "Next time we certainly will. Anyhow, if the water's so precious, we'll pay for it."

"No, forget it," conceded Clayton-Browne. "It's just that we have to be careful these days. There are still hundreds of prospectors combing the countryside looking for gold, but you must agree we station people often find ourselves supplying them with free water and tucker. It becomes a nuisance, not to say - expensive."

Both Paddy and Tim could have argued, but as it seemed he was still going to let them fill their canteens besides watering their camels, it was probably better to keep the peace - especially with a rifle trained on you.

All at once there was a scurrying of sheep next to a patch of mulga about a hundred yards distant. Three coloured station hands were herding sheep into a wing which led into a yard. Though they were all dressed in dungarees and faded check shirts, there was little doubt that two of them were females. One of the shepherdesses had caught sight of Wilga and waved to him. But Wilga had been trying to keep out of sight behind the big stock tank in case he was recognised by his former employer. Wilga knew that because his thumbprint had been placed on a piece of paper by the Clayton-Brownes, he was theirs to do as they wished, even possibly to take his life if he tried again to run away.

Clayton-Browne had now recognised Wilga and his handsome face creased in a frown.

"I suppose you know you have one of my station boys there," he said, still cradling the rifle. "We've had trouble with you prospectors before. One of the McAllum properties further to the north-west has actually had some of their lubras kidnapped."

Tim drew his pistol as quick as a flash, catching Clayton-Browne off guard and forcing him to drop his rifle.

"Right," snapped Tim. "Yes Mister Browne, we prospectors have taken your women. As a matter o' fact, since I came over here by way o' the Kimberleys eight years ago, I've had a lot of experience with you Westralian squatters. Me an' me prospector mates have travelled right down searchin' for gold. The Kimberleys, the Pilbara, the Fortescue, the Gascoyne, an' yes, the Murchison, because I was up there well east o' Geraldton after Connelly made the first strike, which if I remember was on a McAllum station. Yes Mr Browne, we have taken your lubras, but they didn't need much persuadin' I tell ye'. Because it's slaves ye've made of 'em, far more than the bucks, because the bucks, like Wilga here, often go walkabout don't they, an' forget to come back?" He gave a harsh laugh, again waving his pistol. "No Mister Browne, this time I'm afraid you're outa luck. Right, Lennie, Ahmud, Wilga!" roared Tim. "Fill up the rest o' the canteens. We're on our way."

By this time Paddy had grabbed his rifle, training it on Clayton-Browne, while Tim mounted his camel. Tim did likewise for Paddy.

"You'll be sorry!" retorted Clayton-Browne with temper. "There's a law."

Paddy reacted angrily.

"What bloody law Mister Browne? What you mean the law of the Hungry Six? One of my friends was up in Carnarvon when you mob persecuted that poor bloody Gribble, the missionary. Not only do you own most o' the sheep-runs up there, but you also hand out the sentences, don't you? One o' your clan's still the local Magistrate. It's the bloody same in Geraldton, isn't it Mister Browne? If I remember rightly the Magistrate's your brother Desmond."

"There are only a few families in the colony educated enough to take on judicial work," defended Clayton-Browne haughtily.

"An' I'd bet you'd prefer to keep it that way," cut in Tim, scornfully. "But I tell you matey, you'd better make the most of it. With all us t'othersiders over here to take the vote, your days are past."

Tim suddenly became impatient, again waving his revolver.

"Lennie, Ahmud, Wilga! Mount your camels. Quick, before I do somethin' I might regret. Hurry up, now, we're leavin."

Wilga couldn't get out of the place fast enough, but as he went to urge his camel, one of the young station lubras ran over to him, calling.

"Wilga-aa! Wilga-aaa!"

But Tim sent her back with a wave of his hand.

"No sweetheart. You stay for a while. But who knows, the way things are changin', it might not be long before we're back to take you away. In fact, anyone that wants to come."

With that Tim and Wilga urged their ungainly mounts to catch up with the others.

From then on they pressed the camels hard, constantly in fear that Clayton-Browne and his staff might catch up with them on horse-back. Just in case, Tim had armed everyone with a pistol or rifle. Ahmud immediately dropped a parrot out of the air with the Winchester, showing his prowess as a former Afghan tribesman who had fought against the British.

That night they took turns to mount guard. And it was not till late the next day, when having passed a long steel peg denoting the Clayton-Browne boundary, they felt they were safe from pursuit.

They now headed north-east, and by the next afternoon they sighted a prominent feature in the same direction. Lennie had little need to tell them it was part of the greenstone range leading east-nor-east to Mt Margaret, Mt Leonora being more to the north. By the end of the day they had reached the stony foothills area, where they found a small encampment of toughened prospectors who had not seen civilisation for more than six months. But from reports of the rich gold strikes, it was obvious that once word reached the populace, Leonora as it had come to be known, could trigger yet another boom. There was even hopeful talk of a railway from Kalgoorlie to serve the whole Mt Margaret area, which when put through the harsh waterless lands to the east of Lake Ballard would be a Godsend.

After a couple of day's rest, Tim suggested that they establish the boundaries of the greenstone and the alluvial. Riding fifty miles or so due-west, they soon found themselves tracing a narrowish saltlake to the right, with higher border grounds of pinkish sandplain covered in tussock grass, scrub pine, and mallee. Next day they were again in the mulga-lands.

Apart from an isolated hillock, which Tim declared contained traces of copper, it was felt they were now out of the likely gold country. So Tim at the head of the party, now turned right about, to lead east over miles and miles of broken stony range. Three days after passing the prominent Mt Margaret feature itself, they found themselves on a desert-like plain, seemingly endless and covered in a miserable species of spinifex, with the occasional desert oak and scrawny eucalypt. After a good day's ride without change, they decided to turn back, the silhouette of Mt Margaret in the distance a comforting sight.

While wiping off perspiration with his neckerchief, Paddy spat in disgust.

"Christ, what forlorn lookin' country. An' from what I've heard, it's like this all the way to South Australia, an' more."

"You're right at that matey," said Tim. "Still more'n six hundred miles, an' hardly a solid rock, let alone a reef. In fact, from what I know of geology, it's part of an old sea-bed."

"An' not a skerrick o' fresh water, I understand. Ernie Giles crossed it in '75 an' called it the Great Victoria Desert? Christ, if ever anyone deserved a knighthood, it's him."

Tim gave a harsh laugh. "I thought we'd been over that subject before cobber. Over here in the west the only ones who are recommended for titles are the ones who come from the best families; and o' course, that also goes for explorers." The digger-geologist took a drink out of his water-bag. "Anyway, hooshta-aa. Let's be on our way."

Returning to camp, Tim decided to concentrate on the ironstone slopes which had proven so well near Kalgoorlie. And as he happily explained, the other mob had not looked half enough. As soon as Tim had witnessed the dark-topped hills, he recognised their possibilities. He knew that the streaks of brown which ran down the slopes could lead to the gossans which could cover rich seams of quartz, often loaded with gold. Finally, Tim marked out the extremities of four rich areas he believed could rival some of the best strikes around Kalgoorlie.

It had been their intention with the onset of summer to travel nor-west, not only searching for more likely gold areas, but ultimately to reach the Murchison fields which lay inland from the port of Geraldton, and which according to reports since Tim had prospected there in 1890, had grown tremendously. Yet in Leonora, the early summer heat had become so intense that they decided to stay around and cool off in a drive-shaft they had dug into the southern side of an ironstone slope. They had also erected their tents with large flies on top, for added coolness. The location was also close to one of the few gnamma holes in the area which was fed by a permanent spring.

With the continuing century heat, they had even contemplated waiting till around early May, the start of the following winter before they struck out for the Murchison.

What helped them to make up their minds to leave in late February 1896, was a rare half inch of rain from a summer thunderstorm.

They had now accumulated more gold than they could possibly carry on their pack-camels. It was opportune that during their sojourn in Leonora, the assistant government Warden had arrived there from Kalgoorlie. Apart from carrying enough gold to change into ready cash later, they left the rest with the assistant Warden who could take it to Kalgoorlie when he returned. They also registered their claims, which Tim had decided to offer for a high price to a well-known British company. It was also arranged for the assistant Warden to deliver a letter to Daniel, not only asking him to negotiate the mining deal, but also telling of their adventures on the gold-trail, including the confrontation with Julien Clayton-Browne.

Next morning after the rain, with Tim taking the lead, they headed north-west, the air deliciously cool after the rain. They rode for three days, finding rock-holes brimming full, the mulga scrub already green and revived. The party followed the ridges for nearly ninety miles, finding plenty of signs of gold, but without the promise of Mt Leonora. Also here it was obvious it had not rained here for many months, even years, the mulgas withered and browning, the pink soils dry and dusty. The following day, about twenty miles to the north, a feature known as Mt Keith came into view. By nightfall they were close to the base of the mount, the coarse gravel slopes giving little indication of gold. After camping the night, and riding north for two more days, they found themselves more and more in red ironstone country.

Tim always carried a compass in his kit, and also a sextant which he often used at night-time to take a cross-sight on the stars.

"We're almost outa the Murchison and into the Gascoyne," he said to Paddy one late evening over a whisky. "Time we headed sou-west. Remember that assistant Warden talkin' about a new strike in a place called Meekathara. Reckon if we leave early tomorrow, we could just about reach it by sundown."

And Tim was right. In fact, Paddy had come to admire this toughened Victorian more and more, despite his sometimes uncouth comments. Yet there was also a feeling of envy, because it seemed that in the few years Tim had been in the West, he had learnt more about the outback than most Western Australians would in their whole lifetimes.

Though only in existence a few months, Meekathara was already proving itself a bonanza, similar to Cue, which was around sixty miles to the south. Only ten miles further on was Day Dawn, with two pubs, a bank, a general store, and judging by its size another good gold show. Then a day's ride across the huge salt expanse of Lake Austin, with a mine poppet-head rearing in the midst of the lake itself. They then headed south for Mt Magnet, eighty miles on.

The usually taciturn Tim was astonished to see how Magnet had grown since 1891, when though it had been discovered before the glittering Coolgardie, the prospects at the time were only mediocre. But now the town was as thriving and colourful as Coolgardie was at its best, with three newspapers, a dozen trading houses and a half-dozen pubs.

Paddy was struck with it too, as he remarked to Tim while they drank whiskies in the coolness of the Magnet, the most popular pub. "Back in 1880 Daniel had said that this colony needed gold to make it go. He was not far wrong."

"But it will need more than gold matey," replied Tim, wisely. "These places, as lively as they are, could turn into ghost-towns if the gold runs out. It's happened all over the globe. They need somethin' besides gold to keep 'em alive. I guess that's why Victoria was so lucky. Take Ballarat an' Bendigo. After the gold ran out, with the rich red soils an' the reliable rains, the miners were able to turn to agriculture. But with bugger-all rain an' near desert, what have you got here besides gold? You'd never be able to put in a plough, an' even with livestock. Why, it's so bare round here they'd be lucky to run one sheep to every fifty friggin' acres."

"Well, at least it's somethin'," returned Paddy, with a shrug of his shoulders. "But you are right, pretty well right though our gold-areas, even those up north, apart from runnin' sheep an' a few cattle - which need to be flamin' hardy at that - there's bugger-all else to make a quid."

Tim grabbed Paddy's glass, performing his usual ritual of sliding it over to the barman with his own. "Anyway cobber, as long as the gold sees us out, eh? Let our leaders do the worryin', such as they are by God."

Paddy laughed carelessly. "Strange that you should say

that Tim. Remember you were the one who said that the Groves Gang and its kind was finished."

"Yeah, I guess I made sort of a pledge, didn't I matey?"

"More a threat, I'd say," grinned Paddy.

They had already cashed their gold with the Mount Magnet Warden, and next day they headed for Yalgoo, eighty miles west, said to be the last of the gold towns before the one hundred and fifty miles to Geraldton and the sea. They found the track literally choked with horse-teams, pulling huge wagons packed to the hilt with stores and mining gear, most on their way to Cue and Meekathara. They had just settled down to what seemed a quiet section of road when a strong black coach sped past, enveloped in red dust and pulled by six frisky horses with flying manes. It was accompanied by a heavily-armed trooper escort.

"Christ, there goes the gold-coach," yelled Paddy, over to Tim. "Not takin' any chances, are they?"

"Well there's been one or two held up, hasn't there?" yelled Tim. "Not that we've got the time to practise Ned Kellys, I'd rather a breath o' the ocean at Geraldton."

But that was not to be for a long time.

On the second afternoon, they reached Yalgoo, comfortably set among greenstone hills. Yet in the town there was great excitement, because within a week, the railway was expected to arrive from Geraldton, then to push its way slowly to Mt Magnet and possibly up and beyond, even to Meekathara.

Yalgoo was on the western edge of the gold-country, the boundary running approximately along the Gnow's Nest Range. It was the habitat of the mallee-hen, and terminated around sixty miles to the sou-sou-east near a comparatively new gold town called Field's Find.

So after a rest in Yalgoo including a few beers and more talks with the locals, which included a discussion about good prospects along the Gnow's Nest Range, they headed south for Field's Find.

The party had been amongst the mulga for months, but now as they rode south, they noticed it giving way to raspberry jam and bowgada, and in the wide gullies leading into the dry lakes grew a type of York-gum, with an undercover of prickly heath and black wattle. On the ridges the ground was often hard and lateritic, with patches of loose white quartz as could be seen around a tombstone. They soon began to pass small groups of prospectors who were using Yalgoo as their base. Many were on bicycles, the bumpiness of the tyres suggesting they were rammed with sheep's wool, the usual inner tube being too prone to punctures.

They also passed many flocks of sheep. By their generally poor condition combined with the way the acacia herbage was eaten up right out of reach, the effects of the dry seasons were evident.

The flocks were usually cared for by lubras, with the occasional white stockman watching over them. The number of half-caste children accompanying the shepherdesses brought a hard-bitten remark from Tim.

"Us white-fellas have certainly been sowin' our wild oats round here, haven't we chum?"

Paddy nodded his head. "Yeah, looks like it."

"You know up in the Gascoyne we did a bit o' prospectin' in the Kennedy Ranges, where some o' the Myalls, as they call the bucks, had still managed to evade the flockowners," Tim went on. "Sometimes the odd female would return to the tribe an' have a white-fella child. But out in Myall country, the half-white kid was always grabbed off the lubra an' done away with, whether she liked it or not."

"Yeah," replied Paddy grimly, glad that Lennie and Wilga were to the rear, out of earshot. "I guess you couldn't blame the Myalls in some ways. Daniel told me a lot about it after he'd been up north years ago. Remember me talkin' about that poor devil of a missionary, Gribble. Well, one o' the things he was run outa the colony for was because he had complained about the libidinous way the whites were carryin' on up there with the coloured womenfolk."

Tim gave a harsh laugh. Describes a lot, libidinous, doesn't it? But what with the old bucks not allowin' a young buck to touch a female till he's well over twenty, an' with the young females ready for it at around twelve, makes the term even more interesting doesn't it? But I'd say right up a randy station-owner's alley."

"I guess you're right Tim," returned Paddy abruptly, looking to change the subject. "I guess you're right."

Late the next afternoon, they reached Field's Find, established the year previously. There was already a sizeable settlement set in a rich red valley between two quartzite ridges about a half mile apart. To the east was the northern termination of what was known as the Pinyalling Hills. Both the range country to the east and the mining country to the west, drained steeply into a narrow section of Lake Monger, in total a huge, usually dry salt pan, around a hundred miles long, which ran in a strip from the north-east, widening rapidly to the south-west of Field's Find.

Field's Find had already proven its worth in alluvial gold. James Field, its discoverer, had made enough in twelve months to retire to Perth. As yet in Fields there was neither law nor Warden. One self-confessed claim-jumper had taken advantage and had already recovered a small fortune in gold from a claim said to belong to a small British company, now absent.

All in all, the location for Tim had an aura of expectancy about it. Whether it was the gold, which some said could be still picked up on top of the ground like orange peel, or whether it was just the environment, was hard to explain. But the feeling was there.

The first morning the rising sun had turned the northern tips of the Pinyallings a glorious rose-red, while only a couple of hours after midday the same sun cast mysterious shadows from the jagged jasper outcrops over the blood-red alluvial. And as the day waned, there were those few wisps of cloud to the west, reflecting the gorgeous pink and grey of the setting sun. In Tim's words, as pretty as 'neath the wings of a galah cockatoo ...

Tim was so struck with the place - both the gold potential and the environment - that he decided to team up with the claim-jumper. "Just for the heck of it!"

Despite its attraction, the area was suffering from the extremely dry run of seasons, experienced not only in the Murchison, but through the whole of the pastoral areas including Kalgoorlie. That summer thunderstorm which had fallen on Leonora, enabling Paddy and Tim to continue on the gold-trail, had been one out of the blue.

As the red alluvial country of Field's Find made it difficult to find good water, it was being carted from a spring in the Pinyalling's. Here also a small offshoot of the well-known Yamadgee tribe spent their summers, later ranging north south or east as a winter suited them. West beyond the southern tip of Lake Monger however, was out of bounds for the Yamadgees. For here since the beginning of time had roamed the Balardi, now mostly shepherding sheep for the New Norcia Mission, located one hundred and fifty miles to the south-west.

It seemed that both Ahmud and Lennie had also taken a liking to the Field's Find locality, both gaining permission from Paddy and Tim to use the camels to haul the town's water-wagon to and fro from the Pinyalling Hills. Wilga was also content to stay, as could be seen by the way he practised spear and boomerang throwing with other natives who appeared to enjoy hanging around the little mining-town.

Paddy explained to Tim how Wilga had told him that the young native himself was related to the Yamadgees. "Reckons he's been here before with his father and uncles when he was only a boy. He's even been as far up along the Gnow's Nest Range nearly to Yalgoo. From what I can gather the Yamadgees use Mt Singleton down further to the south-east as a sort o' sighting point when they are on walkabout, similar to Mt Churchman further to the south-east. Then there's Mt Jackson, well north o' Southern Cross."

"Yeah," said Tim. "I've seen 'em on a survey map. They form a sort of a big crescent with Mt Singleton on one tip pointin' north to the Pinyallin's an' up here, an' Mt Jackson on the other tip pointin' east. Mt Churchman o' course is more sou-west, in the hollow part o' the crescent. Yeah, the blacks in their own way probably do use the mounts as observation points, similar to our early explorers." Tim's eyes went dreamy.

"You can imagine a crowd o' Yamadgees on walkabout standin' on one o' the mounts thousands o' years ago an' surveyin' the land as it was. So I suppose to the new Yamadgees these mounts are kinda sacred - got their own names for 'em too, I'll bet. Could ask Wilga sometime?"

"Yeah, we could do that Tim," replied Paddy, admiring the more philosophical scientific side of his friend.

But Tim soon revealed the more hard-bitten part of his character.

"Yeah," he went on. "These local lubras are quite comely too, aren't they? Seein' I've taken to the joint, wouldn't mind grabbin' myself a Mary."

"It could be an idea," agreed Paddy, not wanting to appear prudish in an area where white womenfolk were so scarce.

Maybe Tim was being honest and practical thought Paddy. He had remembered as a lad, secretly listening to the conversations of his elders. Grandpa David had spoken about John Hutt who was Governor of the Swan River Colony between 1839 and '44. According to Grandpa David, John Hutt had considered the possibility in a place so short of white womenfolk, and where young female Aborigines seemed over-plentiful, that the authorities should encourage the settlers to take on dusky brides.

Paddy realised however, that though the little mining town was completely devoid of white womenfolk, the South Murchison district was not. Some pastoral properties had been settled as far back as 1875.

Yet Field's Find apart from the odd lubra, was obviously a man's town, and it was a surprise to Paddy when one day the little settlement did have a white female visitor. Not that the surprise was unpleasant. Jenny Dunbar was riding with her father to visit friends at Thundelarra station, around fifteen miles nor-nor-east of Field's. The Dunbar lease lay south-east across the Pinyallings. Paddy recognised the father as Will Dunbar, eldest son of Jim Dunbar - Henry Lovedale's old friend who had first established Mt Rupert, the well-known grazing and farming property eighty miles north of Northam.

Jenny and her father halted their horses outside the store where Paddy and Tim were talking under the verandah. Despite her plain riding habit and battered stock hat, the young woman excited the imagination.

CHAPTER 12

"Meet my daughter Jennifer," said Will Dunbar, after the men had exchanged familiarities.

"Pleased to meet you both," smiled his daughter.

Her voice had that same pleasantness as her father, even a trace of burr, doubtless inherited from her grandfather Angus Macregor, long famous in Swan River as the Shepherd King. Macregor had first leased a huge spread of land southeast of New Norcia, and had helped Jim Dunbar start on Mt Rupert. The American had later wed Jeannie, Macregor's only daughter.

"Please call me Jenny," the young woman said. "I get called far worse on the station during shearing."

Paddy could not help liking her. She appeared to be about eighteen, her light brown hair under the old stock hat showing the occasional glint of gold. Her eyes were grey-blue and her features well-shaped with a small slightly upturned nose. Her jaw was just a little determined. Yes, Paddy thought, a romantic picture of a flockowner's daughter, obviously not one of the pastoral gentry but one who might hold her own anywhere.

"Pleased to meet you likewise Jenny," replied Paddy casually. And as if for something to say, went on. "Been dry round here, hasn't it?"

"I'll say it has." Jennifer's, eyes were now concerned, showing that she shared the worries of the station with her family. "Father and I were just on our way to Thundelarra station to cry on another grazier's shoulder so to speak. About the long drought, I mean."

"Yeah," added Jenny's father in his slow easy drawl. "It's been the worst we've had since coming out here back in 1880."

"But it's nearly the same all over isn't it?" queried Paddy. "Since 1893 they've had it pretty dry round York too."

Will's face grew taut. "My God, it's been far longer than that round here. We haven't really had a good rain since '91."

"Could've been the gold-rush," Tim joked looking skywards. "The Good Lord up there."

"Yeah, probably too many rough heathen prospectors," replied Will good humouredly, yet showing that he had already sized Tim up. "Look, sorry," he went on quickly. "But we must be on our way. We want to get to Thundelarra before dark. Might see you on the way back tomorrow. Cheerio."

After they had left, Tim put his hand on Paddy's shoulder. "I reckon they'll be callin' in all right matey," he grinned. "Especially if young Jenny has her way. Not that she'd be one to chase after a man. Looks too sensible for that. All the same, when she left she had that look in her eye." He laughed out loud. "Yeah, I reckon they might be droppin' in. So we'd better keep an eye out, eh cobber?"

Paddy grinned self-consciously. "I guess so, I guess so. But who says they'll be stayin'?"

"Wanna take a bet?" grinned Tim, pulling a small piece of gold from his pocket. "In fact, if you like I'll lay on a whole twenty ounces."

Jennifer and her father did call in next day, and invited both Paddy and Tim to the Dunbar homestead. But after they rode off, Tim declined, saying that he'd probably be cramping Paddy's style.

"Aw, cut it out cobber," Paddy had protested, while sharing a few whiskies that night with Tim in the ramshackle pub, which like the store was open to all-comers at any time. "Anyway, where can I find a horse? It'd seem a bit queer payin' 'em a visit on a camel."

"My new prospector mate's got one," said Tim, taking

a sip of whisky. "A bit long in the tooth, I will admit. Still, a bit more sedate than a camel."

"Looks like I've got no choice," grinned Paddy.

Next morning Paddy left for the Dunbar property. The station was fifteen miles east-south-east of the mining town. After following a track over the gravelly Pinyalling Hills, Paddy emerged out into light scrubplain, the soil pink and quartzy. The homestead in the distance was on slightly higher ground and as Paddy rode up he was impressed by its setting. Well to the south stood the lone peak of Mt Singleton, while to the west reared the Pinyallings, bounding the huge saltbush and mulga flat, which comprised the bulk of the station.

Mrs Dunbar was well-spoken, reminding Paddy somewhat of his mother. He was surprised to hear that Peg Dunbar was the daughter of an English transportee, Harold Carey, an educated man, who after his conditional pardon had been granted a teaching job in Goomalling. At the time Goomalling was a new agricultural settlement, sixty miles north of Northam and around eighteen miles south of Mt Rupert, the property of the original Dunbars. Harold Carey's wife and daughter had been allowed to emigrate from England even while Carey himself was still ticket-of-leave. The husband and wife later became highly respected citizens of Goomalling.

As Goomalling was the nearest school at the time to Mt Rupert, Will and his brothers and sisters were educated there. It was then that the Dunbar family made the acquaintance of the Careys who agreed to board the Dunbar children during the school week. In years to come, Will Dunbar was to fall in love with Harold Cary's daughter, Peg.

In fact, the Dunbars were so open and honest about their relationship with an ex-convict - still heavily frowned on by the better-class families - that Paddy naturally brought up his own heritage causing Will Dunbar to laugh loudly.

"Of course we know of your father, Paddy. Who wouldn't

know Michael O'Leary, our brave Fenian? He's become a legend." Will grasped Paddy's shoulder in friendly fashion. "Paddy, you've become like one o' the family already, what about sharin' a whisky? I know it's only Monday, but it's like a special occasion. Also with shearin' an' musterin' over, maybe we've got time to listen to your adventures on the gold-trail."

"No, no whisky in the morning Will," ordered his wife with finality. "Better a nice cup of tea."

Will gave a grin. "Well, I guess 'round the house you're boss, Peg. So it looks like we'll just have to settle for a cuppa."

They sat outside in deck-chairs on the station-house verandah, while a pair of smiling Aborigine girls brought out tea and scones. From where they sat, they had a clear view of Mt Singleton to the south, its two thousand foot rising above the plain, clear against the skyline.

"Looks grand, doesn't it?" Paddy remarked.

"Yes, I guess it does," said Jenny, answering for her father. "That's if you don't look too hard at the country between. You must have noticed all the dead mulga and saltbush."

"I reckon I did," returned Paddy. "Still, your sheep look in good heart, far better than some of those we saw on the way down from Yalgoo."

"It's because we're not overstocked," said Will. "Those ewes you saw have been three seasons without lambs. We've now learnt not to put the rams in with the ewes until the season is assured." Will gave a sigh. "But when that'll be, God only knows?"

"Of course," said Jenny, "what Dad hasn't told you, is that our sheep also have the benefit of an extra run. For two years now we've had permission from Templetons to run our flocks on Singleton station, which surrounds the mount down there."

Paddy opened his eyes with interest. "I don't quite get what you mean?"

"Oh, the former owner went broke," explained Will. "Had the bad luck to start in '91, right in the beginning of the Murchison drought. Templetons, the big livestock and loan company finally ran him off."

"But you must admit John Tracy had big ideas Will," broke in his wife. "Tried to fence the whole half million acres when most of the stations around here have still got hardly a wire on them. What with John Tracy putting up the most up-to-date shearing-shed and windmills besides."

"And all that talk from his wife about a big mansion of a house," added Jenny. "Still, we'd just had a run of good seasons, and they'd just come out from England with money."

"An' I guess Templetons were ready at the time to back 'em to the hilt," said Paddy grimly. "But o' course when the company looked like losin' a bit, they decided to run 'em off. Sounds to me like the same old story."

"Yeah," offered Will, handing his tea-cup to his wife to be re-filled. "From my experience in this land, you've got to be prepared to take the good with the bad, which banks and livestock companies won't always do. The trouble is, new chums like John Tracy get caught."

"That's right," said Paddy. "Just like my Grandpa David used to say, and I guess you've heard o' him. He reckoned that even round York, when workin' out your future capital, you had to allow for one bad season in three."

"Which means out here, three bad ones out of five," rejoined Will grimly. "An' worse."

"Yes," said Jenny, a sad faraway look in her eyes. "As you said Dad, and worse. Why, when we last had a good season I was still going to school in Goomalling. Remember that spring holiday Mum, when I brought friends home. Townies, you called them. Remember how they were in rhapsodies about the size of the pin-cushion everlastings compared to those at Goomalling. All colours, and almost up to your knees."

"Yes Jenny," replied her mother, wistfully. "We've almost

forgotten what they look like. Yet when you were little, we had three seasons like that in a row."

Paddy was a little pensive, knowing that with these station families, talk about the better seasons was all so important.

Will broke the silence. "Anyhow Paddy, tell us about the gold."

Paddy told them about his adventures around early Coolgardie with Daniel, the dance-hall girls and the typhoid, the growth of Kalgoorlie and the disappointments of the diggers who had come over to the west with starry eyes, intending to make their fortunes. But they were eventually forced to lose their independence and work down the mines for the big companies.

"Yeah, the *Geraldton Express*, of which we sometimes get a copy, wrote quite a lot about that," said Will. "But how has the gold panned out for you Paddy?"

"Well, not bad." Paddy wondered whether he should tell them about his stake with Daniel in mines both in Coolgardie and Kalgoorlie. But he finished up telling almost all, opening Jenny's eyes wide, especially concerning their rich finds over at Leonora.

"But why did you come down to a dry hole like Field's Find?" she questioned. "When you said it was your intention to travel on to Geraldton and catch the train via the new Midland Railway to Perth."

"Oh I guess I could blame Tim," shrugged Paddy, noncommittally. "I really don't think he ever wishes to go back to civilisation. Even though it's a dry hole, as you say, I believe he's already struck on Field's. But if we get what we expect for our claims he could probably return to his beloved Victoria, and retire for the rest of his life."

"What about you Paddy?" asked Jenny, becoming suddenly embarrassed, because she knew she was fishing.

"Don't know really," replied Paddy, still lightheartedly. "I guess I've done pretty well outa the gold too, an' o' course it was my intention to live it up a bit in Perth, an' then even go back to the old York farm for awhile." He put his hand to his chin. "It's strange isn't it, but like Tim, there's somethin' about this part of the globe I like too?"

As her daughter lowered her eyes a little, Peg Dunbar answered. "Well you're not the first one Paddy, because I liked it right from the start, and still do, despite the droughts." She laughed. "It's so totally ridiculous isn't it?"

"Oh, cut out the sentimentality Peg," said Will, not unpleasantly. He turned to Paddy. "You seem to have a lot of time for Wilga, the Aboriginal."

"Well I do. Remember I told you that he was the one who really put Bayley an' Ford onto the first gold strike in Coolgardie. The big one. As a matter o' fact for some reason he took a likin' to me, of all people."

"I'll bet it's because you treat him with understanding Paddy," smiled Peg Dunbar. "As we try to treat our natives here." She turned to her husband. "Tell him about Worral and Nandi."

"Yes," cut in Paddy. "I've met them both, they called into our farm at York with your parents Will, an' o' course you an' your brothers an' sisters were there too."

"Now I do recall," said Will. "But that was a long time ago. "Anyhow, Worral an' Nandi's nippers are now grown up, an' in fact two are workin' on our station here. The rest of the family is still livin' at Mt Rupert workin' for my two younger brothers. Worral an' Nandi both died only in the last three years."

"Like Aunty Liz an' Uncle Henry Lovedale," said Paddy. "They only went in the last five years too. But they were gettin' on, weren't they? Guess we've all gotta go, sometime. Anyway, with Worral an' Nandi's children here, what's this about the regular natives not bein' friendly with other natives from the west? Or I should say sou-west I suppose, down towards the Darling Ranges."

"Oh, we had trouble on the station here for awhile," said Will. "But now, believe it or not, they get on well. As a

223

matter of fact, the two girls we have here now are from the local Yamadgee people."

"Wilga's close to the Yamadgees too," said Paddy. "Even though his family clan's well over a hundred miles to the south-east."

"Oh yes, that's the isolated group on Clayton Downs station," said Will. "The tribes follow the ridges round not only so they can check on where they are, but usually they can dig for good water down from the stony high country, even after a long dry." Will shifted his position in the chair. "O' course you went through Clayton Downs on your way to Leonora, didn't you?"

Paddy nodded his head. "Yep, an' bringin' up the subject o' Wilga, though I didn't say earlier, that was where we struck trouble with Mister Julien Clayton-Browne himself. He tried to claim Wilga back. Even pointed a rifle at us."

Will gave a whistle. "Well with Julien it's not surprisin', but go on, tell us the whole story."

When Paddy mentioned about some station boys on Clayton Downs being girls, Peg Dunbar interjected.

"That's a custom with those families Paddy, because the real boys are always running away. But you may be sure it doesn't happen here. The only reason we employ girls is to help around the house, and then we pay them fairly."

"But the Clayton-Brownes are a completely different kettle-o'-fish," explained Will, sarcastically.

"They certainly are," continued Paddy. "As Tim McBride pointed out. An' o' course, though a Victorian, he's seen an' learnt more since he's been over here than most Western Australians. Prospected all the way down from the Kimberleys to Kalgoorlie."

"Yeah, an' that includes a lot o' station country," said Will. "Also, as you know Paddy, most of it's either owned or leased by the few top families."

"You mean the Hungry Six," grinned Paddy, still giving Will Dunbar credit for his knowledge. "Before we went chasin' gold, Daniel Hordacre an' I were reporters on the *Fremantle Herald*. It was the editor of the *Herald* who first coined the phrase, as Daniel would say."

"Yeah the Hungry Six, or what's left o' the old nob families," grinned Will. "An' they do deserve it. We used to look forward to readin' the *Herald* when the mail contractor sometimes brought it from Yalgoo along with the *Geraldton Express*. Fact is, I believe at the time the Geraldton weekly had connections with your *Herald*. Yeah, Daniel wrote that long article in the *Herald* about Gribble, didn't he? That poor unfortunate missionary who was forced outa Carnarvon by the pastoralists for tryin' to educate the natives."

"And even penalised by his own Anglican Church," added Paddy grimly. "Like Daniel said, all for just tryin' to change the old order of things." Suddenly Paddy became cautious. "But I guess you people are pastoralists too?"

Peg Dunbar looked hurt. "I'm surprised at you thinking like that Paddy. We try to treat our natives with understanding, as Will's father did before us on Mt Rupert."

Jenny was slightly angry at Paddy. "We know all about the old families Paddy, such as the Clayton-Brownes, McAllums, Mainwarings and so forth. We know the stranglehold they have had on this colony for almost seventy years. We know how they still lease the bulk of the pastoral lands, and how they have claimed the natives on such lands as their own."

"Yeah," said Paddy, cynically. "An' all good Christians, people who should set an example. Still, with the t'othersiders gettin' the vote - like I remarked about what Tim McBride said to Clayton-Browne - their days are numbered."

"And as they all have relatives in Parliament, it means the end o' the Groves Gang too I hope," gritted Will. "All the same Paddy, until such becomes a fact, you'd still better keep an eye on Wilga. You must know the law. He's a runaway."

225

Jenny supported her father. "Yes, the same law which still allows plantation owners to retain their workers, as it was the same law which allowed the old gentry in the American south to have slaves and treat them far worse than their blood-stock race-horses."

"Same sentiments as our Westralian upper-crust," added Paddy grimly. "Except with them you add polo-ponies."

"Pity there weren't a few more like this Daniel, from what I'd read in the *Herald* an' what you tell of him," said Will. "But I guess it takes education, which so many of us lack."

"Oh, it'll come. It'll come," contributed Jenny. "I saw it happening so much when I went to school at Goomalling, helped by our outspoken teacher, himself the son of an expiree, similar to my grandfather, who we told you was himself an ex-convict. There along with children from ordinary families we learnt so many truths about our so-called well-to-do, whom we are supposed to call our betters. Betters, my God!" She screwed up her pretty face.

"Well said Jenny!" returned Paddy, as their eyes met. There was a silence, Jenny trying to hide her feelings by lowering her gaze. Paddy too, had emotions, realising that this young woman, besides being attractive, had sentiments so much similar to his own. Indeed, the whole family attracted him in a way he had not experienced since he had left the farm.

The interlude was broken by the clip-clop of hooves on the drought-parched red-soil. Three riders came into view as they passed the house from the rear. One was a young white man, the other pair Aboriginal youths. As they passed on their way to the big station shed, Will called out.

"Hey Kim, come an' meet Paddy O'Leary. Bring the boys too."

"Meet Bindi an' Badji, youngest sons of Worral and Nandi, and twins I might add," spoke Will, deliberately introducing the native lads before his son.

The lads had a contented look, their features having that

pleasant glow, peculiar only to a healthy Aboriginal. Paddy took each by the hand, each speaking in good English, enhanced more by that soft bird-like quality, again so appealing in an Aboriginal.

"An' this is Kim, my eldest," went on Will, indicating the tall, well-built young stockman.

"Meet Paddy O'Leary," said Will to his son. "Digger prospector who I'm glad to say has taken a likin' to our district, dry as it is."

"Yeah, so dry we'd like to forget it," said Kim. "Anyhow, pleased to meet you Paddy," he went on, taking Paddy's hand in a strong grip.

As he stepped under the verandah, Kim removed his station-hat, revealing his white forehead in stark contrast to the deep-blue eyes, and the reddish bronze of his well-cut features. "Looks like rain comin' up in the north," he remarked.

"Yeah," said his father. "There's been mare's tails in the northern sky for two days now. But we expect it this time of the year, don't we?" He gave a shrug. "Just the signs I mean?"

"But there's a good wind springin' up," insisted Kim, hopefully.

"Oh well, you never know," returned Will, half-turning to Paddy. "I guess we'd better say our prayers." He finished just a little sarcastically, bringing a comment from his wife, aimed at Paddy.

"Oh, Will just cracks hardy Paddy. Just because we don't go to church, doesn't mean we don't pray sometimes. And I guess if the rain really does come at last, we'll be giving thanks from our hearts too."

The tears almost came to Paddy eyes. Peg Dunbar was proving even more like Judith, his mother.

By now the two native girls had raced around from behind the house, Badji and Bindi throwing taunts at them, but in an affectionate way.

After showing Paddy around the homestead which included apologising for the state of the garden because the well was going dry, Peg sent one of the girls down to the shed to tell everyone it was time for dinner. They all sat down to the same big table, Aboriginal stockmen and all. The girls first helped Jenny serve at the table, and then they too, sat down, giving cheeky glances at the native boys, their eyes dancing.

Paddy knew that by having the natives eat at their table the Dunbars were breaking a strict convention, even though the native lads from Mt Rupert had been schooled in the New Norcia Mission. Yet he knew that the native boys in particular, had shared meals with Will's father, Jim, and Jeannie, his wife. The same could have gone on in York with Paddy's Grandma Mary, and Grandpa David, as it could still go on with Paddy's parents. And whether it was right or wrong, the reason Paddy believed in it, was what his Grandpa David had said. By letting all come to our table if they wished, we are acting right and proper as Christians. This kind of sharing, Paddy knew, had been practised so much on the track between Wilga, Ahmud and young Lennie and Tim and himself. After the meal, they all stood once more together under the verandah.

"Sorry Paddy," said Will. "But I guess I'd better earn my keep." He turned to his daughter. "Jenny, my girl, it looks like you've got the job of showin' our guest round the station. As a matter-o'-fact if Paddy's agreeable, you might start off by checkin' on the sheep down at Singleton." He turned to Paddy. "How does that strike yuh? Trouble is it's a good twenty five miles there an' back. You might finish up ridin' home to Field's in the dark."

Paddy gave a grin. "Well it wouldn't be the first time I've ridden at night. An' if Singleton is really as good as it looks from here, I'd certainly like to pay a visit." He turned. "But what about Jenny?"

She gave an appealing laugh. "Well you won't eat me will

you? I'd have had to check the sheep over there in any case, so you may as well tag along."

"Much obliged. But one thing I'd like to beg of you, is the loan of a good horse."

Will laughed loudly. "You rode over on a real bag-o-bones, didn't you? Yes Jenny, let Paddy take his pick o' the station hacks. In fact, if he wishes he could take one for keeps."

"No Mr Dunbar, I'll buy it," said Paddy.

"Just as you like Paddy," replied Will, as he walked off. "An' for Pete's sake call me Will."

"That's a command," laughed Jenny to Paddy, as she grabbed her hat and they prepared to walk over to the stable.

Paddy took his pick of the stock-ponies. Jenny was surprised when he chose one that was flighty - indeed, an Arab Cross which had thrown her brother Tim only in the very last week. But once in the saddle, she could see that Paddy was no slouch as a rider, teasing the stock-pony and making it dance before he took off at a gallop. Her old stock hat flat back with the wind, Jenny was soon racing beside him, thrilling to the chase.

Within an hour they had reached the rich red flat at the base of the mount. On the south-side of a dry creek-bed, stood a well-built shearing shed and quarters, far more elaborate than on the Dunbar property. Paddy was impressed.

"Ideal set-up," he grunted. But where's the homestead?"

"Oh, remember we said that it was all talk. That big pile of station rocks there past the windmill, was about as far as they got before Templetons foreclosed. Anyhow, with such a hot dry wind, it looks like most of the sheep are here waiting their turn to drink at the trough. Just the same, I'd like to check, and fortunately a quick way is to ride up the mount where you can see all over the station."

They rode up the mount, winding their way between York-gums, white-barked flood-gums, and scrub acacia; the lower flora made almost leafless and barkless through the gnawings of hungry sheep. Nearer the crown of the mount grew short tamar and heath, harshly red-brown from the lack of rain. The riders now spiralled the mount to make it easier for the horses, finally reaching the little plateau on top.

"Whew, what a beautiful view," yelled Paddy over the wind, as he looked north-east across virtually millions of acres of mulga and salt-bush plain, broken by the odd dry watercourse and saltlake. To the south lay a much larger stretch of saltlake, its whiteness shimmering in the heat.

"That's Lake Moore," said Jenny. "Around fifteen miles wide on average and more than eighty miles long from north to south. But the view's much better this way," she went on, pointing more south-west. "Down there you can see Mt Gibson, around five hundred feet high, and really just a massive lump of blackened ironstone." She took out a pair of field-glasses from her saddle-satchel and handed them to Paddy. "Now if you look closely, you can make out what has recently been called the Gunyidi Track, which runs the ninety miles from Gibson to Gunyidi on the new Midland Railway. Naturally, our station and Field's are connected to Gibson by different routes." She again pointed. "If you look well out from Gibson along the Track, you can see the edge of the salmon-gum and gimlet timberlands, which they say in the future could be released for agriculture - wheat and so forth."

"Yes, so they were telling us at Field's," replied Paddy, subconsciously correcting his English in Jenny's presence. "Also they were saying that before the Midland Railway went through, there was a rough winding track from the Lower Murchison here, all the way to Geraldton on the coast."

"Yes, that's right. And there's always been a track of sorts to Perth from here as well. All the way to Bindi-Bindi pastoral station, where you can either carry on south-west to the native mission at New Norcia, or journey due south to Toodyay on the Avon."

"But you went to school in Goomalling didn't you, and

often stayed at Mt Rupert? You must have cut off what is now the Gunyidi Track, somewhere shorter?"

"Yes," she laughed, hanging onto her hat in the wind. "In fact we still branch off at a place called Jibberding. Another track winds a little west of south all the way to Mt Rupert."

Paddy gave a wide grin, and like Jenny, hung grimly onto his flapping hat. "But still a long way from home isn't it?"

"Oh we get used to long distances. For example, from here to Mt Rupert, even across country on horseback which I've done more than once, is a good one hundred and fifty miles. As a child I particularly enjoyed travelling with mother and father to Mt Rupert and Goomalling by buggy, and sleeping and eating on the way."

"A bit different from only three miles to school like I had," grinned Paddy. "But even before the stations were begun, Bishop Salvado ran his flocks out here didn't he, all the way from New Norcia?"

"Yes, as far back as 1860 the Mission had an outstation right by this very mount. The well where the windmill now stands in the flat was put down by Salvado's Benedictine monks."

"My God, they did cover some territory in those days!"

"Yes, and a lot of it was illegal ... and still is. Crown land, not yet gazetted for lease. What I mean is that despite the station-owners taking a lot of the Mission run, as we call it, the Benedictines still graze their flocks illegally over a huge area of Crown land. Pretty well all that area you can see to the west from here, including the forest lands, which run in patches nearly all the way to New Norcia."

"What ho, the Catholics," joked Paddy. "Even though I'm supposed to be one. The Benedictines now own much of Perth's real estate too. Yet I suppose someone has to rival the Hungry Six, who after all pretty well run the Anglican Church here, includin' the Bishop."

Jenny was amused. "Yes, it's just what Dad says. My goodness, look at that black line of clouds in the north. And the wind, it's really starting to blow."

"Could be the end of the drought at last," grinned Paddy hopefully.

"Well I'm keeping my fingers crossed," laughed Jenny, showing both hands.

"And praying in your heart too, I'll bet. Just like your mother said," replied Paddy, suddenly grave.

"Yes Paddy, yes I am." Her eyes though serious, were beautiful. She had removed her hat, putting it under her arm from the wind. Her gold-tinted hair, usually tidy, was now gorgeously unruly.

"Anyhow Paddy, it's getting on," she said, as she took the field-glasses from him, and gave a good final sweep of the station area, still with her hat under her arm. "I can't see any stray sheep anywhere, so I guess we'd better start riding down. There's also that windmill to put out of gear. As Kim would say, the wheel must be just buckin' in the wind."

It took a good half hour to reach the red flat near the shearing shed, the millhead as Jenny had predicted, just bucking in the wind.

"Jesus," cried Paddy, forgetting himself. "The outa gear wire's snapped. Looks like I'll have to climb up the tower an' re-connect it."

"NO YOU'RE NOT!" screamed Jenny. "Let the mill go! If it blows over, we'll build a new one."

"Windmills cost money!" yelled Paddy, and with that he was climbing the fifty foot tower, struggling his way over the platform under the mill machinery. To Jenny, the huge wheel was whirring so fast that the razor sharp blades seemed as one.

As brave as she was Jenny closed her eyes, sure that Paddy had little chance. But there he was coming down, having connected the reefing wire and yelling over the wind.

"Righto Jenny, pull her outa gear."

It was then she could have kissed him gladly, but it seemed

Paddy had become totally practical, pointing to the shed.

"Look, some of the corrugated sheets are flappin', have you any tie-down cables?"

"No, we keep some over home, but I'm afraid there's none here," replied Jenny, feeling helpless.

"Well looks like a fence is gonna be shorta some wires," yelled Paddy. "Come on!"

It seemed that the visitor had taken over, Jenny not caring and obeying his every command.

"Grab a pair o' pliers from the shed," yelled Paddy, which Jenny did. Then cutting it each end, they both dragged the wire from a long line of mulga posts. Paddy expertly scaled up the side of the shed in the gale, running over the roof and leaping off the other end, causing Jenny to scream and hold her breath once again.

Next task was to tie extremely heavy weights on each end of the wire. As the shed needed two tie-down cables, the same ritual had to be carried out once again.

"Jesus," yelled Paddy. "Looks like we'd better do the same to the quarters."

By the time they had finished and had raced to the safety of the shed, the whole sky was as black as pitch, the rain starting to fall in torrents.

"Looks like your prayers were answered sweetheart," Paddy heard himself saying.

Jenny too was in a thankful mood, and it took all her will-power to stop throwing herself into his arms and kissing him. But instead she answered him gaily, deliberately talking carelessly.

"Yep, they are an' that Patrick. Looks like you payin' us a visit has changed the Dunbar fortunes."

"But I don't know about you an' I Jennifer, my lovely," he laughed, carrying on with the hilarity. "Remember we both have to ride home. Also I'm due back at Field's."

Jenny had the feeling that Paddy might not be doing either. It was now growing dark, the rain roaring and hitting the corrugated roof like countless steel pellets. Although she was glad of the rain, she had a feeling of panic, knowing that she was trapped alone with a grown man, a man she hardly knew. Certainly she had dreamt about such things. But here it was really happening. At the same time a delicious warmth had crept over her despite her panic, proving that if she had chosen to be isolated with anyone else bar one of her kin, it should be Paddy O'Leary.

But she still avoided his eyes as he yelled something over the crescendo of rain. Something she fully expected.

"My God, it looks like we're stuck here for the night, doesn't it?"

CHAPTER 13

To combat the roar of the rain on the tin roof, Jenny put her mouth close to Paddy's ear.

"Paddy, I'm worried about the sheep. If the creek starts to run a banker, the whole flat could be under water."

"Well they've got a free run to the mountain, haven't they?" yelled Paddy. "Anyway, it's too dark for us to do much about it now."

"Yes, I suppose it is," replied Jenny, her voice thin, wondering whether it was because she was trying to be heard over the rain, or because she was nervous.

"What about the quarters?" suggested Paddy. "They look well-built. I guess they'd be lined. Certainly a bit more comfortable than this tin shed. Want to make a run for it?"

"All right," said Jenny, still unsure. "Sometimes Kim and the boys camp over here during mustering, so I guess there's some tucker there too."

In the quarters, they found some hard tack, jerked mutton and biscuits packed away in a sealed barrel. There was also a stack of dry wood under the quarter's verandah. With some difficulty, Paddy lit the big wood stove, which was used to cook for shearers. In the meantime, Jenny had discovered and lit a hurricane lamp. A big deal table, chairs and an old sofa with the now blazing fire gave a touch of homeliness. Paddy felt that all that was needed was for Jenny to roll her hair in a bun, and change into a house dress and apron rather than her too practical riding habit. All the same, she had tidied her hair and had straightened her rain-soaked shirt, accentuating her swelling breasts.

They had also discovered the inevitable tea and sugar, and using the rough utensils soon had a reasonable repast laid out.

"You'd make a good wife for some lucky beggar Jenny," joked Paddy, wiping his mouth after the jerked meat and biscuits.

"It's all right feller, I'm not the marryin' kind," laughed Jenny, carrying on with the banter, even though her heart was quaking.

"Well my girl," said Paddy, "seein' the sleepin' section is only one room, looks like I'll be dossin' in the kitchen."

By now Jenny had become serious.

"But I couldn't go to sleep if I tried Paddy. Not with the din of the rain. Anyway, I like the sound of it, I don't want to miss a drop."

"I'd say by now we might have had a drop too much," grinned Paddy. "All of two inches I'll bet. Better another lot in a month's time."

"But it just doesn't happen that way in the station country Paddy." She became more earnest.

"You should know that! As Dad says, when it wants to come, let it come, because you could be a darn long time without it."

"Yep, I guess you're right. I only hope everyone else gets it too, even the Clayton-Brownes, if only for their poor bloody stock." He stopped. "Sorry Jenny, bit coarse with the tongue aren't I? Look how I was this afternoon before the rain. No way to speak in front of a lady."

She laughed. "Me, a lady Paddy?"

He became serious. "Yes you are Jenny. Even dressed in your station clothes you are still a lady, an' always will be."

"Thanks Paddy, I must admit, my mother did try to teach me certain good manners. But on a station it's difficult, and as far as swearing's concerned, well I swear sometimes too. But what I don't like is a man swearing just for swearing's sake in front of a woman. Which I know was not your intention Paddy."

Paddy gave a grin. "Well I hope not Jenny. Anyway, seein' we are goin' to wait up, reckon I'll make another cuppa.

He stood up to move the kettle over the stove, but Jenny just beat him to it.

"No, that's my job," she commanded.

"There we go again," he said amusedly. "Acting like an old married pair."

Jenny tried to hide her feelings, yet knowing that if there was anything she wished in the world now, it was to spend the rest of her life with Paddy. By the look in his eyes in the lamplight, she instinctively felt that he might have similar thoughts.

"Paddy," said Jenny, after they had sat there in silence, the tea-cups empty, the only sound the eternal drum of the rain. "That girl you were talking about in Coolgardie who caught the typhoid and later died, did you think much of her?"

"Well, I did a bit," returned Paddy, surprised at Jenny's questioning, but assuming it was just something to pass the time. "You see, I knew her before while I was workin' for the *Herald* in Fremantle an' Perth. But why do you ask? With her death I was only tryin' to bring out a point about the rottenness o' the plague?"

"I could tell you liked her by your eyes Paddy," she said, looking at him even more closely. "Tell me more.... Did you love her?"

He spoke after a silence, his voice softer. Jenny had to lean closer to hear him over the rain.

"I don't know Jenny. She was certainly different from girls I had taken a shine to at school. She always made me feel good when I was near her. Yet it wasn't that I wanted to be near her all the time. You see when Daniel an' I first went prospectin' 'round Southern Cross, I guess I forgot all about her. Anyway, she later got work in Northam, an' then again later in Coolgardie."

"Yes, you said she was an entertainer, a pub-girl."

Paddy spoke more abruptly. "But not one o' those I tell you. Ann was a sweet kid."

"Sorry Paddy."

"No, I may as well tell you the lot, even for Ann's own sake."

"Yes, she said close again to his ear. "Yes, I'd like to hear it, just for Ann's sake."

Paddy told Jenny how he'd hired the coach and taken Ann with the help of one of the other girls, all the way from Coolgardie to Ann's parents home in Perth, and how they had been fearful in case they too should catch the typhoid. How he'd had to look after Ann almost like a baby till they'd found her a hospital bed. How he'd thought her troubles were over, till one day he received a letter from Ann's mother saying she had consumption and was not expected to live.

It was then Paddy halted his sad tale, telling Jenny that seeing she knew that Ann had died, she had heard enough.

"No, tell me the rest Paddy. If it had been me that died that way, I feel I would wish that all the story be told. You say when you heard about her being in a special hospital, you sent her a telegram saying you were coming."

"Yes, but you won't like the rest ..." At Jenny's silence Paddy went on, talking about the mournfulness of the sanatorium compared to the beauty of spring outside, and even more so, where Ann lay dying. He told of how Ann had simply asked him to hold her, which he had done till she passed away hours later.

Jenny's eyes were glistening in the lamplight.

"She must have waited for you Paddy, when she got the telegram."

"Yes Jenny, the hospital sister who read her the wire said the very same thing. She waited."

Paddy suddenly put his head in his hands.

"Ann was one in a million Jenny. The trouble was I didn't care enough. Even in Coolgardie, she had to lower herself and remind me. It seemed I preferred the company of my boozy mates. Not that Daniel's like that. But the trouble was that he wasn't impressed with me chasin' round with someone like Ann neither."

"Yes, but I guess the problem was that Ann did love you Paddy. But did you love her? As I've already asked."

His face looked tragic.

"I don't know Jenny. I don't know? I really don't know."

Jenny had almost placed her hand over his as it lay on the table, wondering whether the desire to do so was just to give comfort, or to add to the delicious sensation she felt in her breast, so mixed up with feelings of sadness for the departed Ann.

Believing that Jenny's silence was one of sleepiness or even boredom, Paddy suddenly spoke loudly above the rain.

"'Bout time you turned in my girl. You'll need all your wits about you tomorrow battlin' through the flood, which with the rain still pourin' down, there surely will be."

"Yes Paddy," said Jenny, grateful to him, but knowing that if he now asked her to lie with him and comfort him, she would not hesitate. She now knew that he was a man who would never take advantage of a woman.

He spoke. "It's got a bit cold. Are there any blankets?"

"Yes there should be, in the bunk room." She disappeared through the door into the bunk-room, throwing out a couple of blankets.

"I've given you the moth-eaten ones," she joked. "Now remember I want eggs an' bacon for breakfast. Goodnight."

"I'd say by my pocket watch, it's already goodmornin'. Probably too late for that goodnight kiss."

She ran across and kissed him, somewhat disappointed when he only kissed her back like a brother, yet feeling the trembling of his body and knowing he was using all his will-power to hold himself back.

Jenny also later lay there trembling, desiring him so much she burst into muffled tears. Finally she slept, and next thing she knew she was being shaken by Paddy.

"Come on sleepy-head, I've got breakfast on. Certainly not googs an' bacon, but believe it or not I've found some flour an' made a few pancakes filled with chopped up jerky. Goes well on the track, anyhow."

She answered gaily. "Thanks friend. Yes, I've had pancakes on the track before. But why didn't you wake me earlier? Cookin's my job."

"No it's not sweetheart." He had almost said, "not yet!"

She knew now he was teasing her, possibly because the night was over and he had himself under control.

It was then she almost dared to reach up and pull him closer. He at the same time savoured her delicious sweetness, forcing himself not to slip under the blankets with her.

"The rain's eased," she said as she came into the kitchen, "but it's still coming down."

"Yeah," he answered casually. "An' I'll bet by now all the station-owners are prayin' for it to stop. Just take a look outside."

Jenny looked through the window, her face comfortably close to his. The early sun was beginning to penetrate through the thinning cloud, which with the wind having abated, seemed determined to shed its every last drop.

"Goodness," she gasped, coming to reality. "The water's above the first section of the windmill and lapping the shed. Why it's like we're on an island."

"Yep," said Paddy, appreciating their togetherness by the window. "Lucky the stable where we left our horses is on high ground like the quarters here. When the rain clears I guess the best bet would be to ride to the top o' the mount an' take a look 'round."

"Yes, good idea," said Jenny, a little sad in the thought that the romantic interlude with Paddy was now over.

Riding up the little mountain was no cake-walk. Pushing their horses into the swirling flood, they kept clear of the creek, which was defined by the absence of the mulgas. The waters, well over stirrup height, grew shallower as they approached the base of the mount. The riders at last were able to rest and comfort their horses by the edge of the woodlands. The air was filled with the croak of frogs, causing Paddy to make humorous comment.

"Would you listen to 'em?"

"Yes," laughed Jenny. "It's a good five years since I've heard one. Where they materialize from after a big rain God only knows. Oh, look, there's the sheep." She pointed into the timber, where the bedraggled animals were hunched in their hundreds.

"By the size o' the mob, it looks like they could be all there too," remarked Paddy hopefully.

"Yes, but I wouldn't say that for the main flock," replied Jenny, her mood changing. "Apart from the eastern slopes of the Pinyallings, there's only the homestead area which is on high ground."

Paddy jumped on his horse. "Anyway, let's get to the top an' take a look."

The view from the crest of the mount, showed thousands of acres to the north-east under water, the only sign of life the tips of the mulgas.

"Mother Murphy!" gasped Paddy. "Talk about too much of a good thing."

Jenny looked frightened. "Goodness, I've never seen anything like it. I'm worried about the homestead. Through the binoculars I can just make out the roof, but I'm still not sure whether the house is clear of the flood."

"Well what do you reckon then? Should we wait another day, or chance it and make our way back."

The thought of just the two of them spending another night alone gave Jenny a delicious thrill. She pointed to the sun, now blazing merrily out of a clear sky.

"Looks like the rain's finished. We could keep to the shallow patches by following the mulgas. They'll indicate the depth of the water."

Paddy looked at her with admiration, realising that unlike

241

most women, station life had encouraged her to think in a more practical way.

"Good thinkin' Jennifer my girl," he laughed, wheeling his horse.

"Thanks cobber," she answered casually. "Let's get on our way."

Once down the mount the pair rode through the flood, following the winding track, as indicated by the absence of the little trees. They forced their way towards the far-off stationhouse, often having to stop and extricate near-dead sheep from mulga branches. In silence Paddy would take his rifle from its saddle-scabbard and despatch each stricken animal swiftly. Though he knew Jenny was hardened to such things, he realised that with her it was no place for sick wisecracks, as he knew would have occurred between himself and Tim McBride.

The horses waded and swam for more than three hours, the sun now well past midday. The sky was clear, the air tropical, the flying ants swarming from the tips of the mulgas. More and more branches stuck with sheep. More and more sheep to be shot.

"Oh, look!" yelled Jenny, pointing ahead. "The station-house. It's safe!"

"Yeah, but not by much," replied Paddy, grimly. "The water's almost up to the sheepyards."

They reached the surrounds of the shearing shed, the ground literally covered in soaked miserable sheep. Will Dunbar, his son and the stationhands were so concerned about the animals, that they hardly noticed Jenny and Paddy approaching. It was Peg Dunbar who ran down from the homestead to meet them, followed by the native girls.

Jenny raised a smile. "It's all right Mum. You should have known we'd be safer over at Singleton than back here. The biggest danger was yesterday, when Paddy insisted on fixing the reefing cable on the windmill when the gale was at its worst. Paddy insisted on tying down the sheds too, with fencing wire. By that time it was pitch dark and raining in torrents." She halted, looking slightly guilty.

"Just the same, I suppose we could have made an effort to come home."

"How could you in such rain?" said Peg. "Anyhow, the quarters are over there with tucker and so forth. Why shouldn't you use them!"

"We did Mum!" Jenny still felt she was making apologies.

By now Will Dunbar was there. He gave a forced grin, deliberately putting out of his mind the fact that his daughter had spent the night alone with a man.

"Well Paddy," he said. "Looks like it's come with a vengeance."

Paddy was relieved. "Yes Will, it has an' that. As I was sayin' to Jenny, a bit too much of a good thing. How much rain did you measure?"

"More than eleven inches; the most rain at one time since we started the station back in '80."

"Jesus!" Paddy had again made a slip of the tongue. "But seein' it rained heavy most o' the night, I shouldn't be surprised. How many sheep do you reckon you've lost? Don't worry about the ones over at Singleton, they're safe up the mount."

Will stroked his chin. "Well I guessed that, an' we are also hopin' a big mob might have got up into the Pinyallin's. But even barrin' that, I'd say we could've lost a good two thousand."

"Jesus," said Paddy, forgetting himself once again.

"Oh well," said Will. "With the way the mulgas were dyin' before the rain, I guess without it we could have lost the whole flock. All of twenty thousand."

"Yes, we should be very thankful," broke in Peg. "Anyhow Will, these young people must be starving."

"You're right Peg," added Will. "Seein' it's so close to afternoon tea-time, we'll just give these ponies a bite to eat an' come up the house as well." He gave a wink towards his wife. "It bein' well past midday, we might even indulge in a whisky. That's what I mean by givin' thanks."

Later, while Kim and the two native lads went back to mothering the sheep, Will and Paddy went on talking and drinking, consuming a whole bottle of Scotch. It was then that Paddy made the suggestion about getting himself back to Field's.

"You'll be battlin'," grinned Will. "Remember Field's is situated on the west side o' Lake Monger, an' I'll bet by now the lake's just about up to the town."

"But Field's itself is on pretty high ground," argued Paddy.

Will gave an amused grunt. "But even that narrowest part of Lake Monger which we call The Crossing, could be six foot under. It happened way back in 1885, after around five inches. O' course, the mining town wasn't there then, but the location's the same. Like I said, the water could be lappin' the town."

"Looks like you're still stuck with us Paddy," joked Jenny, who had been listening.

"Looks like I am," said Paddy, with pretended solemnity. "Still, I guess you could do with a hand with the sheep anyhow?"

Will drained the last of his whisky. "Yeah, I can see us pullin' sheep outa the mulgas for days."

It was a good week before Paddy was able to cross Lake Monger into the mining town. While successfully hunting for sheep in the Pinyallings, he and Jenny had ridden to the crest of the range of hills, the whole southern expanse of Lake Monger laid out before them.

"It'd still be a good five feet deep, even at The Crossing," observed Jenny. "You see the water flows into Lake Monger from as far up as Meekathara, two hundred and fifty miles away. It could be flowing in some measure for weeks. With a big rain Lake Monger flows through Jibberding into other big lake systems, eventually finishing south-west as far away as the Moore River, then into the sea."

"Yep, by the amount of water down there I'm not surprised," he grinned. "Anyway, I've got used to waitin'. In fact, the way I feel right now, I could wait forever. With you I mean Jenny."

Jenny knew that this time it was no play-act. He meant what he was saying. She felt herself blush, scared to meet his eyes.

"I like you around too Paddy," she tried to say casually, her lips trembling. "But I guess when you get to Perth and start living it up, you'll forget all about little Jenny Dunbar out in the backblocks."

Paddy pushed back his hat, his eyes crinkling in the sun.

"Well yes, I do still intend to journey on to Perth. But now methinks I'll be makin' different arrangements. As a matter o' fact, I'm goin' to call on Templetons an' have a go for the lease o' Singleton station. With all the recovery after the rain, you won't be needin' it so much now will you?"

She was still afraid to meet his eyes, not sure she should reveal what she felt in her heart.

"No, I guess not," she went on levelly. "Anyway, it would still be a long time before we could afford to buy it. Just the same Paddy, with all the money you could make out of gold sales, why choose a lonely life on a station?"

He laughed carelessly. "I told you before Jenny, I like it here. Even without the good rain. Yes, if your Pa is agreeable, I'll take over the Singleton lease. I've even been lying awake at night thinkin' about the sort o' homestead I'd build. All walled with those different coloured rocks which the cove who went broke carted down from the mountainside. Believe it or not, I might even go to the expense of a slate roof, like some o' the more expensive buildin's in Kalgoorlie. I'm hopin' you'll help me design it, Jenny."

"Could be a waste on a station, building such a mansion," she replied calmly, yet with her heart almost ready to burst.

"Still, with the pretty mount not far away it might just be appropriate. If you could afford it that is. What I meant about the mount being pretty, you wait till you see it this spring after the big rain."

"Anyway," she went on, still feeling decidedly but deliciously uncomfortable, "we'd better get back, looks like we've got good news for Dad about the rest of the sheep."

"Yeah, I s'pose we'd better, Jenny," said Paddy seriously, having almost said "sweetheart", this time not in jest, his whole frame as with Jenny's, tingling with a growing love.

When Paddy again met Tim, after at last crossing Lake Monger, Tim's comment was typical.

"Yeah, we reckoned you'd be stuck over there for a while. Anyhow, there wasn't much to do here in any case. What with the mines fulla water, as they still are. It was lucky the pub had just put in a big store o' whisky. Which reminds me, we may as well step over an' breast the bar now."

"Haven't changed, have you Tim?" laughed Paddy good humouredly as they walked under the pub verandah. "Anyway, how are the others?"

"Oh you mean Wilga, Lennie an' Ahmud. Well for a start Wilga cleared off before the rain."

"HELL! Why?" Paddy was surprised.

"Well, we had neglected him a bit since we've been here, you must admit."

"But he seemed happy throwin' spears an' thing's with the local Yamadgees."

"No matey, it was just to pass the time. I really believe Wilga liked workin' for you Paddy. You probably should have given him a bit more attention. Now he's gone."

Paddy was downcast. "But where, for Chris-sake?"

"Well Lennie reckons he could have gone back over Clayton Downs way. Round by way o' Mt Singleton, Mt Churchman an' Mt Jackson way, well over a hundred miles."

"But the Clayton-Brownes could grab him!"

"Wilga's too smart for that," grinned Tim. "Especially when he's by himself usin' bush tactics. Yeah, I reckon it might be his intention to sneak out that pretty little lubra. You know that bright little shepherdess who came runnin' over."

"But that could have been his sister."

"No, Lennie was tellin' me. She's a sort o' third cousin. O' course little clans like Wilga's do interbreed a bit."

"But you can't say it's still not a risk Tim, Wilga tryin' to take her out with a bastard like Julien Clayton-Browne. I know they haven't probably gone as far down here. But they're still the same families as up north where they've shot so many blacks just for runnin' away."

"Yeah, an' stealin' away a good reliable shepherdess could be worse couldn't it? It means money." Tim put his hand on Paddy's shoulder. "You feel kinda responsible for Wilga, don't you matey? But I wouldn't worry too much about him. I'd reckon he could be back with his little Nardi any day now."

Paddy brightened. "As a matter o' fact I could have a permanent job for him. I've decided to buy Singleton station."

Tim almost dropped his glass.

"You've what? I didn't even know there was such a station. O' course we've all heard o' the mount. "What'n hell's been goin' on over there with the Dunbars? Better let me in on it."

Paddy told Tim most of the story, without going into the details about Jenny. But Tim had already caught on, letting out a loud laugh.

"Well cobber, I don't know who's trapped who? But I will say you've made a good choice. That Jenny's as sweet a kid as I've ever seen. An' I tell you, I'm not a bad judge o' women. Though I've spent a lotta time in the outback, I've still knocked around the city an' met all sorts. Anyone who lived in Melbourne in those hectic days before the crash in '88, would know what I mean. Females, my God, I could write a book about 'em." Tim put down his glass. "Just the same Paddy m'lud, you could've picked a bad time to buy a station. With the big rain, the prices will be up to hell. Still, you'll have all your gold cash won't you?"

"Yeah, that's why I'm still goin' to give it a go. I'll be straight around to Templetons when we get to Perth."

"So it's off at last to Perth now, is it? And who said I was keepin' you company?" Tim gave his customary grin. "Still, I might tag along. There's all our gold business to fix up."

"Thanks Tim. We could travel as soon as possible by way of the Gunyidi Track to the new Midland Railway. Jenny was tellin' me about it."

"Yeah, I know about it too. But you've forgotten somethin' else haven't you? I mean Ahmud an' Lennie."

Paddy looked shame-faced. "Yep, sorry."

Tim laughed, taking another swig of whisky. "It's all right chum, if you're agreeable, things could work out fine. We owe 'em a bit more than wages, so I was thinkin' about not only givin' 'em the camels, but buyin' 'em a decent wagon."

Paddy grinned, giving Tim full credit for his generosity. "Why, that's a hell of a good idea. But where'd we get a big wagon like that?"

Tim knocked his long dead pipe on the bar. "Well, they say since the rail went through there's a heap for sale in Yalgoo. Could be cheap as dirt. Young Lennie's no fool, he reckons that this rain could be the start of a run o' good seasons, an' with the stations growin' more an' more wool a good camel team in front of a wool-wagon is the answer, especially with a teamster like Ahmud. O' course, we'll have to buy 'em a heap more camels too."

"I don't mind," nodded Paddy. "Especially if Ahmud's keen as well."

Tim stuffed tobacco in his pipe. "O' course Ahmud's keen.

He's never been more contented. Lennie an' Ahmud have become real good mates. Lennie says Ahmud was captured by the British years ago while fightin' on the North-West frontier. Till he managed to get sent out here as a camel-driver he'd been a prisoner for years in India. Yeah, seein' the climate here also suits him, he should be as happy as Larry."

"The whole thing fits in well, doesn't it?" said Paddy. "Even though the rail's through to Yalgoo, it would be cheaper for these stations down south here to have their wool carted to Gunyidi on the Midland Railway. If the dry seasons come again, which they surely will, and with the wells dryin' up, the camels could just about travel the whole ninety miles without water."

"Well it's a bit further than ninety miles," grunted Tim, putting a wax match to his pipe. "Gunyidi's only a spot where it's convenient for the Track to meet the railway line. The loading stop is twelve more miles south to Watheroo, said to be a railway town. The railway runs the pub an' all. But they say it's still a lively joint."

Paddy laughed. "You've certainly found out a bit since I've been away. Here's me tellin' you about the Track, as was pointed out to me from Mt Singleton, an' you know about that an' more."

"Yeah," said Tim, blowing smoke between sips of whisky. "An' that Mt Gibson you were talkin' about. They've just struck gold there. On the way we could take a look-see."

"Well when do we start?" grinned Paddy. "As you noticed, I've bought myself a decent nag. But what about you?"

"Oh, that apology for a horse you led back will do. We don't have to parade 'em through Perth anyway. Before we jump on the train at Watheroo we can leave 'em in a holdin' paddock."

"Yep, an' while there we could wire Daniel tellin' him to catch the train from Kal' to Perth."

"Yeah maybe we could paint the city red together. But

Daniel's such a flamin' wowser."

"Yep, an' I might be goin' a bit quiet too, remember I want to buy that station."

Tim laughed loudly. "God Almighty, here's us worryin' about money, when we'll probably get enough outa sellin' the claims to last us the rest of our lives."

Paddy gave a grin. "I told that to Jenny. How if Tim McBride wanted, he could go back an' live in fancy style in dear ole Melbourne Town."

"Well, I could since it's recovered. But no, I'm goin' to settle in Field's. I like it here." He became confidential. "Fact is I've still got my eye on that little lubra. She's a real sweetie, an' apparently it's all right with the bucks. Only needs a bottla beer now an' then or a shotta whisky."

Once again Paddy was disgusted, but what could he do about it? If Tim didn't fraternise with the girl one of the other diggers would.

"Looks like we've both found our niche round here," he went on, still avoiding his friend's eyes. "Anyway, I had ideas about headin' for the city day after tomorrow. Too quick for yuh I s'pose?"

"No, not at all cobber. Not at all! As I said, the mine's still flooded."

CHAPTER 14

Just after daybreak, Paddy and Tim rode their horses across the narrow section of Lake Monger, negotiating the water with some difficulty. The horses were heavily laden with satchels as well as the riders.

They rode due south, and by late afternoon had covered the forty five miles to Mt Gibson, which was as Jenny had described to Paddy, just a huge protruding boulder of blackened ironstone. South-west of the mount, was the new mining settlement. Besides tents, it already contained its share of hessian-walled tin-roofed buildings. Tim was extremely pleased to find that one rough structure housed the inevitable pub, run by a Dutch woman migrant, who with her strong blue eyes and determined jaw, looked according to Tim, as if she knew how to handle all types of men, including prospectors out on the spree.

Paddy and Tim were in no great hurry, and after seeing to their horses, indulged in a few whiskies. It was while they were in the pub listening to the local diggers that they decided to spend time fossicking around. Tim soon set his practised eye on a small ironstone knob just up from a quartz ridge which had already been taken up. "Might travel down from Field's later an' put down a shaft," said Tim. "Might even get myself an old spring-cart to cart a bit o' gear."

"You'll need a better nag than you've got at present," grinned Paddy.

"That's for bloody sure," said Tim. "Matter o' fact I might latch onto a coupla mules. They use 'em a lot in Queensland on short difficult runs. Far more reliable than a horse, I tell ye'. Need less water an' tucker too."

Though Paddy and Tim again drank freely with the other prospectors during the evening, the next morning saw them up bright and early. They found the Gunyidi Track, winding approximately south-west through a mixture of bowgada acacia and eucalypt timber. That day they covered nearly thirty five miles, and after riding through an extensive tract of greyish sand covered in wodgil acacia and broom-bush ti-tree, found their way barred by the usually dry southern tip of Lake Monger, now covered with muddy red water, a good five miles across.

"Jesus," swore Tim. "If I'd known this, I might have talked you into ridin' the seventy miles north to Yalgoo along the Gnow's Nest Range. We could've caught the train up there, even if it is a roundabout way to Perth. The trouble with this track, no one seems to know enough about it. Those diggers back there all came south from Magnet an' Yalgoo."

Paddy shook his head. "But from what Jenny says, about five miles past the lake is a place called Jibberding, where the Dunbars turn off to travel the seventy miles sou-sou-west to Mt Rupert, the old Dunbar ranch, as Will sometimes calls it."

Tim pointed across the water. "But that's not to say that beyond Jibberdin' we won't find more lakes, filled to the flippin' brim like this one."

"You could be right." Paddy nodded his head towards the sun disappearing down behind the trees beyond the lake. "Anyway, looks like we'd better make camp - could be dark before we get across?"

"Yeah, that wind across the lake's turned mighty cold too. Lets get to it an' gather some o' this dead timber for a fire."

The moon rose early, and the blaze of the campfire was reflected in the lake from the higher ground. After a quick meal, Paddy and Tim while enjoying the warmth, yarned and took it in turns to take swigs from the whisky bottle. It was a part of bush life Paddy really appreciated. Yet he knew it was a man's life, rather than a woman's. After falling in love with Jenny, he had thought much about a permanent home and a family.

Next morning they crossed to the higher ground on the other side of the lake. The loamy rich red soil made Paddy remark that it was similar to some of the better wheat country east of York. By mid-morning they had reached Jibberding, where the Dunbars had gouged a neat sign into a piece of plank and nailed it to a tree. A couple of acres had also been cleared out, in which lay a stable and wire yard. Tim was impressed.

"I reckon this could be a good spot for a wayside store an' tavern. Once all those diggers at Gibson get it into their heads that this track heads towards the city, it could be pretty popular."

"There's all the grazier traffic too," agreed Paddy. "Includin' Lennie an' Ahmud an' their camels."

"Yeah," said Tim, as they rode on. "I've always had a mind to own a bush pub. As a matter o' fact, when we get the money for our claims, I might even make an offer for the one at Field's."

"Pubs will always do well out in the backblocks as long as the gold holds out," nodded Paddy. "Anyway, with all the money you should be gettin' after the sale of our claims Tim, you could start your wayside inn back there, buy the Field's pub, an' still run your mine into the bargain." Paddy realised a lot of their discussion was just pure track talk. Yet in an exciting pioneering situation, how inspiring even just to imagine.

"Yeah," said Tim. "Talkin' about the mine, while in Perth I might send a cable to the owners in London an' make an offer. Could also look round for a good-sized engine an' pump to clean out the mine-shaft."

"Good idea," said Paddy, yet wondering why Tim even contemplated buying and working the mine, when with the sale of their Leonora claims he should have enough to set him up for life. But that was Tim, as with other roving t'otherside prospectors, who no doubt stood by that now well-worn clique, 'the searchin' was better than the findin'.

Also Tim had his eye on that little black Mary he'd spoken about, just as Paddy had his eye on Jenny Dunbar.

"Yeah." Paddy was emulating Tim's lazy drawl. "Buyin' an engine an' pump could be a right good investment, especially if we're in for a run o' wet years like they say. You could hire the gear out to other small miners too."

They chatted on, as was the wont of travellers making a slow journey through the bush. By mid-afternoon, they found themselves in far heavier timber. The red clay, though dry, showed deep wagon or dray tracks, mixed with sunken hoof-marks. They also passed the occasional flock of sheep, tended by native men. One group of dark shepherds was under the attendance of a black-robed monk.

"What Jenny calls the New Norcia run," remarked Paddy. "Even though it's all Crown land with the mission more'n ninety miles away. In the early days, accordin' to Jenny, the monks had their flocks right out as far as Mt Singleton."

"Yeah, they were tellin' me in Field's," said Tim, after the big rain when there was nothin' else to do but loaf an' drink an' talk." Tim indicated the rich carpet of young native grass between the salmons and gimlets. "My God, with this timber cleared, you could grow a whopper of a wheat crop here this season couldn't you?"

"You could at that Tim. Jenny was sayin' there's talk about openin' it up sometime. That'll bugger the monks usin' it as a free pasture won't it? But even if it is released for agriculture, I guess it's still a long way to cart grain to the Midland Railway. From my calculation, we've still got around fifty miles to go."

"Yeah, I guess we must also remember this wet season could be just a flash in the pan. From what I know of heavy soils like this in Victoria, they need a bloody lotta rain at the right time. You could find yourself takin' up land, all sweetness an' light after a good winter, then after a run o' rotten seasons like we've just had, you could find yourself right on the bones o' your proverbial bum."

"You could be right matey. You could be right. Still, accordin' to the papers, they reckon the last five years have been the driest on record, which means they mightn't come again for a long time. I guess we've just got to live in hope, like you buyin' that mine-shaft pump Tim, an' findin' that apart from this year, you might never need it."

Tim brushed away a fly. "Well, if we are in a for a good run, maybe some o' those broken down prospectors back at Gibson an' Fields could make their stakes here. Most have wives an' kids over t'otherside, like the other diggers in Coolgardie an' Kal'. Apart from the prospector adventurers like me, most were hopin' that gold could help 'em settle down permanently some place. It's damned ironic, isn't it? Though the diggers are always slingin' off at people who own land, it's mostly what their frantic fossickin' for gold's all about. Take the Eureka Stockade now, most o' the diggers there were hopin' to make enough cash to be able to start a little farm an' work the soil. Fact is, many of 'em who had farmin' backgrounds later became Victorian wheat cockies. But the poor bastards got so shorta money later that they were forced to get together an' form a cooperative. O' course it broke down, just like I said would happen if the diggers formed that gold co-op in Kal'."

Apart from the fact that Tim had brought up the eternal problem of the smallholder or battler, Paddy was amused.

"So it's you Victorians who manufactured the term cocky for the little independent settler," he mused. "Since they've been usin' it here the last few years, I thought it had naturally derived from our cockatoo farmers in the '50s an' '60s, who had grown wheat illegally while workin' for the likes o' the McAllums an' Clayton-Brownes. This was before the gentry families were forced to take their flocks out into the backblocks."

Tim laughed. "Oh, the cockies got their name much earlier than that matey, even well before they did in Victoria. It first came about in New South Wales when the conditional pardon con's practised the very same thing as your convicts later did here, growin' wheat illegally. But their plots were so small that all they appeared to be doin, accordin' to the critics, was scratchin' round like white cockatoos, besides plantin' extra tucker for the parrots themselves. Hence the term cocky, held in some endearment by the cockies themselves, but regarded with profound contempt by the rural upper-class."

With the horses moving not much faster than a walk, Paddy nodded his head. "Yeah, same over here. Anyway, my Pa an' grandpa used to talk a lot about cooperatives. But like Daniel said about miner's cooperatives in Kalgoorlie, they need outside help to get started. Probably government."

Tim was sarcastic. "Jesus Paddy! Could you imagine the Groves Gang agreein' to a scheme like that, not only with minin', but land or anythin'? Apart from buyin' sure-fire shares in the big companies, it's not in their nature. As they've proven with land before, they'd rather grab all the best for 'emselves, which they probably will when this stuff's released for agriculture. An' even if they can't do that, with all the push they've got, they can easily arrange to have first pick o' the land by persuadin' the government to put a high price on it. Yeah, they'll probably get the Groves Gang to put in another rail-link too, an' get this colony even more in the shit to dear ole Britain, like what's happened with the Midland Railway."

"Well they can soon build railways for gold, can't they? Still, aren't we aimin' to get rid o' the Groves Gang in the next election? We've talked so much about a government by the people an' for the people, an' not for the chosen few, just like Daniel said."

"But I've changed my mind a bit since that," growled Tim. "Durin' the flood, we had nothin' to do in Fields 'cept drink an' talk. Like in Coolgardie an' Kal' when there's an election in the winds the t'otherside diggers love to talk politics, especially if there's a chance to walk the streets with the good ole Eureka flag." Tim became more disconsolate.

"The trouble is to find a candidate. Politicians don't get paid m'lud. So similar to the last two elections, we could wind up with a heap o' fake liberals feted an' financed once more by the Hungry Six an' its mouthpiece the *West Australian*." As he sat easily in the saddle, Tim began to fill his pipe from "the makins" cut from a plug the night before.

"Well why don't you put up yourself Tim?" grinned Paddy. "You'll have wealth enough after we sell our gold claims. An' what with you bein' a registered geologist, you could be like Peter Lalor who got elected to the Victorian Parliament after Eureka. As my Grandpa David used to say, as yet the lower classes still need someone to look up to. Someone liberal an' learned like Lalor, an' more in sympathy with the ordinary folk."

Tim lit his pipe and took a puff. "Well, I'm mighty proud that you feel that way matey. But unlike Lalor, I'm a shepherder not a leader. I like urgin' 'em on behind the scenes. Anyway, though it wouldn't be the first time I've decked myself out in glad rags, I now doubt if I could stand it. No, bugger it matey. Not that I won't be involved."

"But as you intimated, we must find a candidate Tim. Looks like it's somethin' else we've gotta talk to Daniel about besides gold."

"Yeah," grunted Tim. "Daniel's good friends with the editor of the *Geraldton Express*, who incidentally was a good mate o' mine in Melbourne and an agitator to boot."

"Hell Tim, you have had connections! An' with Daniel friendly with him also, I guess the wires could have already been twangin' a tune between Coolgardie an' Geraldton."

"That they could have matey. That they could have. Anyway, let's stop an' boil the billy."

That night they camped in a spot denoted by a sign as Miamoom. Close by was a big pile of granite where the New Norcia monks had carved out and plastered one of their round wells.

"Maybe this is another good place for a wayside shanty," suggested Tim, though mostly just for something to say. "Goin' by my calculations, it could be still another thirty miles to Gunyidi on the Midland Railway, let alone the other twelve down to Watheroo."

"Well, till they put in another rail connection, it certainly could be another good place for a bush tavern Tim. But we'll have to be callin' the whole shebang McBride Enterprises, won't we?"

But where'd I find all the good managers?" questioned Tim with good humour

"You might rake up a couple like Gretchen back there in Gibson," grinned Paddy.

"My God yes. She's one in a million, got those tough diggers toein' the line already."

"Anyhow," went on Paddy, as they tethered out their horses. "If I remember about wayside inns, it's hard to get a liquor license."

"Don't worry about that," laughed Tim. "I haven't knocked around with prospectors for nothin', I tell you I've seen whisky made out of anythin' that'll rot, be it vegetable, fruit or grain. Even those wild red berries you see all through the backblocks in spring, called quandongs. The kernel from the sandalwood nut makes a good brew too, I tell you. One digger who'd travelled, reckoned it was just like a potent brew made out o' coconuts in Ceylon, called arak or somethin'. Still, you can't beat barley or wheat. Probably buy a few bushels from a broken-down cocky up the Midland Railway a bit towards Geraldton."

Paddy knew Tim was deliberately romancing, but thoroughly enjoyed the lightheartedness.

"That you could matey. I can just recall an old ex-convict character on the farm called Timothy, who besides makin' a good brew of ale, could also manufacture what they called colonial spirits."

"Yeah, colonial spirits," bantered Tim. "It was called that

in Victoria too. You see what I mean, makin' a good local whisky would be no trouble."

Before reaching Miamoon Hill, Paddy and Tim had to negotiate more flooded areas. Early next morning after crossing a rich red flat bounded to the north by a huge natural, well-filled salt-lake, they found themselves trekking over an extensive area of sandplain. The foliage was tamar and a short species of ti-tree, besides the occasional wild pear, a pale-barked sprawling little tree. But the pears, though shaped accordingly, looked even tougher than the tree.

"It's strange lookin' country all round," said Tim. "Hard goin' for the nags too, the gullies are so soft in the low patches, the poor bastards are sinkin' past their fetlocks. You were talkin' back there about cartin' grain to the Midland Line. My God, I reckon even in summer a loaded wagon would be mosta the time half down to the axles in sand."

Paddy flicked his reins in disgust. "Lennie and Ahmud could be battlin' with their wool wagon too, couldn't they? Probably could do with a few extra camels."

"Yeah, they could at that," nodded Tim tiredly. "Still, you never know, a few miles up ahead we might run outa the pesky stuff."

But both riders and their mounts were disappointed. Apart from the occasional quartzy timbered ridge, the seemingly bottomless sands continued and they did not reach Watheroo till late the following day. Although Watheroo itself was situated in lightlands, the railways had excavated a huge dam into a patch of tough grey subsoil. Next to the dam was the steam-driven pumping station, with the necessary tank on a high stand, used to replenish the locos.

The pair left their horses in the holding paddock owned by a middle-aged couple. Though the paddock looked over-grazed and virtually packed with the mounts of travellers, the holding price was exorbitant, bringing a scathing comment from Tim.

"Jesus, they say the husband works on the railways, but goin' by the paddockin' charge, I'll bet they both make their fortunes inside a year. Anyway, let's make for the railway pub. It's handy to the station platform, so we shouldn't miss the train even if we have a few too many."

"Well, we could," grinned Paddy. "It doesn't come through from Geraldton till about midnight."

"It's all right, I've come across this sort o' thing before," joked Tim. "We just give our names to the barkeeper, an' if we're too drunk they'll throw us on the train with the rest."

Paddy put on a serious face. "If that's the way we're goin' to carry on, my wild Victorian friend, methinks before we breast the bar I'd better send that wire to Daniel in Coolgardie. Looks like the telegrams go from the station. This dear old English Midland Railway Company runs everythin' doesn't it?"

"Well they've been given millions of acres of land on either side o' the railway for layin' the track, so why not make the bastards run the post-office? Anyway you won't want me to hold your hand while you send the wire, so I'll go next door an' order a coupla beers. They say they've got kegs on ice, like in good ole Kal'."

As Tim predicted, when the train eventually did arrive around half past twelve, the barman rang a bell and had a roll-call. Those beyond helping themselves had to be assisted aboard the train with their belongings. Though Paddy and Tim had had their share of booze, they were still sober enough to manage by themselves. Expecting at least to be able to rest their posteriors for the trip, they found to their dismay that there was standing room only. The train was loaded with diggers taking a break from the Murchison goldfields. So all Paddy and Tim could do was be patient and join the throng, which largely meant quaffing down bottled beer, the diggers having supplemented their supply from the Watheroo Refreshment Rooms as the railway pub was known.

"Jesus!" swore Paddy rocking about from passenger to passenger as the train put on pace. "If we'd have used our brains we'd have booked a first-class carriage. There's a whole swag of 'em up towards the engine."

Tim's reply was typical. "Well, it wouldn't be the first time I've ridden first class m'lud. An' I don't mind travellin' with upper class wimmen an' kids. But I tell you, if any o' the menfolk up there are like that Clayton-Browne character we ran into, I might find it hard to hold my tongue."

"Me too," mouthed Paddy into Tim's ear, still pushed with the rock of the train. "Though it could be a far more comfortable trip, we might have just find found ourselves in trouble with the law."

They arrived in Perth station around nine o'clock. On the way they managed to get to the carriage window and catch a glimpse of Midland Junction, the new terminus to the north, situated around three miles east of Guildford in the shadow of the ranges. Having recovered their satchels and handed in their tickets, the pair along with the rest of the diggers moved out into the metropolis. Paddy had not visited the city for more than three years, and he was amazed at the growth.

"Jesus," said Tim. "Talk about the roarin' nineties. It reminds me o' Melbourne before the crash. Still, the Melbourne boom was propped up by wool. This one's propped up by gold, an' seein' there's plenty more out there to be won, I reckon Perth's safe for a few years yet."

"I don't know so much," replied Paddy, as they dodged a stream of horse-drawn cabs. "Coolgardie was on the way out before we left."

"Yeah, but apart from Bayley's Reward, Coolgardie was only surface gold. But Kal' will last for donkey's years. Those gold seams get richer an' richer as they go down. The British companies, the devil-take-'em, will probably never reach the bottom. Anyway, before we run ourselves ragged, we'd better find a place to sleep. What about that flash new pub advertised so much in the papers? The Palace, down on the corner o' William St an' the Terrace."

Paddy knew that Tim was referring to St George's Tce. "Know your way round for a Victorian, don't you, my friend?"

"Well, I have spent time here. Me an' me mates spent a whole three months in the joint after we first came down from up north in '92, after you mob first struck gold in Coolgardie. Got rid of all our gold money too, by golly. There's nothin' like the bright lights for doin' that. An' o' course now they're a whole lot brighter."

"That means we'd better watch out for the female o' the species, hadn't we chum?"

"Yeah, you can't teach me much about them neither. Still, if we want to play round a bit, we'd better get some money for our claims. I spent most o' my spare cash in the pub in Field's."

"But I guess we won't be able to do much about the claims till Daniel arrives from Kal'. That reminds me, I asked him to send the reply to the Perth Post Office. There it is right over there."

After receiving Daniel's wire that he would be arriving in Perth in two day's time by train, Paddy and Tim walked along Hay St to William Street - then they carried on over the hill and down to the Palace. Paddy was tremendously impressed by the elegance of the womenfolk. Many were dressed for winter in ultra-expensive velvet street gowns - of rich burgundy or green, or an appealing brown - all with saucy hats to match. The few inches of chiffon under the skirts only added to the glamour.

"Jesus," exclaimed Tim. "It's marvellous what gold can do."

"The cinderella colony has really come into its own. Thank Christ for the Victorian digger."

"Yeah, otherwise you Sandgropers in the west could still

be gropin' in the sand - just as your South Australian neighbours used to say. Anyway, here's the Palace, lead me to the bar, I'm as dry as a wooden God."

"While you wet your whistle Digger, I'll book in to the pub. I'll order some breakfast too. For a grown lad that pie an' tomato sauce we had on the train hardly touched the sides."

"Looks like we could be coolin' our heels for a coupla days," said Tim, over the breakfast table. "What's on the agenda besides drinkin' grog?"

"Well, I think I might take a walk back up the road a bit to Templetons an' see about buyin' that station lease."

Tim laughed. "Still haven't forgotten her, have you sport? Anyhow, I think before you front up to those Templeton office-Johnnies, it might pay you to indulge in a hair-cut." Tim fingered his strong black beard. "An' I might even treat myself to the luxury of a shave."

"Oh no Tim, without that beard, your mates won't even recognise you."

"Well, bar the moustache, it's comin' off," swore Tim. "I want to look my best for these city gold-diggers, especially if they're as good-lookin' as some o' those females we saw walkin' down the street."

Paddy carried on with the small-talk, wondering whether Tim really meant it about making the most of a good time on one of his rare visits to the city. Paddy might have urged him on further. But despite the natural excitement of all the temptations of a thriving city, Paddy couldn't get his mind off Jenny, just as Tim had intimated.

Besides a shave and a hair-cut, Paddy also purchased a new outfit of clothes. Not shiny shoes, pin-striped suit, waistcoat and bowler hat, but better quality station togs, including a new broad-brimmed hat with rakish edges similar to Julien Clayton-Browne. All the same he didn't want to appear to the livestock company manager as a dude with little experience, apart from the ready cash close at hand.

Paddy need not have worried. One look at him by the Templetons manager was enough. Then the voice and the strong handshake with the smile with the eyes rather than a toothy grin. Here was a true man of the outback. The manager himself had originally come from the outback also. The Queensland cattle country, Templetons having originated from t'otherside, the company still preferring to select their managers from over there.

"Yes Paddy, the lease is yours. In fact, if you don't get as much for your gold claims as you expect, we could arrange extra finance. And because you've had such good rains in the Lower Murchison, we could fully stock you up with sheep."

"Thank you Mr Woodhams," said Paddy.

The manager smiled, shaking Paddy's hand again. "No matey, call me Bill. It's a pleasure to have met."

So Paddy's visit to the livestock company was successful, even if he only turned up with a token amount of money. He now walked down the street with his mind on Jenny Dunbar even more, thrilled with the thought of telling her the news.

Later in the busy main bar of the Palace, he told Tim.

Tim laughed loudly. "You didn't have to tell me, Paddy lad, you look as happy as a pig in manure. But what if she knocks you back after all? You haven't even asked for her hand yet, have you?"

Paddy had become serious. "No, I guess I haven't. But really Tim, there's somethin' between us. Somethin' different."

"But I remember you tellin' me you had been that way about little Ann Fogarty."

At the angry look in Paddy's eyes, Tim hesitated. "Sorry cobber, but you would reckon I should know all about women. I never told you before, but at one time when I returned to Melbourne for a time after prospectin' up near Hall's Creek with a quite a bit o' money in me pocket I

might add, I latched onto someone I thought was special."
Tim's eyes clouded.

"But just when we were due to be married, she decided
to leave me for someone else. O' course, losin' my gold
money in the Melbourne crash didn't help. That's when I
came back an' joined my digger mates up north again."

Though feeling a certain sympathy for Tim, Paddy was
still annoyed. "What, you mean that without my bein' able
to buy Singleton station, Jenny would probably pass me by?
You know she's not like that Tim!"

Tim placed his hand on Paddy's shoulder.

"No, I didn't mean that matey. "If looks an' personality
mean anythin', Jenny's one in a million. But it's just that
I don't want to see you get hurt m'lud. Anyway, let's walk
round town an' try all the new drink joints. Sorta pub crawl
like we used to do in Kal'."

"All right Tim, but just to look round. Just at the moment,
I'm not in a drinkin' mood."

Two days later Daniel arrived on the early morning train.
Paddy and Tim met him at the station. It was not surprising
that most of Daniel's talk over breakfast was about the
coming election.

"As a matter of fact, I've got so sick of trying to raise
candidates among the diggers for the new gold provinces,
that I've decided to have a go myself."

"Jesus," said Paddy. "But you'd hardly have the time
Daniel."

"I'm going to make time," replied Daniel, with firm lips.
"You just don't realise how hard it's been, even though
there's now tens of thousands of diggers frequenting the
Eastern Goldfields. It's not that they lack interest in politics.
They're eternally talking about Eureka and freedom in the
pubs, but that's about as far as they get."

"Yeah," said Tim. "Paddy an' I were only talkin' about
it while whilin' our way between Field's Find an' Watheroo."

Paddy gave a grin. "I even suggested that Tim be a candidate for the new seat o' Murchison."

Daniel showed interest. "Well, you could be Tim. You've had the learning. And with it you've got that special ruggedness which the diggers appreciate. Yes Tim, and now you'll be able to afford it, why not?"

"As I told Paddy, No... No... No...!" swore Tim. "But otherwise I'll help every bit I can."

"My God Tim, I've heard that story from diggers so many times in the last few weeks, I'm fed up." Daniel suddenly dropped his knife and fork on the table and looked at Paddy.

"Well now, what about you old friend? Now I come to think of it, you've got the lot. Son of a smallholder farmer which could get the more ordinary station-owners and cockies in, and a proven digger besides."

"And a flamin' successful one," laughed Tim. "Someone ordinary who's struck it rich. Why didn't I think of it before?"

Paddy put up his hands in protest. "Hey, steady on for Chris'sake!"

Tim would not be beaten. "But you said yourself Paddy, how your grandfather talked about ordinary folks needin' someone liberal an' learned to look up to. Who better than you ole chum? Yeah by golly, why didn't I think o' that before?"

"Well matey?" asked Daniel, his eyes unusually eager.

Paddy looked imploringly at Tim. "Tell him why cobber, for Chris-sake? An' even then I wouldn't be in it."

"He's gone an' fallen in love," said Tim scathingly. "An' gone an' bought a sheep station in the bargain."

Daniel's eyes showed a flicker of annoyance, reminding Paddy so much of the time when Daniel had been unhappy about his relationship with Ann Fogarty. It was one of Daniel's more unfortunate traits, the tendency to want to possess people, or use them for his own ends.

"What, when?" gasped Daniel, recovering a little.

"Oh Jenny Dunbar," said Paddy. "You remember Jim Dunbar up at Mt Rupert. Well, his eldest son Will took up a station in the Lower Murchison back in '80. He an' his wife Peg have a daughter, Jennifer, round eighteen. But Tim's all wrong, though I did take a shine to her there's nothin' serious yet, I tell you." Paddy felt like a little boy, trying to explain a misdemeanour.

Daniel was more sympathetic. He even smiled. "But what about this station?"

"Well, apart from Jenny I liked the look o' that too. I fixed up the lease with Templetons yesterday, awaitin' o' course, the money for the claims."

"That part of it's all right," said Daniel. However his face still showed disappointment over Paddy's purchase. "So it looks as if you are going to settle down, despite all that independence you showed in your younger days on the farm at York." Daniel smiled at Tim. "He was quite a rebel."

"I'm not surprised," said Tim. "But let's get onto business. By what you just said, it's good news about the claims."

"Yes, I got the best deal by quitting the lot to one British company," explained Daniel. He looked at Paddy. "Our two mines in Coolgardie and Kal' besides."

Paddy was eager. "Well, what was the price?"

"Satisfactory, of course. You know me Paddy, if it wasn't, I wouldn't have made the deal. Thirty thousand pounds for yours and Tim's prospects up at Leonora, and twenty thousand for our shows in Coolgardie and Kal."

Tim gave a whistle. "My God, a fortune. We'd better celebrate."

"Oh, there's a few signatures involved in Perth here first." Daniel became more serious. "As a matter of fact, now that I've become a genuine liberal candidate, selling the claims to an overseas company did make me feel like a hypocrite."

"What do you mean, for Chris'sake?" asked Tim.

"You should know what I mean Tim. The British companies are gobbling up all the best mining leases, as they did in Victoria and Queensland. The trouble is that Westralia, with the mess it was in before we found the gold, can least afford it."

"Well, I do agree we should try to stop it matey, I do agree," said Tim. "An' I've talked so much about this with other diggers. That's what carryin' the Eureka flag is all about. Self sufficiency for good old Australia, which means not lettin' these hungry British companies grab the best ore-bodies, not only like they're doin' in Westralia, but like they've done in South Africa, Canada, New Zealand, Victoria and Queensland. You name it, in every flamin' British colony - all the profits finishin' up in London. An' o' course now we've got the Yanks here too. See in the *West Australian* this mornin' a big write-up about a Herbert Hoover who's just landed here to manage that big new mine the Americans put down north o' Mt Magnet." Tim drew a breath. "Yeah, I totally agree with you Daniel. But without us havin' ready capital to buy machinery to mine the deep gold, what'n hell can we do about it? You know the old sayin', that beggars can't be choosers. So we just have to put aside our utopian principles as you call 'em, an' grab a bit while we can."

"Yes Tim," replied Daniel quietly. "But remember, as a people's candidate I have to talk not only about the needs of the digger, now forced to labour down the mines for the industrialists, but also about the future of our colony."

"But you're a bloody Victorian like me Daniel," argued Tim. "Why the hell should we worry about a land usually full o' heat, dust, an' flamin' flies?"

"But we do, don't we? And of course, as a newspaperman who believes in social justice, I could worry far more. As a newspaperman I also study statistics. If I told you how much gold has been taken out of this country without Westralia gaining any benefit, besides a few jobs and a few shares bought by the old landed gentry, you'd be shocked."

"No I wouldn't matey," returned Tim, soberly. "The

trouble with you Daniel, with your intellect, you imagine the ordinary bloke doesn't think or even talk sense. Why, after the big rain when Paddy was stuck out on the Dunbar station, an' I was stuck with the other diggers in the Field's Find pub among other things we talked about the need for better roads an' railways. O' course then it came up about how this foolish government, despite Westralia bein' in the midst of a world-shatterin' gold boom, has had to give a British railway companies millions of acres of our best agricultural lands just to put down railtracks an' supply locomotives."

"I agree," said Daniel. "Why, with the wealth of gold Kalgoorlie has already produced alone, we could have railways and macadam roads galore, with diamond-studded cars and coaches to go with them. Yes Tim, I totally agree. But I'll bet that most of the politicking in the Field's Find pub was brought on by yours truly, Tim McBride. What I mean is that you do think far deeper than the average worker or digger." Daniel turned to Paddy. "You too matey. That's why I've always appreciated your company. And that's why you'd make an ideal candidate for the seat of Murchison."

Though Paddy answered in the negative, he still couldn't deny that the talk had inspired him. It so much brought out all the ideals his grandfather and his parents had talked about for the future of the battling colony. It was so frustrating now that its fabulous mining potential was being revealed, that the profit should be taken away to add to the coffers of England - and now America. It needed someone to stand up and shout about it from the electoral platforms.

Indeed, he felt now that if it wasn't for Jenny and Singleton station, he might, as Tim would say, come down from his perch and have a go. Yet though he wasn't even betrothed to Jenny, and probably might never be, he still felt that at least he should discuss it with her ...

CHAPTER 15

After a week in the city Paddy and Tim returned to Field's Find, making their way back by way of Watheroo and the Gunyidi Track. Once back in Field's, Paddy was anxious to get out to the Dunbars to break the news to Jenny about purchasing the station. It was not unnatural that he was still the butt of jokes from Tim.

"Can't get there quick enough, can you cobber? But do be careful," he grinned. "Otherwise, with your eagerness, you could easily lose her."

Paddy took notice and as he rode, his mind toyed with what he was going to say. Since the drying up of the flood, the station country had already shown a miraculous change, the earth under the re-enlivened mulgas, showing green shoots already six inches high. The sheep, rather than scuffing their way along red dusty trails in search of food, were now lying contentedly in the mild late Autumn sun.

When Paddy rode up to the homestead, Peg had just sounded the gong for morning tea. At sight of Paddy, Jenny forced herself not to race ahead in front of the men. Today, rather than the inevitable riding-habit, she was dressed in a blue calico house dress with white piping, the simple garment only accentuating her shapeliness. Paddy drew a breath, still wondering what he was going to say.

Jenny spoke first, still trying to keep the gladness out of her voice.

"So our Prodigal is back from the big city. Painted the town red I suppose?"

"Well, we did a bit," grinned Paddy. "You see we got such a good price for our claims." Paddy realised he was showing off once again, something Tim had warned him about. But he went on. "The city does stir one's blood a bit. But my God, the place has grown."

"That's gold for yuh," smiled Will, walking up with Peg.

"Just what Tim McBride said," returned Paddy, trying desperately to be casual.

"But the important thing is," said Will, "what happened about the Singleton lease?"

Paddy couldn't keep the enthusiasm from his voice.

"I got it!"

While Jenny held her eyes down, it was Peg Dunbar who brought out the feelings of the family.

"Oh that's marvellous Paddy. We couldn't have asked for a better neighbour. Are you going to live on the station?"

Paddy's eyes crinkled. "Well I had a mind to. As I said even before the breaking of the long drought, I like the district. So does Tim. As a matter o' fact, he's bought that mine I was tellin' you about, made arrangements with London by cable."

Jenny looked at Paddy, her heart still thumping.

"Well Paddy, I suppose you'll be buying sheep?"

"Yes, I've already arranged with Templetons. They've offered to stock the place up for me - accordin' to the manager, even if I was still a bit shorta cash."

Will became cautious. "I'd watch 'em if I was you Paddy.

"But the manager seemed a decent bloke."

"That's why he was given the job," said Will. "But you must remember he's got to do what he's told. Sure it's a good time to give out loans for sheep. But with the stations right down in numbers after the long drought, the sheep will be hard to come by. So those sheep will most likely be purchased from families such as the Andersons, Clayton-Brownes an' so forth, who besides their formerly parched station runs, own extensive properties in safer rainfall areas, closer to the coast, like round Geraldton and Greenough. An' o' course, along the Avon Valley, and on the other side o' the ranges, near Guildford. Just think of the commission that Templetons will get. Also most of the old families have shares in Templetons, even though it's a t'otherside company."

"Yes, Tim McBride warned me about the buying rings, controlled by the big pastoralists and the big companies like Templetons, on the way back from Perth.

"That's right," said Will. "Livestock companies like Templetons rely mostly on share capital, the shares being mostly owned by the squattocracy. The tie-up between the livestock companies an' the big pastoralists, is even more blatant in the north, with the export of cattle from Wyndham an' Derby, where the buying rings are at their best - or I should say at their worst. Yes Paddy, and you may be sure that though the manager may have seemed on your side, Templeton's stockmen may not be. Many of 'em have been to finishing school and have been sired from the nob families. And we know who they are, businessmen graziers like the Andersons, McAllums an' Clayton-Brownes."

"Yeah," broke in Kim Dunbar, who had been listening. "Those young stock rep's could be onto you like flies to a jam-pot Paddy, especially if the new client has money to burn. Which you certainly have!"

Paddy nodded his head in agreement. "Doesn't give the battlin' station-owner much of a go either, does it? Especially ones who've lost most o' their sheep. Tim talked about the stock boys. He reckons their main aim seems to be to put it over the next mug." He laughed cynically. "Which I guess coulda been me. Anyhow, thanks for the good advice. But the trouble is, where do I get my sheep?"

Jenny's eyes were now full of interest, her natural sense of economics, inherited not only from sensible parents, but also from the tough, simple life on a station.

"Paddy could probably buy sheep from Ben Ryan in Northampton, north of Geraldton," she suggested. "His brother Jack has also got that station north-west of Thundelarra, which being closer to the coast, survived the drought far better than the rest of us."

"Good thinkin' Jennifer," spoke her father. "But it all depends on Paddy. He may be committed with Templetons."

"I'm not!" Paddy said. "It was just that I thought that them bein' the only big livestock company here, they'd be the logical ones to make arrangements." He looked up almost helplessly. "Well, what do you all reckon? Should I ride up an' see the Ryans?"

"To be sure," said Will. "As a matter o' fact Paddy, I might ride up there with you." He turned to his daughter. "I guess you'll be comin' along too Jenny?"

"Well, yes, if Paddy wouldn't mind." It came out naturally, Jenny finding it hard to stifle a blush.

Paddy too, felt the emotion, forcing himself to speak offhandedly. "You could make up for me Jenny. As far as selectin' the right ones are concerned, I probably wouldn't know a sheep from a goat, as my elder brother John used to say when I wouldn't take an interest in the farm."

"Well now you can prove him wrong," smiled Peg. "But with our help if you need it." She turned to her husband. "Seeing there is not much doing on the station at present Will, you should be off to the Ryans as soon as possible. They've probably already had enquiries from other station-owners wishing to stock up."

"First thing tomorrow Peg," drawled Will. "So looks like you'd better camp here for the night Paddy. Anythin' you want at Field's we could pick up on the way through."

"Suits me Will. But I'm so beholden to you all."

"Don't worry," laughed Will. "As Peg says, just at present, we've time on our hands."

The Ryans received Paddy with open arms. Not only because the name O'Leary gave sure indication of an Irish background, but because the Ryans like most other Irish families in the colony, also revered Paddy's father. The bond was further strengthened by the fact, that one original member of the now extensive Ryan group of families in the colony, had been transported for horse-stealing. Here the easy-going Big Jack Ryan laughed uproariously, saying it was just that his uncle Dinnie had been unlucky enough to get caught. "Anyhow," he went on, "these sheep you require, I can supply around five thousand, but for the other six, it may pay you to ride over to the brother's place in Northampton. It's a long way Paddy, but it's worth the effort. Ben's been importin' top quality merino rams from South Australia. Last year his wool fetched top price."

Paddy looked helpless. "Good idea. Guess I'd better start out for Northampton right away."

Big Jack gave a loud laugh. "Oh, not by yourself lud. I'll be in your company. Haven't seen brother Ben for quite a while." He turned. "How about you Will? Comin'?"

"O' course Ben - Jenny too I guess?" He glanced at his daughter.

"Yes of course Dad," smiled Jenny. "Why did you even ask?"

"But why go to all this trouble just for me?" protested a worried Paddy.

"It's all right, we'll take it outa your hide later Paddy," laughed Big Jack. "But just right now we've got the time. Not like the cockies over near the Midland Railway who have to get their crops in, all we have to do now apart from odd jobs is wait for the wool clip in spring. An' by the looks o' this early winter feed by gad, the clip looks like a good one." He turned his head, the greying black hair, mane-like. "Don't worry about Peg Will, I'll send word over with one o' my station boys."

"Thanks," said Will. "The lad had better also let Peg know we could be a bit longer. If we buy the sheep we may as well help drive 'em back."

"Yeah," said Big Jack casually. "Could take a while though, it's well over a hundred miles, even straight as the crow flies. Still, seein' I'm ridin' with you, I may as well keep you company on the way back too - pushin' the woollies."

Paddy enjoyed the casual friendliness of this man, himself said to have originally come out as an illiterate shepherd. Indeed, Paddy appreciated the good neighbourliness of all these local station people. The good opening rains had no doubt lifted their spirits and enhanced their natural friendliness. Yet he wondered how the traditional graziers fared in comparison - the old rural well-to-do. From his experience at York and along the Avon Valley, besides his more recent experience with Julien Clayton-Browne, Paddy knew that they lived in a different world. As his Grandpa David had said long ago, the influential families only did their exploring and conquering for one reason, wealth and power, not to get on with their neighbours, especially if the neighbours were of a lower caste. The aim for most of the gentry colonists, as always, was to return to England - the ultimate of course to receive a knighthood for their colonial accomplishments, even though thoughts of a better more equalitarian world, might never enter their minds.

To Paddy, the Dunbars and Ryans were so different.

The whole operation, buying the sheep over at Northampton, and herding them back took more than three weeks. Paddy offered to pay the Dunbars and Ryans handsomely for their trouble. He realised he had got such a bargain with the sheep, mostly because the other Ryans over at Northampton also liked his looks, especially with a name like O'Leary. But when Paddy kept on harping on it, Big Jack told him off in no uncertain terms.

"Look Paddy, for Chris'sake pipe down about it, we may need help ourselves one day."

So Paddy just left it at that.

During the drive, Paddy naturally spent much time with Jenny. The young woman, after her experience alone with him on Singleton station now trusted him completely.

One evening after bedding down the sheep in a large wire yard close to a convenient government well, Will and Big

Jack smoked their pipes after a whisky, as Jenny and Paddy walked off in the twilight.

"Well-matched pair aren't they? said Big Jack, indicating the young couple. "How long before the weddin'?"

"Not even engaged yet," laughed Will, not too loudly. "In fact I feel like eggin' 'em on."

"No, don't," replied Big Jack, wisely. "Just let nature take its course. An' I'd say with them, there's a lotta commonsense mixed along with it." He laughed, with another puff of his pipe. "Lucky you Will, you've got little to worry about."

"Don't I know it," said Will.

Before the drive was over, Paddy did propose to Jennifer, but it was not quite as peaceful as Big Jack had hinted. Jenny responded by throwing herself into his arms. Paddy then brought up the urgent need to have contractors build the homestead.

"You don't have to worry Paddy," insisted Jenny, putting her hand to his cheek. "Why, I'd marry you if you had nothing."

"But a good station an' a nice new homestead helps a bit, surely," burbled Paddy.

"But that's not what love is all about," insisted Jenny. "Love is simply wanting to be close to someone you love, like I do with you Paddy."

"Yeah," drawled Paddy. "But you have to use your head a bit, don't you? What I mean is, if everyone who loved each other was like that, my girl, nothin' might get done. Lovin' between a man an' woman means children, an' the children need to eat, as do the married pair. An' o' course every married pair needs a house."

"My mother told me almost the same thing Paddy, but what I really meant was that you didn't need to go to the trouble of buying Singleton. And now it's not just an ordinary house but a real expensive one." She began to cry. "I just want you Paddy, without any strings attached."

Paddy knew she was trying to tell him how much she really loved him, and he felt humbled, thanking his Maker for the first time in years. It made him think again of his mother, Judith, and how she had reminded him that there would be times in his life, when sweet gifts would be laid at his feet for no apparent reason, and for seemingly no deserving.

The next afternoon, they told the good news to Will and Big Jack.

Later as the young pair walked off together alone, Big Jack brought out a fresh bottle of colonial spirits from his satchel.

"Mother Mary, it's time again for a whisky," he yelled joyously to Will. "I wonder when the wedding'll be? Reckon it could be a good year to get married in Yalgoo. A bit more rain this winter an' the countryside couldn't look better."

Will took a swig from the bottle. "Yeah, Jack ole man, I certainly agree. In a year like this, Yalgoo could be ideal. Also people could travel all the way up from down south by train for the weddin'. But it's not for us to decide."

"Well, the bride's old man has to pay for the doin's," countered Big Jack. "I should know, I've had two daughters married already. Lucky you've struck such a good season."

"Wouldn't matter," said Will, drawing on his pipe. "Peg an' I would still make sure we'd manage, because we both like Paddy."

"Sure enough," said Big Jack.

When Paddy eventually returned to Field's Find, he broke the news about the coming marriage to Tim.

"Jesus old mate," said Tim, realising it called for another visit to the bar. "Let's step over for a drink."

"So you've gone an' done it," he said with a wink, almost

277

draining his glass in one gulp. "Any problems?"

"Well you were right. Buyin' the station an' so forth almost buggered things up. She loved me in spite of it."

Tim laughed loudly. "Told you, didn't I? In fact I knew from that first day when she set eyes on you here in Field's. Anyway cobber, you don't have to worry about labour for that station either. Wilga's back with a half-dozen other blacks, four of 'em women, one bein' Wilga's chosen. You know, the one who ran over to him that day. An' one o' the lubras is in the family way."

"Jesus," gasped Paddy. "So Wilga's brought 'em back from Clayton Downs?"

"Yeah, an' Lennie reckons that Mister Julien Clayton-Browne's ropable. In fact, one o' the blacks had his shoulder clipped with a bullet. Nothin' to worry about though. Anyway, they're all now camped with the local Yamadgees."

"Hell, it was probably all right with just Wilga goin' walkabout all the time, but what with him clearin' off with all the others, I guess the Clayton-Brownes will be usin' their legal rights to claim 'em back."

"Yeah, like the rotten bastards do up north, they've got the niggers' thumbprints. The quicker that putrid old English Master an' Servant Law is cut out the better, especially with these poor bloody natives, who'd willingly give their thumbprints just for a bit o' flour or even a kind word."

"Yes, Tim, I'd certainly need no thumbprint. If a native didn't want to work for me, he wouldn't have to, like I told Wilga in Coolgardie."

Tim gave a knowing grin. "But that's your nature matey. You learnt from your parents. Everyone in this world has a soul an' has feelin's. Not like the Clayton-Brownes who read a passage from the Bible every night, an' treat their black servants like dogs durin' the day. Yeah, it's your kind of attitude which makes us want you for a candidate for the Murchison, cobber." Tim was apologetic. "Sorry Paddy, I said I wouldn't bring it up again, didn't I?"

"You did Tim. Anyhow, I'd better go an' see Wilga."

"Yeah, you'd better. Fact is, accordin' to Lennie, he already knew you'd bought the station before he even got back here."

"How, for Chris'sake?"

"Oh, he knew all right. Haven't you ever heard how these Aborigines communicate from a distance. Certain ones like Wilga are probably given special powers in these initiations they have. If he's like that, seein' he's so close to you he could've tapped into your thoughts too Paddy. Probably why he came back with all those extra sheep-hands."

"I'll put 'em all on with Wilga then If they want to. An' my God, if the Clayton-Brownes do come on the place, I might run 'em off with a Winchester."

Tim laughed harshly, downing another whisky and ordering two more. "Not by yourself matey. I could have all the diggers across from Fields in no time. Any excuse to have a go at those damned troopers. Though with all us diggers now around, I doubt if the Clayton-Brownes'd be game. The squatters learnt too much of a lesson up north when they accused us o' stealin' their shepherd girls for camp-mates."

Paddy's sudden quietness, brought a quick response from Tim.

"Reckon I'm a bit of a hypocrite, don't you? But remember those lubras weren't forced to go with us diggers. Like this one who has elected to live with me here in Field's. It's not like givin' one's thumbprint an' bein' made to work for the gentry - besides bein' forced to open their legs occasionally for the wealthy graziers an' their sons." Tim downed his whisky. " Sorry, I do get crude at times don't I?"

"No, you couldn't have explained it better. Also I get your point about the native women electin' to go with prospectors of their choice. But as my Grandpa David used to say, it's all part of the whole Aboriginal tragedy, the breaking down of the old tribal laws, which as weak as they were, at least encouraged the Aboriginal male to protect his womenfolk."

"Yeah, your Grandpa David was dead right. In fact, what's

left of the Abo's have picked up such bad habits from us whites, particularly with smokin' an' booze, most o' the bucks would hire their wives an' daughters to a white man, just for that proverbial shot o' whiskey or plug o' tobaccy. You're right matey, so havin' decided that the lubra is entitled to some sort o' choice, we must help 'em fight for their rights against bastards like this Clayton-Browne."

Paddy grabbed Tim's hand. "Thanks cobber. Anyway, it's gettin' late. After I've seen Wilga, I want to get back to the Dunbars."

"Yeah," grinned Tim. "Don't forget to give Jenny my regards."

Next morning Paddy and Jenny rode over to Singleton station to find Wilga and his companions already there. In fact, the natives had made straight for Mt Singleton, following an ancient trail over the Pinyallings.

Apart from being barefoot, the natives were all dressed in their station clothes, except for the young woman expecting the baby, who wore a plain calico dress, her thinnish calves looking out of place against her distended belly. Paddy noticed how the shepherdesses, including Wilga's chosen, always kept their eyes down, their dark lashes now fluttering with pleasure.

"We ready for work," said Wilga, running on the spot.

"But where'd you all camp matey?" asked Paddy, indicating the still locked shearers' quarters.

Wilga pointed towards the mount. "Old kalleep, been there long time."

Jenny broke in. "I didn't show you Paddy, but there's an ancient native camping ground around the base of the mount a bit. Goodness, but there's nothing left."

Wilga smiled broadly.

"Plenty all right Missus. Plenty kangaroo for tucker. No worry. Now, we look round sheep eh? Bad blowfly this year. We catch struck sheep - fix up."

"Yes Wilga," smiled Jenny gratefully. "The green Autumn blowfly is bad this year owing to the big rain. Thank you so much."

"No worry Missus," smiled Wilga, trotting off with his companions.

"Looks like you've put 'em on the pay-roll sweetheart," said Paddy to Jenny. "Thank God I'll have a wife who knows plenty about sheep. If I was on my own here, the green blowfly woulda probably got all the flock before I woke up."

She laughed. "Well my lad, if you want to run Singleton station you'd better learn, or my goodness, you'll be gettin' the boot." She became more serious. "Anyhow Paddy, we should feel honoured that Wilga and his capable friends are here to help. Had it been me who'd been made a virtual slave just through a thumbprint and I'd finally got away, I doubt if I'd want to work again for a white person, ever."

Paddy put his arm around her. "I feel the same way, but it seems that if given a go, the natives are not really averse to station-work - especially the womenfolk, an' with sheep, I mean. As you already impressed on me durin' the drive when I was gettin' in a temper - sheep are contrary animals you can't hurry. As you said - let 'em go their own pace. From what I can see, it's like that with these natives."

"Well Dad has said the very same thing about our own boys on the station. Don't push 'em, give 'em good tucker, pay 'em fair wages, an' you've got 'em for good."

"Probably the best way to treat any worker," said Paddy. "Black or white. By now the genteel families should have learnt their lesson. Accordin' to my Grandpa David, it was the reason this colony was turned into a convict establishment, because the very same families had refused to pay their white shepherds decent wages."

"Yes," agreed Jenny. "And the same white shepherds went out into the backblocks cutting sandalwood while others left the colony for far better pay in South Australia. That was just why the pastoralists had to bring in convicts. It was well drilled into us when I went to school in Goomalling." She put her arms around him. "Anyhow my darling, with the natives not needing the quarters, it looks like we'll be right for a home for awhile." She giggled. "That's after we're married of course."

Paddy laughed nervously. "But I've already booked contractors to put up the homestead. Real good ones. I discussed it with Big Jack Ryan, even before the end o' the drive. He was sayin' how they'd made such a good job o' the Yalgoo courthouse. Expert with stone an' so forth. So I told him to go ahead an' arrange it. The builders could be here any time. Big Jack reckons that usin' local stone, they could whack up a decent size house in a coupla months."

Jenny put her hand to his mouth, playfully. "Sh'sh, I thought I told you to forget about the house."

"Well you hush too sweetheart," said Paddy, grabbing her and kissing her. "It's my turn to be realistic like you with the sheep. We'll need a homestead sometime, so why not have it ready an' waitin'? I'm goin' to tell the builders to make sure it's ready, because I want it to be my weddin' present to the most delectable gal in the colony."

"Talk like that won't get you anywhere," she laughed. "Anyway, what about the preacher? You're Catholic aren't you? Do you want me to change?"

Paddy laughed. "You know, my mother said the very same thing to my father in far more dangerous circumstances."

"I know that your mother insisted she turn Catholic, because she believed it would not worry her as much as your father. I feel the same as her Paddy."

"But Jenny dear, my parents are very liberal about it, not that they don't care. My elder brother John married Hannah, daughter of Franz Heindrickson, the Northam cartage contractor. They got married in the Northam Lutheran church. It seems the only time I attend church now is at weddin's or funerals. Anyhow, whatever church your folks got married under, it'll do me, as I'm sure it'll do my folks."

"Well, if you put it that way, my folks were married Congregational, mainly I think because the Congregational minister in Goomalling was so popular. He used to mix so much with the ordinary folk."

"Well, who's the most popular preacher in Yalgoo then?"

"It could be the Congregational minister up there too. He seems to be the only one who gets about. Sometimes visits our station in his horse and trap."

"Righto it's Congregational then," said Paddy, kissing her again. "But what's Big Jack Ryan goin' to say about an O'Leary not marryin' in a Catholic church?"

"Well, out here I doubt if he'd care," she laughed. "Like us, he takes people as he find 'em. No Paddy, don't worry, the Ryans will be along to the wedding because they like you as a person, similar to the way they like the Dunbars as a family, that's what it's all about."

Paddy had tears in his eyes. "Yes it is sweetheart, an' right now I'm givin' thanks to Jesus as my mother taught me. I hope you don't mind."

She kissed him. "Of course I don't my love. As a matter of fact, I was well ahead of you."

It became September, and with more good rains in the station country that winter, the land was indeed a picture. While the mulga and bowgada flats were a carpet of pink and white everlastings, the perennial shrubs along the Gnow's Nest Range made the most of a good winter. The display was truly magnificent.

Most of the people who attended the wedding from down south, travelled up to Yalgoo by train via the Midland Line and Geraldton. Among these was Daniel, as well as Paddy's younger brother Rory, who now ran the O'Leary farm at Merredin.

But Paddy's parents, Judith and Michael, chose to travel by horse and buggy from York. John and his wife Hannah and their two children rode with them. On the way north, they stopped at Goomalling, where Peg Dunbar's family joined them in another conveyance. Then there were the Dunbars from Mt Rupert. So it was quite a procession.

After a night on the Dunbar station, it was off with more buggies across to Field's to pick up Tim McBride. Then it was north along the edge of the Gnow's Nest Range to Yalgoo, the Fergusons from Thundelarra and the Ryans from Bindamundra joining them on the way.

As the Congregational Church had still not been built in Yalgoo, they held the ceremony in the new Town Hall, attractively faced with local stone, similar to other public buildings. In Yalgoo, Tim discovered more of his digger friends, and with him gaining permission for them to attend the wedding, the hall was filled to capacity. For convenience, it was also decided that the reception be held under the same roof, one of the local publicans supplying refreshments. The editor of the *Geraldton Express*, Mike Beaumont, was there with his note-book and camera, ready to record the first wedding in the Yalgoo Town Hall. Both being in the newspaper game, it was not surprising that Beaumont spent most of his time with Daniel Hordacre of the *Coolgardie Miner*. Even so, though Paddy was happy enough to renew his acquaintance with Daniel and meet the editor of the *Express*, he became annoyed after the wedding when Daniel again made the suggestion about Paddy becoming a candidate for the seat of Murchison. To make matters worse, it seemed that in cornering Paddy, Daniel had made sure that Jenny was away talking to other guests.

"Steady on Daniel," said Tim, who was also with them. "Let the man have his honeymoon before you pester him again, for Chris-sake."

"Sorry," said Daniel, half-apologetically. "But we are getting desperate." He turned to Paddy. "I guess you haven't heard who's won pre-selection for the conservatives here? Or I should say, the one who's standing for the Groves

Gang."

"Wouldn't have a clue?" replied Paddy, more concerned about getting back with Jenny.

"Well, it's Ashley McAllum."

"Oh no!" Paddy failed to control himself.

"Yes, it's true," went on Daniel. "Of course, he's now married, and living on one of the big McAllum holdings out from Geraldton."

Mike Beaumont, well-known for his support of the underdog, now said his piece.

"Ashley unfortunately, is pretty tough opposition. Having had so much experience with the *West Australian* as a reporter, he's learnt how to get through to the average Joe Blow."

"I'd call him more a con-man," added Daniel. "Not that he wouldn't be any good as a politician."

"Well yeah, he could be," returned Paddy casually. "An' if I wasn't gettin' married, I could think about puttin' up against the bastard, but hell Daniel, not now."

The Geraldton editor answered for Daniel. "It's still a while before the election Paddy. Not till next April. Think about it, because if this wider Murchison electorate, with all its new digger voters is virtually gifted to the Hungry Six families just for the want of a candidate, my God, I think I'll close up my paper."

"Yeah, it wouldn't be too good would it?" returned Paddy, still trying to shrug it off.

Paddy was forced to admit that the prospect of putting up against an old rival like Ashley McAllum, stirred his blood. Also by refusing to put up as a candidate when he was apparently so popular, he felt he was letting his side down.

He was relieved when they were joined by Jenny, still radiant in her white taffeta gown. With Tim making a wisecrack about the young pair wanting to get away to enjoy the bliss of the nuptial couch, they walked away arm in arm, later to pose for their photograph outside the Town Hall.

Certainly Paddy's thoughts now were wholly devoted to

his new young bride, not only grateful for the fate that had brought them together, but grateful also that they could now share the future as man and wife.

Jenny's thoughts were similar, her feelings enhanced by the tremors of sheer rapture which swept through her as she experienced the look of tender worship in her husband's eyes.

It had been arranged that the bride and groom spend their first night in the new Yalgoo Arms hotel, itself an imposing stone-walled edifice.

"Better do the right thing an' carry the bride through the bed-room door," said Paddy, gathering Jenny in his arms.

Though joining in the hilarious ritual, Jenny felt a tinge of nervousness. While they were courting, though often aroused, Paddy had never gone beyond the usual caressing and cuddling, even though Jenny herself had felt so overwhelmed with love she might have let him go further.

But now though she would let herself go with abandon, she was as worried as any virgin might be.

By the light of the electric lamp, Paddy caught the mixture of fear and desire in his young bride's eyes, and in preparation for bed let her undress and change into her nightgown in private, he doing the same.

"Paddy, please don't hurt me," she whispered, as he held her close.

"I never will sweetheart," he breathed.

"I know that my love," she said, her voice trembling as he gently laid her on the bed.

Their love-making continued through the night, their pleasures ever sweeter, their love ever more consuming.

The newly-weds decided to spend the rest of the honeymoon in their new homestead at Singleton, but on passing through Dunbar station, they received shocking news. Wilga and the other male natives over at Singleton had been arrested by the police, put in iron neck collars, chained together and led away behind the troopers' mounts.

According to the native girls, who had fled over to the Dunbars, the police had told Julien Clayton-Browne, who was with them, that it wasn't their policy to arrest womenfolk. Apparently Clayton-Browne had still tried to coerce his former shepherdesses, but they had refused, running off into the mulga to hide.

CHAPTER 16

"The rotten bastards!"

Paddy's outburst was immediately followed by an apology to Jenny and her family. The rest of the party, after spending the night further north on the track from Yalgoo, had parted company at Field's to proceed on the long trek south.

"It's all right Paddy," Will almost spat. "You are only speakin' out for the rest of us. The mongrels must have known about us bein' away at Yalgoo for the weddin'. Otherwise they wouldn't have been game, even with the police."

"Yeah," returned Paddy angrily. "The dirty swines knew I would've put up a fight to protect the natives, besides enlistin' the aid o' the diggers from Field's." He sucked in his breath. "But now Wilga an' his friends have been taken away." Paddy turned to one of the shepherd girls.

"Any of the boys hurt Yandi? Did they put up a fight?"

The girl nodded her head. "Yes, fight bad. Policeman chase Wilga. Kick policeman, say not go back to station - only run away again. Boys in chains all kick other policemen. Spit at Mr Clayton-Browne. All say no go back to station. Run away again."

"What did the policemen do then?"

"Policemen say, kick policemen, spit on Mr Clayton-Browne, not stay on station, all boys be sent to Rott - nest."

"Oh, my God!" said Peg. "Rottnest Island, once natives go there they never come back!"

Both Peg and her daughter began to cry.

Paddy gritted his teeth. "Look, I think I'll take a trip to Perth and blow someone up. Or I should say argue the natives' case. It's so damned unfair. I don't know whether I told you or not Will, er Dad, but Wilga was the one who helped Bayley and Ford find Coolgardie."

"As a matter o' fact Paddy, you did tell me. But after all, Wilga's only a black man." Will became cynical. "No special mentions for them. I doubt if it would help Wilga and the others one bit. Still, with an election comin' on next year, with all the new digger voters askin' for a change, maybe you could throw in some threats."

Jenny, already worried about Clayton-Browne and the police taking away the native boys, became even more concerned. She realised that if Paddy brought politics into it, he would have people again pushing him to put up as a candidate.

"But I think first of all we should get over to Singleton to see if everything's all right." Jenny was also eager to settle into the recently completed homestead, which they had furnished.

"You're right Jenny," replied Paddy, quickly. "We'd better take the shepherd girls back too. Yandi an' Teeta were here a while back. Where've they gone now?"

One of the Dunbar house-girls gave answer. "Other girl sick. Have baby."

"Oh my God, yes," Peg Dunbar almost shrieked. "That's why they weren't all here, and the strain of having to run over from Singleton."

She turned to the house-girl. "Lullagi, where is she? Where are they?"

"Out behind house, in mulga. Me show." She barred her hands at the men. "Only lady."

"Yes," said Peg, turning to the men. "With them it's the law, only females look after females during a birth. Jenny and I will go."

But just as they were about to move off, the other three shepherd girls came around from behind the homestead, including the formerly pregnant one, her figure now almost back to normal. The lubra herself looked decidedly relieved, and in fact, had pulled on a pair of men's trousers, glad to be more like her sisters or cousins.

"But where's the baby?" Paddy questioned, a horrible thought in his mind.

"They said they decided to get rid of it," Jenny almost whispered. "I know it's nothing unusual Paddy, but my God, when it happens so close."

"But why?" asked Paddy, turning to one of the shepherd-esses, the chosen one of Wilga.

She fluttered her lashes in anger, her attractive lips drawn back, showing her teeth.

"Baby too much white-fella Clayton-Browne! Baby no good!"

Peg Dunbar took over, her voice firm.

"Look, it's done, so there is little we can do about it. They do the same to a new-born child if it is deformed, or even if it is a girl when they've had too many."

"Yeah," said Will, catching the mood of his wife. "And why not the likes of a Clayton-Browne, the bastard. Anyway by God, it's one less half-caste whom the families of the Hungry Six have sired. And by hell, out on their stations, especially up north, there's been plenty." He turned to his daughter. "Sorry Jenny."

"No, it's all right Dad. Anyhow, as I said before, I'd like Paddy and me to get over to Singleton before dark."

"Good idea," said Will. "But with all your gear, you'd better borrow the buggy." Jenny turned to the shepherdesses. "You girls want to ride back with us?"

Wilga's chosen pointed to the lubra who'd had the baby.

"She ride. We run." And with that the girls were off, the formerly pregnant one, pacing after them before she could be stopped.

"Hey," yelled Paddy. "Come back, you'll hurt yourself."

Peg smiled. "I doubt it, they are not like us white women you know. No lying up after giving birth for them."

Later as Jenny and Paddy drove off, Will gave a parting word. "You'll be shearin' in a coupla weeks Paddy, but now that you've lost your boys, don't worry about it, the Dunbars will hop in an' give you a hand. The same team is doin' both sheds anyhow."

"I feel like a waster," said Paddy to Jenny miserably as they rode along in the buggy. "What with knowing practically nothing about sheep, an' now your parents offering to organise our shearing."

"Well, we were going to work in together in any case," Jenny consoled him. "It's just that with the loss of Wilga and the other three boys, it makes it difficult for mustering before shearing."

"Yeah, I suppose the girls can do so much."

"Yes, although we haven't had the experience, they tell me that women are excellent at flock-watching. But yarding up near the shearing shed, when one has to move fast, and tempers get frayed, well Paddy, I don't think it's really a woman's place. Do you?"

"So we'll be short an' here's me runnin' off to Perth?"

"No, I didn't mean that. You forget there's Kim and our native boys. She squeezed his arm. "So you can still go. The girls were telling me they've also had experience helping cook for shearers, so what with that, besides bringing the flocks up to the yards for shearing, they are going to be pretty useful."

Sitting there bouncing along in the buggy, Paddy put his arm round his young wife. "Not much of a honeymoon, is it sweetheart?"

She leaned her head on his shoulder. "Oh darling, don't say that. What more could we want? A night in style in the Yalgoo Arms, a night under the stars along the track, and now a night in our own brand-new home. Yes Paddy, what more could we want?"

As Paddy drove with her across the little creek to the new homestead he could well agree. Although the house paddocks were drying off, the fact that they were still untouched by sheep, had left them covered in a panorama of pin-cushion daisies, not only in the usual pink and white, but in cornflower blue and heliotrope. It seemed that in this bountiful season after five years of drought, fickle Mother Nature had at last condescended to give her all.

Now with the sun about to set behind the Pinyallings, and Singleton rearing delightedly just to the south-west, the new homestead looked all the more luxurious.

Certainly it was well-appointed for a station homestead. Walls of local stone as planned, the reddish-yellow jaspers and sandstones complementing the metallic-green diorites and the grey granites. Different to the conventional square station-bungalow, the homestead was built more like a manor-house, two rectangle buildings with roofed promenade between, angled to make the most of the odd cooling breeze from the south-west.

In addition, rather than the corrugated galvanised-iron now all too common to farm and station buildings, the roof had been covered with treated sheoak shingles - not the expensive slate as Paddy would have wished - yet still giving the whole building a far more gracious effect.

Before the wedding, Jenny had again protested about all the cost. But Paddy had again consoled her.

"Why shouldn't I spend the extra? Why, with my gold profits I probably would have built a mansion in Perth anyhow, so why not build one right here?"

But after surviving those five years of drought on the station with her family, Jenny on that day, still could not help feeling concerned.

"But, my darling, we are falling into almost the same trap as that English family who had leased Singleton earlier. They were wealthy too you know, only to be thrown off by Templetons. They started off in a good year like this, and never even got their swanky homestead built."

"At least we'll have the swanky homestead," he joked. "But please stop worrying sweetheart. Or do you think we should have built our mansion in the city, probably up Mt Eliza overlookin' the Swan River an' right close to the McAllums an' Clayton-Brownes?"

"Well it could be a better investment there than a flash home on a station, I will admit. But if living in the city meant I had to live close to that lot, I'd rather stay here, even if I had to take the risk of going broke."

In answer he had put his arms around her and swung her off her feet. "So we've decided on our mansion out in the backblocks. Now stop actin' like a station-owner's daughter an' more like a gold-digger out to get her chop."

She laughed prettily. "It's all right Paddy, I think I could play the part if I want, and all the trimmings."

After spending those glorious nights with her since the wedding, Paddy could well believe it. With her looks and charm and her response as a partner, he believed she could leave any chorus girl for dead. It seemed with Jenny, she had the lot - all woman.

The fact that Jenny had already found so much fulfilment with her new husband, made her look even more desirable. The mood for both was even more enhanced as they contemplated having their first meal in their new homestead together. Then into their new bedroom, already tastefully appointed, to share once again those delightful mysteries.

Early next morning it was back to earth again, Jenny getting breakfast with the help of two of the shepherd girls, who had gently insisted that they should help, especially with the washing-up. Leaving Jenny to instruct the girls about their station-work, Paddy got ready to ride to Perth to vent his anger concerning Wilga and his friends. But Jenny became a little annoyed when Paddy said that rather than taking the track straight to Gibson and the Gunyidi Track, he would divert by way of Field's to talk to Tim. It worried her that any involvement with Tim would end up in something political. Even so, there was still the growing feeling that to secure the release of Wilga and the others, it might be the only way.

As expected, Tim's reaction to the story about the arrest of the natives was similar to that of Will Dunbar.

"The bastards, not that I blame the police so much, it's those mongrel Clayton-Brownes. An' here it is nearly 1900, Christ, you'd think it was back in the Dark Ages."

Paddy gave a harsh laugh. "I guess that rotten Master an' Servant Law does go back that far." Now Paddy realised he had made a mistake, because Tim came up with the typical answer.

"Well Paddy, we'll just have to get rid of it, won't we? An' a lot of other putrid old English laws as well. That's why we want you to represent our district matey." Tim coughed in mock apology. "Anyway, if you don't mind I might ride to Perth with you. There's a few little trinkets I want to buy, I'm settlin' down too, with Meei-a. Buildin' a cabin just off the jasper ridge up there by that patch o' York gums an' raspberry jams. Also want to order a coupla big corrugated iron tanks. Even with the big rain before winter, we've run outa good water already." Tim looked hard at Paddy. "I won't be crowdin' you out matey?"

"Hell no," said Paddy. "You're such good company along the track my friend." Paddy knew that he could have gone on to say in fact, that Tim was really too good a company - especially when he would want to stay that extra time in the Gibson and Watheroo pubs, and of course, live it up a bit in Perth. Nevertheless, there it was, Paddy had little choice but to accept Tim's offer.

But one suggestion that Tim did make along the track, was that Paddy should demand to see no one less than the Premier, William Groves, who, he said, though married into the Hungry Six mob, was still regarded as being among the more liberal of the sitting members.

Tim explained ... "Though the Groves Gang has let all the gold profits be taken out by those damned British companies, and now the Americans - at least Groves has conceived some big projects beneficial to the country. Take his backin' of the engineer C.Y. O'Connor in at last building a decent harbour at Fremantle. Also Grove's backin' of O'Connor's plan - said to be crazy by some, mind you - to pump water from the Darlin' Ranges, the whole three hundred an' sixty miles to Kalgoorlie."

Sitting there on his horse, biding his time along the Gunyidi Track, Tim flicked away the flies with a mallee-switch. "What I'm tryin' to say, is that at least Groves wants to do somethin' for Westralia, not like that Hungry Six mob with him, who are only in Parliament for their own ends. Like for instance, protectin' this rotten Master an' Servant Law." Tim gave another flick with the switch. "So you see Paddy, outa the whole filthy bunch, Groves himself would be the best."

"Yeah, that I could quite believe," said Paddy. "But the question still is, will he see me?"

As he feared, Paddy was to be disappointed.

Leaving Tim drinking in the Palace hotel, Paddy took a horse-cab along St George's Terrace up to Parliament House, situated on the eastern brow of Mt Eliza. The first setback for Paddy was at the military barracks, the gate of which had to be entered before he could gain access to the Parliament grounds.

The Guard, decked out in white pith helmet, red tunic, navy-blue trousers and polished boots, ran his eyes over Paddy's rough station clothes.

"Well Mister, what's your business?" he asked unsmilingly, his bayoneted rifle still half at the ready.

"I want to see the Premier," said Paddy, itching to say something impolite to the soldier, who had already annoyed him with his arrogance.

"Well you'll be flamin' lucky," replied the soldier, still holding the rifle. "Got an appointment?"

"No, I'm afraid not. You see something suddenly cropped up. Also I've come a hell of a long way."

"Doesn't matter," said the soldier. "Without an appointment you may as well clear off back home." When Paddy still stood there with a determined look on his face, the soldier relented slightly. "Anyway, what's your business about?" he questioned, now half at ease, his rifle and bayonet down by his side.

"It's confidential," returned Paddy, aching to smash the soldier in the face, despite his armoury. "Look mate, give us a go, surely I can see someone up there?"

"All right," said the guard. "You don't look, like you'll rob the joint. I'll take you to our Relief Sergeant."

The Relief Sergeant had almost the same questions as the Guard, except possibly couched more formally. His final verdict was also necessarily the same, except that he advised Paddy to talk to the Parliamentary Secretary.

That much over, Paddy saw the Secretary, where he had to repeat almost the same story he told to the Guard and the Relief Sergeant, except that the Secretary informed him that all communications with the Premier by any ordinary citizen was usually by letter.

"But, Sir, it's urgent," replied Paddy, hoping the "Sir" would help.

Paddy must have created an impression, because the Secretary suddenly told him to wait, as there might just be a chance of Paddy being able to talk to one of the Ministers.

Paddy was then left sitting on a hard wooden stool for a good two hours.

"Well my man," said the Secretary on his return, "you are fortunate, the Minister for Labour is able to give you time - Edwin Mainwaring."

"Oh Jesus," swore Paddy under his breath. "Bloody Ten Foot Ned. O' course he's now Minister for Labour as well as Mines, it was all in the paper."

"Yes," the Secretary went on, as if reading Paddy's thoughts. "And I'll have you show him the respect he deserves. We have just received word by cable that he has been granted a Knighthood in this year's Honours Listings."

"Oh Mother!" swore Paddy again under his breath.

Paddy was led upstairs to a huge tastefully furnished office, with desks and wall-panels done in polished jarrah, the chairs of the best imported leather. Sir Edwin was dressed in a fashionable pin-striped suit, with waistcoat to match complete with watch-chain. The only difference between now and when he confronted the diggers in Kalgoorlie, was that owing to his splendid victory over the alluvial protestors, the watch chain complete with watch, was now 21 Carat. The grateful mining companies had expressed their sentiments in gold.

After Paddy was presented, Sir Edwin looked him up and down, and similarly to the Guard, the Relief Sergeant and the Secretary, was not very impressed with the outback attire. Furthermore, after Paddy had tried to explain about his wish to reclaim Wilga and his friends back from Rottnest Island, Sir Edwin positively glared.

"Indeed, no!", he roared with high dudgeon. "A law has been broken!" Before Paddy could protest, the Minister pontificated on. "Do you want the blessed country to go to ruin Mr O'Leary? We've had enough trouble with labour here. For an employer to have the power of life and death over a worker, especially an Aboriginal, is an inherent right. An inherent right!"

Paddy again looked hard at Mainwaring, wondering why all the males of such families looked much the same. Like Julien Clayton-Browne, Mainwaring was undoubtedly of noble appearance. Tall, strong-jawed, Roman-nosed, thin-lipped - looks alone denoting him as having come from one of Britain's better families. As during that day on the stand against the miners, he not only epitomised the arrogance inherited from almost seventy years of family supremacy in the colony, but from hundreds of years of feudal rule in Britain. Yes, thought Paddy looking at Mainwaring, if physical characteristics meant everything, one could easily believe he was among God's chosen.

Paddy stood his ground, remembering his parents' teachings about thinking what Christ would do in certain difficult circumstances. It made Paddy turn his mind to Wilga and his friends having steel bands clamped around their necks and all chained together and made to trot behind the troopers' horses. He imagined what was happening to them over on Rottnest Island, and Mainwaring's thorough-bred look now changed to that of Satan, even to the horns sprouting out of the handsome head.

Filled with righteous courage, Paddy let forth:

"YOU HARD-HEARTED OLD BASTARD! Here I've come two hundred and fifty miles, mostly on horseback, and you tell me the country will go to ruin if an employer can't own his workers. My God, it's bad enough with an educated white man, who at least knows what he's done when he puts his cross on an employer's ticket, but a poor simple Abo', my God."

Mainwaring reared to his full height.

"Calling a Minister a vile name is an offence my man. I could have you arrested like your black friends."

"Bloody arrest me, you dirty mongrel," roared Paddy, trying to think what Tim would say. "And here's you one o' the bastards who try to never miss a Sunday's church. My God, you'd not even make a good Christian's arse'ole, none of ye'."

The Irish had come out in Paddy, and he knew that he'd gone too far. It was not long before he was grabbed and hustled out by four more of the uniformed Parliamentary Guards, who were obviously there for that very reason, to protect the Members from people like Paddy. But as he was marched out, he gave a last vicious parting shot.

"Anyhow, come this election you miserable lot will be finished. The diggers an' cockies will have you all out on your necks for sure. MARK MY WORDS!"

Paddy returned to tell his tale of woe to Tim over whiskies in the Palace Hotel. It was then that Paddy was finally convinced that he must think seriously of putting up as a candidate.

"Yes Tim," Paddy conceded. "I'm right on the edge. But what sort of a representative would I be to let myself use abusive language like I just did in Parliament House?"

Tim gave his usual chuckle. "The diggers an' cockies will all love you for it matey. That's what Eureka's all about. Free expression, not that stiff-necked bullshit front we've inherited from England. I guess you've heard the story about Thomas Jefferson who after he became President in the new American Republic, tied his pony to a hitch-rail outside an' attended his first Congress in simple homespun farm-clothes, just to be different. Probably swore like blazes too."

"Yes of course," laughed Paddy. "Mark Twain told the story when he was over here back in the eighties. Made Jefferson a sort of Australian hero. Though to the more educated diggers like you, I guess he already was Tim. Also Henry Lawson took it up, if you remember, in the *Bulletin*."

"Yeah, the *Bulletin*, voice o' Eureka! As a matter o' fact, it would be a better title for it. Anyway matey, so you've decided to stand."

Paddy became angry, feeling that in his ideological quest the wily Victorian was trying to take too quick an advantage.

"Don't push me Tim, if it means securing the release of Wilga and the others, yes, I could stand. But there's Jenny to think of. We've talked about it, and she says that if there was anything she'd hate to be, it's the wife of a politician."

"Yeah," returned Tim, with a slow smile. "I guess she would have to spend part of her life in the city. You'd probably have to buy a posh residence in one o' the well-to-do areas. Anyway, with all that extra gold money you got from the sale o' yours an' Daniel's Coolgardie an' Kalgoorlie claims, you could easily still afford it."

Paddy took a gulp of whisky. "Jesus, I thought you were trying to talk me into politics, not out of it. Carry on like that about living in the city, which I know Jenny's against, and I'll say "No" to the election right here and now."

"Sorry cobber, but you've forgotten we have to do somethin' about Wilga an' his mates. As a matter o' fact, it might be an idea to wire Daniel in Kal' an' get him to take it up in his paper. Also there's Mike Beaumont of the *Geraldton Express*. Pity we couldn't do somethin' here in Perth, but with the city's only newspaper the *West Australian* bein' backed by the McAllums an' the Hungry Six mob, we're buggered. So we'll just have to make do with the *Coolgardie Miner* an' the *Geraldton Express*. Maybe we could kid the editors to make a few threats, like if they don't release our black friends, the rotten Groves Gang could lose the election."

"Yeah," drawled Paddy. "Will Dunbar suggested somethin' like that before I left. Anyway, if it does save Wilga and his mates, it could save me putting up."

"Yeah, it could," grinned Tim. "An' it could make you all the more popular as a candidate too, because if I've got anythin' to do with it, the papers will be quotin' the story about you an' Sir Edwin. An' I mean, in full."

About to protest, Paddy's mind went back to his recent confrontation with Mainwaring. He firmed his lips and gritted his teeth.

"Well then, though I reckon the *West Australian* might take it up and slander me to hell, if it will help get Wilga and the others back from Rottnest Island, I guess it's well worth it."

Paddy returned to Singleton to find Jenny and the girls

mustering the sheep for shearing which was due to start in a few days. Jenny also had to get things organised to cook for the shearers and shed-hands. As they walked up to the homestead, she was eager to find out about the results of his quest. When he told her about his confrontation with Sir Edwin, she was not surprised.

"Well Paddy, you had to expect it from a member of the Hungry Six didn't you? I suppose Dad and I are as much to blame for egging you on. I'm sure Dad did anyhow."

"It wasn't completely wasted," said Paddy. "We've already wired Daniel and also the editor in Geraldton to get the story in the papers. My language to Sir Edwin an' all."

She kissed him. "Well, I don't mind darling, especially if it helps those poor natives."

"Wait on, there's more." Paddy spoke tentatively. "After what happened with Sir Edwin, I'm tempted to put up for Parliament after all."

At her silence Paddy put his arms around her. "Sorry sweetheart, nice way to greet my new wife isn't it? Especially with me clearin' off three days after the weddin! Look, I promise to say no more about it, unless you bring it up. Now, let's go to bed?"

She giggled, rubbing her full breasts against him. "No, can't you see I have to get lunch. Then I have to get out again and help the girls with the sheep."

"That can wait," laughed Paddy. "And so can dinner." And with that he picked her up like a baby and carried her into the love-nest, which indeed for the next half-hour, it was.

Later after she had dressed, Jenny teased him. "Well, with that taken out of you, I suppose you think you're going to lie down after lunch for the rest of the afternoon, but there's work to do. What do you prefer, the house or the paddock?"

"Well, I guess seein' you've probably forgotten more than I ever learnt about sheep," he laughed, "maybe I'd better put on the apron."

"No, it'll be out in the field with you, my lad," she commanded. "The girls will show you. It's only sorting the wethers from the ewes anyhow. Lucky we've got such good holding and drafting yards here, much better than on the home place." Paddy knew that "home" meant the Dunbar property.

When Paddy arrived at the yards, the shepherd girls were already busy. He marvelled how they moved the sheep without much yelling and cursing as had been his experience as a lad in York. In order to make up as large a flock as he could over at Northampton earlier, Paddy had been advised to purchase two thousand wether male sheep among the ewes, which now had to be separated. Most of the ewes had lambs, already sired to rams before Paddy had purchased the flock. So the eight thousand ewes now had around six thousand lambs at foot, which made the mob all the harder to handle. But the girls were expert at it and soon sacked Paddy from working the swing-gate on the drafting yard, because they said that he didn't know the difference between a ewe and a wether. Later towards sundown, Wilga's chosen, with the archful lashes, suggested she go up and help Jenny prepare tea. Not that the girls ate in the homestead kitchen. They refused to, only taking the offer of a piece of meat, a loaf of bread, or bits of tea and sugar, the beverage to which they had become addicted while working for the Clayton-Brownes.

Shearing came a fortnight later than expected, and now Paddy was able to be in attendance as any station-owner should. But Paddy often felt like a passenger. He was so grateful to Will Dunbar and Kim, and the rest of their crew. Even Peg Dunbar drove all the way over to help Jenny in the kitchen, leaving the homestead at daybreak. All to be ready for the shearing-day at seven thirty.

The four contract shearers were tough though humorous types who shore all the year round, working through from sheds as far north as the Kimberleys right down to Esperance on the southern coast. Theirs, they said, was a station run, which did not include the cocky farmers, who were settling on the richer soils along the new Midland Railway. These families were now growing grain and running sheep on lands which previously had been under lease like the stations.

It was now that Paddy wished he had taken more interest in shearing shed work on the home farm at York. Not that he was without experience, but there appeared to be so much expertise around the place, that he decided to relegate himself to the position of rouseabout. Such action on the part of a station-owner attracted certain wisecracks from the hard-bitten shearers, Will joining in.

Shearing finished, the hundred or more bales of wool had to be loaded onto Lennie and Ahmud's huge camel-wagon, now the pride of the station country and ready to cart wool from the Lower Murchison to Watheroo, to be loaded on rail-trucks.

It was just after the completion of shearing in late October that Jenny pulled Paddy aside one day, a mysterious expression in her eyes.

"What's the matter darlin?" laughed Paddy. "You look different, not that I'd say you're unhappy."

"I think we're going to have a baby."

He gathered her in his arms. "Oh, sweetheart, sweetheart." Then he stopped, handling her as if she was made of delicate china.

"Eh, it's all right," she giggled. "I'm not due till another seven months or so."

He was concerned. "Anyway, how do you know for sure?"

"It's a natural thing. If I didn't know what was happening to me, I'd be ashamed to call myself a station-owner's daughter."

"Just the same, I'd better get you to a doctor."

She now laughed out loud. "Goodness me Paddy, I told you, it's a natural thing."

Paddy was still worried. "But the birth, surely. You told me the story of the young wife who died during childbirth while camped on this very station back in the early '80s. You know, before that family from England took it up."

"But that was in the days when the nearest hospital was in Geraldton, nearly two hundred miles away. There's one now in Yalgoo."

"Yes, and that's why you'll have to stay up there. Or even in Geraldton for a while before the birth."

"Oh no!" she laughed. "None of this waiting for weeks being pampered in the city, like the McAllum or Clayton-Browne wives. When I go, I'd prefer to have the baby in Yalgoo."

"But Yalgoo's still a long way?"

She became more serious. "Of course, I'd have to allow a few days. Anyway, some pregnant wives out in the backblocks take in a midwife. There's one travels round in a sulky, fully equipped. Mrs Ferguson of Thundelarra station has had her in. In fact, a couple of times, one time a girl, one time a boy."

Paddy could have argued further, because with Jenny pregnant he only wanted the best for her. Also he realised now that he'd better keep quiet about the coming election, even though the copies of the *Geraldton Express* which were dropped weekly by the mail-carrier, were full not only of Paddy's verbal duel with Sir Edwin, but of the iniquities of the Master and Servant Law, which had caused all the trouble. The paper also wrote of the British and American mining companies taking out all the gold profits and leaving the colony to borrow money for much needed projects, such as railways and the highly-vaunted Goldfields Water Scheme. The paper alleged the venture could have been paid for ten times over from gold profits withdrawn by overseas companies.

The Geraldton editor also talked about the liberal-democratic stance, which he said was only another name for the ideals which had inspired the Eureka Stockade. In this way he was not only getting to the diggers, but also to the cockies, who like the original miners, only wanted to be free to run their farms or claims on an individual or family basis.

One aspect the editor had to be cautious about however in regard to the cockies, was the Master and Servant Law and its effect on the natives. Because they worked their own properties on a family basis, the cockies had little need for black labour. The editor was of the opinion in fact, that if they had needed black labour, many of the smallholders might have been as well possessed of the slave-owner mentality as the gentry pastoralists. Yet by the very fact that the cockies were the natural enemies of the well-to-do, he was able to induce them to take up the liberal cause.

Still, the Hungry Six and their mouthpiece the *West Australian*, had not been idle.

The Worker's and Miner's Unions had formed what they called Political Labor, which they had hoped would be made legitimate so that candidates could be fielded in the coming election. But under pressure from the old families, the conservative-dominated Parliament refused to allow the new party to be registered - for obvious reasons. They'd also recently refused to pass a reform for politicians to be paid salaries.

Tim put it cynically to Paddy one day over drinks in the Field's pub. "The bastards are scared outa their wits. Anything to stop the diggers puttin' up." He suddenly put his arm round Paddy. "But they've forgotten about you, haven't they old chum? One who's still got the wherewithal, the cash to get by in Parliament, the same as those Hungry Six mongrels."

Paddy was half-angry again.

"I haven't really said yes yet, have I Tim? Remember I've got a wife to be concerned about." He gave a short laugh. "An' a baby on the way!"

Tim grasped his hand. "Hell, that calls for another whisky. Even so, it still won't stop you runnin' for the Murchison matey, you're committed. Remember Wilga an' Co."

A week later, while Paddy was riding up Mt Singleton on horseback as he never tired of doing, enjoying the view from the crest, he found two of the native stock-girls comforting Unkee, Wilga's chosen. Unkee was just sitting there, sobbing silently. At first thinking she had been hurt physically, Paddy halted his horse. "What's the matter Unkee?" he asked.

"Unkee sad," said one of the girls. "Want Wilga."

The distressed Aboriginal girl now turned towards Paddy and lifted her head, her eyes imploring, holding more appeal than he had ever seen in a white women, including Jenny or even his own mother, Judith. Paddy was deeply concerned for this girl, who with her bright nature, had borne the abduction of her beloved so bravely. As Paddy knew, whites, particularly high-bred Anglicans were inclined to tell themselves not to be affected by the emotions of coloured peoples, especially those who were heathen. But Paddy had been taught differently, and he felt the tears come to his eyes, ashamed to have to turn away his head so that he might not show weakness in front of the black girls.

As Paddy rode slowly back to the station-house, he knew that he must do something about Wilga, otherwise the young Aboriginal and his friends would certainly spend the rest of their lives on the bleak grey island. Whole black families had done so since Rottnest had first been made a penal institution for natives back in 1841. He also knew that his unusual compassion for Aborigines had sprung from the beliefs of his grandfather and his mother, Judith. This, coupled with his understanding of the needs of both the digger and the cocky, made him the logical candidate for the Murchison, just as Tim had told him.

CHAPTER 17

Paddy did not need to tell Jenny that something was wrong. In the comparatively short time she had known him, particularly as they had proven their love for each other, she believed she could read his moods.

"What's the matter darling?" she asked concernedly, as she met him at the kitchen door.

"Oh it's Unkee, Wilga's chosen. She's become suddenly distressed about Wilga. I could almost believe Tim McBride when he says that certain Aborigines can reveal each other's thoughts to one another over hundreds of miles."

"Yes, I believe it too," she said. "And with two people in love like Wilga and Unkee, it could be even more probable." She frowned. "Maybe Wilga's been hurt or something."

Paddy's lips drew into a thin line. "Whatever it is sweetheart, it makes me feel it is now almost my duty to stand for Parliament. Even just to fight to have that damned Master and Servant Act abolished."

She began to cry. "Yes darling, I guess it's the only way. Now I suppose Daniel and Tim will believe that Wilga and his friends being taken away in chains might have been the best thing that could have happened."

He put his arms around her. "I don't know whether they are as tough in the hide as that my love, but both having political minds, I guess you could be not far wrong. Anyhow, I'll ride over to Field's and give Tim my decision. Seeing that he reckons he's the diggers' representative there, I'll leave it to him to pass the word up to Yalgoo, where it'll soon get to Mike Beaumont the Geraldton editor. He can organise the rest."

For Tim McBride it was welcome news. He'd become worried about Paddy's family commitments, even though he had failed to admit it. In his determination to be rid of the political domination of the Hungry Six in the Murchison, Tim had been dwelling on putting up as a candidate himself after all. And certainly Tim believed that as far as backing from the diggers was concerned, he was probably second to none. But there were those damned cockies and small station-owners who would no doubt prefer a Hungry Six candidate to an ex-Victorian, who unfortunately had a reputation for blowing his bags in the bar about dear ole Melbourne town.

"Yeah cobber," Tim declared. "You've really brightened my day. Looks like we'd better make tracks up to Yalgoo tomorrow."

Paddy shook his head. "You might, but I'm not. It's not fair on Jenny. It is only owing to the worry about Wilga and his friends that she has agreed. Anyway, the election's nearly four months away yet, so why not let things move slowly for a while?"

"That's not long when there's an important ballot like this one comin' up," said Tim. "Anyway, have it your own way, I can do the early organisin'. I guess I'm just thankful that you've come to your senses, even if it is due to the worry about Wilga."

They shook hands. "Thanks Tim, give me till after Christmas an' I'll probably be at your beck an' call. Anyhow, now that I've decided, I'd better start thinking about all the nasty things I know about dear old Ashley our opposition candidate. Not that I've ever hated the silly bastard, it's just that he's been sired from that rotten Hungry Six mob."

"Yeah now you're talkin' feller," grinned Tim. "It's just us an' them, that's all it's ever been about. Otherwise you're runnin' soft. Anyhow, expect to see your nomination in the next issue of the *Geraldton Express*. Also if you don't mind I'll give the editor the story about the distress of Wilga's chosen. Not that it'll worry the majority o' the diggers an' cockies. I'm sorry to say that like the gentry, there's still too many of 'em who reckon our blacks don't have feelin's. Just the same, it'll help stir the stewpot."

"It's all right by me," rejoined Paddy. "Still, if I do any campaignin' it'll probably only be about what's got me fired up - that cruel law which banished Wilga an' his friends to faraway Rottnest Island."

Tim laughed quickly. "If I've got anythin' to do with it, you'll be doin' a lot more than that. Not only about the rotten way they've treated us t'othersiders by not allowin' us the vote in the last two elections, but also for not lettin' this Political Labor be registered as a party to fight on behalf of the diggers an' workers. Not that I hold complete truck with the party, mind you, because I believe that parties as such can take away a man's independence - but it's the principle. Also o' course, there's this business of lettin' the Brits an' Yanks take out most o' the gold profits."

"Well yes, I guess I could have a bit more to say," replied Paddy with a half-smile, as he picked up his hat.

"You will all right ole chum, 'cause I'll be right behind you urgin' when you're makin' your speech."

"Speech, Jesus!" Paddy was horrified. "What's this about speeches? I thought I only had to do the rounds o' the public an' talk to the odd bod who we know's on our side."

Tim gave a guffaw. "Why, speech-makin' is an essential part o' the contract my lad. Anyway, if you're worried, I can word your missal beforehand."

"Helped by Daniel an' that Geraldton editor too I'll bet," Paddy responded as he walked away. Not that Paddy was angry. He hadn't had much practice at speechmaking, that was all.

It was now late February, 1897, three months having gone by since the audience between Paddy and Tim in Field's. In the meantime, Jenny had been suffering the usual complications of early pregnancy, morning sickness and emotional instability. Her mother Peg had consoled her about the problem and had promised the nausea would soon go away. But even the sight or thought of mutton distressed her, particularly making her wonder what was happening to someone who was determined to spend the rest of her life on a station where meat or mutton was almost the staff of life. Neither had Paddy made it easier, having suggested that her sudden phobia might cause her to change her mind about living out in the outback. She might now even prefer to live in the city after Paddy had won his seat.

"We could build a posh house in Mount Street, near Mt Eliza next to the nobs," Paddy half-joked.

Jenny was not amused. "I told you before, I don't want to live next to that lot!" She burst into tears. "I don't want to be a politician's wife anyhow. I just want to stay here on the station."

He held her close. "There, there, sweetheart, I'm sorry."

"No, it's all right Paddy. I'm such a grouch, aren't I? Even though Mother tells me that in my condition it's just normal. But, uhh, the smell of meat cooking, and the smell of Dad's pipe! Thank goodness you don't smoke. And as far as your entering Parliament's concerned, well, I'll just have to do my duty, even for the sake of Wilga and his friends." She suddenly brightened, kissing him. "And talking about the natives, how about hopping out and helping the girls with the last of the mustering. They'll be again threatening you with the sack."

"Yes Ma'am," replied Paddy, giving her a mock salute, yet so glad she could be getting over her condition - not dangerous, but sometimes hard to live with.

On the first day of March, Paddy and Tim boarded the train at Yalgoo en route to Geraldton. It was packed with diggers from Meekathara, Day Dawn and Mt Magnet, as well as a host of smaller mining towns which had since sprung up. The Geraldton editor had done his work well, writing in his columns about Paddy, the man chosen by these tough t'othersiders, mostly ex-Victorians, as their "Man of Eureka". The Geraldton paper had gone on to say how Paddy would be giving a rousing talk in Geraldton. Tim too, had done more than his bit, having ridden three times to Yalgoo, each time catching the train on to Mt Magnet, then to journey on by coach to spruik at the more far-flung gold settlements.

Already primed with liquor, the diggers on the train were in a happy mood, determined to show the Bastards of the Strip - such also included the gentility of Geraldton - that they meant business. Another attraction in Geraldton in summer, was the glorious sight of the sea, as well as the refreshing touch of the ocean winds, often more than gentle.

Although Paddy enjoyed his share of the jollity and booze, while rattling along in the train, his eyes still searched the landscape through the open carriage window. After Yalgoo and the gold country, the terrain gradually flattened, as they neared Mullewa. This was a well-known droving stop - popular well before the mining boom. As the engine came to a halt to take on water and coal, the diggers raced over to The Drover's Retreat, the one and only pub, not only to drink tap-beer but also to stock up with bottles.

With the engine again in motion, the red dusty soils of Mullewa soon gave way to huge areas of sandplain, which apart from supporting a few kangaroos and emus, were still regarded as useless either for running livestock or growing grain. After more roistering and more booze, Paddy had thoughts about going a bit easier and keeping his head for the next day's speech.

The clattering train was now winding its way through productive farmlands. Yet while some held tall white wheat stubble, other far larger stretches ran cattle and horses, the soil red and bare through overstocking. These were the coastal domains of the gentry station-owners - as indicated by the elaborate farmsteads, each built on the lines of an

English manor. Paddy knew that it was here in one of these that his old rival, Ashley McAllum, now spent much of his time, happily married and with his wife too expecting a baby.

They were now steaming through the Geraldton rangelands, more like small mesas, flat on top with their steep parapets towards the sea. An indication of the strength of the prevailing west winds, especially in late winter, was shown by the larger species of eucalypt, their red-white gnarled and twisted trunks bent grotesquely to the east. The shorter foliage was a hardy heath-type species of dwarf native-oak, or tamar.

One by one towards the rear of the long train, carriage windows had begun to open, doubtless not only to let in the invigorating ocean air, but to drive out the smell of grog and of stale tobacco-smoke.

Down below lay the orderly town-port of Geraldton, its streets in precision, marked out back in the 1850s by the military. Beyond the town stretched the azure-blue sea with the Abrolhos Isles clear across the horizon. Closer in lay anchored steamers and tall-masted sailing-ships, waiting to dock to load wheat and wool.

As the engine puffed lightly down the grade, the passengers took stock of the commercial houses and pubs with their sheer walls and steep-pitched roofs - in stark contrast to the cool-looking French-style bungalows.

At the Geraldton station - an imposing looking building of local inland stone - passengers were already busy alighting on the opposite platform from a train just in from Perth. A waiting crowd had made way for some notables from the big city.

"Well, would you look who's here!" said Paddy, as he and Tim stepped from the Yalgoo train with the diggers. "It's our dear friend, Sir Edwin."

"Yeah," grimaced Tim. "Bloody Ten Foot Ned! Looks like he's arrived in a special carriage, police escort an' all. O' course, he's got a big property up here, like most o' the land-grabbin' bastards." Tim laughed. "Jesus, I guess he's really up here to hold dear little Ashley's hand tomorrow."

The editor of the *Geraldton Express* who met them outside the ticket-office confirmed Tim's premonition.

"Sir Edwin Mainwaring will be there all right," he explained. "Not only to introduce Ashley McAllum the candidate, but also to open proceedings. In fact, although I suggested the meeting, it seems the powers-that-be have taken over."

Tim gave a harsh laugh. "Well, with that mob, are you surprised?"

"No, not one iota," replied the editor. "Anyhow, I've offered them a dare and suggested that they run the meeting like a forum asking questions and so forth. The meeting has become so important that they've gained special permission to hold it in the assembly-hall section of that big new government building over there, due to be completed later this year."

They were standing in Geraldton's main thoroughfare, Fitzgerald Street, the editor indicating an imposing two-story edifice with a good three-hundred foot facade. While the main centre section was fronted by a series of arches above squared columns, tacked on each end were more conventional structures. The roofing was of Georgian design and tiled with slate. Across the whole was at least a half-dozen brick chimneys. Yet the mix created a pleasing effect and the design was a credit to the architects, even though at present much of the facia was laced with steel scaffolding with plasterers busy on their platforms.

According to the editor, the end section without the scaffolding was all but finished, and it was here where the coming political meeting was to be held.

"Jesus," said Paddy, commenting on the whole building. "Going to be really posh, isn't it? Better'n anythin' in Kalgoorlie, even Perth."

"Well, since the diggers have been invading Geraldton in the last few years, the Groves Gang has become worried,"

313

laughed Beaumont. "Of course, my paper's been stirring things up a bit too. There is a rumour that the diggers may take over Geraldton and make it the capital of a separate state taking in all the north as well as right around to Kalgoorlie. This would leave the Groves Gang with only about one twentieth of Westralia. Far smaller even than the old original Swan River."

"The old coastal strip bar Geraldton!" grinned Paddy. "From Perth around to Albany, an' only inland as far as York an' Northam. The way they treat the common folk, they don't even deserve that."

"Yeah," agreed Tim. "We've talked about it in Field's. It's to do with this coming Federation, which the Hungry Six mob's against. While they want Westralia to stay with dear ole Britain, the diggers want to form a separate province an' join up with t'otherside in self-government for the whole of Australia." He looked closely at the editor.

"But why waste money puttin' up flash buildin's in Geraldton if that's likely to happen?"

"Oh, the old Geraldton families believe that the government hasn't been caring about the place enough, and virtually letting the miners take over. The laughable thing is that Edwin Mainwaring, Minister for Mines is the one who has successfully pushed for the new building. But for Geraldton it has not been before time, up until now, apart from the hotels, the Mechanic's Institute, and of course the Anglican church, there has been hardly a place where more than about fifty people can get together. The well-to-do families have their large entertainment areas in their homesteads a la 18th century style. They take it in turns to hold private dances and I guess that's why the Clayton-Brownes, McAllums and so forth have never asked for even a Town Hall. And here's Geraldton been settled now for more than fifty years."

Tim shrugged his shoulders cynically. "To hell with the old families. All we want is enough space at the end of a hall to pin up the good ole Eureka flag." He turned to the editor. "You've got one I hope?"

"Of course!" laughed the editor. "Per favour of our Geraldton seamstress. She's a real rebel."

"Yeah, we had a nice lady like that in Kalgoorlie," remarked Paddy. He turned to Tim. "Jesus, not that the flag did much good over there in the fight for the alluvials. We still lost, didn't we?"

"Yes, you did, didn't you?" replied the editor, glumly. "Mainwaring put it over you. When I heard the news, I must say I was damned disappointed."

"This is different," returned Tim brightly. "Once caught, twice shy. These Murchison diggers have all pledged to forget about the grog an' concentrate on the meetin'. They've come to realise that the only way they can get their demands through now is through politics. That's why on my rounds o' the gold centres I've inspired 'em all about our young candidate here." Tim indicated Paddy.

"Cut it out Tim," grinned Paddy. "You're makin' me nervous."

"What, nervous lud, with an opposition candidate like Ashley McAllum. Why, you were tellin' me on the train that if ever you had the mettle of someone it was he."

The editor's tone was cautious. "But I wouldn't take him too lightly Paddy. You should know that. As we agreed after your wedding, Ashley's got a way about him. That's why they've been grooming him."

Paddy could well agree. "Oh Ashley's no fool. When he was with the *West Australian*, he was a damned good reporter. An' I'd say no one gets a better insight into politics and politicians than a journalist." He gave a grin. "I guess on the train it was just the beer talkin'."

"No, you meant it matey," said Tim. He turned to the editor. "Anyway, now talkin' about papers, who's doin' the reportin' for the "West" tomorrow?"

"Gloria!"

"Gloria, who the hell's she?"

"Oh, sorry!" The editor looked almost sardonic. "Ashley's younger sister. Don't you remember I did a write up about her two months ago in the *Express*. I was virtually forced to do it by the well-to-do families here. Even Desmond Clayton -Browne, the local Resident, was at me."

"Yeah, I remember," said Paddy. "Jenny pointed the article out to me. "Gloria'd just come back from England after study over there, just like Ashley did years before. Supposed to have done well at literature or somethin'"

"Yes, supposed to, is the right word," replied the editor. "She actually failed her first year, but the family kept her at it and paid her way the whole five years just like they did with Ashley. Of course, that part of the story I cannot print. All I can print about the well-to-do is about how they pioneered Geraldton and about their prowess at breeding racehorse winners, polo and tent-pegging and of course about Gloria. Anyhow, she's been put on the staff of the *West* to report on the meeting tomorrow."

"Jesus," said Tim. "I'll bet that'll be worth readin', I wonder what she'll put about the diggers?" He gave a mischievous grin. "Anyway, what's this Gloria look like?"

The editor smiled back, having known Tim of old. "I should have expected you to ask that McBride. Well, she's twenty two, and with plenty of class to go with it. Or I should say what the top families call class. Just the same I haven't got much time for her, too much of the affectedness common to her breed. Besides that I don't trust her."

"Hell, she must've cut you up the wrong way," grinned Paddy. "I'd like to have a look at her myself."

"You will at that," returned the editor. "She'll be interviewing you tomorrow on behalf of the *West*."

"But enough o' Gloria," swore Tim. "She sounds as dull as can be." He turned to Paddy. "Time we booked into a pub. With all this crowd here, we'll probably have to sleep in the park."

"I've already booked you into the Geraldton, the best pub

in town," laughed the editor. "And you've also got the best room."

"What, with a touch o' fluff an' all," bantered Tim.

"Not quite, but it's available if you want it."

The editor looked at Paddy. "Looks like you'd better spend the night home with me and my family Paddy. This cove, Tim here, could lead you astray. Remember we want you hale and hearty for tomorrow."

Paddy laughed somewhat nervously. "I know this cove of old, he's all bloody talk." Yet Paddy wasn't so sure. With Tim certain to be mixing with his digger friends later, anything could happen. Paddy was no angel, but he desperately wanted to remain true to Jenny.

Geraldton town was in an expectant mood; even the natives had joined in. Though it was now close to sundown, most were moving along Fitzgerald Street in groups, some of the younger men dressed in station clothes and wide-brimmed hats. These were those with some semblance of dignity, not of the ancient ritual and tribe, but those who had been fortunate enough to be working for some kindly station task master, similar to the Dunbars, who treated the natives more as equals. While some of the young lubras with their expressive eyes and fluttering lashes wore well-fitting figure-revealing simple floral dresses, others wore their gowns like sacks, the hems untidy, the skinny legs protruding through like sticks. It was in the features of these people that the hopelessness of a badly subjugated, beaten race, was revealed.

Yet these people were up with the news enough to know that Mike Beaumont's *Geraldton Express*, as well as Daniel Hordacre's *Coolgardie Miner*, had taken up the cause of the natives with regard to the Master and Servant Act, the heinous law which had made these Aboriginal people no better than slaves to their white masters.

The very fact that these two outspoken newspapers had taken up the cause of the natives, even if only for political reasons, had begun to worry the Groves government. There was even a rumour that the Groves Gang might engineer a Bill before the election to have the Master and Servant Law abolished.

Julien Clayton-Browne of Clayton Downs station was also in town, or rather on the old family property ten miles south-east of Geraldton in the rich Greenough Flats. The property was now run by Julien's brother Desmond, the District Magistrate.

Gathered outside the Assembly Hall on the meeting day were both friend and foe, the conservatives being conspicuous by their dress. Relatives and followers of the old families looked their best, as was only expected of them when they were under public gaze. The menfolk had on well-cut suits, and while the town businessmen wore bowlers, the wealthy pastoralists sported the equivalent of the stock-hat. But unlike the careless floppy brims of the diggers and the cockies, the hats of the graziers were edge-sewn, the brims sightly curled. The womenfolk were dressed elegantly in the latest street gowns, the station wives wearing smaller versions of their husbands' stock hats, complete with silk puggaree.

Not that all the fine regalia impressed Paddy, dressed simply in blue cotton short-sleeved shirt, moleskin trousers and station boots - plus the new stock-hat he had bought in Perth, but because he had kept on wearing it, now somewhat battered.

More important than dress to Paddy and the diggers were their beliefs, flamboyantly represented in the huge blue and white Eureka flag, even larger than the Union Jack which graced the hall behind the dais next to a painting of Queen Victoria. Other smaller versions of the Eureka flag were also in evidence, all manufactured by the sympathetic Geraldton milliner and now waved and held aloft by the diggers.

Some of those more radical, and generally with Irish

backgrounds besides being spurred on by the popular t'otherside weekly, the *Bulletin*, were talking openly about a future republic after they had kicked out those English related "Bastards of the Strip" - or those fornicating members of the Hungry Six.

Not backward in expressing colourful and appropriate phrases, it was also the rebellious Irish-Victorian digger who donated the bulk of the literary chapter and verse to Beaumont's *Geraldton Express*. As the editor had remarked privately, it seemed the so-called educated well-to-do of the colony had nothing creative to contribute. Their minds were apparently absorbed too much in grabbing land and making money.

The crowd surged into the Assembly Hall. Sir Edwin and his retinue had already taken their places to the rear of the building near the stage. Part of the entourage besides Ashley McAllum - Ashley's heavily pregnant wife was absent - were the Clayton-Brownes and their wives.

Gloria McAllum was there also, not only because she was a member of one of Geraldton's influential families, but as the journalist for the *West*. She appeared desperately anxious to have an interview with Paddy as the opposition candidate. But though Paddy was at first impressed with her shapely figure in the expensive street-gown and her dark hair and well-cut features similar to her brother Ashley, he was put off by her tone of voice.

"Too much the friggin' plum in the mouth!" was Tim's later appraisal.

The leading lights of the opposition, including Paddy and Tim, had now taken their positions in opposing corners down from the stage. Sir Edwin had decided to open the meeting formally, and he even went as far as to suggest that as the conservatives were already in power, that Ashley McAllum, the new Murchison candidate speak first.

"No!" yelled a digger. "You can go to bloody 'ell. We'll

toss a flamin' coin. It's the fairest way."

So toss the coin they decided on, Tim using the standard kip, which meant two coins up instead of one.

After a whispered conversation with Paddy, Tim looked across at Ashley. "What's it to be laddie? Odds or blinkin' evens?"

Having often been a witness to a game of two-up in Kalgoorlie, Ashley gave a friendly smile.

"No, why not let Mr O'Leary make the choice?"

"Go on Ashley," grinned Paddy. "What the hell difference does it make? Call, for Chris'sake!"

Thus urged, Ashley called and won, electing to speak first, prompted by Sir Edwin.

Ashley was the essence of articulation:

"Ladies and Gentlemen, I am proud to stand before you as your conservative candidate. Proud I am indeed in my praise of the existing Groves government, who since its inception has brought so many improvements to the colony. Most prominent among them so far, I believe, has been the construction of Fremantle Harbour by C.Y. O'Connor."

A loud hurrah came from the conservatives, with a murmur from the diggers and cockies, because they were forced to admit, that the conversion of Fremantle from a dangerous rock-strewn anchorage was certainly a boon.

"... and to take stock of our new communication systems," went on Ashley, "besides thousands of miles of telegraph line, the magnificent new railway from Perth to Geraldton, the Great Southern Railway from York to Albany, the Eastern Goldfields Railway from Northam to Kalgoorlie, and more spurs out into the goldfields." Ashley now turned to the Murchison diggers. "And of course, talking about important links to the goldfields, we have your own Yalgoo line, which I'm proud to say has now been gazetted by the Groves Cabinet to proceed beyond Mt Magnet."

The diggers again cheered along with the gentry. "And besides scores of new roads and bridges, is the incredible plan by C.Y. O'Connor to pipe water with a series of steam-pumps the whole three hundred and sixty miles to the dry and waterless Kalgoorlie from a reservoir high in the Darling Ranges near the coast."

"But who's payin' for it all?" suddenly yelled a digger. "I've heard this government's had to go inta hock for everythin', even despite all the flamin' gold. Yeah, who's payin' for it all?"

"Yeah, let Paddy tell us about it," yelled another digger. "Yuh bloody toff, git orf the flamin' dais."

But Ashley wasn't beaten. He began to talk about the political acumen of the landed families, and how it was still important to put people with influence and education in Parliament.

"Yeah, yuh rotten mongrels," yelled the same digger. "That's why you bastards over here never encouraged the poorer kids to go to school, in case the kids took over when they grew up. Like when you refused to give us t'othersiders the vote in the last election, 'cause you reckoned we were only the rabble. But you've had it now chum, I tell ye'."

"Yeah," yelled another miner, once more waving his flag. "Up Eureka!"

It was then Paddy felt a pang of sympathy for Ashley. He heard himself call out loudly and wondered why.

"For Godsake give the man a go!"

This brought cheers from both sides of the hall, even from the two dozen dismounted troopers who had accompanied Sir Edwin.

"Come on, hurry up. We want Paddy!" yelled a digger from the back of the hall, waving a bottle.

As Paddy was pushed up onto the dais, he felt his legs trembling, his lips dry. As usual it was a time when he remembered his mother, and whispered one of his infrequent prayers to the Almighty.

"Ladies and gentlemen," he began. "I now stand before

you as a genuine liberal. Not a fake middle-of-the-roader, with platitudes about a better future for us all; asking you to have faith; to trust in us, because we are for the people. To let us carry on as before because we've done so well. But I ask you, during those golden years just passed, what else could a government do than do well? My God, with all the gold that has been uncovered in the five years since Coolgardie, a government should be doing quite a bit better than just doing well. In fact, my friends, it should be doing bloody fabulous."

A raucous cheer came from the diggers as Paddy raised his fist in the air.

"But who is doing fabulous, my friends? Not us, nor our government, but these British and American mining companies who are now over here exploiting us as well as other colonies. Mr McAllum has just spoken about all the grand projects mooted since gold was first discovered in the late eighties. The Midland Railway, for example, from Perth to the port of Geraldton, where we are now standing. A boon to be sure my friends, and certainly justified as we begin to realise the wealth of our colony through gold. But there we have it, to get that line through, we've had to gift millions of acres of some of our best agricultural land to an English railway company. While I do not disagree with some of the landed families having to pay agricultural prices for their rich feudal redlands round Moora, Carnamah and Mingenew, I do disagree with the company demanding unfair prices from battling farmers, whom I'm proud to call cockies."

Now a cheer rose from the smallholders.

"But that is not all," roared Paddy, now with his ire up. "The Great Southern Railway from York to Albany has been the same. Anthony Hordern, the British financier, had similar giftings - millions of acres of choice red loam, still more of the colony's best agricultural land. As Anthony Hordern has since died, there is talk of forming a Western Australian land company to buy it back. But at what cost, when it should not have been gifted away in the first place?"

"Yeah, and what about this Kalgoorlie Water Scheme?" yelled a digger. "I know it's needed, but who the hell's goin' to pay for that?"

"Yes, that's the burning question," retorted Paddy, realising he was not following the line of his speech. "Yes, I agree, it is a great idea. But the latest I've heard is that most of the money will have to be borrowed again from dear old England. But if they suddenly cut off our lending as they did with the Melbourne land boom back in '88 bringing on the crash, what then, my friends?"

Paddy nodded towards the prospector. "That's about all I can say, digger. So maybe you should ask some of the well-to-do, who so much support the Groves Gang." Paddy called across to Ashley. "Hey, Ashley, maybe you could shed a bit o' light?"

"No, Mr O'Leary," replied Ashley pompously. "I'm afraid I cannot."

From the way he half-glanced across to Sir Edwin for his cue, Paddy knew Ashley was lying.

With a glare and a quick nod of the head from Tim in the crowd, Paddy now took more care over his speech.

"But my friends, I'm not standing up here today just to talk about the companies taking out our gold and robbing us right an' left. Besides here to support the cocky and small station-owner, I am also here to support the digger, even if most of 'em did come from t'otherside."

Amidst friendly heckling from the diggers, Paddy gave a roar. "Yet most o' the diggers now want to be Westralians like us. The majority want to bring their wives an' kids over from Victoria an' settle here permanently. An' I must say, that thousands of these diggers have been in the colony ten years or more?" Paddy again raised his fist skyward. "But has the Groves Government allowed 'em the vote up till now? No, not likely, because Mr Groves knew where that vote would go, didn't he?" Paddy glared pointedly at Ashley.

"As it will in the coming election, right where it should - with a good liberal candidate like me!"

Paddy knew he was blowing his bags, but he didn't care, he was beginning to enjoy it.

Claps and cheers came from the crowd.

"Good on you Paddy," a mob of diggers yelled in chorus.

Paddy realised his time would soon be up, and he hadn't mentioned one word about the Master and Servant Law, the reason he had run as a candidate. It was the Geraldton editor who reminded him.

"Mr O'Leary," he called. "Could I ask a question? Why have you put up as a candidate?"

Paddy set his jaw.

"You all read the *Geraldton Express*, or I hope you do anyhow. A few weeks ago I had five of my black station workers taken away by the police, just because they preferred to work for me rather than someone else. So I'm here to talk about that iniquitous Master an' Servant Law, which enables a station-owner to retain his black workers - mostly claimed in the first place by means of a tarred thumbmark from the poor unsuspecting local tribespeople."

Despite murmurs from the well-to-do, besides a few from the smallholders, Paddy went on, choosing his words carefully.

"Yes, ladies and gentlemen, what about a bit of decency in this colony? I must tell you about Wilga, a dear friend of mine. He was one of those many black men who have led our explorers and prospectors to water. In this case with Wilga it happened to be Bayley and Ford's fabulous Coolgardie, which Wilga's people had previously named Colgardy." Paddy's voice rose.

"But just because Wilga an' his friends preferred to work for me rather than Mr Clayton-Browne there."

Clayton-Browne and his wife were in the forefront of the conservative crowd, and they now looked as if they wished to be anywhere but there.

"Yes," went on Paddy. "Because they had elected to work for me, they were led off my station in neck collars and chains by the police. It was also typical of Mr Clayton-Browne and the police that they didn't have the guts to do it in the open. They had to sneak in and take Wilga and his friends while I was being married up in Yalgoo. Many of you know my wife, Jenny."

Cheers now came for Jenny from the diggers, besides hoots at Clayton-Browne and the police.

Now it was Sir Edwin's turn. Paddy gave him a full glare before he let forth.

"You probably read in the papers about how because Wilga an' his friends protested too much they were all sent to Rottnest Island. I travelled all the way to Perth, hoping to get some compassion from our good Minister here. But, no sir! Not dear ole Ten Foot Ned of alluvial fame, who's now also Minister for Labour besides havin' been also gifted a knighthood. No, as far as our Minister's concerned, those black rascals can stay on that rotten island forever."

Paddy's strong eyes again waved over the gentry.

"Aren't you ashamed, and you call yourselves Christians."

"Yeah, thank Christ I'm an atheist!" yelled a digger, who didn't really mean it, because as an Irish Roman Catholic he always carried rosary beads in his pocket.

"Me too," yelled another digger, a husky ex-Queenslander, who no doubt had had his share of dusky concubines. "In fact, we should all be ashamed, the whole flamin' lot of us." He turned. "What say you mates, we're all behind Paddy? A man's entitled to pick his job whether white or black. Out with the rotten Master and Servant Law."

As the diggers yelled loudly for Paddy, they in turn looked scathingly at the cockies, who still seemed reluctant to take the side of the traditionally despised Aborigine.

All at once a burly wharf-labourer raised his fist.

"Aye, out with that rotten Law because it not only affects blacks but white workers as well."

325

The man himself like so many white servant-types, cared very little about the blacks, except that there was a danger that if the Aborigines were encouraged to lift themselves, they might compete for the jobs of white workers.

But now three-quarters of the hall yelled in unison, leaving the genteel folk ashen-faced. Many had already begun to leave the hall, though still maintaining dignity, especially the ladies. One or two half-turned with noses in the air, as Paddy was surrounded by his supporters.

"Jesus matey," said Tim to Paddy, clutching him by the shoulders. "You were a sensation! I couldn't've believed it of yuh."

"I couldn't've believed it of myself cobber," sighed a relieved Paddy. "I guess someone up there likes me."

"I'm far from religious, but I'd say He does an' all," went on a happy Tim. "Let's all over to the Geraldton pub to celebrate."

"Eh, steady, we haven't won yet," grinned Paddy.

"After that, I'll already be layin' two to one on, an' that's for bloody sure," laughed Tim.

That evening in the Clayton-Browne mansion out on the Greenough Flats, there were concerned faces. Sir Edwin and his wife had been invited out for the evening meal. Certainly if ever the British upper middle-class lifestyle was upheld, it was during dinner on the Clayton-Browne's Geraldton estate.

Also invited was the Anglican Vicar with three leading female members of his vestry. Recently vestry members had talked about the Anglican Church formerly a power in the land, losing its grip, and how the district of Geraldton had become infested with sots and wine-bibbers.

"... besides not going to church," a well-known and talkative vestry lady and spinster, Esme Anderson had explained "... they appear content to inhabit the Geraldton district for the rest of their lives, never to enlarge their minds with frequent trips to the city, or with the occasional trip overseas."

Also typical was a letter or portrait penned by Esme to a relative in the old country.

"... and in the last five years, Heaven help us, especially with gold and the invasion of those ruffians from the Eastern Colonies - most I might add being suspected of having convict forebears - there has been a change for the worst. Also sadly, the breaking up of our pastoral estates for agriculture, has seen an influx of the dreadful cocky types. Indeed, the way they carry on when they visit Geraldton, they too could be possessed of a very dubious ancestry."

In the Clayton-Browne dining-hall lit by oil-fired crystal chandeliers, the table was laid out with spotless white lace-embroidered linen, the cutlery of Sterling silver, the crockery of English bone china. A butler and a brace of white female servants attended the table. The gentry families still would not trust an Aboriginal to attend the table on special occasions. Decorating the spread were roses and carnations from the well-kept garden, as well as chrysanthemums, which bloomed so well in Geraldton in this time of the year.

Determined to keep to tradition despite the social setback in Geraldton, the womenfolk had changed into fashionable dinner-gowns, the gentlemen, including Ashley, complete in dinner dress.

After the meal the gentlemen relaxed over the table with cigars and port. The ladies, still attended by servants, retired to the drawing room while the children were assigned to a nanny.

The women were just as eager as the men to discuss the day's events, and later they all sat in the lounge section of the library in imported chairs of Gascoigne leather, the men in the excessive heat, having obtained permission to remove their jackets.

Lady Angela Mainwaring, Sir Edwin's wife, surveyed the

scene, still very angry over what had occurred during the day. She felt that her husband had been deeply humiliated, and wondered why men like this O'Leary and those creatures behind him could not show more respect for one who had been placed on the top of the Australian honours list by Queen Victoria. Lady Angela had been eagerly looking forward to a voyage to Britain to witness her husband's knighthood capped off with the touch of Her Majesty Queen Victoria's sword at St James Palace.

Gloria McAllum was also hurt, having been snubbed by the editor, when she had suggested to him after the meeting that he might care to print her point-of-view of the proceedings in his paper.

"No, I'm afraid not, Miss McAllum," he had replied. "If you wish to publish your opinion, leave it all in your report to the *West*. It's mostly owned by your family, anyhow."

"But I want to be unbiased," she argued.

"Well now, so you do admit the colony's only daily is biased," the editor had retorted abruptly, avoiding her attractive brown eyes. "Admittedly it is a very subtle bias. Regretfully however, they have influenced many an ordinary reader in the city - but thank goodness not in Geraldton. Anyhow Miss McAllum, best of luck, save it for the *West*."

With that the editor had left, saying he had to prepare his next print.

But Gloria with her bent for literature, wanted desperately to mix with the people. A few days before the meeting she had even dared to visit the Geraldton Hotel with her brother Ashley, and dressed inconspicuously, had even sat with him in the private lounge, viewing through a half-open doorway what went on in the main bar. Indeed, it thrilled her, especially when the pub-girls performed in front of the men. As one who had read a mixture of Jane Austen, Fielding, Thackeray and Dickens, she so much yearned to portray life from both sides - even to disguise herself and work as a hotel barmaid or even a kitchen-maid. But what chance had she in Geraldton? Or even in Perth? She would be betrayed by her manners, her speech.

A branch of the Salvation Army had recently been set up in Geraldton, and if she had not been such a devout Anglican, she might have joined the feminine soul-savers who would courageously enter a pub - good speech and manners notwithstanding - not only seeking donations for a worthy cause, but to enquire about the welfare of those whom drink had left in need.

Oh to be a man! Especially a newspaperman like the Geraldton editor, who appeared to have a license to go anywhere and mix with all and sundry. If she was to become a genuine journalist, she desperately needed this liberty.

During the discussion that evening, Gloria was not sure whether to be annoyed with or to admire her brother Ashley, whose experience as a reporter, especially among the goldfields diggers, had given him the maturity needed to face a changing world.

"After what happened today, we've just got to face up to facts," was Ashley's first salvo, bringing gasps from the womenfolk. "With the digger and cocky vote, the whole political scene will change."

"Well, we've known this for years," agreed Sir Edwin, loosening his collar. "That is why our *West Australian* has been out to capture the middle ground, and with some success, I might add."

"Yes, I should know that in my years as a newspaperman," said Ashley. "Also I have found that though they might detest us, once they get on, most people do appear to want to copy our ways, even our speech - especially women. In fact, I've found it most amusing."

"What we call Philistine types," suddenly spoke out Madelaine Clayton-Browne, the wife of Desmond, and the hostess. Not so many years ago, Madelaine knew that after-dinner conversations especially about politics, would have been strictly for the menfolk. In fact, among the gentlewomen, characters such as the diggers and cockies would have hardly rated a mention. But after what had gone on at the meeting today, right now it was an emergency, tantamount to war!

"Goodness gracious," Madelaine went on. "It takes years of tradition to build up families like ours." With her fan, she waved towards two large family paintings of 18th century origin, done in baroque style. One depicted a private garden with fountain and Romanesque-style gazebo. The comfortably seated husband and wife looked aristocratic and elegant, the five children likewise. The painted smiles on their faces belonged to cherubs more than children.

Ashley's wife, also a Clayton-Browne and a second cousin to Ashley, could well agree. "Yes, Aunt Madelaine," she said. "But we've seen much change even before the meeting today, haven't we? The cockies, as they call them, had already begun to dominate Geraldton. Why, I've heard that one has recently applied to be appointed as a Justice of Peace."

"Heavens above," expostulated Madelaine Clayton-Browne. "It must be a joke. Why, I doubt if any have ever been to school."

"Well, as I said before, we'll just have to accept it," admitted the more realistic Ashley. "Our families have pretty well ruled this colony since 1829. Instead of regarding the inevitable change with horror, maybe we should be realistic about it. We have already accepted that those trying to get on will try to ape us in our ways." Ashley gave a slow smile. "And furthermore, as most of our political institutions have been created by our kind, the Mobocracy would have to admit, that with the right man at the helm, our ideas could be reasonably democratic."

Madelaine Clayton-Browne looked horrified.

"My goodness Ashley, but with all the riff-raff having the vote the man at the helm could soon be one of them, don't you realise?"

Ashley uncrossed his legs, placing his feet square on the floor - noisily.

"But as I said, Aunt Madelaine, we will just have to accept it. Who knows, if we call ourselves true Christians, maybe it is a part of God's plan to have people like us pave the way, even though in the process it may have seemed right that we grab most for ourselves - as you must admit we have done in this colony. Now is the time to share." Ashley gave a gulp, his eyes avoiding his Aunt's.

Sir Edwin smiled cynically. "Your years as a reporter have made you more liberal, dear Ashley. But never forget this, young man. The very fact that as the rabble get on and try to copy our ways, shows we are the quintessence of British culture. So while you descend down among them, Ashley, regard them more as children, but dangerous at times, I will admit."

Ashley laughed pleasantly. "I don't know about dangerous, especially when they make unpleasant jokes about you within your hearing. My God, as a reporter, it was often my experience in a rough Kalgoorlie bar."

Madelaine Clayton-Browne clicked her tongue.

"Ignorant fools, more's the pity Ashley."

"Anyhow," said Sir Edwin. "Let's look on the bright side. All is not lost. As Ashley pointed out in his speech today, we have proven ourselves, the acumen of the colony's lower ranks is yet to be established."

"Agreed," spoke up Ashley. "It is also the line of our astute paper, the good *West Australian*. Do not change the rulership if it is performing its task well."

"Especially if the rulers are good upstanding citizens," added Madelaine Clayton-Browne. She now looked hard at her nephew, Ashley. "And that also means good Christians, despite the opinions of those ... those abominations at the meeting today. So I believe as good Christians we should devote part of our daily prayers to the coming elections. Success for our kind."

Ashley as a journalist had mixed with the ordinary folk, and it was almost on his lips to declare cynically that those abominations his aunt was referring to, especially the Roman Catholic Victorian Irish diggers, might be praying as good Christians for success in the elections too. But he kept quiet.

CHAPTER 18

With Geraldton in gala mood in the days before the election, Tim decided to hang around, as he put it, with a crowd of his digger mates. Not so Paddy. He was soon on his way back to Singleton to be close to the six-months pregnant Jenny.

He had tried to persuade Jenny to travel back to Geraldton with him for that special day, but she had refused.

"No Paddy," she said, clasping her midriff. "Not only do I feel uncomfortable travelling, but who'll vote for a candidate with a gadabout wife in the family way. Ashley McAllum's wife is heavily pregnant too, isn't she? I'll bet she doesn't present herself. Especially with her kind, it's not decent."

He kissed her. "I suppose not. Still, I'd reckon if you were there, the diggers an' cockies would respect you all the more for it."

"No," Jenny replied firmly. "I'll vote in Field's with my family." She suddenly gave a laugh, half-burying her head against his chest. "Anyhow, I'd have thought you'd have preferred to be in Geraldton without your wife. What about all those new Geraldton fancy ladies, mostly there to entertain the Murchison diggers?"

Paddy realised she did know a bit more than he had bargained for and was almost about to tell her about Tim McBride still up there enjoying himself, despite his pregnant Aboriginal wife in Field's. But he thought better of it. Anyhow, he had already lied to Jenny about Tim having returned with him from Geraldton to the mining town. He kissed her again lovingly, feeling once more that blissful content, and wishing he could forget the hustle and bustle of politics and stay with his young wife on the station.

But next day when Unkee, Wilga's chosen, clasped his hand with that soulful look in her eyes - the other lubras grouped around with the same expression - Paddy was reminded yet again that he had a mission.

He knew however, that the scrapping of the dreaded Master and Servant Law was not enough. The trouble was that with the decimation of the tribes, most natives now looked to the whites for subsistence. This meant that despite the station-owners having no legal claim to them, many would stay on the sheep-runs, especially the womenfolk. The irony was that these females appeared not to dislike looking after the flocks. It was just that the big station-owners in particular made too much of it, including the well-known fact that the wealthy pastoralists and their sons, were using the lubras as concubines. What the answer was, Paddy found hard to fathom. All he knew was that his parents and grandparents had taught him that the whites owed the natives a deep debt, and until that debt was paid in full, the guilt would remain, truly the white man's burden.

Paddy had decided to ride all the way to Geraldton on horseback. A special coach had been arranged to travel from Field's to Yalgoo, to link up with the train for the election. But Paddy declined, knowing that the whole trip to Geraldton with the diggers, including the coach run, would be a never-ending bout of drinking. The one hundred and fifty mile trek in the saddle, was just what he needed before the excitement of the polls.

He kissed Jenny once more, with a further smile and a wave to the shepherd girls. The sun stood just above the eastern horizon, red-gold and molten, heralding another scorching day. They were already in the middle of a heat-wave, unusual for the time of the year, for it was now April. Though he carried two two-gallon canvas water-bags, Paddy had left without a packhorse, knowing that after a flush year, there was good water in a government well a few miles west of the Koolanooka Hills, around seventy miles west-nor-west of Singleton. Forty miles further west was Mingenew, now a railway stop, and with its huge railway dam, a good watering-point.

After riding over the southern section of the Pinyallings and crossing the now mostly dry Lake Monger, he followed an old stock-track, first through mulga and bowgada, then wodgil followed by salmon and gimlet forest. On that first day, in a silence only broken by the squawk of white cockatoos and the occasional snort of his horse from the dust, Paddy mused over the past and future of the colony. Even apart from a better deal for the natives, there was still so much to do both socially and economically ... Also to do justice as an M.P., if elected, Paddy knew he must rein himself back from his old ways - which he was already doing since he had married Jenny. Yet to be a good politician did not mean that he must forsake what his parents and grandparents had taught him. Though not all human beings were born equal, each was entitled in the language of the digger, to a fair go. Here he knew was the difference with the attitude of the Clayton-Brownes and McAllums, who believed that their families were among God's chosen, and were entitled to the fruits of a workman's labour - the workman only to receive a mere pittance - while God's chosen shared the loot.

Though not of the chosen, Paddy still realised he himself had been fortunate to have educated parents as well as educated grandparents. It was up to people like him who were far closer to the ordinary folk - so pitifully uneducated - to do his bit, as Tim had informed him in far rougher terms. He compared himself to his rival, Ashley, knowing that in intellect he could match Ashley any time, though possibly not in manners and speech. They were both excellent horsemen. While Ashley was tops at fox-hunting and polo, Paddy was almost unsurpassed in the more domestic tasks for which a horse was often so necessary. Ashley was also physically capable as was needed in a good polo player.

Likewise physically, Paddy was no slouch, as he had proven more than once in those rough and tumbles as a youngster, and in later life in a bar-room brawl. His mind went back to his rough-house scrap with the wall-eyed young prospector in the Coolgardie Pub when he had defended the honour of Ann Fogarty, the dance-hall girl.

Still, Ashley in his own way might have been every bit as gallant.

Yet there were tens of thousands of men as capable as Paddy or Ashley who had never been to school. Paddy was reminded of so many diggers, their kids likewise, many now residing with their mothers in towns similar to Mt Magnet and Yalgoo. Yet the equal opportunity his Grandpa David had so often talked about, no different to the "fair go for all" as vouchsafed by the diggers, must also be for the Aborigines. There was the need to prevent the Anglican gentry from treating these people like sub-humans. And indeed, if they condescended to let them be educated, not to simply regard them as a convenient servant class - a selfish trait inherited from the feudal days and applied to the conquered natives.

Paddy had often discussed this problem with Daniel, who had declared that despite the so-called humanist doctrine brought out in the Renaissance and enlarged during the Enlightenment, the more compassionate egalitarian aspects of the philosophy had been conveniently halted in order to protect the superior status of the white man.

As he rode along, Paddy pulled a switch from a jam tree. The flies had become troublesome. His mind still active, he remembered listening to his father and grandfather discussing Charles Darwin and Herbert Spencer and their combined theory of evolution. Survival of the fittest. How well this theory fitted into the philosophies of the McAllums and Clayton-Brownes, even though it threw out the origins of man as declared by the Bible.

This only gave the established gentry a certain legitimacy

- because with their money and power, they were already sitting in the box seat, as Tim would say. So the works of Darwin and Spencer to them could be conveniently defined as just part of the Divine Plan, even though the founders had indeed declared themselves atheists.

But now with this coming election, all could be changed in Westralia at least. He imagined himself in a new digger's parliament similar to after the Eureka Revolt in Victoria when Peter Lalor the people's hero had become one of the leading lights in the new government. All those huffy selfish aristocratic types kicked out.

Fortified with such exciting thoughts, Paddy rode on.

The terrain he rode through now was rugged and broken, with the odd steep hill of blackened ironstone, similar to Mt Gibson, well to the south-east.

Next morning he rode through the Koolanooka Hills, though prominent, really just a low strung-out range, the red-black ironstone knobs all bobbing up in line. By noon he had reached the government well, just down from a red gravel ridge running into a rich basin of salmon and gimlet forest. The well, as with most other government stock wells, was not equipped with a windmill, only a windlass, with the usual well-bucket in which water could be drawn and poured down a sluice to a trough. After satisfying his horse and topping up his water-bags, Paddy hooked up the well-bucket and replaced the well-cover. Besides green parrots eager for a drink, three crows had alighted on the edge of the trough pushing out the parrots, their black feathers sheeny in the sun, their eyes baleful and unmerciful. Paddy in the mood he was in, was reminded of the arrogant inhuman attitude of Sir Edwin Mainwaring that day when Paddy had confronted him in Parliament concerning Wilga and his friends. God, how he detested the whole rotten crew, and all that the Hungry Six stood for.

After a bite to eat, and still in a pensive mood, Paddy rode on towards Mingenew - first through about ten miles of the

ironstone hills, still dipping down into the forested gullies.
Topping the last gentle rise, he found himself on the edge
of a plateau, looking down over a vast timbered flat, beginning
almost a hundred foot below. Though not a geologist like
Tim, he realised that here had occurred some enormous
ancient cataclysm, heralding a dramatic geological change.

Letting his pony take the steep descent cautiously, he was
soon impressed with the fertility of the country, although he
had been told that thirty years previously before they had
shifted most of their flocks up into the Gascoyne and even
further north, families such as the McAllums and Andersons
had let their sheep and cattle eat out all the natural grasses.

Another ten miles and he reached the first of the cocky
selections, the farmstead area denoted by a brush-covered
stable and tin shed, the rough cottage walled with hessian
and roofed with secondhand rusting corrugated iron. These
settlers, as Paddy knew, were all heavily in debt to the
Midland Railway Company, which had been granted the land
by the government for the convenience of the railtrack and
service.

Feeling that it was his duty as a candidate to pay at least
one of the settlers a visit, Paddy halted his horse by one
of the abodes. He was not surprised to find the young cocky
red-faced and stocky, uneducated and yeoman-like, the
heavily-pregnant wife still retaining an Irish brogue from her
mother who had been one of the Irish stitch-girls, given free
passage to the colony to make wives for the expirees.

"G'day cobber?" was the greeting from the man, his
speech and attitude being not much different from a Victorian
digger. "How yer goin'?"

"Not bad at all matey. Not bad at all," returned Paddy,
easily copying the language, "'cept it's so flamin' hot. Just
about drunk all me water." Paddy decided that right now,
it was not the time to mention politics.

"Got just what the doctor ordered," answered the man,
inclining his head. "That well just there's as fresh as a daisy.

Unusual in these parts, I tell yuh. Mosta the water if not salt, is fulla magnesia, gives you the flamin' runs no end. Matter a fact, the neighbour's missus had the runs so bad last year, she lost 'er second nipper." The cocky spat. "Yair, we're lucky all right."

"Yeah," answered Paddy, his vernacular still matching the man's. "In this country anyone who's got permanent good water is damned lucky, I do agree."

"Yair," the man went on. "Specially round here." He again jerked his head towards his wife, who after being introduced, was still obediently standing a few yards away, as if awaiting further orders.

She now received her command. "Hey Meg, what about makin' a cuppa an' rustlin' up a bitta tucker for our visitor?"

"It's still three hours till tea-time," half-joked Paddy, as the wife obediently left for the house.

"No, come in just the same," invited the man. "Bitta hay for your nag behind the stable too."

"Yep, much obliged," said Paddy.

The interior of the rough homestead was Spartan to say the least. The only modern convenience appeared to be the square cast-iron stove, backed by a couple of sheets of corrugated iron, wired together and standing on end behind the range to form a chimney-piece. The shelves and cupboards were just ordinary packing cases, with drop-downs of hessian, the heavily-scrubbed table just a series of pine boards, nailed to a frame which in turn was held up by four bush timber posts resting in old meat tins filled with arsenic sheep-dip poisoned water. This no doubt was to ward off the ants which in a streak of sunlight, now scurried in their myriads over the red earthen floor. But what Paddy noticed or felt most of all, was the intense heat radiating from the bare tin roof above.

Paddy compared the habitat of this young married pair, with the veritable mansion he had built for himself and Jenny out on the station. The comparison made him feel guilty, knowing that he, Paddy O'Leary, and Jenny were lucky exceptions, as she had reminded him so many times. Yet if the ordinary folk were to gain independence enough to own their own farms without substantial government assistance - which was not offering - this was the only way. An early life of hardship till they had made good - the way of the cocky battler.

The wife had now regained her speech, asking Paddy whether he preferred Kangaroo rissoles or Quandong pie? Paddy laughingly replied that as it was still only afternoon tea-time, the Quandong pie would suffice, and not to worry about heating it up, straight out of the cupboard would do. In fact, Paddy now had a desperate desire to get out. The ants had begun to run up his legs inside his pants, one already nipping at his thighs. The wife was apparently still unconcerned, being now too busy brushing the ants from her quandong pie.

Paddy realised after he had left, that he had forgotten to mention politics. But he turned his mind away from it with a shrug, believing that seeing that voting was not compulsory, the young cocky and his wife would have been too engrossed in their farm and themselves to worry about placing a vote anyhow.

As he neared the railway town of Mingenew, the land became more open and cleared, the orderly paddocks covered in yellowing wheat stubble from the excellent season before. Paddy knew that much of this valuable land closer to the railway line and formerly under a peppercorn lease by the old families, had been purchased by them from the Midland Railway Company. The former pastoralists now practised mixed farming, growing grain as well as running sheep and cattle. Thus from Mingenew north to Geraldton, families such as the Clayton-Brownes, McAllums, Bartletts and Andersons still held domain over millions of acres, despite the intrusion of the smallholders or cockies.

Paddy's first impression of Mingenew town, was of a big locomotive taking on water from the inevitable high red tank. He returned a cheery wave from a man with a shovel, sitting on top of a tall wedge-shaped coal-chute, waiting for the engine.

Paddy decided to stay the night at the Mingenew pub. Most of the talk that evening was about the coming election the day after tomorrow. Naturally when it was found that Paddy was the diggers' and cockies' candidate, he was well patronised, including free drinks and an order to stand on the bar and preach his piece. But here, despite too many grogs, Paddy was cautious, failing to mention his real reason for standing - to attempt to be rid of the iniquitous Master and Servant Law, so that Wilga and his friends could be released from Rottnest Island. Though the Mobocracy had shown sympathy during his speech in Geraldton, Paddy knew it was not a good subject to bring up in the pubs where the blacks were usually referred to as "... those useless bloody niggers...!"

After the few words on the bar, came still more drinks, and in fact by next morning with his aching head, Paddy felt he might just as well have travelled up to Yalgoo by coach from Field's, and risked the carousings of the diggers. He had almost decided to put his horse in an empty stock-car which was part of a waiting train. But instead he rode, jogging along the track which ran a chain or so out from the railway line. The line after its northern route to Mingenew, now ran west-nor-west on its thirty mile run to Dongara on the coast.

The countryside had now changed dramatically into a vast undulating lightland plain, odd locations extremely high, reminding Paddy of age-old sandhills, spawned from the fury of the westerlies in ancient times when the sea lay closer.

He reached the little sea-port and agricultural centre of Dongara around three in the afternoon, impressed by the sudden change from the sandplain into the rich pink flats which abounded the Irwin River. Around here also, the gentry families still held sway, their manor-like farmsteads, including tall, coned-peaked silos and steep-walled red brick and shingle-roofed granaries, bespeaking prosperity. Yet Paddy knew that most of these well-appointed structures were the result of cheap convict labour, particularly during the reign of the enterprising but tyrannical Governor Hampton.

A less imposing but popular structure was the Dongara hotel, which apart from filling his waterbags from a nearby watertank, Paddy religiously avoided. He feared that similar to Mingenew, he could be trapped by the locals. Also knowing that he still had a good seventy miles to travel north to Geraldton, he felt it better to press on till well after dark. He would sleep in the open somewhere along the track.

By midday next day he was riding along the highly productive Greenough Flats, still the domain of the gentry, the heavy stubbles giving indication of the crops which had gone before. What trees still existed after the initial clearing, stood revealed as those strange wind-ridden bent-over eucalypts, the odd rich-red fallow-paddock acting as a dramatic contrast to the huge snow-white sandhills rising to the west before the sea.

Late in the afternoon, Paddy rode into Geraldton, being careful for the time not to look for Tim and his digger mates. But it was not to be - Paddy was already too well-known, and he was grabbed by a couple of prospectors from Yalgoo and hustled into the Geraldton pub where stood Tim, elbows firmly anchored. Though he had inhabited the hotel most of the day, as usual, he was well in charge of his faculties. In fact, Tim in anticipation, had even saved a spare bed for Paddy in his lodgings upstairs.

For Paddy that evening it was again more whisky and beer except that, different from Mingenew and its kerosene lanterns, the bar-room here was lit by huge electric chandeliers, now clouded in tobacco smoke. Also different to Mingenew, here in Geraldton there was plenty of feminine entertainment. Besides the barmaids, there were the scantily-clad chorus-girls, who at present kicked their legs high while a man in a long-sleeved striped shirt with armbands and smoking a cigar, expertly struck rhythm on the piano.

Paddy's mind went back to Ann Fogarty, remembering how despite her so-called low vocation, she had always maintained her dignity. He wondered about some of these damsels. One, knowing he was the candidate, had already given him a wink. Not so many months ago, he knew he might have let himself go, especially while trying to get over the death of Ann. But now there was Jenny.

The chorus-girls had begun to mix with the crowd, acting tantalisingly, and generally touting their wares. The well-endowed cheeky one came up to Paddy, deliberately brushing against him, her nipples almost exposed.

"Eh steady on Marie," spoke Tim by Paddy's side. "This fellow's the candidate. He's got to remain respectable. Married too!"

Marie pursed her painted lips seductively.

"As if that matters. Just let me alone with him for a while."

Paddy raised a laugh, the election still uppermost in his mind. Also there was Jenny, even though Marie had looks enough to entice the most respectable married man. He pursued the middle-road, acting a little devil-may-care.

"You're right Marie, you'd certainly be hard to resist, but I'm a reformed character, I've made a pledge."

She pouted, now pushing her near-naked hips close to his - mistaking a playful gleam in Paddy's eyes.

"Once a man's had a taste of the forbidden fruit, he never forgets," she murmured. "What's your room number dearie?" She was now teasing him.

"Clear off Marie, for Pete's sake," scolded Tim. "Try someone else." He laughed. "What about the saloon? There's a few o' the gentry in there?"

"By Jove, surely not Ashley?" mocked Paddy, glad to be

343

rid of Marie.

"Yeah, Ashley," returned Tim. "The very one. Part of his tactics is to hobnob with the town businessmen and even the carters an' contractors. Once they've climbed up moneywise, as usual they prefer to indulge in the saloon with the bank Johnnies an' livestock rep's."

"And for that reason a target for the Groves Gang," agreed Paddy. "Not that Ashley would abhor what he's doing. As a reporter, he's had plenty of experience yakkin' to the same types in the gold-towns."

Marie had returned, waiting for a cue from the piano-player.

"And other types in skirts too," she cut in sweetly. "Don't you worry about our gentry lads, I've been in Geraldton hardly a month, and yet, my God, I could already tell some stories. Of course, with them it must be all done behind the scenes. Also I've seen the odd high-class female hanging about too. Not that they're always so discreet. In fact one little lady has become far too nosey for her own good - asking about the welfare of us girls if you like."

Tim looked at Paddy. "Oh, Gloria!"

"Yeah," laughed Paddy, "Gloria, our Geraldton rep' for the *West*. Though she's got such a hoity toity voice, not bad lookin' for a toffy-nose, is she?"

"Yes, from what I've seen of her, not bad at all," admitted Marie. "Even dressed in those dowdy clothes she wears while hanging about here. But if she really wants to do a story on how the other half lives, I can teach her plenty." The look in the entertainer's eyes showed she was not joking. There was contempt there for Gloria and her kind.

"What, you mean about what goes on when you're entertainin' a customer upstairs Marie?" scoffed Tim. "You do fancy yourself. Now be on your way an' get into your act, it's all ready to go."

Before she left, Marie fluttered her lashes alluringly at Paddy, envying the woman who was his wife. With all her experience, if there was ever a man who attracted her, it was this one.

"Well, enough groggin' on for awhile," declared Tim. "What about a hand o' poker or pontoon?"

As Paddy knew, here Tim was back to his favourite pub pastime besides grog. It was the reason the tough digger-geologist was able to retain his faculties while out on the spree. There was nothing like having to use one's wits at gambling to sober one up. Those who had to be carted out, were nearly always the characters who clung to the bar.

But though Paddy sat down to a game, it was not long before he threw in his hand. His mind was still too much on Jenny.

Surprisingly Tim also pushed back his chair.

"Think I'll hit the sack as well," he yawned. He turned to the other players. "There's plenty o' time to win all your cash tomorrow."

"Not if we can help it, you bastard McBride," shot back a digger. "Sump'n tells me your luck's just about due to run out."

"Never," laughed Tim, and picking up a bottle of whisky from the bartender, he walked up the stairs with Paddy.

Tim and Paddy talked for a long time, including about Gloria.

"Mike Beaumont's been tellin' me that the nobs, includin' our good Resident, Desmond Clayton-Browne, have engaged her to write Geraldton's official history," informed Tim.

"Jesus," said Paddy. "How could she be allowed to do that while still a journalist with the *West*?"

"Well seein' she's a McAllum, she's allowed to do anythin'." Tim took a slurp from the bottle. "I guess Gloria might try to be sincere enough herself, it's the bastards she works for. Mike Beaumont reckons her thesis will be carefully censored, or gentrified as he calls it."

"If they had any decency or sense of democracy, they'd encourage Mike Beaumont to write it."

"Christ Almighty, Paddy. What! Those mongrels take the

view of the majority? You must be jokin'!" Tim passed over the bottle. "Anyway, as usual you're draggin' your feet. Have a swig."

"No thanks mate, I think I'll get some shut-eye."

But it was Tim who fell asleep first. Paddy lay there awake for a long time again thinking about his young wife. Jenny and the shepherd girls were also on the station by themselves, not that they all weren't capable. Tim's heavy snoring didn't help much either.

Next day, the day before the election, Paddy, rather than playing on with Tim and his mates, decided to stroll around Geraldton, passing the time. But if he expected to escape unnoticed, he was mistaken. Besides the Geraldton editor having more than once published Paddy's photograph in his newspaper, most remembered him for his stirring speech a fortnight previously. To be sociable, he was even forced to have a few drinks in the other two Geraldton pubs.

In the endeavour to still be alone with his thoughts, Paddy walked casually along Fitzgerald Street. It seemed typical of the time, he mused, that the main streets of two of the colony's important rural towns, Northam and Geraldton should have both been named after Captain Charles Fitzgerald, sent out from Britain in 1848 to make certain that Western Australia at the time was turned into a Penal Establishment. Britain's gaols had been full to overflowing, and she desperately needed somewhere to send her miscreants, many of them rapists and murderers, as well as those due to be transported for stealing a rabbit from an estate or some similar insignificant little crime.

Paddy had heard the story so often from Grandpa David, who with the editor of the *Perth Gazette*, Robert Black, had fought so hard to prevent the "brutalisation of a former free colony" - words spoken over the pulpit by Doctor James Hardy, spiritual leader of the colony's Methodists.

One of Perth's main streets had been named Fitzgerald also

as well as a river in the colony's south-west. Yet the man Fitzgerald had not arrived by any choice of the people - as his name now splashed around the colony should suggest. It made Paddy contemptuous. But he also realised with a sense of pride that he was at least having a go to rid the government of the types of citizens who would honour such a man. In fact, he felt that if he did gain the Murchison seat, he would suggest that the main street of Geraldton change its name at least. If enough digger-liberals like himself did get into Parliament, they might even name it after one of the two hundred courageous Aboriginals who had all been transported south to Rottnest Island because they had stood up against the first Geraldton settlers.

"Jesus", he grinned to himself. "What a stir that would bring about!"

Still greeting the odd person, Paddy strolled down to the wharf where lumpers were manhandling bagged wheat from a railway truck, which in turn had carried grain from huge stacks stockpiled from the excellent harvest. Further down the wharf were the fishing boats, many just in from the Abrolhos Islands loaded with schnapper, dhufish, and Spanish mackerel, as well as rock lobster. The bulk of the fisherman were comparatively recent immigrants. One darkly sunburnt Greek called out.

"Paddy, halloo. Goot on you cobber, we're all goingt to vote for yoo-o-oou."

"Yeah thanks," called back an embarrassed Paddy, knowing that the votes of these new Westralians would be valuable, but wondering if they would keep to their word, because voting was not compulsory.

Despite all the popularity, Paddy still yearned to be home with Jenny. With his recent experience of the less toadyish elements of the common herd in Geraldton, once you got them to the polls, they would vote for anyone as long as he was opposed to the Groves Gang. In Tim's words ... "rather than vote for the swells, they'd just as soon vote for a drover's dog."

All at once Paddy was jerked to reality and reminded of the real reason he was putting up as a candidate. He had walked well beyond the end of the long wharf, where a small sailing vessel, a schooner, had tied up to a lone jetty. The dark stain on its sides showed it had come a long way, probably from as far up as Carnarvon, or even further north. But what held his gaze were the dozen or so dejected-looking blacks being herded to the edge of the boat by three policemen, themselves unshaven and generally unkempt looking.

Clamped around the necks of the natives were the dreaded steel neck-collars, the policemen now coupling the poor unfortunates to each other with chain and padlock. Though people ambled by as if such an event was an everyday occurrence, Paddy half-hesitantly slowed his pace.

One of the policemen jabbed a pistol into the ribs of the lead savage.

"RIGHT, NIGGER, GET MOVIN'!" he snarled.

Without a murmur the native in front stepped out of the craft, the chain rasping on the gunwale, as his companions were forced to follow.

With deathlike indifference the condemned men began to move in file, the chain-links clinking in unison - the policemen all in step with revolvers cocked.

Paddy realised what was happening. The dark prisoners had been brought down from up north to serve sentence on Rottnest Island. But why they had been brought into Geraldton he had no idea. Unless there was fear of a storm out to sea and they thought it wiser to bring the prisoners into Geraldton, there to be despatched south to Fremantle by train, and shipped from there to Rottnest, weather permitting.

With an election in the offing, Paddy thought what a bad time it was to land the prisoners in Geraldton. Then he smiled cynically as Tim again invaded his thoughts.

"Don't build up your hopes on that score matey. As I told you before, most o' the lower ranks just couldn't give a damn about the Abo's, they want the nobs out for far more selfish reasons."

A cool almost bleak wind had sprung up from the sea, not helping the fit of depression which had come over Paddy as he walked slowly up towards the town centre. He wondered whether his fight for the betterment of Wilga and his kind was all in vain, and whether behind the scenes on both sides, he was really a laughing stock. What was the use of him thinking romantic thoughts about a Digger's Parliament, when the diggers themselves didn't care a hoot about the blacks either?

Why those five thousand or so black miscreants now on Rottnest, if not locked up, might not only have prevented the pastoralists and cockies from opening up the lands, but might have also prevented the diggers finding the gold. And the other five hundred or more who had died on that bleak isle from other than natural causes, well, it was no more than the proportion out of the total which might have succumbed by the same means in any prison.

Yes, he was just a laughing stock, as his grandfather had been in the old days.

All at once the wistful agonised features of Wilga's chosen came into his mind, pining for her beloved, and Paddy found himself thinking of his mother and murmuring a prayer to the Almighty that justice would be done.

But almost in the same breath he felt insignificant and ashamed that Tim and his mates might have overheard his prayer.

"Oh, to hell with it," he mouthed out loud to himself, and with that he pushed open the swing-doors of the Geraldton pub, just in time to meet Tim and a couple of mates on the way out.

"Well, look who's here!" grinned Tim. "We're just off to have a bite o' fish an' chips down the track."

"Think I'll join you," said Paddy.

"'Bout time," said Tim. "We're into another handa poker later. Wanta make up a four?"

"Could do," said Paddy, now very glad to get away from his own despairing thoughts.

But later though there was plenty of entertainment in the bar besides drinking and cards - prominent being the music and the entertainment girls, Paddy again went upstairs to bed, this time without waiting for Tim. He felt at least he might get a bit of sleep, before Tim started his snoring.

Next morning voting began at eight-o'clock, the two candidates each at his position and dressed appropriately. Ashley McAllum sported a well-cut suit, waistcoat, watch-chain and bowler hat, while Paddy wore simply a clean version of his station clothes, wide-brimmed hat, check-shirt, moleskin trousers and polished boots. Behind the candidates were their immediate backers. With the absence of Sir Edwin, who had his own electorate near Perth to attend to, Ashley was accompanied by Julien and Desmond Clayton-Browne and their wives. Other influential couples were also in evidence, having travelled in from their Greenough and Irwin estates.

A well-kept lawn adjacent to the new Assembly Hall, was the venue for the well-to-do, who had set themselves up with tables under huge silk-lined sunshades. As the Union-Jack fluttered gaily in the breeze, more well-appointed coaches began arriving, discharging their genteel cargoes, including children. What had largely caused the early influx of the better families was that a polo match had been planned for soon after midday between Geraldton and Northampton a neighbouring town to the north. This was the domain of the sheep studs, unlike Ben Ryan's, mostly owned by the Geraldton elite.

But as far as voting attendance was concerned, it seemed that apart from one or two, the diggers and cockies were noticeably absent.

Accompanying Paddy in his loneliness beside the Eureka flag, was Tim. Even the Geraldton editor was missing, his role being to run around with his note-book and camera keeping a kind of neutrality, so that he could at least take close-up photographs of the Geraldton sophisticates. Sophisticated, certainly they were, especially the womenfolk, who, with their stylish hats and elegant summer gowns could grace any the best of English garden parties. Gloria McAllum was also there, but unlike the editor, she carried her notebook in an elaborately embroidered handbag.

It was the opportunity for Tim to begin his clowning. "Whew," he said in a low voice. "Makes the old heart miss a beat doesn't it? They know how to present themselves I must admit. Look at those teen-age daughters. An' would you look at Gloria McAllum in that big picture hat an' white lacy gown. What a difference from when she hangs round the pubs, dressed like a plain Jane or one o' those suffragettes. Would you look at the way she's swingin' her hips. She's tryin' to attract attention, there's nothin surer."

Paddy joined in, glad of the diversion, because he was worried.

"Thought you didn't like her cobber?"

"Just right now I've changed my mind. Whew, what I couldn't do to her!"

"That's if she'd let you."

"Oh, she would all right, just given the right conditions an' locality," grinned Tim. "Look how she's glancin' our way. She's not only after information, but after a he-man an' no mistake."

"You do pride yourself, don't you matey? Anyhow, where's all our digger an' cocky voters, it's now eleven o-clock, an' we've hardly had a one."

"All in the pubs after a taste o' the dog what bit 'em," returned Tim, sarcastically.

"But if they're on the grog again, who says they'll worry

351

about knockin' off drinkin' to vote?"

Tim gave a quick laugh. "You should know our diggers better than that, Paddy. I don't know about the cockies, but the diggers'll keep their word - that's the reason they've all come to Geraldton..... Oh all right!" went on Tim, having noticed that Paddy was still not convinced. "I'll go an' rouse the rotten bastards out."

Paddy looked happier. "Yeah, good idea. Now make sure you don't get stuck in the pub yourself."

"Don't worry, I won't," grinned Tim. "Hey, here comes our editor wavin' a piece o' paper. What the hell's up?"

The editor was all smiles. "Just received a telegram," he said, handing it to Paddy. "Here, read it."

As Paddy read the telegram, his eyes widened.

"WELL, I'LL BE BUGGERED...!" he yelled, forgetting where he was. "So if elected Mr Groves has pledged to get rid o' the rotten Master an' Servant Law. Christ Almighty! I've done what I set out to do!"

"Like hell you have!" swore Tim. "There's a lot more to change in Parliament than that. What about our rights? The rights of the digger, includin' the rights of the workers to have their own party."

But Paddy was hardly listening. He was so happy. High ideals about what he was going to do when he was elected were forgotten. He could not wait to get home to tell Jenny the good news - and in particular Wilga's chosen and the shepherd girls.

Tim broke into his reverie, the quick-witted digger, as usual holding supreme in an emergency, despite his weakness for gambling and drink.

"Jesus Paddy, wake up! If the Groves Gang wins, their leader hasn't the power to shove a reform through like that. Just imagine our illustrious Sir Edwin agreein' to that. Or Darcy McAllum, Ashley's old man. Or any o' the rest o' the bastards. Why, I wouldn't believe a promise from that mob till Wilga an' his friends are safe back at Singleton."

He grabbed Paddy by the shoulder.

"Come down to earth matey. Can't you see that tossin' out the Master an' Servant Law could be just a ruse to get the labourers an' wharfies to vote along with the nobs. That rotten Act was not only to do with blacks but ordinary workers too. Most o' the workers like the cockies couldn't care less about the treatment of Abo's, but when it affects them it's a different story. In fact, it now might pay to remind 'em that it was pressure from us - mainly you - which has forced Groves to make such a promise. Yes, by Gad, we'll capitalise on that message. You'll be more of a hero than ever."

With that Tim was off, to pass the word around the pubs, as well as to the fisherman, wharf-workers, and servants and labourers generally.

The editor was now talking to Paddy. "Yes, Tim's right, you'd better stay on. Also you must remember we don't expect to win the Geraldton ballot in any case, even though they've allowed the visiting diggers to vote here. It is the votes from the new mining towns which will win the Murchison, like Yalgoo, Mt Magnet and Meekathara."

Paddy gave a slow grin. "Yeah, I s'pose I'd better. But it looks like we've given 'em a bit of a hurry-up though, doesn't it? Look over there!"

They were just in time to see Julien Clayton-Browne and his wife walking stiffly away, the wife's features unusually pale. Also many of the other well-dressed folk were folding their umbrellas and picking up their picnic articles.

Beaumont gave a cynical laugh. "Oh, I guess they've got a good excuse. They're all off to polo."

The editor left, and all at once Paddy realised someone was standing beside him. He was surprised to see Ashley holding out his hand, with a not unpleasant smile.

"I must congratulate you Patrick," spoke Ashley warmly. "I am sure that what you said in your speech that day brought on the decision. I think it stirred a few hard hearts, even

353

on our side."

"Thanks matey," replied Paddy, with another vigorous shake of his rival's hand. "But I haven't won yet, have I? We've got to wait till they count the ballot box tonight."

"Well, I didn't mean you were going to win Geraldton," said Ashley. "Maybe the mining towns, but certainly not Geraldton. Why I was congratulating you, as I said, you moved a few hard hearts."

Paddy could tell that Ashley was glad to be rid of the Master and Servant Law also. It had become an embarrassment to him as it was apparently to his leader, William Groves.

"Thanks once again Ashley," said Paddy, returning the handshake. "An' for Chris' sake from now on call me Paddy."

"I will that and all," smiled Ashley once more.

But after the ballot count, Ashley had little reason for humour, for as Tim put it, Paddy beat the Geraldton swells by a mile.

By three-o'clock the diggers had come in droves, they whom the gentry had called the Rabble. Geraldton had now become a centre for the ordinary folk, as it was to remain. The only boxes that showed a majority for the conservatives in the whole of the Murchison were Irwin and Northhampton, regarded as gentry strongholds.

Besides the employed staff, only a certain few were allowed in the Assembly Hall atrium as the votes were counted. On one side of the room were seated the conservatives, namely Ashley McAllum, Julien Clayton-Browne and his brother Desmond, the District Magistrate. None of the wives were there. The only females were Esme Anderson, who it was said, still poked her nose in everything, and Gloria McAllum.

Against the opposite wall, besides Paddy, Tim and Mike Beaumont, sat Fred Burgess, a tough scrutineer for the cockies, and Jock Bryant, a similarly tough representative for the wharfies.

The hotel bars had been deliberately closed for the count-out. Outside the Assembly Hall surged a great pack of revelling diggers, cockies and workers, the gentility not getting a look in.

When the results were called from a window, there was a roar from the crowd.

"WE WANT PADDY...! WE WANT PADDY...!"

But just as Paddy was about to obey the request, he was again confronted by Ashley.

"Congratulations again Paddy. This is getting a bit of a habit, isn't it?"

But behind Ashley's somewhat valiant smile, Paddy could see disappointment, almost shock.

Accompanying Ashley was his sister, Gloria, who too congratulated Paddy - not to shake his hand, for with females from the best of circles, this was just not done.

Since that first day of the meeting, it was the first time he was able to appraise her right up close, and he was a bit disappointed. Maybe the shock had affected her, similar to Ashley. But he could see she was a bad loser. Her lips were now tightly drawn, the normally appealing brown eyes a little slitted. Certainly in Tim's words, she'd be still nice to take to bed. Yet she was supposed to be about to write Geraldton's history and he wondered with her sheltered upbringing whether Gloria had the capacity to write history from the ground-level as generations to come would want it. Instead, as the Geraldton editor would say, it would suffer from gentrification, written from the point-of-view of the landed or the old families. In this case, the views of the Hungry Six.

"WE WANT PADDY...! WE WANT PADDY...!" again came the cry from outside.

"Go on, you'd better get out there," said Tim, grabbing him by the shoulder.

"But it's only Geraldton," protested Paddy.

For the benefit of Gloria, who for some reason still stood

there watching, Tim let out a happy roar.

"ONLY GERALDTON! ONLY GERALDTON....! Jesus, matey, it's the nob stronghold. Or was! Besides that, you've got all the gold towns sewn up without a doubt. So, come on! Let's celebrate!"

Outside the diggers carried Paddy shoulder high to the Geraldton pub.

Paddy did celebrate and gladly, and when the wires came through confirming his win, who could blame him for later stripping down to his underdrawers and dancing an Irish jig on top of the bar urged on by the diggers and dance-hall girls.

Nonetheless, Paddy was sober enough next morning to leave at daybreak for the long three-day ride to Singleton, anxious to tell the good news to Jenny and the shepherd girls. Certainly he pressed his horse, and at last within sight of the homestead, he urged it to a gallop.

Jenny and the shepherdesses were standing by the sheepyards and as they ran towards him, Paddy yelled out, waving his hat.

"WE'VE WON...! WE'VE WON....!"

Jenny, despite her condition, ran into his arms as he jumped from the saddle. Also the excited shepherd girls were all around.

Paddy suddenly released Jenny, realising that Wilga's chosen was very close, her expressive eyes deep and intense.

"Wilga come back?" she asked simply.

"Yes, Wilga come back Unkee," he replied, holding back tears. "They've already agreed to release our boys from Rottnest Island."

"Not straightaway?" she went on, with doubt still in her tone.

"No, not straightaway Unkee. It has to be passed through Parliament first. But it's a foregone conclusion, I tell you."

But she became downcast again, her large eyes deep and

troubled. It made Paddy realise how important it was to get to Perth for the opening of the new Parliament in three weeks time.

Daniel Hordacre had also won his seat in Kalgoorlie, and other goldfields seats had fallen to independent liberals like Paddy and Daniel. Yet barring Fremantle, regarded as a worker's town, and North Perth, the old Coastal Strip seats such as Perth, Rockingham, Mandurah, Bunbury, Busselton and Albany were returned to the conservatives. The agricultural seats of York, Toodyay and Narrogin also fell to the old guard while Northam was taken by the liberals. But the new goldfields-pastoral seats, including the Murchison were all easily taken by the digger-liberals.

The new Parliament now stood about even between the digger-liberals and the conservatives. William Groves had again been elected Premier, and he now held the deciding vote. It was to his credit that he kept to his promise and voted to oust the antiquated Master and Servant Law, allowing thousands of natives on Rottnest Island the right of freedom. Apart from the murderers and thieves, most of the unfortunates had been banished to the dreaded Isle, just because they had refused to work for some pastoralist, or had speared sheep or cattle on some station located on their former age-old hunting grounds.

Even so, the Hungry Six members who had regained their seats were cautious, and as some had recovered their positions in the new Ministry, including Sir Edwin Mainwaring, they were able to bring in a proviso that only a selected number of Aboriginals be freed at first. The excuse was that apart from the so-called thieves and murderers, there were many known inciters among them, and it could be dangerous to let too many loose at the one time among the public.

Mike Beaumont had travelled to Perth to observe the first sitting of Parliament. Discussing the outcome with Paddy and

Daniel, he had made a prediction. "... Though we still haven't completely cleaned out the Hungry Six, owing to their backing in the old electorates, I'd say by the end of this term they'll be packing their bags."

"Yes," agreed Daniel. "What could help them on their way is that there is a good chance that Groves with his deciding vote could back most of our reforms, which includes both officiating Political Labour and paying a Member's salary."

"Bloody turncoat," grinned Paddy happily. "O' course, he always reckoned he was a genuine liberal. Still, with him I guess it's the old story of runnin' with the hares an' huntin' with the hounds."

Daniel smiled cynically. "Probably what he believes is best for Western Australia. Yet I must say that Groves is a true pragmatist. With the continuing increase of digger and worker types in the colony and all getting the vote, he can see the writing on the wall. As the promoter of the Goldfields Water Scheme along with C.Y. O'Connor, he wants to stay in the limelight when there's sure to be that change of government in 1901. He's even altered his mind about the coming Federation at the end of 1900. Previously he was dead against breaking political ties with the old country like the rest of the Hungry Six crowd, but now he's on the side of Federation."

"Certainly I favour Federation too," rejoined Paddy. "But I'm wonderin' which is the worst, to be at the beck an' call of Britain, or be dictated to by t'otherside."

"Yes, and that could mean being called to order by either Sydney in New South Wales, or Melbourne in Victoria," returned Beaumont, gloomily. "The cities are already fighting over which should be the Federal capital."

"It is a bit of a farce, isn't it?" cut in Daniel. "Especially as under our so-called independent Constitution, the British Governor will still have the final say."

"Yeah, they call it the Royal Prerogative don't they?" added Paddy sarcastically. "If only we could be rid o' the bastards completely an' become a republic under the Eureka flag, like the *Bulletin* writes about."

"I don't know about the Eureka flag," smiled Beaumont. "But a republic will come, never fear! It is the only way we can establish our true identity as a nation - even if it takes a hundred years."

"Christ Almighty, I hope it's much sooner than that," swore Paddy. "Fancy havin' to put up with pukka types like Sir Edwin an' Sir Darcy McAllum, even as governors. Oh, my God, I think I'd migrate to America or somewhere. Surely we've got a better future than that." Paddy suddenly went quiet. "Anyhow, I'd better see what's doin' about gettin' my boys back from Rottnest."

"That's been arranged," supported Beaumont. "The first boatload will be arriving at Fremantle about midday tomorrow. As a newspaperman I'll be tagging along with you."

"Thanks," acknowledged Paddy as he turned to Daniel. "Look matey, give my apologies in Parliament on Monday, will you. I believe it's my duty to ride back with my boys."

"Yes, much more a duty Paddy," smiled Daniel. "Give my regards to Jenny."

The day turned out bleak and grey, not surprising because it was now early June and the start of winter. The coastal steamer *Wadjemup*, the native name for Rottnest Island, was wooden and clinker-built, and served not only for pleasure cruises around the island for the whites, but also as a transport to carry native prisoners, mostly on a one-way trip. For a change, she was now loaded with two hundred and fifty souls on the way back - albeit without chains and neck-collars.

The decks were packed with thin and emaciated Aborigines, many of whom had become desperately sea-sick during the rough crossing. Yet the look in their eyes as they began to file down the gangplank was akin to starved animals about to be released into a fresh new pasture.

All at once Paddy recognised one of his native boys, then another, then another, then another two.

Paddy felt a sinking sensation in the pit of his stomach.

"Where's Wilga, for Chris' sake?" Paddy asked the most intelligent of the young natives.

"Wilga die," said the native simply. "Been dead long time."

"OH, GOD! NO! NO-O-OOOH!" shrieked Paddy, dropping his head in his hands.

Beaumont was beside him. "Steady now old man, steady now."

But Paddy pushed the editor aside, rushing over to an unshaven and heavily pock-marked police-sergeant, who had just stepped off the boat.

"You mongrels!" swore Paddy. "One of my station boys has died over in that rotten place. Why the blazes didn't you let me know?"

The tough-minded sergeant, already mystified with the liberal attitude the authorities had suddenly taken concerning the locked away boongs, as he called them, immediately regarded Paddy's performance as comical.

"Eh, listen ere now," he replied coarsely. "What de ye' think we've got over there? A flamin' holiday camp or somethin'. What's this sendin' word to the mainland about a sick nig prisoner. Jesus, that'll be the day!"

"You bastard!" roared Paddy, grabbing the sergeant by the throat. "You mangy pox-ridden bastard!"

While other policemen crowded around, one jabbed a pistol in Paddy's ribs. "Looks like we've got a real bleedin' 'eart, 'ere. Could be the lock-up for you my lad."

"It's no use Paddy, it's done. It's done," cried the editor, also pushing his way in. "Make the best of it Paddy, and take these lads home. You may be sure I'll be writing a good story about this in the *Geraldton Express*."

"Yes, I s'pose I'd better," replied a subdued Paddy.

"Right, come on lads," he said kindly to the rest of the

station boys as he shook himself from the policemen as if they were lepers. "I've already left horses at Watheroo for us all to ride back to Singleton. Guess we'll be leadin' one."

That night they caught the Geraldton express, stopping off to pick up their horses at Watheroo. They rode through the rest of the night and as they drew in sight of the homestead around midday, Paddy tried to steady himself, wondering what he was going to say to Wilga's chosen. As he had sat those hours in the saddle with the native lads also silent beside him, he had wondered whether his attitude was too idealistic, too weak - too much influenced by his mother and his Quaker-Evangelical grandpa. He found reassurance in the knowledge that outspoken newspapermen such as Daniel Hordacre and Mike Beaumont were of the same mind. And of course, there was Jenny, how lucky he was to have a wife like her.

As they rode over the creek-bed, flowing a little water from a recent rain, Jenny ran down from the homestead to meet them, despite the discomfort of her pregnancy. As she got closer, the shock in her eyes was obvious.

"WHAT'S HAPPENED? WHERE'S WILGA...?" she cried.

Paddy jumped down from his horse and took his wife in his arms.

"Wilga's dead, sweetheart. According to the boys here, he died almost a month ago over on that God-forsaken island."

She held onto him, sobbing. "Oh Paddy, what are we going to do? Poor Unkee. Anyhow, I'm sure she knows. It's been agony to look at her."

He stroked her head, as she pressed against his chest. "Yeah, I'm certain now her an' Wilga were in touch. It suddenly stopped, that's why she knew. But where is she? Where's the rest o' the girls?"

His young wife lifted her head, becoming more practical. "Oh, we've had another burst of the green blowfly from

361

the early rains. The girls have been busy down at the sheepyards. Wait on! Here they come now!"

The native boys still sat in their saddles, and whether it was the sight of the extra riderless horse, or simple intuition, but Wilga's chosen suddenly began to wail, high-pitched and terrifying.

"WILGA-A-AAAA—! WILGAAA-A-AAAAA—!"

The other shepherd girls began to imitate her, and now the native boys joined in, jumping from their saddles and running to their opposite numbers, quickly embracing them. By now Wilga's chosen, left alone, had raced screaming over to the mount.

"My God," said Jenny. "What are we going to do?"

"Oh, I guess she'll get over it in time!" Paddy replied.

"No, never Paddy," cried Jenny. "What if it was you? No, never!"

"Sorry sweetheart," soothed Paddy, as he held her close. "Bit callous, wasn't I? Anyhow, at least Wilga didn't die for nothing. It was mainly fighting for his release that got rid of that damned Master an' Servant Law."

"Paddy," she asked tremulously. "How did Wilga die?"

"Well, I did get most of it from the boys on the way back. Yes, Wilga was treated harshly early in the piece. He an' the boys got out one night an' stole a boat, but the sea was too rough an' they were washed back on the rocks. The guards later caught them and they were all heavily whipped. But seein' the rotten bastards knew Wilga was the leader they put him in solitary confinement for a whole fortnight. The trouble was that after he was let out he still refused to eat."

"Probably he just didn't want to," sobbed Jenny. "He was still mentally in touch with Unkee, and it was so terrible that he would probably never see her again. He really died of a broken heart." She buried her head in his chest. "Oh, Paddy!"

Paddy gently stroked her hair.

"Yes, and the very fact of an Aboriginal being locked up in a black windowless cell, which the authorities do deliberately. It's somethin' that's right against their nature. Also the bleak greyness of Rottnest is so different from the rich redness of the inland."

"Yes," she whispered. "Putting them over there is like taking away their life, their very soul."

"Yeah," drawled Paddy, releasing her and realising it was about time they all pulled themselves together. "Of course, the rotten police know this, that's why the bastards get so much pleasure out of it. Anyhow, darling, as soon as you're well enough after havin' the baby, I guess we'll be movin' to Perth."

"Dad and Kim say they'll watch over our station," said Jenny. "Just the same Paddy, seeing that the terrible Master and Servant Law has been tossed out, I suppose you could put in your resignation. M.P.'s still have that right you know."

"I had thought of it my love. In fact, just to have what's left of that rotten Groves Gang gapin' at me from the opposition seats, makes me feel I've already had a gutsful. The trouble is, the numbers in Parliament are just about even an' if I get out, who knows, Ashley McAllum could get in. What I'm tryin' to say is there's a lot of important reforms we want to bring in, includin' the women's vote. We could be next in the world after South Australia. Also I want to make sure those Hungry Six mongrels don't go back on their word about later releasin' the rest o' the prisoners from Rottnest Island. If I had my way, I'd like to see the whole rotten place shut down."

"Yes Paddy," she whispered. "Still, even then, the natives will be far from compensated. God knows if they ever will be for the loss of their tribal lands."

He put his arms around her.

"No sweetheart, I guess it's goin' to take a long time. It's goin' to take plenty of understanding, as well as patience, which most of us whites don't have. Anyway, talkin' again about stayin' in Parliament, I promise it'll only be for the one term. I want to settle down with my family on the station. By the time three years is up, I reckon I'll really have had that gutsful."

She eased herself from his grasp, her state of pregnancy uncomfortable. "Well, I suppose I could put up with it as a politician's wife Paddy, especially if it's for a good cause."

He held her more gently, but lovingly. "An' don't say there won't be some aspects of livin' in the city in a flash house an' mixin' with other politicians' wives you won't enjoy, my sweet little Jenny. Especially when I show you off in some expensive elegant gown."

"I am capable of fronting up like a good wife. But just at the present I'm not in the mood to think about such things - maybe later. Right now, just say we're doing it for Wilga."

"Yes, for Wilga. And a bit o' decency round the place."

"Yes," she replied. "A bit of decency. For surely this colony needs it."

Now read on ...

The final novel to be published in the *A Land in Need* series:

Book 3   The Gully Road